D1405757

# CELESTIAL

# BLIGHT

## BOOK ONE OF THE FARSIAN TRILOGY

BY VALENTINO MORI

ISBN (print): 978-1980559245
ISBN (ebook): 978-1370821853

Cover Design by Les Solot

Map Design by Samuel Busch

For Shauna,

who supported and guided me for over a decade
and also let me write fantasy novels instead of book reports.

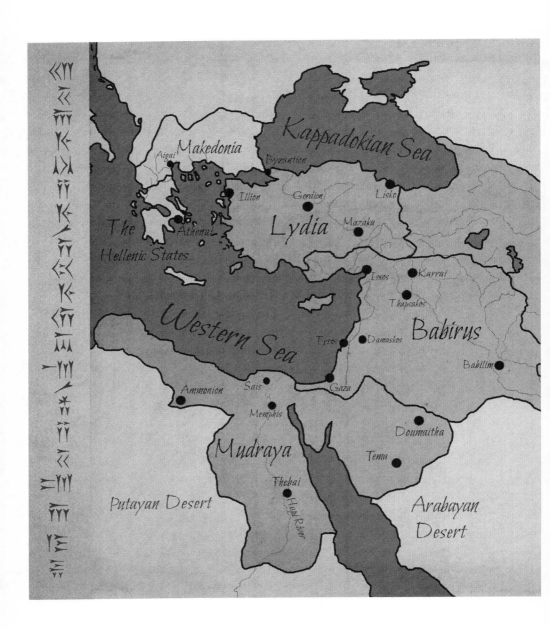

# Table of Contents

# Chapter 1 – Unclasping

Zemfira was daydreaming about what an ocean would look like when the temple bells started ringing. The ladle slipped from her fingers into the pot of bubbling rice. Zemfira glanced at her aunt to confirm the sound meant what she thought. Her aunt smiled and nodded. Today was Unclasping Day.

"I can't believe it's finally here," Zemfira whispered, tugging off her apron and running her fingers through her hair in a futile attempt to make it behave.

Her fingers went to the Iron Necklace at her throat. Every child across the Kingdom of Farsia wore one just like it: the Iron Necklace prevented them from accessing their Casting. Once Zemfira was free of it, she would discover and develop her powers—she would be an adult. Then she might finally venture beyond the village, and see what lay beyond the foothills and the valley.

"You should hurry," said her Aunt Gozeh, hands occupied by the bread dough. "Those who arrive first get unclasped first. But please take the rice from the fire before you go."

"Yes, Auntie," said Zemfira. "And I'll do extra chores tomorrow. Who knows, maybe I'll be an Infernocaster and I can heat the rice all by myself."

Gozeh shook her head. "Children always underestimate the Cost of Casting. You'll see, soon enough. It's not always an easy exchange to make."

Zemfira rolled her eyes and pulled on her scarf. "I was joking, Auntie! See you later!"

Nebit was one of many villages dotting the foothills. Under the summer sun, the dirt road snaked between the cottages and the sentry tower, up to the stone temple that overlooked the valley. The bells still rang out, louder than ever. Zemfira headed uphill, past the mules turning the little flour mill, mouth dry with anticipation.

"Zemfira!"

She turned to see her friend Paniz emerge from between the trees on the side of the road. Paniz kept her hair short and rarely wore her scarf, and strangers often mistook her for a boy. Her tunic, although covered in dirt, was not frayed like Zemfira's. But Paniz's father was the village blacksmith, and blacksmiths earned more than goatherds.

Zemfira was returning the greeting when she noticed a bruise on Paniz's cheek.

"Paniz! What happened?"

The girl blinked and touched her face, then grinned. "Just a little scuffle. A few boys were kicking my little sister, so I had to teach them a lesson. Come on, let's get to the temple!"

Paniz wanted to explore beyond their little village almost as much as Zemfira did. Many times they had promised each other they would venture out as soon as they were unclasped and gained control of their Castings. But Zemfira knew it wouldn't be quite so easy. Paniz might be ready for adventure, but Zemfira couldn't just abandon her little brother and her widowed father.

They rounded a corner and almost ran into Old Navid as he vomited beer and mysterious chunks into a barrel.

2

"Disgusting," muttered Paniz, stepping around the inebriated old soldier and continuing up the hill. Although her stomach twisted with nausea, Zemfira stepped forward and put a hand on Navid's shoulder.

"Are you alright, sir?"

"Me? Oh, I'm fine," said Navid, waving her off. "Never been better in my *damned* life. Enjoy my retirement, eh? Isn't that what I'm supposed to do?"

"He's drunk, Zemfira, let him sleep it off," said Paniz, impatiently. "Let's go get unclasped."

Zemfira glanced up at the temple's bell tower, saw other children hurrying up the road, then clenched her jaw.

"Come, sir, let me bring you home," said Zemfira, putting a shoulder under his arm. "Your wife will be worried about you."

"Zemfira!"

"Go ahead Paniz," said Zemfira. "I understand."

Paniz scowled, spat once into the dirt to indicate her sentiment, then lifted Navid under his other arm. "Today, of all days."

"You don't have to make a fuss about me," slurred Navid. "I'm not—I'm not really as old as I look, you know. I'm a Stormcaster with the Cost of Aging."

"We know," said Paniz.

They had heard Navid's war stories as much as anyone in the village.

"In service to the royal army I gave my youth so that my king could achieve victory," grumbled Navid. "A true patriot, I am. So why does the Satrap reject me from the summer campaign?"

They guided Navid onto the forest path which led to his isolated cottage.

"The Satrap rejected you? But aren't you retired?"

Navid chuckled. "Those northern raiders are making him nervous, so he sent out a call to all the veterans in Baxtris. I go all the way to his citadel, I report for duty, and do you know what he says to me?"

"No idea," said Paniz, kicking a pinecone with her bare foot.

"Says I won't be nimble enough for his mobile army. Nimble enough! I was renowned for my swordfighting! And a decent caster too!"

"I blame you for this," muttered Paniz to Zemfira.

"Almost there," said Zemfira, looking straight ahead.

Navid's cottage sat by the creek, nestled on two sides by thorny berry bushes. Zemfira's heart sank when she saw the door closed. Was his wife not there yet?

"Oh, this should be good."

Zemfira turned to see Navid's wife crossing the stream with two dead rabbits in one hand and a limp pigeon in the other. Her eyes flashed fury at her husband, but softened when she regarded Zemfira and Paniz.

"Thank you," she said, dropping the rabbits and taking Navid's weight from the girls onto her shoulder. "He doesn't deserve such concern, but I appreciate it nonetheless. The moment I go out hunting he slinks into town."

"I'm allowed to drink," protested Navid. "I've earned it, haven't I? I've served my king, even if he is a bit of an idiot."

"Navid!" his wife snapped.

"Bah, it's the truth. I cannot help it."

Navid's wife glanced at the girls, at the necklaces they still wore, then in the direction of the temple bells. "Why are you wasting time with this drunken fool? Get going! Get unclasped already!"

Paniz pulled Zemfira along before she could offer any more help, and in a second they were hurrying back down the forest path.

"That wasn't so bad," protested Zemfira. "We won't be too late."

"I have vomit caked on my shoulder," grumbled Paniz.

Zemfira chose to ignore this. "I can't believe it's today! We're going to discover our Castings! Unless they turn us away."

"They won't turn us away," said Paniz firmly. "Last time a thirteen-year-old got unclasped. Fifteen is definitely in the age range."

Zemfira knew that age wasn't the only marker of adulthood. Sometimes the monks denied those who were still emotionally immature. But she kept this to herself.

"What do you think you're going to cast?" asked Paniz, already out of breath but not slowing down. "Storm, maybe? Or Sprout? I could see you as a Sproutcaster."

Zemfira grimaced at the thought. Her father was a Sproutcaster, though he only used his Casting to provide extra food for the goats in winter.

"I hope I get something a little more exciting."

They reached the main road and joined the dozens of children moving uphill. Many were too young, but optimistic enough to try. All looked nervous and eager. All wore the Iron Necklace.

Beyond the last cottages rose the Thirst Temple of Nebit —a mossy structure with bird statues flanking the gates. The monks inspected each child at the entrance, either letting them enter or turning them away if they were too young.

Zemfira and Paniz found seats next to Malek, the son of the tanner, who was trembling. At only thirteen, he was lucky to make it past the monks' scrutiny.

5

"What's wrong Malek?" asked Paniz, putting a hand on the boy's shoulder. "Anxious about what your Casting will be?"

"It's not my Casting I'm worried about," whispered Malek, his teeth denting his lower lip. "But my Cost. What if my Cost turns out to be Depravity? I don't want my Casting to turn me into a monster! I just—"

"You won't be a Soulbreaker," said Paniz. "They're incredibly rare. Your Cost will be Fatigue or Hunger, most likely."

"How can you be so sure?" Malek shuddered. "How can everyone be so excited if—if we might..."

Zemfira couldn't remember a Soulbreaker ever being unclasped in Nebit. Those who corrupted their own souls in order to cast were very rare. The subject of Soulbreakers was taboo and questions were not permitted, but everyone knew Soulbreakers quickly turned from the path of virtue and lost their humanity. Aunt Gozeh often said the only difference between a Soulbreaker and a Shadow Beast was the number of legs.

The courtyard was almost full, and still the bells sounded, on and on, beckoning children from across the valley. Finally, the Targu stepped forward, and raised his hands. The children turned and the bells went still. The echoing peals continued until silence returned.

"Welcome, children," said the Targu. A red headband encircled his wrinkled forehead and white hair, indicating his seniority. "Unclasping Day is a very special occasion: a cause for celebration and solemnity. Once your Iron Necklace has been unclasped, you can call upon your Casting. Misuse your new power, and you will be punished as an adult. There is a reason we do not allow children to play with such power. It should never be taken lightly."

The Targu looked around, folding his arms behind his back.

"We have three Insightcasters in our temple who will identify your Casting and your Cost, once your necklaces are removed. Those with Thirst, like myself, will be invited to join the temple. Those with Hunger, Fatigue and Aging shall be given our blessing."

He paused again, as if silently acknowledging the possibility that someone with the Cost of Depravity could be uncovered. Zemfira wondered if a young Soulbreaker would be put to death on the spot, or imprisoned first. They certainly couldn't be allowed to deplete their own soul and unleash destruction on innocent people.

"There are nine expressions of Casting," said the Targu. "Sprout, Storm, Obedience, Inferno, Stone, Insight, Temperature, Light and Shadow. Some Castings will complement your Cost: others will present a greater challenge."

The children whispered excitedly, each hoping they'd be revealed to possess an impressive Casting, like Storm or Inferno.

"Some of you will gladly pay the Cost of your magic," the Targu continued, once the children had settled down again. "It will ease your life, and open new possibilities to you. For others, the price will be too great, and there is no shame in refusing to cast. Through careless use, people have dried themselves out, starved to death, and withered away. Becoming a true Caster is a great achievement, but refusing to cast embodies prudence, and without prudence, no one achieves wisdom."

"Can't we just get to the Unclasping?" whispered Paniz, her knee bobbing rapidly. Zemfira suppressed a smile.

"Wait patiently while we examine your peers. Those who create a disturbance will be examined last. Let us proceed."

The monks started at the front, touching one child or another on the shoulder and guiding them into the temple chambers. Birds sang beyond the walls. Shadows moved across the mountains as afternoon gave way to evening. Still they waited. Children entered with necklaces and exited as adults, their throats bare.

A monk tapped Paniz on the shoulder. She rose and walked confidently through the center door, but Zemfira could see her fists were trembling. She vanished from sight, and Zemfira closed her eyes.

She thought about the mother she could barely remember. She had died when Zemfira was four. Her father seldom even spoke her name. More than ten years later, his grief was still too sharp. Zemfira did not feel sad about her death; but she constantly sensed the maternal absence and wished her mother had been alive to see Zemfira reach adulthood.

Paniz emerged, beaming. The monks tried to steer her towards the exit but Paniz whispered in passing, "Infernocaster with Fatigue."

Zemfira tried to smile, but seeing the strip of pale skin where the necklace had been on Paniz's neck unnerved her.

Most children had left the courtyard and the first stars were pricking the sky when a monk finally stepped up to Zemfira's side. She followed the monk, heart hammering, into the chamber on the left. Like all Thirst Temples, miniature canals ran between the stone slabs of the floor. Little gardens of moss and fern grew in the shadows, but on a circular dais she saw a monk, bathed in lamplight. He sat cross-legged, eyes closed.

"You mustn't be nervous, my child," said the monk.

He was young, Zemfira saw, as he scooped his shallow cup through a canal and took a sip. The hair, constrained by his headband, was black and wild, but his eyes revealed monastic

8

tranquility. The tattooed prints of an eye were visible on both wrists. If he removed his headband, she would see a third eye drawn with ink on his forehead.

"Can you see my mind?" she asked the Insightcaster, as he put down his cup.

"Only its most obvious fragments," replied the monk, serenely. "Insight is one of the most difficult Casting arts, and comes at a risk. If you look too deeply into someone's mind, you might lose your own. Please take a seat, with your back facing me."

She obeyed. Two more monks approached, bearing the tattoos for Temperature and Stone. They stood behind her, each placing a finger on her necklace and focusing their powers. She felt the material grow hot, then cold, then the iron links loosened. The necklace fell in pieces to the floor.

She had expected a rush of energy—to become acquainted with her own powers in a second—but nothing happened. She almost felt disappointed. Slowly, Zemfira turned to face the young monk. He had gathered up the iron fragments and was setting them aside delicately.

"Not so complicated, was it?" he said with a smile, as the other two monks bowed and departed.

"No," agreed Zemfira. "That was much faster than I expected."

"We're not done quite yet," said the monk. "I still have to take a gaze into your soul and gauge the nature of your powers. In addition, it's my duty to answer any questions you have. You should not leave the temple feeling confused or afraid. Now, relax and open your mind. It will make the process much easier."

Zemfira nodded, absentmindedly touching her exposed neck. She took deep, slow breaths.

"That's good," said the monk, closing his eyes. Immediately, he opened them again. "Zemfira, your energy is blindingly bright."

"And that's—that's good, right?"

"Yes," he said softly. "I barely had to probe to see your inner illumination. You are a Lightcaster, dear child."

Zemfira's stomach relaxed while her pulse accelerated. Lightcasting was almost as rare as Shadowcasting, and quite powerful. Navid had talked with reverence about Lightcasters he had known in the army, soldiers who damaged enemies and healed allies with equal skill and grace.

The monk closed his eyes again, mouth tightening, eyebrow twitching in concentration. Then his eyes shot open and he stared at her in alarm. With great effort, he composed himself.

"My apologies," said the monk. "I was just...no matter. Your cost is Aging. Your Casting comes at the price of your youth. And that concludes your unclasping."

The monk would not meet her eye. Although he knelt in the posture Zemfira associated with meditation, the monk's left palm was open, as if ready for instant casting.

"Are you sure my Cost is Aging?" said Zemfira, slowly.

"Yes, yes, quite certain."

"But you seemed—"

"Didn't I say there is sometimes difficulty with Insightcasting? Well, I am still learning." The monk's forehead glistened in the lamplight. "So, have a good evening, and best of luck."

"I thought I was allowed to ask questions if I had any," said Zemfira.

"Oh," said the monk, jaw tightening. "I did say that, didn't I? Well, if you have a question or two, go ahead."

She wanted to ask, *why are you lying to me about my Cost?* There was no doubt this man was hiding something from her. But what about her Cost would cause such terror? There was only one plausible answer, unlikely as it was: Depravity.

She was a Soulbreaker.

That horrible fact would explain the monk's reaction, his lies. He didn't want her to know. He wanted her to leave, unaware that she was poised for evil. That meant the temple would not detain her. Someone else would handle her, when she was not expecting it.

"Is it true that Lightcasting can have healing properties?" she asked.

She needed the interview to end as well. Unfocused as the monk had become, he did have the power to gaze into her thoughts. She couldn't let him know what she suspected. He had to think she was just a dumb, gullible girl.

"Healing properties, yes," said the monk, adjusting his headband. "It's quite difficult though...a technique that requires a...mature touch...and I might wait a few months, perhaps even a few years, before you attempt—"

"That's good advice," said Zemfira, rising to her feet, making the monk flinch. "I don't think I want to use Lightcasting that much. Not if it ages me."

"Very wise," said the monk, smiling with relief. "I wish you a good evening."

Zemfira bowed, and hurried out of the temple chamber. The ascending moon rose from beyond the mountains, heralding the night. Curious eyes turned in her direction as she made her way to the exit. Tears gathered at the edges of her eyes and as she hurried through the temple gates. Once she was out of the monks' line of sight, she started to run.

11

# CHAPTER 2 – THE ZEALOT

As a Royal Zealot, Volakles had a sacred duty to protect the royal family of Farsia at all costs. He tried to bear this in mind as the stewed peach sailed through the air and collided with wet impact against his forehead.

"Princess Stateira!" cried one of the eunuchs, as the eleven-year-old princess giggled at her mischief. "You must not throw food, not at your Zealots."

The stewed peach had already fallen onto the garden pathway, but sticky syrup was now sliding down Volakles's cheek. He wanted to wipe it away, though he wasn't sure he was allowed to. Two years as a Zealot, and he still didn't know if wiping away fruit juices would be considered nonverbal communication with the princess, which was forbidden.

The palace gardens were saturated with song, spices and silks. Dancers pirouetted over the lilyponds, poets sung with vibrating voices, eunuchs hurried forward with ebony trays and silver dishes. The evening entertainment for the eldest princess was opulent, but even opulence became mundane after a while.

"I was only trying to be nice to the Zealot," said Princess Stateira, picking up another stewed peach from the silver dish and sliding back across the pillows to evade the tentative hands of her eunuch. "He looks so serious, and I heard his stomach gurgle and thought he might be hungry."

"Princess, please, you mustn't—"

"Hey, Zealot," called Stateira, the diadem on her head tilting to one side as she assumed a crouching position. "Zealot, open your mouth, I think this time I can make it land right inside. It's a very tasty peach."

Volakles loved peaches, a fact which the princess certainly didn't know, but no love of fruit would make him open his mouth. While disobeying the crown princess was a severe offense for most palace staff, Volakles reported to the Captain of the Zealots, and through him, to the king himself. He was here to protect Stateira, and to do so with decorum, no matter how much the girl's antics made him want to laugh.

"The reason the Zealot's stomach is gurgling," said the eunuch, blocking the thrown peach with remarkable swiftness, "is because he bears the Cost of Hunger."

"He's casting?" asked Stateira, suspiciously. "Why is he casting?"

"He scans for enemies, Princess. Do you see the markings on his helmet?"

"The eye of Insight," said Stateira. "He's an Insightcaster."

"Yes," said the eunuch, patiently wiping his long sleeves clean of peach syrup. "He ensures no enemies lurk nearby. Thanks to him, no one will approach you with ill intent."

Instead of confirming this verbally, Volakles closed his eyes and focused. He cast his mind out in spirals around him, taking note of nearby souls. He had not been promoted to the rank of Zealot for his skill with a sword, but because he was one of the sharpest Insightcasters in the kingdom.

His awareness sorted through eunuchs, musicians, actors and fellow Zealots. He sensed them as vague clouds of intent: the desire to serve, the admiration of the palace gardens, the alertness of those sworn to protect the family. Nothing was out of place: no mind with murderous ambitions lurked near the princess. Volakles felt his stomach tighten with his Cost of Hunger, but he didn't let the discomfort show.

"He looks so serious," said Princess Stateira when he opened his eyes again. A quick flick of his eyes told him the princess was lying on her pillows, staring at him. Her bracelets jangled and there were food stains on her silk dress. "Is he not allowed to look happy? Does he not like the music? Maybe we need more dancers, then he'll smile."

"I think it's time for bed, Princess," said the eunuch, wiping a trickle of sweat from his forehead. Volakles did not envy his duty. "Come, you have reading lessons in the morning, and you're going riding with your mother before luncheon."

The princess beamed at this news, clapping her hands delightedly. "Do I get to ride my favorite horse?"

"Whatever you wish, Princess Stateira," said the eunuch with a deep bow. "Will you walk to your room or would you like the litter to carry you?"

The girl considered this, finger on her lower lip. "I'll walk," she said, eventually. "The litter smells so musty."

It was a relief to leave the boisterous gardens and follow the princess's entourage at a respectful distance. Once she was within her chambers, Volakles and his fellow Zealots could relax their expressions, address their hunger and stretch their limbs. Volakles pulled a piece of dried goat meat from a pocket and chewed it, the savory flavor subduing his gurgling stomach. Then he wiped the fruit juice from his face.

"Your composure in the face of stewed peaches is an inspiration to us all," grinned Golzar, Volakles's closest friend among the Zealots. "I'll bet she starts throwing all sorts of things at you, in order to get a reaction out of you."

Normally Volakles would have appreciated the humor at his expense, but tonight he just nodded his acknowledgement.

"I'll take the first patrol," he said.

"You feeling all right?" asked Golzar.

"Yes," said Volakles, adjusting his sword sheath and his round buckler. "I'm fine."

Golzar and the other Zealots took up positions in front of the door and along the corridor. Servants stood there too, equipped with anything a princess might need in the night. Volakles took a deep breath and began his patrol.

Silence slowly settled over the palace as festivities concluded for the evening. Volakles walked along the edge of the garden, still smelling the hints of smoke in the breeze. The moon gleamed. Crickets and nightingales filled his ears with their songs, but otherwise all was quiet. All was peaceful.

Volakles closed his eyes and sent out another controlled spiral of Insight. His stomach twinged, and he slowed his expenditure, trying not to waste any stamina in his output. He tried to remember the advice given to him by Royal Targu of Hunger: *Only cast when your mind is clear from distraction, otherwise your Cost of Hunger will take more than it must.*

There was a gentle rustling in the royal gardens, a breeze through the pomegranate canopies or perhaps an owl shifting position. Volakles took a step toward the sound, and stood still. Even with his scan, there was the chance he had overlooked an assassin. New Casting styles were always being developed. Old Casting styles were being rediscovered. He could not rely on his Insight alone. And so he stood still and listened.

As children, Volakles and his brothers would hide in the sea caves along the craggy coast and search for each other. He remembered crouching against the salty stone, listening to the ocean roar outside, hoping that if he stood still, his older brothers would mistake him for just another rock. Those days had made him a very good listener.

Suddenly Volakles felt a surging presence, a powerful aura of Casting. The air grew bitter, the earth rumbled and the illusion of calm shattered. Volakles drew his sword, the blade catching the moonlight. He ran back to the corridor, mentally reaching out to his fellow Zealots and alerting them.

Tapestries hung askew. Lamps had crashed to the ground and little fires were sparking up on the carpets. In front of Princess Stateira's chamber, two servants and Golzar sat cowering by the door. Volakles could pardon the terror of the servants, but not of his fellow bodyguard. He grabbed Golzar and shook him.

"It's some divine punishment," Golzar whispered to him, eyes wide.

"Then we shall fight the Celestial Ones," snapped Volakles. "We protect the royal family at all costs. Gather yourself: this is a human evil, and we will quench it."

Golzar's expression cleared, the fear in his eyes receding. "I'm sorry—my mind was—I don't understand—"

"Not now, brother," said Volakles. "First, our duty."

Golzar drew his sword and turned to the princess's door. It was death to enter the room of a royal with a weapon, but this was an emergency. Volakles could now sense the murderous intent as clearly as he might hear laughter in an empty room. Slamming through the ornately carved door with his shoulder, Volakles rolled forward over the splintered wood and stumbled to his feet.

16

It was a devastating sight. The wall facing the garden had collapsed entirely. Bricks lay in dusty heaps on the smashed bookshelves. Debris was strewn across the flowerbeds. The princess sat awake atop her pillows, devoid of royal mystique. In her fear, she could be any other young girl. She stared at the moonlit silhouette of a stranger, approaching her with a long knife in one hand.

"I guess she missed a few," said the stranger, voice like gravel. His bare torso was etched with an array of tattoos, which rippled as his muscles flexed.

Volakles's pulse pounded within him. Who was this man? How had he breached so deep into the palace?

The stranger raised his free fist and the rubble began to tremble. Broken bricks and rock rose into the air and hurled themselves at the two Zealots. Both dodged in different directions, Volakles rolling forward, between the stranger and the princess's bed. He tried to remember his lessons—what was the best way to counter a Stonecaster? Swiftness. It took incredible energy to maintain speed with Stonecasting. Rocks, by nature, did not want to move.

Golzar ran forward, channeling his Casting into his sword so that flames roared up around the blade. He slashed at the man, but the Stonecaster blocked with his knife and slammed Golzar in the stomach with a rock, knocking him backwards. There was a hollow cadence to this Casting, a yawning absence which told Volakles a simple, horrible fact. The man was a Soulbreaker.

"Get out of here, princess!" Volakles shouted, placing himself between the assassin and the child. "Flee, now!"

He had no time to consider etiquette. Her safety was his only concern. Stateira didn't reply, nor did she move. Fear had overwhelmed the princess.

Volakles focused his Casting on the assassin, clenching his fists as he tightened his grip on the man's mind. He could not subdue him. The man's spirit and Casting were too strong. But Volakles could cause him mental anguish: a headache without peer.

"Zealot swine," spat the Stonecaster, holding his temples with his free hand. The mental vicegrip was not strong enough—Volakles still struggled using Insightcasting as a decisive weapon in battle.

The Stonecaster slammed his right foot down and the bricks beneath Volakles exploded up, throwing him into the air, then crashing down again. The landing was painful even with his leather-padded armor. Volakles's stomach growled with menace.

Golzar struck again, but the assassin pushed him back with a hail of pebbles. Volakles struggled to his feet, picked up his sword, and watched in horror as the Stonecaster raised his arms and brought all the stones and fragments into the air, creating a whirling maelstrom of debris. How was he able to raise and control so much stone, after already exerting himself so much? This was the awful power of a Soulbreaker.

The man laughed and the stones swirled faster. Volakles knew he could not dodge them all, not in his current state. He covered one eye and stared straight into the man's shadowed visage. Volakles did not know his name or his mission, but he could still gaze into his immediate intent.

Aimgazing was costly. He instantly felt the bite of Hunger intensify, but he had no choice. When the man hurled the bricks and stones at him, Volakles could see their trajectory. It was similar to the afterimages burned into one's eyes after looking at the sun. Trails of translucence showed Volakles where the Stonecaster was intending to strike.

Volakles dodged forward, wove left, then right, then down. He braced himself against the hail of stone fragments, and slammed the man in the jaw with his buckler. Ceasing his Aimgazing, he stabbed his sword through the man's shoulder and heard him cry out in pain. Volakles stabbed again, missing a killing stroke, but slicing into the man's right arm, his blade cutting through tendons and hitting bone.

Then he felt a cold pain sink into his back—a pain so shattering that his sword slipped from his grasp. He sank to his knees. He could sense another presence, one that had been hidden from him until now, but he could not turn around. All of a sudden the world was ending.

Volakles saw the palace ablaze, the king lying dead in the road. The Celestial Ones lay broken, wings tattered, as the stars faded from the sky. Shadow Beasts roamed across broken cities. His mother, his brothers, his niece and nephew—all struggling to breathe as they suffocated in front of him, but he was helpless to save them.

He heard a scream, but not from the thousands drowning and being devoured by Shadow Beasts. This scream was nearer, more real. Volakles focused his mind, closed himself off from all the images and fought against his terror. He staggered upright, his eyes full of chaotic visions, and turned to face the princess's bed, where a woman in black stood, tendrils of darkness curled around her fists.

"Impossible," she said. "You should be losing your mind."

The princess was lying on the bed, whimpering. She didn't look injured, but Volakles suspected she had received a similar dose of her greatest fears.

"You're a Shadowcaster," said Volakles, increasing his output of Insight, so as to keep himself from the valley of horror behind him. "And you've learned how to manipulate fear."

19

The woman slashed her hand toward him, sending a shadow lunging for him but he absorbed it on his buckler. She smiled. "You're going to starve if you keep that up. Just let go and surrender to your madness. It will make your death almost painless."

"I will kill you before—"

The Stonecaster, on his feet again, slammed Volakles into the ground with his good shoulder. He was bleeding badly, but his bloodlust was staggering.

"Careful, Sargon," said the woman. "You're injured."

"Deal with the girl," the Stonecaster growled. "I'll kill these Zealots."

Volakles tried to roll out of the way but Sargon smashed a rock down onto his shield arm. The pain was incredible. Something must have broken. He was trapped. Pain coursed through his body while hunger clawed at his stomach. His vision was blurred. He tried to reach up and stab with his sword, but the man's boot stamped down on his forearm, pinning him.

"Goodbye, Insightcaster."

In that moment a burst of fire shot out and hit Sargon in the face. Volakles hadn't realized Golzar still clung to life. The unexpected flame made Sargon recoil, releasing Volakles's arm just long enough for Volakles to thrust his blade into the Stonecaster's stomach. Sargon, clutching his cheek, stared at the sword. Then, blood spilling out of him, he collapsed to the ground.

Volakles could not hold on any longer. He was famished. His thoughts lacked coherence, and the Shadowcaster was beyond his perception. He was losing consciousness, and she would kill him. The pain in his arm throbbed as all faded into darkness.

# CHAPTER 3 – HOME

Paniz was waiting, halfway down the hill, sitting against a gnarled tree.

"So?" she said, jumping to her feet.

Zemfira looked at her friend, trying to shake the sense of hollowness inside her. There was soot on Paniz's fingers, as if she had been experimenting with her new abilities. Zemfira swallowed and tried to look calm.

"So what?"

Paniz rolled her eyes. "What did the monk say?"

"I'm—I'm a Lightcaster."

Paniz tilted her head, giving the matter some consideration. "That's not bad. What about the Cost?"

Zemfira cleared her throat, and started walking, so that Paniz could not see her face. "He said my Cost is Aging."

Paniz made a noise of disgust. "Ugh. You'll have powerful magic at your disposal. I assume you're not excited about aging prematurely like old Navid, but your abilities will be far beyond—"

"I need to get home," said Zemfira, dully.

"Wait," called Paniz, running after her. "Why so dejected? Were you hoping for something else?"

Zemfira shrugged. Moonlight and memory guided them

down the road.  The smell of lentils and roasted vegetables drifted from cottage windows.  Zemfira knew if she thought too much, she would start being afraid.  She couldn't let that happen.

"You're acting very strange."

"Go home, Paniz."

"What's wrong?  Why won't you tell me?"

"See you tomorrow."

Undeterred, Paniz kept prodding Zemfira for more information until she finally shook her off at her front door. Paniz stalked off, muttering to herself.  Zemfira, swallowing, turned to face the cottage.  Smoke was rising from the chimney of the cottage and Zemfira could see the glow from inside.  Heart heavy, she opened the door.

Kuzro was a stocky man with a scruffy beard and a weathered face.  He sat cross-legged on his pillow, one bare foot tapping against the dirt floor as he ate.  Jabo was animatedly recounting his daily adventures to their father, about his swim in the creek, his race across the valley.  Both looked up delightedly when Zemfira entered.

"My daughter!" he cried, rising to embrace her. "We've been waiting for you!  Congratulations."

Zemfira closed her eyes while her father pulled her tight. After a second, she embraced him too. "Thank you, father."

"Your aunt decided you deserved a little something special, so she added some salted meat to the rice.  Here!"

He scooped a bowl into the pot simmering above the fire. The rich savory smells did nothing to incite Zemfira's appetite. She sat down, tried to smile and listened to her little brother finish his story.  Two young goats sat in one corner, bleating occasionally.  Kuzro had a fondness for these two in particular and refused to subject them to the crowded chaos of the town's shared barn.

"A Lightcaster, eh?" her father said, pouring himself more beer. "Your grandmother was a Lightcaster. Your mother's mother, that is. At the age of forty she decided to pursue the spiritual life and even rose to the rank of Targu in her temple. A remarkable woman."

"What sort of a Caster was our mother?" asked Jabo, leaning against one of the goats.

Kuzro's face drooped for just a moment, before he smiled again. "She was a Temperaturecaster—and a very good one. She could slice the frost off a winter day and dispel a heatwave. Together we grew a fine garden, the best saffron and tea in the valley."

Aunt Gozeh and many others had pushed Kuzro to remarry and provide a mother to his newborn son and five-year-old daughter. If Kuzro had tried to find a bride and remarry, he had not tried very hard. He had devoted himself instead to raising his children. Zemfira had never seen her father raise his voice, even when Jabo stole a sweet lime from a traveling merchant, and he had to give up a goat to protect his son from local law. But what would he do when he discovered his daughter was a monster?

Kuzro put down his beer. "What's troubling you, Zemfira? Are you nervous about casting?"

Zemfira shook her head.

"Light is one of the most diverse of the Casting arts, you know. It can heal, it can harm, and do everything in between. They say Lightcasting is how the Celestial Ones administer their divine justice. I have said for years that you are an angel, but now I have my proof!"

Zemfira felt sick to her core. "Father, please."

"Are you concerned about the aging?" asked Kuzro. "It's understandable. Youth is certainly precious. But there are ways to control your Aging. With enough practice, you can expend a great deal of magic and only shave a day off your life."

"Father—"

"If you want to study at a temple, and learn how to use your Lightcasting to maximum effect, that could be arranged."

This offer took Zemfira by surprise. "You would let me study at a temple?"

"Of course," said Kuzro. "Jabo is old enough to start herding the goats with me, and the two of us can probably handle your daily chores."

"With or without Aunt Gozeh's help?"

Kuzro laughed. "I'm serious, Zemfira. Your cleverness makes me wish I was a rich man. I wish I could afford scrolls for you. Given the chance, you would be a great reader."

She turned away from the praise. "I can't go. It would be too hard."

Kuzro smiled. "No need to decide now. There is time, and the summer is warm. If, when the leaves begin to fall, you want to visit an Aging Temple, we'll find one together."

That night, Zemfira moved her little straw mattress further away from the red embers of the fireplace. She could hear her father's gentle snores and her brother's sleeptalking. Only when she was certain they were asleep did she allow herself to cry. The tears seeped onto her wool blanket and she pressed her mouth against it, so that her sobs would be inaudible.

She was going to die. That was the fate for all Soulbreakers. Perhaps the monks would contact the provincial Vazir, or the Satrap, or maybe the king, and they would send someone to hunt her down. If she stayed here, they would kill her. If she tried to run away, they would track her and kill her anyway. How long would it take them? A few days?

Maybe she deserved to die. Maybe she was a monster after all, and only the necklace had constrained the beast within. Was it safe for her to sleep in the same building as her family? Why did the monk let her go? A Soulbreaker. A *Soulbreaker*.

She thought about Paniz becoming an accomplished Infernocaster, joining the Farsian army and achieving great glory. Paniz often spoke of visiting foreign lands and returning with treasure and better stories than Old Navid. As a Soulbreaker, Zemfira would never see Paniz's triumphs. She would not see Jabo grow up. She would never get the full story of her mother's life from her father's reticent lips.

Unable to stand it any longer, Zemfira crawled out from under her blanket. After glancing towards the slumbering forms of father and brother, she made her way out into the darkness. The night was heavy with the perfume of petals and grass.

Barefoot, Zemfira moved from the dirt and gravel of the road to the pine needles of the forest path. She did not know who to talk to, did not know where to go. Only one person came to mind, one person who knew of the world beyond the village.

Navid's cottage was draped in foliage and shadow. The moon was sinking and only the stars glowed above the tree peaks. Blood pumping in her head, Zemfira assumed the cross-legged position she had seen the monks adopt, and prayed to the Celestial Ones, in case her gambit failed.

Hours passed as the nocturnal world moved around her. Bears were rare in the foothills and no wolves had troubled the area in years, but Zemfira's fear didn't come from predators. She waited while the sky turned pink and the clouds scattered like broken boulders. Then she moved through the wild grass and knocked on Navid's door.

25

The gnarled veteran answered the door, sword in hand. He appeared to have slept off his intoxication, but looked displeased by the disturbance.

"You? What's the meaning of this? Zemfira, is it?"

Zemfira was glad she didn't have any tears left. She swallowed heavily.

"If you're here for some sort of compensation for yesterday, no one asked you to take me home, that was entirely your—"

"I need advice."

"Get out of here. Any questions you have can wait until —"

"No," said Zemfira. "This is very serious."

Navid leaned his sword against the wall, looked over his shoulder where his wife slept, then stepped outside. "What is it?"

She had been formulating the right question all night, but now the words failed her. She sat down in the grass. "Do the monks tell unclasped children if they're Soulbreakers?"

"Of course," said Navid, gruffly. Then he hesitated. "At least, I assume so."

"When is the last time a Soulbreaker was discovered in Nebit?"

Navid stared at the discolored sky for a while. "Which Cost did they say you had?"

"Aging."

"And you don't believe them?"

"The monk recoiled from me when I was unclasped. He told me not to use my Casting."

Birds were starting to sing timidly between the branches. Little mountain flowers of purple and yellow were opening to the first rays of the sun. Navid tugged at his beard, expression hard. "Have you told your family?"

26

"No. I didn't. I didn't know what to do."

The old soldier muttered a curse. "You're in danger."

"What is going to happen to me?" Navid turned away again. "The Cleansers."

"Who are the Cleansers?"

"A division of the King's secret police. Unlike the Judgement, they serve only to eliminate Soulbreakers—those who use their Depravity to cause devastation, and—"

"And the children."

Navid's eyes closed. "The recently unclasped."

"So the Cleansers are coming to kill me."

"It seems likely, my child."

"But why?" pleaded Zemfira. "Why does the king need to kill Soulbreakers? I swear I never want to use my Casting. I won't allow myself to become a monster. I—"

She broke off at the expression on the veteran's face. "It doesn't matter. The king, despite his fine words, won't kill you for the sake of your fellow villagers. His Cleansers will kill you because it is foretold that a Soulbreaker will topple the noble House of Haxamanis, and bring the kingdom to its knees. It is in the interest of the king to prevent that, no matter how wicked it may seem."

Zemfira shivered. "How long do I have?"

"They will first eliminate those unclasped near the capital, the inner provinces. Then they will fan out and tackle the other Satrapies. Children here, in Baxtris, have more time before they... disappear. As long as they don't suspect you know anything, you have a month or two."

She took a deep breath. "Maybe I can run away. I can hide."

"They'll be watching you now, Zemfira," said Navid. "You are under constant mental surveillance. If you leave Nebit, the monks will know. They will mobilize the villagers and hunt you down. And once the Cleansers arrive... well, their Insightcasters are specifically trained to detect Soulbreaker auras."

Zemfira twisted her finger around a stalk of grass and pulled it from the soil. "So I have no chance."

"The king does not want to give any Soulbreaker a chance. Your options are limited."

He waited while Zemfira sat there, dawn breaking over the mountains. Her brother and father would be waking up now, wondering where she had gone—perhaps imagining she was at her daily chores. Her eyes itched from exhaustion.

"Would you train me?" she asked, quietly.

"What?"

"I can't use my Casting," she said. "I'll die before I wreck my soul. But I need to defend myself. I need to know how to fight."

"Cleansers come in groups of two. You can't fight them off without casting."

"Even with training?"

"Doesn't matter," said Navid. "I have been in wars, Zemfira, and I could not fight one Cleanser without calling on my Casting."

Zemfira stood up, eyes burning from lack of sleep. "What would you do with my fate? Would you sit around and wait for your murderers to do their duty? Would you kill yourself right away and avoid the dread? If I can't survive, then I will use the rest of my life to fight for it. When they kill me, they will find me ready to die honorably, having never cast Light or broken my soul."

Navid watched her as she breathed heavily. "You're brave. I don't know if I would be as bold in your place."

"So you'll help me?"

The old man inclined his head. "I will, but don't assume it'll save your life."

Relief flooded her. "When do we begin?"

"Get some sleep," said Navid. "You can barely stand. This afternoon, come and knock on my door."

"Will you be sober?"

"Bah. Get out of here."

Zemfira started walking back to the path, then stopped.

"Are you afraid of me?" she asked.

Navid turned at his front door and examined her. "I don't know," he said. "Perhaps I should be. Sleep well, girl."

He entered his cottage and closed his door.

# CHAPTER 4 – THE CLEANSER

Volakles awoke in pain and semi-darkness.   His skull throbbed, his arm hung useless and his stomach roared.   He knew this intestinal agony—his Cost of Hunger unfulfilled.   Even as he struggled to figure out where he was, he smelled the soup.   It sat in a bowl beside him, lit by distant lamplight.   With numb fingers and a keen desperation, he scrabbled for it.

He resisted the urge to finish the bowl in a single helping and took a controlled sip.   The hot liquid slid down his throat, burning and invigorating him.   His tongue detected chunks of meat in the broth, and using his good hand, he transferred one to his mouth.   Chewing was difficult and he had to rest before before taking another.   Each mouthful cut his hunger, and slowly the beast within retreated.   He let out a long breath.

He was lying in a jail cell.   A lamp glowed from a stone corridor and shone on the iron of his bars.   Judging by the uniform of the guard outside, Volakles was imprisoned in the palace dungeon.   He was now a prisoner of the king.

Still gathering fragments of his hazy memory, Volakles heard boots on the stone floor and looked up.   It was difficult to discern the figure, so swathed in shadow, but judging by the shape of the helmet, Volakles knew this was no soldier or guard.   This was an officer.

"Awake? Good, I have no time to waste."

Volakles tried to rise into a presentable position, but his injuries prevented him. The crisp voice of the man was unfamiliar. He stood with his hands behind his back, looking down at Volakles through the bars.

"I am Sahin, Captain of the Cleansers. Your shameful failures last night have resulted in terrible misfortune for the royal family and for the kingdom."

"Please, sir," said Volakles, "What happened?"

Sahin eyed Volakles with distaste. "It seems we are both ignorant of certain details. I can tell you that a Soulbreaker lies dead, as do many Zealots. The few survivors are struggling to regain their mental faculties. And the princess is gone."

Volakles pressed his eyes closed in shame and horror. Sahin continued.

"My soldiers have moved the royal family to the citadel and swept the entire palace. We did not find a trace of her, so we suspect she still lives. But in the hands of a Soulbreaker, she will not be alive for long."

"I can find them," Volakles said hastily. "I know the flavor of the criminal's soul, as I do that of the princess. I can identify both of them, if I am near."

Sahin smiled, pacing back and forth. "The king wants you executed as soon as you deliver your testimony. Perhaps tortured too. He is quite enraged."

Volakles tensed and swallowed. "No punishment is too great for my failure, Captain Sahin."

"I appreciate your contrition," said Sahin. "But a painless death for you will suffice. You failed in your duty but you did vanquish one Soulbreaker. However, what if I offered you something worse than death, as an alternative punishment?"

"I don't understand," said Volakles.

"No," agreed Sahin. "But surely you know your value. A powerful Insightcaster, loyal to the crown and gifted with the sword. It would be a shame to discard someone who survived two Soulbreakers. The kingdom is too fragile to waste its assets."

"The king will pardon my life?"

"The pardon comes at a price. Should you accept, you will join the Cleansers and begin purifying our kingdom from the next generation of assassins, rebels and murderers."

Volakles's throat locked up. Sahin was right. The assignment was a rival for death. Even if an unclasped child was a vessel for evil, Volakles wasn't sure he could kill one. Sahin saw his discomfort.

"Without the Cleansers, there is no Farsian state. The provinces would be helpless against rampaging Soulbreakers, who become more powerful and more wicked each time they cast. I trust you understand the stakes."

"Yes."

"You cannot join the squadrons that pursue the missing princess, but you can ensure the kingdom's safety in years to come. What do you choose, soldier?"

Volakles was a Zealot. He had fought in the infantry, proved himself to the Satrap of Lydia, and always struggled to be worthy of higher honors. But he had not struggled enough. His failure tasted bitter in his mouth, but he didn't want to die with dishonor. He wanted to serve, even though he dreaded the implications.

"I will do whatever you ask," said Volakles, quietly.

"Excellent," said Sahin, voice soft. "Then we can proceed."

\*\*\*

The inexperienced Lightcaster who healed Volakles's arm almost botched the endeavor. After a painful hour, Volakles's arm was tender but functioned satisfactorily. He waited in the darkness and tried to meditate, but he found he could not empty his mind.

It was not Sahin, but another Cleanser who came to his cell to release him.

"My name is Firuzeh of Thebai," she said to Volakles. "Follow me."

She led him up the staircase without a word. Volakles noticed the tattoo on her neck. She was an Obediencecaster, though with her hardened body and muscular physique, she would not need to cast much to assert her authority. Her skin was darker than his, but this was hardly surprising—Thebai lay far to the south, in the Satrapy of Mudraya.

"I have been informed of your recent actions," said Firuzeh. Her words were precise, her tone unemotional. "I suppose the kingdom is fortunate that a good Insightcaster was not executed. But not all Zealots make good Cleansers."

"I will serve my king to the extent of my abilities," said Volakles.

"Yes," said Firuzeh, simply. "I understand you are recovering from injuries, both physical and mental."

"I am."

The Cleanser nodded. "You have ten days before we set off on our assignment."

Volakles blinked. "We?"

"You are my new partner, Volakles," said Firuzeh, bluntly. "Cleansers work in pairs, so that we always outnumber our prey. My former partner died two years ago, while attempting to kill a Soulbreaker. Since then I have worked alone. Now we have been paired together."

"I'm sorry to hear—"

"I do not tell you to win your sympathy," said Firuzeh. "I tell you to put you on your guard. This work is dangerous."

Volakles bowed his head and chose his words carefully. "I would be grateful for your guidance, Master Firuzeh. How do you suggest I prepare for this assignment?"

Firuzeh looked unimpressed by his deference. "It is crucial that you strike without hesitation, but you will not learn that in the barracks. That must be learned through experience."

She deposited him at the Zealot barracks to retrieve his possessions. Volakles walked past his former comrades, who did not meet his eye. He wondered if they blamed him for the disappearance of Princess Stateira. Golzar was not among them, and Volakles did not have the courage to ask if he had survived.

He changed out of the prison tunic and into his spare uniform. He washed his face in the basin, then filled his sack and left the dormitory forever. From now on, he belonged to the Cleansers.

\*\*\*

Volakles spent his first days as a Cleanser in isolated misery. The Cleansers' barracks were built more like a large temple than military quarters, each Cleanser taking their bed mat and sleeping wherever they felt comfortable. Among the soldiers were experienced monks, available for guidance in matters of Casting should a Cleanser desire it. No matter where Volakles went, one or two monks would follow him. Had Sahin asked them to watch him? It seemed possible.

Volakles had not tried to befriend any of the other Cleansers. They knew who he was, and what he had failed to do. He managed to find a little garden in which he meditated and reflected on his new role. Had he been stronger, had he channeled his Hunger more efficiently, perhaps he could have kept the princess safe from the Soulbreakers. It meant only one thing: he needed to refine his Insight.

There were thirty-six Targus in the temple complex—one Targu for every combination of Casting and Cost. A monk told him to seek out Master Hettie, the Targu for Insightcasters with Hunger, whom he found sitting with a scroll in her lap.

"Young Volakles," said the Targu. She was his mother's age, her gray hair in braids. Like every Targu, she wore the red headband. "You are troubled."

Volakles bowed low and assumed a kneeling position. "I am afraid, Master Hettie. I've recovered my strength. I've resumed my morning exercises. But I know it's not enough."

"Swordplay is never the totality of a soldier, this is true," said Hettie.

"I must amplify my Insightcasting," said Volakles, "if I wish to confront these Soulbreakers."

"Indeed," said Hettie.

Volakles shivered at the thought of Sargon lifting hundreds of rocks and bricks into the air, swirling them without effort. Hunger would never grant a Caster as much pure power as that offered by Depravity. His thoughts drifted to the other Soulbreaker, the Shadowcaster.

"One of the assassins cloaked both their presences not only from sight, but from Insight. A Shadowcaster, wielding all the power of a Soulbreaker. I want to know if there is an Insight technique I can use to pierce a Shadowcaster's veil for the next time."

Hettie placed the tips of her fingers together. "I cast Insight to discover truth and wisdom. I am not versed in all combat forms of our Casting art, but I will delve deep into the scrolls, and see if there is any way to break a Shadowcaster's web once it has been spun."

Volakles grimaced. "Thank you, Master Hettie."

"In the meantime, train with a few Shadowcasting monks, and fight them while observing their minds. Once you develop a good sense for their trace, you will be able to identify the presence of a Shadowcaster even while they are blocking you."

"That won't tell me who else they're hiding."

"It won't. But this is a step forward. Practice, and whenever possible, meditate: it is difficult to gain insight into others. It is near impossible to know yourself. Your mind is the final bastion you must infiltrate in your pursuit of enlightenment."

Volakles bowed his head. It was advice he had received before, from previous Targus and the drillmaster in his infantry unit. Gaining Insight about oneself from within oneself required intense endurance and mental clarity. Golzar and the other Zealots would snort with derision when he had tried to explain the difficulty. *All you have to do is think better,* Golzar had said, giving him a shove. *Do you know how hard it is to create fire without physical fuel? You've got it easy.* Volakles repressed anguished thoughts of his fallen comrades and instead hardened his resolve, determined to master self awareness.

***

The Cleansers' barracks had five training areas to prepare Cleansers for combat in all terrains. Volakles practiced his swordfighting in the glacier, swamp and desert environments, then engaged in his Insight training in the forest zone. Even through the ordeal of rigorous training, he had to commend the Temperaturecaster monks for recreating the impediments of snow

36

and desert. But extreme weather was simple compared to the training for withstanding Shadowcasting.

"You're letting us get to you," said Garguk, one of the two Shadowcaster monks, leaning against one of the saplings and drinking water from a wineskin. "You need to shake our influence in order to concentrate. Without concentration, you'll misread our intent."

Hajgo, the other monk, nodded. Both wore the trousers of the barbarian style, which served well in hand-to-hand training. Volakles grimaced, chewing on his piece of dried meat, and wiping the sweat from his forehead.

"I can handle one of you," he said, touching the bruise on his shoulder. "But when you're both casting, it's—"

"The equivalent of a Soulbreaker, perhaps?"

Volakles said nothing, but swallowed his mouthful and assumed his position again, bending his knees and raising a fist. His older brother, Aniketos, had taught him how to fight—had toughened him at Volakles's request. Fists were little help against the pirates of the Kappadokian coast, though they had at least protected him from the older boys of the village. But both Garguk and Hajgo were the equals of Aniketos—and they were both skilled casters.

Garguk lunged first while Hajgo clouded Volakles's Insight. He struggled to perceive where Garguk would strike, but it took more attention to break through the mental clouds than to dodge. Volakles stepped back and blocked the second punch.

"No relying on your eyes," said Garguk, and he spread a veil of shadow around the two of them. Volakles grimaced. Without access to sight, he had to break Hajgo's embargo on Volakles's casting.

A fist hit him in the chest, not a powerful punch, but a blow to put Volakles on the defensive. He retreated, bracing for the next blow and readying a counterattack. Another blow hit his cheek. Volakles tasted blood and stumbled back, head spinning. He could feel Garguk's shadowy energy on his cheek, and could sense the greater energy of it within Garguk himself, not even a meter away.

Volakles was so surprised by this realization he almost took a kick to the stomach. Until now he had perceived Garguk's shadows and Garguk as a single entity—an indistinguishable amalgamation of his Casting and his being. But there was a difference he could sense now—not in quality, but in movement. He could not break Hajgo's veil, but he was hazily aware of Garguk. At least he knew where Garguk was.

Volakles ducked beneath a swath of motion, which he assumed was Garguk's arm, and punched directly into the center of the presence. Blind to everything, Volakles heard the monk give a grunt and stagger back a few steps, obviously surprised. Hajgo clamped down harder on Volakles's Insight, but Volakles was not looking at Garguk's intent anymore, just at his output of energy.

"You're improving," said Hajgo, when the sparring was over. "But you still must work faster to break through the Shadowcasting should you encounter a Soulbreaker."

Volakles nodded. Even with his general sense of Garguk's presence, he had taken a hefty beating when Garguk stopped toying with him. Being able to sense an opponent was not the same as being able to stop him.

"Better," said Garguk at the end of the lesson. "Let's see if you can keep it up tomorrow."

Volakles thanked the monks and returned to his mattress for a brief respite. Firuzeh was there, waiting for him.

"We leave tomorrow before the sun rises," she said. "You have recovered sufficiently, and we cannot delay any more. Cancel all training sessions and prepare your gear."

Firuzeh had been absent from the temple complex for several days, out on assignment with Sahin. No one knew the details, but Volakles did not read success in Firuzeh's expression. He noticed she didn't carry the standard saber. Instead, two short swords were sheathed on her back. Cleansers of a certain rank had the privilege of choosing weapons that best matched their style.

"Where do we ride?" asked Volakles.

"We have received word from the temple at Chadrakarta, the temple at Arakhotoi, and the temple at Nebit. Those are our destinations."

"Understood," said Volakles. He hadn't heard of Nebit before—it was likely a small village—but Arakhotoi was the capital of Harauvatis, the eastern-most Satrapy. He had only started adjusting to the customs of the capital and the Fars dialect, after growing up in coastal Lydia. He could not imagine what strange worlds lay in the east.

"Captain Sahin wishes you to see the kingdom, in all its complexities. This work requires an understanding of the kingdom's various local customs. No matter how well the royal cartographers sketch the kingdom, it is always better to visit yourself, and understand personally."

Volakles felt his cheeks grow warm as an embarrassing question formed on his lips. "Do—do they speak Farsian in—"

"They speak Farsian in the East as they do in the South and the West," said Firuzeh. "It is the royal language, the language of trade. Be ready at dawn tomorrow. I have no patience for tardiness."

# CHAPTER 5 – TELL ME

"Stop trying to be aggressive," said Navid, blocking the strike from Zemfira's wooden sword, and tripping her to the ground. "You're not ready for it yet."

The bruises and torn skin on Zemfira's fingers and knuckles showed the intensity of the last few days. She clenched her teeth, got back to her feet and picked up the practice sword.

"I can't just block your blows and win."

"You won't win any other way either. Don't think in terms of victory. Think about surviving."

The clearing glowed with warm sunshine. A scattering of clouds and breath of wind reduced the heat, but both combatants were sweating. Zemfira wanted to walk down to the creek and wash herself, but knew she couldn't stop practicing. Not yet.

"Again," she said.

Over the years Zemfira had suspected Navid's war stories were exaggerations to delight the villagers, but those doubts were fading with each lesson. The old man moved with the speed of a cricket, darting to Zemfira's left and swiping at her. Zemfira blocked, the impact shuddering into her bones and muscles. She took a step back, swiping another attack aside and resuming her stance. Navid had instilled the defensive position in her with hours of practice. It was almost instinct by now.

Navid feinted to the left, swung around and slashed at Zemfira's ribs, which she deflected with effort. The veteran struck again and again, occasional blows getting through and making the girl retreat—but she never struck back.

"Better," said Navid. "Your body is already developing the instinctual reaction to each attack."

That was when Paniz stepped out of the trees. Zemfira felt her heart quicken and her throat grow wordless. There was anger on Paniz's lips, and in her fists.

"This is where you have been all this time? You said you were helping your father with the goats."

Zemfira looked at her feet. Navid glanced between the two girls, then pushed the wooden blade into the grass and leaned against the handle.

"Why did you lie to me?" demanded Paniz. "What are you keeping from me? Why don't you trust me anymore?"

"There's nothing going on," mumbled Zemfira. "I just don't want to use my Casting if it uses up my youth, and I need to learn how to defend myself."

"That's dung," spat Paniz. "You've been upset ever since your unclasping."

"I didn't tell you because I'm ashamed," said Zemfira. "I didn't want you to think I'm vain because of my refusal to cast."

"I don't believe this," muttered Paniz. "You're actually lying. Lying to me! Fine, I won't ask anymore. I'm going to the temple."

"What—why?"

Paniz was already walking away. "To learn what you won't tell me."

"No!" shouted Zemfira. "Don't! Don't do that!"

"Why not?" said Paniz. "What don't you want me to learn?"

Zemfira didn't say anything. Paniz shook her head in disgust, then started walking again.

"You have to tell her," said Navid, quietly.

"I can't," said Zemfira, eyes hot from restrained tears. "She'll hate me and fear me and—"

"Trust her, Zemfira."

She swallowed and then ran after Paniz. Paniz, realizing Zemfira was in pursuit, started running too.

"Stop, Paniz!"

"No!"

"Listen to me," said Zemfira. "I'll tell you. Just—just stop, please."

"Eat dirt!"

But Paniz did slow down. She turned, facing Zemfira and folding her arms. Zemfira swallowed.

"The monk said my Cost was Aging but I know he was lying."

"Monks can't lie."

"This one did."

Paniz chewed her lower lip. "Why would the monk lie?"

"Because," Zemfira took a deep breath, "because I'm probably a Soulbreaker."

Paniz stared at Zemfira. Then she scowled, made a fist, and struck Zemfira.

"Ow!" The pain made Zemfira stumble to one side and she clutched her cheek. "Why did you do that?"

"You kept *that* from me?" demanded Paniz.

Zemfira winced at Paniz's anger.

"Did you think I'd rat you out to the monks? I can't believe you, Zemfira."

"Paniz, I'm—"

"What?"

Zemfira's mouth was dry. "I'm really scared."  She explained what Navid had told her about the Cleansers and watched Paniz's eyes widen. "Navid says I have...maybe another twenty days.  Then they'll arrive here and kill me."

Paniz gritted her teeth. "We won't let them."

"Paniz, there's nothing we can do."

"Run away!  We can run away together, find a mountain cave where they'll never look, and—"

"They've got Insightcasters.  They'll track us immediately. There's no point."

"Then why are you training with Navid?  You think you'll beat them in combat?"

Zemfira stared at the dirt. "No.  Training is just something that feels productive—I know it won't save me."

Paniz stood up. "We'll find a way.  I'll do some thinking."

"Paniz—"

"Don't give up hope, okay?  Keep practicing with Navid —and I'll work on a solution."

Paniz jumped up and ran off, bare feet swishing through the grass.

***

As the days passed, Navid gave grudging acknowledgement of Zemfira's improvement.

"You're no soldier," he said. "But you've grasped the basics, I'll grant that."

Zemfira's heart sank at the faintness of the praise. "You still haven't taught me how to attack," she said, blinking sweat from her eyes.

"Attacking is the last thing to learn," said Navid. "You won't be attacking. Only strike first when you have surprise on your side. Otherwise, counterattack—that I will teach you."

They started sparring again, Zemfira again defending herself from his blows.

"Don't aim to hit my weapon," said Navid. "Aim for me. Strike decisively."

"And how do I strike decisively?"

Navid smiled, smashing his wooden sword against hers. "Wait for your opponent to make a mistake. When your opponent overextends, you finish them. Go for the neck or the sword arm."

Navid struck three times more, then went in for a stab that Zemfira evaded. Seizing the moment, Zemfira struck at Navid's arm—but the veteran spun away from the blow and struck Zemfira's shoulder.

"Not bad," he said, "but you're still hesitating. Either commit fully to the attack, or maintain your defensive stance. Remember, you can wear down an opponent with strong defense, and a worn-down opponent will make mistakes they can't recover from. Again."

\*\*\*

Many in the village overlooked Kuzro as a simpleton for his occupation and placid demeanor, but he was no fool. He had not missed the scratches and bruises on his daughter's hands and body, nor had he believed her excuses of clumsiness. He was also aware that Zemfira had been miserable ever since her unclasping.

He had been mulling the problem over in the field, sitting with Jabo on a rock covered in lichen. His son would chase after the occasional goat that wandered into the trees, leaving Kuzro to his reflection. From time to time he would encourage a stalk of grass to grow faster, while his thoughts drifted to his daughter. What sort of issue did she not want to discuss with him? Was it a female problem? Possibly. Was it heartbreak of some sort? That didn't feel right. A fight with Paniz? A bully?

As much as he loved his daughter, he often struggled to find the right words before inevitably changing the subject. He was not good at serious conversations, and he knew it. He pondered the problem as the afternoon faded into evening. He sent Jabo home, then guided the goats to the town barn. Other goatherds used bells or dogs to guide their flock, but Kuzro guided the fluffy creatures with a sprig of a nameless plant, tied around his staff. There were benefits to being a Sproutcaster, after all.

The smell of goat dung and hay in the barn didn't even register with him now, after so many years. He wondered if perhaps Zemfira would like some honeycakes. The goat milk had sold well in the morning, so he could afford the luxury. He exited the barn, picking the straw out from between his toes, when one of the monks greeted him.

"Good evening, Kuzro."

It was Avalem, a Sproutcaster monk. Kuzro had visited him when his wife was struggling with Jabo's birth, asking for medicinal guidance. After her death, Avalem had helped him through those dark days following the funeral. Kuzro didn't blame Avalem for the failure of the Sproutcasting to save Roshni's life, but the monk clearly still felt guilty.

"Hello, Avalem," said Kuzro. "What brings you out of the temple?"

Avalem patted one of the pockets in his robe. "I have been out looking for seeds. A new disciple joins the temple tomorrow and I must teach him our art, as best I can."

"You must be honored to have an eager acolyte to educate."

Avalem smiled and bowed his head. "It is an honor to pass knowledge to new casters."

"My daughter, Zemfira—you remember her, no? She was just unclasped too. A Lightcaster, just like her grandmother."

Kuzro was surprised to see a fall in Avalem's expression, as if Kuzro had announced the scattering of his herd or the illness of his children. With effort, Avalem regained his composure and pushed forward his delicate smile. He was a lean man with hollow cheeks and watery eyes. Not all monks fasted as regularly as Avalem did, but Avalem's father had taken his Cost of Hunger as his own philosophy, and Avalem had absorbed it as a method for purification.

"You must be proud," he said, quietly.

"Of course," said Kuzro. "She will do great things yet, I am sure."

Again, Avalem's reaction was one of sorrow, but before Kuzro could inquire, the monk asked, "And has your daughter started experimenting with—"

"Oh no," said Kuzro. "She's a little nervous about casting. I am thinking about taking her to the nearest Aging Temple. She seemed open to the idea, but I have to ask her again."

Avalem, looking queasy, nodded. "That is—good. Have you asked the Targu for permission to leave?"

"Permission? I am under no obligation to the Targu. If I wish to leave the village for a while, that is my right."

"Naturally. I'm sorry Kuzro—I meant for his advice."

Kuzro frowned. There was something uncomfortable in Avalem—in the tensing of his shoulders, in the flatness of his mouth. "Is something on your mind, Avalem?"

The monk shivered in the evening chill. Monks, more than regular citizens, were obliged to speak the truth. It was part of their simple living, part of what made their habits so difficult.

"I am sorry, my friend," said Avalem. "Sometimes I feel you stand beneath the darkest star."

"Bah, why is that?" said Kuzro. "No life comes without pain, and I have been rewarded with two beautiful children. I cannot protest such fortune."

Avalem had no response to this, but simply said his goodbyes. Kuzro walked back home, and watched Zemfira ladle out the thick stew of pickled vegetables and rice from the day before. She looked exhausted as she took a few hardened crusts and heaped them with generous portions of goat's cheese, which brought a broad smile to Jabo's face.

While Jabo ate and Kuzro drank beer, Zemfira told them that her cousin, Gozeh's daughter, had received a marriage proposal from the miller's son. Gozeh, according to Zemfira, was less happy than her daughter was, since she felt the miller was a miser and a cheat.

"And so his son cannot be much better, she thinks," finished Zemfira.

"A monk came looking for you today," said Jabo, between bites of goat cheese.

Kuzro watched his daughter stiffen, saw her hand tighten on her spoon. "What did the monk want?"

"He didn't say," said Jabo.

"I ran into Avalem this evening," said Kuzro. "And he was curious if you had started Lightcasting yet. I told him no."

Zemfira looked sick all of a sudden. Noticing how his daughter was squirming, Kuzro decided to change the subject. He instead told the story of Baj, a cartographer from the province of Arabaya, who had traversed the entire kingdom, heading east into the lands where the Celestial Ones had different names and the people saw the entire world as a circle. He told his children how Baj ventured through the small realms of the princes, about the elephants and the tigers and the jewels buried in forgotten temples, the palaces swallowed by the jungle.

He could see a little curiosity flare up beneath Zemfira's eyelashes—she had always loved his storytelling. He had started telling the stories of adventure, of heroes, of myth, as soon as his wife's funeral was over. He would take the stories she had learned while she had served as a scribe, and bring them to his daughter, so that she would know more. In this way, Kuzro preserved the memory of Roshni, his beloved wife.

"What did Baj do in the land of Nanda?" asked Jabo eagerly, though he had heard the adventures of Baj many times before.

"He did what all good traveling cartographers do," said Kuzro. "He went to the court of the Nanda Emperor, and begged an audience with the royal cartographer to trade maps. But the cartographer looked down on Baj as uncouth, so he refused."

Jabo growled in annoyance, and Kuzro went on.

"Baj knew how to deal with vanity and pride. He challenged the cartographer to a contest of a geographic nature. Whoever could best draw the road from Parsa to Pataliputra from memory would receive a map from the other. The royal cartographer liked the idea of adding to his own collection and agreed. Scribes brought each of them identical blank scrolls of parchment.

48

"The Nanda man finished quickly, and proudly displayed his work to the Emperor. Baj did not look up at the clamor. He kept working until his route was perfect. When he brought the map to the Emperor to compare, the Nanda ruler studied them closely. He declared Baj's work was far more like the official records, and applause rang out for Baj, much to the humiliation of the court mapmaker."

Jabo cheered, and Kuzro glanced over at Zemfira, who was eating a little stew, distracted from her woes.

"But Baj was no fool. He didn't claim his map and leave, though he had every right to. Magnanimously, he handed his map of Farsia to the Emperor as a gift and as thanks for his hospitality. And thus the royal court at Parsa learned more about what lies beyond the Indus River, just as they learned about us."

\*\*\*

Sleep did not find Kuzro that night. Jabo muttered to himself as he tossed and turned, but Kuzro listened to Zemfira's breathing. He heard how quick it became before she forced it to slow down again. He watched as she sat up in the moonlight, and stared out the window. As he observed her, a possibility dawned on him.

He stood up, neither disruptively loud, nor entirely quiet, and Zemfira looked over at him. She did not hide her face this time, but watched him walk over, her lower lip trembling. He sat down next to her, and wrapped his fingers around hers.

"Why didn't you tell me?" he whispered.

She shook her head. "There's nothing you can do, father."

"Did the monk say you're a Soulbreaker?"

She confirmed his suspicion. "Not with his words...but with his fear."

Kuzro put his arm around Zemfira and held her tight.

"Please don't tell the monks."

He stared at his daughter. "Why would I ever tell them?"

The first tear leaked out of her eye. "Because if you don't tell them and they find out, it might put Jabo at risk, and since he isn't a Soulbreaker, he's still worth protecting, and you should—"

"Stop it," said Kuzro. "I'm not abandoning you. I'm going to keep you safe."

"You can't. They'll know if I leave the village and they'll alert the Cleansers and they'll always be faster, and—"

The words caught in her throat. Kuzro took his daughter's hand and squeezed it.

"You're scared, of course you are, but there is always hope," he said. "And you are not alone. Remember that."

Zemfira gave a few very small nods of her head. Kuzro embraced her and did not let go until Zemfira's breathing had relaxed. What could he do to safely guide his daughter from this calamity?

# CHAPTER 6 – IN THE ALLEY

Chadrakarta rose up above the harbor with rich edifices of sandstone and brick. The city walls—a hodgepodge of materials hastily constructed to ward off various sieges over the years—now stood proud and draped in the royal colors and emblems. Long ships—both Farsian and Hellenic—docked in the glittering bay.

Volakles was exhausted from riding. He had never taken to traveling by horse. His neck was stiffer than preserved meat, his thighs burned with a rash and he couldn't feel his lower back. The epic poems never alluded to the discomfort of riding with armor. Firuzeh rode without a complaint, and after the first day he had stopped commenting on his pains.

"Stay close," Firuzeh said to him, as they followed the cobbled road up to the main gates, weaving between travelers and merchants. "Once inside the city, we will ride straight for the Vazir's palace, give a brief report to his deputy, and take up temporary residence."

She had explained the procedure a few nights before. Maybe she thought he was too dim to remember. The guards instructed the Cleansers to dismount once they were in the city, then waved them through, knowing their objective. Once inside, Volakles posed his question quietly.

"Why do we report to the Vazir at all? The Cleansers are under the sole authority of the king. Why bother with the Vazir and his minor court?"

"It is good form," said Firuzeh. "The Vazir can provide assistance and will vouch for our arrival, which is necessary if we both perish. If we don't report our success to the Vazir, he will know that trouble occurred and that other Cleansers can finish our work."

Volakles took a sip from his wineskin, thanking the Celestial Ones for the hundredth time that he didn't bear the Cost of Thirst. Firuzeh walked ahead with her gray horse at her side, no reins needed to have the beast follow obediently. Volakles had to keep a grip on his steed. His brain was fizzling from the oppressive midday heat.

Within an hour they found the Vazir's compound. It was modest compared to the palace at Parsa, but Volakles was still been awed by the sight. Towers with flapping banners rose above the copulas. Music and laughter echoed between pillars and statues, but Firuzeh guided Volakles to the stables, where the trappings of luxury were fewer. A trembling stable boy assumed care for their horses.

"From this point," said Firuzeh, as they exited to the courtyard "we do not draw attention to ourselves when we traverse the city. We cannot risk alerting our target. Endangering nearby civilians through carelessness is an unforgivable offense."

Volakles nodded, trying to keep his anxiety at bay. Now that the traveling was over, he had to earnestly reckon with the implications of the assignment. They removed their weapons, took off their armor and cloaks, then made themselves presentable for the Vazir's steward.

"Vazir Amarxes left yesterday," said the steward, guiding the Cleansers into his office and sending a girl off to prepare tea.

"The Satrap of Baxtris needed reinforcements to handle the Skythians, and so our Vazir mustered some forces and led out the troops. I will mention your successful arrival in Chadrakarta when he returns."

"Is the Satrap of Baxtris allowed to do that?" asked Volakles. "Can he call on the Vazirs from other Satrapies for help? Surely the Satrap of Baxtris can only command the provinces within Baxtris."

"Satrap Bessus is trusted by the king," said the steward. "And security of the kingdom will always trump protocol."

"We thank you for your warm reception," said Firuzeh, smoothly. "We would like to make our stay brief and minimize our impact on the Satrap's generosity. What is the status of our target?"

The steward's lips twitched. "The Insightcasting monks stationed in the western district have been keeping a mental eye on Behrouz since his unclasping. He believes he has the Cost of Aging, and will be escorted by two monks to the Aging Temple in Chadrakarta. He lives with his mother—a whore who has no time for the boy or his brother."

"How old is the brother?" asked Volakles.

Firuzeh shot him a look. "Have you procured the monks' robes I requested?"

Volakles blinked. "Monks' robes?"

"One of our many tactics," said Firuzeh. "Monks are trusted, and we can employ deception to lure the target away from the home."

"Deception." The word was bitter on Volakles' tongue. It violated the oaths he swore as a soldier, and as a Zealot. But he was a Cleanser now.

"My eunuch will provide you with all the equipment you need," said the steward. "How soon will you be finished?"

"Unless we are delayed, by this evening," said Firuzeh. "We will humbly accept the Vazir's hospitality for one night, and leave in the morning."

"You are welcome to stay longer," said the steward. "But I am sure you have other business to attend to—other cleansings to complete."

"Indeed," said Firuzeh. "We would like to start immediately."

***

The heat of the afternoon and the woolen robes suffocated Volakles, though the headband kept sweat out of his eyes. He had to remind himself of his new oath to King Artashata: to cleanse the kingdom from the seeds of evil and to cleanse himself of mercy against the merciless. But the denial which had protected him until now was fading. They weren't going to duel the Soulbreaker from the princess's quarters. They had to kill Behrouz, a fourteen-year-old boy. There was no glory in this task.

"I will perform the cleansing today," said Firuzeh. "You will observe and assist if danger arises."

Volakles nodded, mouth dry. He wondered how much damage the boy's soul had sustained—how far down the path of depravity he had already traveled. He felt unprotected in his robes, but said no more.

The slums reeked of poverty. It was far worse than the fishing village where Volakles had occasionally gone to bed with a grumbling stomach—there at least one could breathe. In the Faveh, fetid rats skittered over greasy cobblestones, darting in and out of shadows in broad daylight. Malnourished children watched the Cleansers pass with eyes hidden by disheveled hair.

The smell of rotten fish, decaying garbage and human excrement made Volakles wince.

"We shall scout the area," said Firuzeh, not in Farsian, but in Hellenic, Volakles's native tongue. "I think a secluded alley will suit our purposes."

"You—you speak Hellenic?"

"Naturally," said Firuzeh. "And I speak Koptic too. Keep your eyes open."

There was much Volakles did not know about Firuzeh and she proved to be more intriguing with every terse interaction. Unfortunately, she seemed uninterested in sharing her story and Volakles had never been good at asking personal questions.

When they found an alley between a brothel and a rowdy tavern, Firuzeh put two fingers in her mouth and whistled sharply. The sound rose, carried by the power of Firuzeh's Obediencecasting, up through the air, into the sky. Volakles squinted into the pristine blue above, and soon he could see small black specks circling in the sunlight.

"Birds?"

Firuzeh nodded, releasing a slow breath. "They will assist us when the time comes."

She made a quick examination of the little canal running beneath the back wall of the alley, a mess of feces and tepid water. Then she straightened, apparently satisfied. "Let's go."

They reached the apartment building and Volakles scanned the area, sorting through the multitude of human presence until he discerned the boy Behrouz. It was not obvious that he was a Soulbreaker, but his energy did not have the spark of Thirst, the acidity of Hunger, the bluntness of Aging nor the rumble of Fatigue. That absence clinched the matter.

Climbing to the fourth floor, Firuzeh knocked on the open door and waited for the boys inside to stop scuffling. The room was poorly lit: the single window had been boarded up and only a single sunbeam pierce between the crooked planks. Volakles swallowed when he saw that Behrouz's brother was several years younger than the Soulbreaker boy.

"Who are you?" called Behrouz.

He might have had a trace of Skythian blood in his veins, for his hair was red and his eyes were green. The boy reminded Volakles of the withered donkey his father sold to the local butcher when he was five: defiant, emaciated and mangy. Volakles tried to ignore the stereotypes he had heard about people from Mada, but it was difficult. The boy jutted his chin so arrogantly.

"We are monks from the Aging Temple," said Firuzeh, voice calm but direct. "We are here to escort Behrouz to our temple and train him to become an expert caster."

"Where are you from?" demanded Behrouz, looking suspiciously at her. "Your skin is so dark."

"My origin is not important," said Firuzeh.

"Are you a barbarian?"

"I am as Farsian as you are, Behrouz," she said. "And there is a lot I can teach you, once we reach the temple."

"Show me something," said Behrouz.

Volakles was astounded by Firuzeh's decorum. He thought she might kill him right there, in front of his brother. Instead, she raised a hand, and all the rats in the various corners and crevices of the apartment skittered out across the floor. The little brother screamed, but they all ran towards the curtained window, climbed up onto the ledge, and flung themselves into the open air. Volakles's stomach squirmed at the distant sound of rodents hitting the street below.

Behrouz scrutinized Firuzeh. "You look the same age. Why aren't you older if you have the Cost of Aging?"

"Such exertions only cost about a day of your life—if you know how to use your energy correctly. Do you wish to learn?"

Behrouz nodded and started looking for his shoes. His younger brother ran after him, tugging on his tunic. "Wait, Behrouz, wait until mother gets back, to say goodbye!"

"She's with a man," said Behrouz. "She won't miss me."

"But—"

The little brother looked terrified at the prospect of these strangers leaving him alone in the decrepit room, but Behrouz was seizing his chance to escape. Volakles could see that intent behind Behrouz's bluster, the hope he had for a life within the temple, the freedom that came with controlling his powers. The boy walked past the two false monks, and down the hall, not even waving goodbye to his brother. The little boy stood in the doorway watching them go, tears streaming down his face. Firuzeh remained close behind Behrouz as they descended the creaking stairs.

Once on the street, the senior Cleanser took the lead and proceeded toward the alley.

"Hey!" snapped Behrouz. "This isn't the way to the temple!"

There was only indignation, no suspicion, in the outburst.

"We have a route in mind, young disciple," said Firuzeh. "First we will find you a tavern, and feed you as much as you desire."

It was not just the substance of the lies, but Firuzeh's direct, indisputable tone, which was so effective. Why did those who served the king most faithfully have to break their oaths and speak falsely? Behrouz's eyes glittered at the prospect of a proper meal, and he stopped protesting. He went ahead into the alley, and frowned when he saw it was a dead end. By the time he turned, Firuzeh was already holding the knife.

"What—"

Volakles flinched as she slashed the boy's neck. Behrouz fell to the ground, clutching the fatal wound, and quickly expired. The smell of iron penetrated Volakles's brain. He recoiled from the sight of blood flowing into the greasy gaps between the stones. Firuzeh slapped him in the face.

"Do not remove yourself from the situation," she said. "Always be alert."

He nodded, and watched with insides churning as she dragged the body to the edge of the canal. Then she whistled to the sky once more. The birds descended. Volakles saw crows, pigeons, vultures and many others cover the boy's corpse, consuming the child. He could not watch. It was an honorable funeral rite to have one's body picked clean by carrion birds. The ritual transferred one's physical form into the nutrients for the servants of the Celestial Ones. But the funeral ceremony rarely occurred in greasy alleys.

Firuzeh walked back to her junior partner. "They pose too great a risk to be left alive, but we must treat them with respect if we can. Their spirits deserve to be freed from their flesh—to join the Celestial Ones without the trial of decay."

"They'll never know what happened to him," said Volakles, quietly. "They'll think he forgot about his family."

"Most likely so," agreed Firuzeh, watching the birds under her control peck at flesh and fabric, as even more fluttered down from above. "And it is better that way. The hand of the Cleansers is best shrouded in mystery."

"What will happen to the brother?"

"Perhaps he will become lonely," said Firuzeh. "Or perhaps he will have more to eat now, and won't be bullied by his older brother. It is not our business."

"We have shattered his family, Master Firuzeh."

"And we have saved it. It is never simple."

They stood together in silence until the birds flew into the sky, leaving only bones. Firuzeh raised a fist and released it, breaking her control. She rubbed her forehead, taking deep breaths. She looked very tired—which was understandable after so much casting. She walked over to the skeleton and pushed the bones into the canal with her boot. Each splash was small, and soon the evidence was gone. Not even a fragment of cloth remained.

"It is done," said Firuzeh. "Let us return to the Vazir's compound, and rest."

Volakles said nothing. He wondered, as they walked through the streets of the Faveh district, if he had made the right choice—to murder children rather than die himself.

***

After reporting to the steward, they were approached by an Insightcasting monk.

"I have just received a message from the temple at Nebit," she said. "An alert from the Targu there. The Soulbreaker girl and her father are traveling to the Aging Temple at Kapisa."

"Is this confirmed?" demanded Firuzeh.

"The father has asserted his right against the recommendations of the Targu. Without revealing the girl's Cost, the Targu could not stop them. They leave soon. The girl from Nebit is now your top priority."

Firuzeh nodded. "Understood."

"Will they reach Kapisa before we do?" asked Volakles, nervously.

"Most likely so," said Firuzeh. "But if the monks have been briefed, they will stall with empty purity rituals, to buy time.

59

Let us make use of that stalling.  Volakles, you are to ask the Vazir's steward for a map and a guide to Kapisa."

"Yes, Master Firuzeh."

Firuzeh looked at him, as she removed her headband. "You showed unexpected fortitude today, even faced with our dark duty.  One's first Cleansing is always difficult.  You have my praise."

Volakles bowed his head low, not sure if he wanted such an unexpected compliment.  He straightened and walked back to the steward, mind brimming with what they had committed, and what they would commit next.

# CHAPTER 7 – THE KING'S LULLABY

Zemfira woke to her father's gentle touch. "We must go, before the sun touches the far side of the mountains."

She sat up immediately, wide awake in the darkness. "You said we would leave at dawn."

"I lied to you," said Kuzro. "We have to leave before anyone is even awake."

"Why would you lie?"

"So that you would deceive Paniz and old Navid without knowing it. And since you don't know that you were deceitful, your soul remains serene."

Kuzro, already wearing his boots, tugged his patched cloak over his tunic. The dark morning was crisp, and he looked grim.

Jabo was sleeping at Gozeh's cottage with his cousins. Like everyone else, he would think they were merely heading to the temple in Kapisa. And they were headed in that direction, certainly—but Kuzro had other plans for their destination. Zemfira could see that leaving Jabo behind, even if only temporarily, was tearing her father apart. But Jabo would be safer if he remained ignorant of Zemfira's Cost and where they were going.

Zemfira had never seen her father so intent. He had sold one of his goats to gain a handful of coins, then went to speak with Gozeh. He didn't share the specifics with Zemfira, but she knew he had offered his cottage for Gozeh's daughter and future husband if Gozeh took Jabo into her home. He then went to the temple to misinform the monks of their destination.

"I want them to suspect nothing," Kuzro said when he had returned. "We will stop by a few temples on the way, so that they know where we are headed. As long as they trust our destination and believe we are in their clutches, they will not bother intercepting us with tempest-riding Stormcasters."

Zemfira nodded, trying not to think of the king's agents descending from the clouds upon her. Leaving now meant she could never return to the village that had been her home for her entire life.

She had said goodbye to Paniz the previous evening, telling her the same story they were telling everyone. But Paniz knew. She said nothing, only ran off. Navid grimaced when Zemfira told him, and then surprised her by offering Zemfira a sword. She refused, but he insisted.

"They are my trophies of war," he said, solemnly. "Taken from the men I killed. Each has its own story and holds special significance to me... you will need this more than I will."

She took the saber with the blue cloth and leather grip. The sheath bore an alphabet even more incomprehensible to her than the Farsian one. The sword had belonged to a Hellenic mercenary. It was meant as a one-handed weapon, but it was still heavy for Zemfira. Now, in the dark cottage, she picked up the sword, sheathed it, and strapped it to her back with the leather fastenings Navid had provided.

"Paniz wanted to say goodbye," said Zemfira. "I promised we would see each other before departing."

Fear and hope had dominated most of her thoughts. Now sadness at leaving home, leaving the only world she had ever known, welled up and threatened to overwhelm her.

"I'm sorry, Zemfira," said Kuzro, rousing the two goats that had been sleeping in the cottage with them. "One day, perhaps, you shall see her again—but not today. I cannot risk the monks stopping us—I cannot protect you from them."

Zemfira lowered her head and pulled on her boots—the ones she normally only dusted off when the first frosts arrived. It felt strange to be wearing shoes again, after so many months. They could not afford leather for summer footwear.

She followed her father and the goats out into the darkness. Above, clouds shuffled across the majesty of the stars, outlined by the fading glow of the setting moon. Starlight was not a lot to navigate by, but it had to suffice. They hoisted their packs and started walking.

"What if they know?"asked Zemfira, quietly, following her father down the road. "Some Insightcasters can read intent."

"Some, yes," said Kuzro, adjusting the pouches around his belt. "But only if they are close to you—and only if your emotions are—unprotected. I suspect none of the Insightcasters are skilled Aimgazers. And none of them want to get close enough to you to peer into your thoughts."

"But they can sense me."

"Yes. Your Casting signature will be obvious—but we're not hiding that."

Zemfira was worried her father had come unhinged. She had never seen him so animated. As much as she wanted to trust this fierce, unexpected passion, she couldn't. She didn't know how her father, whom she loved, could save her from her fate.

63

They broke away from the road and took an old shepherd path through the trees and the boulders. Carts and oxen had to take a longer route, but this trail wound southeast to the larger village of Himdook. The shadows flickered as the breeze disturbed the leaves, patches of darkness shifting with each step. Kuzro led the way, holding his staff with the sprig tied to it, and Zemfira followed.

Despite the fear, Zemfira was starting to feel almost excited. Within a few hours she would be further from the cottage than she had ever traveled—that, at least, was an accomplishment she could cherish before she died.

"Did you hear that?" asked Kuzro, coming to a stop.

Over the gentle bleating of the goats and the wind in the leaves, Zemfira heard nothing. The forest smelled rich, mossy and secretive. After a second, Kuzro shook his head, and started walking again. Zemfira unstrapped the sword from her back and pulled the blade from its sheath before following Kuzro.

They were descending into the valley between boulders and along twisting paths. Kuzro stopped again at a clearing and stiffened. This time Zemfira could hear it too: a pounding on dirt, distant footsteps and the occasional rustle of a branch, the complaint of a dislodged rock. Something was behind them.

Zemfira tightened her stance and Kuzro pulled a handful of seeds from a pouch. Both stood still in the starlight, waiting as the footsteps grew louder and drew closer. Blood pounded through Zemfira's head, and she wondered if she should attempt to use her Lightcasting, as a last resort to fend off the Cleansers.

Then Paniz stumbled out of the shadows, panting.

"Paniz?"

"Why—why did you leave so early?" she gasped, clutching her side. "You said you'd leave at dawn, and I woke up before that to make sure—"

"You ran all this way to say goodbye?" Zemfira was touched.

"No. I'm here because I'm going with you."

Zemfira's mouth fell open.

"Absolutely not," said Kuzro. "You are going straight back home."

"I'm doing no such thing," said Paniz. "If Zemfira's life is in danger, I'm not letting her go by herself."

"She isn't by herself," retorted Kuzro. "She has me: her father. I cannot protect you too. You will be executed as a traitor to your king if we're caught."

"Who cares?" said Paniz. "I don't want to stay home and wonder what is happening to you both. I've been practicing my Infernocasting."

Kuzro stuffed his seeds back into his pocket and tugged on his beard in frustration. "Unbelievable," he muttered.

Paniz ignored this. "So, where are you going?"

"I can't tell you," said Kuzro. "Because if you know, the Cleansers might force it out of you."

"They won't be able to force it out of me, because I won't be in Nebit. I'll be with you two."

"Zemfira," said Kuzro. "Talk some sense into your friend."

Zemfira looked at Paniz, at the sweat on her dirty tunic, at her shoes and the travel pack slung over her shoulders.

"I want you to be safe, Paniz," Zemfira said, softly. "But I would be lying if I said I wanted you to go back."

Kuzro's scowled. "Zemfira!"

Paniz grinned in triumph. "So I'm coming along then?"

The goatherd closed his eyes for a moment, then looked at his daughter. "Are you sure?"

She nodded. "We can't stop her from following, even if I didn't want her here."

Paniz hugged her friend tightly. Kuzro grimaced, and stretched his arms. "Let us waste no more time. We must reach Himdook as soon as we can."

They started off again, Zemfira's spirits far more buoyant, even though Paniz was risking her life when she didn't have to. The anxiety of an additional loved one being at risk was tightening the knots in Zemfira's stomach.

"Look, the sky's beginning to brighten!" said Paniz excitedly. "I love dawn—the way the sun pushes the darkness up and out of the heavens."

The gray light of morning slowly revealed the world to the wanderers, creeping over tree trunks and boulders. Birds were beginning to sing. Small insect clouds rose to speckle the air. Dew hung on every moist leaf.

The path emerged from the trees and they descended a long grassy slope, just as the gray above was turning blue. The mountain flowers were opening their buds: violet and gold and brilliant red. Zemfira felt her pack cutting into her shoulders, and her boots pinched her feet, but the morning was breathtaking.

"So where are we going?" asked Paniz.

Kuzro leaned on his staff to keep his balance as they descended. "I already told you, it's safer if I don't say."

"That was before you knew I was coming along," said Paniz. "Can't you tell me now?"

"No," said Kuzro, pushing one of the goats forward so he could follow it around a boulder. "Just think, if an Insightcaster —"

"Bah," said Paniz.

Kuzro glanced over his shoulder. "Your parents did not insist on discipline, did they?"

Paniz laughed. "I'm not a child anymore—we've been unclasped. You should treat us as equals."

Kuzro turned without a word and continued down the trail. But as they walked through a large meadow, he surprised Zemfira by giving Paniz an answer. "We're seeking asylum with Zemfira's family."

Zemfira and Paniz exchanged looks of surprise. "Father, you have family beyond Nebit?"

"No," said Kuzro. "Not my family. Your mother's brother may be able to help us."

Zemfira stared at her father's back. He had never discussed any living family beyond Nebit. She knew her mother had been born in the Satrapy of Harauvatis, but Roshni had distanced herself from her family when she became a royal scribe, and then further when she left the service to live with Kuzro. Whenever Zemfira had asked her father about her mother's family, Kuzro had replied that Roshni rarely talked about them. Perhaps that was not the full truth.

"Who is this uncle?" asked Zemfira.

"Omid is a merchant," said Kuzro. "A successful one. I ask the Insightcasters at the temple to send him a message every year, to see how he is doing. Occasionally he responds—but he does not care for me."

"Did he come to the funeral?"

Kuzro shook his head. "He has put business first in his life. He and his wife have no children."

"If he puts business ahead of his family, why would he risk his life and wealth for us? For me?"

"Because," said Kuzro, scratching his ear. "His wife is a Soulbreaker."

"That's impossible!" said Paniz. "How did she escape the Cleansers? Wouldn't an Insightcaster have seen her during her unclasping?"

"She was not born in Farsia," said Kuzro. "She did not arrive until she was older than you are now. She comes from the land of the Zhou, where they don't put the Iron Necklace on their children—and the Cost of Depravity isn't a capital crime."

"Then why is his wife here?" asked Paniz.

Kuzro patience ran short. "Ask her when we arrive."

Zemfira looked at the orange streaks across the mountain range. "You think Uncle Omid can help me?"

"If he has a way of hiding Jia-Fan's identity, he will have a way to hide yours. Then we can start a new life, with new names, and new hope."

Zemfira knew in her heart it would never be so simple, but she was relieved to have a plan.

They reached Himdook after the sun had crested the mountains, and Kuzro immediately went to search the market for goatherds, merchants and butchers. He gave Paniz and Zemfira a few coins to buy hot rice, cabbage and mutton while he found a buyer for his goats. The village was larger than Nebit, with several intersecting roads and the constant clucking of chickens, but it had no temple. The girls watched the passing farmers as they ate. Kuzro soon returned with more coins in his pockets.

"Not the best price," said Kuzro. "But it will pay for our passage—even with Paniz joining us."

"I hope Jabo is okay," said Zemfira.

"He's resilient," said Kuzro. "And Gozeh will keep him in line."

"Why wouldn't you bring him along?" asked Paniz.

Kuzro knocked some pebbles from his boot. "The monks would be twice as suspicious if we made a complete departure, and Jabo's presence would make us more conspicuous."

"And if we fail, at least Jabo lives," said Zemfira, quietly.

Kuzro did not reply to this.

They did not linger in Himdook, but set off with their packs stocked with dried meat, flatbread and fruit. It was easier to walk without the goats, following the flat road of the valley. The sun crawled up the sky to their left, reaching for noon, but they kept their pace. A merciful wind lessened the heat. They waved at the occasional farmer pushing his plow through the fields. Several orchards showed the first traces of fruit: young apples and a few hints of apricots.

When they were certain no one was around, Kuzro put his hand on one of the smaller apricot trees and gritted his teeth. The trunk groaned, the leaves blushed a deeper green and the little apricots blazed a rich orange. Delighted, the girls filled their pockets with the ripe fruit and soon thick syrup trickled down their chins. Kuzro ate a few pieces of dried meat to recover, smiling.

They walked straight through the valley and up the mountains in the south, along the cramped path forged by centuries of travelers. Zemfira felt the journey in her lower back and her shoulders. She was relieved when Kuzro called a stop for the night. Sunlight was fading from the horizon, and they still had more to climb the next day but they had made good progress in fifteen hours.

"Tomorrow we will stop briefly by the Fatigue Temple by Velvu Hill, before leaving the trail," said Kuzro, gathering twigs and fallen branches. "I told the Targu we would take the road from Himdook to Kapisa, which will buy us more time. They won't expect us for several days more, and when they realize we are not coming, we will be long gone."

He put a few rocks in a circle, then assembled the kindling.

"Can I try?" asked Paniz.

Kuzro looked at her, eyes narrowed, then nodded. He backed away, and Paniz crouched over the pile of twigs. Her eyes sharpened with intensity, and she held out her hand like a claw. Face contorting as if she were having violent cramps, she tightened her fingers and a small ball of flame appeared. Zemfira watched, enthralled, as Paniz pushed the little flame toward the twigs, but in her excitement the flame extinguished itself.

"No," said Paniz, as Kuzro took a step forward. "One more time."

Grunting this time from the exertion, she created a slightly larger flame, and pushed it onto the twigs. The kindling caught, flames licking their way up the tender branches, producing a modest blaze.

"Impressive," said Kuzro. "Though your technique is abysmal."

"What—do you mean?" asked Paniz, yawning. She blinked twice and shook herself.

"You've exhausted yourself to light a fire."

"I exhausted myself by hiking all day. And I have plenty of energy to spare."

Saying this, Paniz curled up beneath her wool cloak, yawned again and chewed a single bite of meat before sleep took her. Zemfira watched the fire as Kuzro added a few logs and placed some spare wood next to his pack.

"You must be tired too," said Kuzro.

She nodded, but her mind still felt terribly alert. She could see the exhaustion in Kuzro's face. He had not slept much in the last few days and it showed.

"Father," she said, putting down her jerky and taking another sip of water from her wineskin. "Would you tell me a story to lull me to sleep?"

Kuzro raised his eyebrows. "If you would like one, of course. Any story in particular?"

"Perhaps you could tell me about Baj's survey of Farsia."

"But that's not a story! And you've heard it so many times."

"Please, father."

Kuzro smiled, and leaned back against his pack, wrapping his cloak around him. "Very well, Zemfira. The king of Farsia, though a powerful man and chosen by celestial judgement, sometimes had difficulty falling asleep. When this was the case, he would have his servants wake up Baj, his cartographer, and ask him to list the Satrapies and the provinces. Baj would struggle out of bed, put on a fresh tunic and gold-trimmed robes, and he would sit at the base of the king's bed, in the middle of the carpet. The king would give the instruction, and Baj would always give the same speech."

Kuzro cleared his throat. "'My king of kings, your lands extend from the citadel of Byzantion across to the holy city of Taxila—from the Iaxartes River down to the coast of the Southern Ocean.' 'List my Satrapies and provinces,' the king would say and Baj would bow. 'Oh king of kings, your wise ancestors divided your lands into seven Satrapies, so that trusted officials could protect the land with ferocious devotion.

"'The first Satrapy was Fars, where your capital lies, from which your kingdom springs. It contains five provinces, and five loyal Vazirs who oversee them.

"'Next came Mada, the plains to the north and those ancient cities to the west, conquered gloriously by your ancestors. So large and ancient is this Satrapy that nine Vazirs monitor the lands and collect your taxes.

"'After Mada followed Lydia, the peninsula of Hellenic colonies, city states that bent the knee to Farsian authority. This fertile land and bountiful sea needed even more careful attention, so the sitting king made ten provinces, a Vazir for each.

"'Babirus was next, a land older than Mada, with that great municipal jewel, Babilim, which gives the Satrapy its name. Some say Babirus is where the Celestial Ones taught humans to unleash their Casting. This prize Satrapy extends to the coast of the Western Sea and seven Vazirs assist the loyal Satrap in governing it.

"'Then there is Mudraya, which lies to the south. A territory taken from the ancient pharaohs in an epic war, but Mudraya is more than the Hapi River and its fertile valley—the Satrapy includes five provinces, including Putaya to the west and Arabaya on the eastern edge of the Satrapy.

"'Expansion moved east then, conquering the lands we now know as Harauvatis—a large Satrapy that includes the faithful client kingdoms of Tatagus and Hindusia, with seven Vazirs and six petty kings.

"'Finally, to the north of Harauvatis lies Baxtris, the wildest territory—shadowed by towering mountains and flushed with surging rivers. Much blood was spilled and the royal treasury almost ran dry in the conquest of these lands, but finally Baxtris submitted to royal glory, and the ten Baxtrian provinces are undisputedly yours. And so, my good king, this is your birthright. You are master of Fars, Mada, Lydia, Babirus, Mudraya, Harauvatis and Baxtris. You control fifty unique provinces, all paying tribute to your grandeur, here in the glowing capital of Parsa.'"

Zemfira's eyes closed gently.

"And this recounting would calm the mind of the king, and let him find sleep. Baj would depart, return to his room and fall asleep next to his wife, staring up at the beautiful maps he had drawn and written, glowing in the lamplight."

Zemfira's breathing had become soft and steady. Kuzro smiled, leaned forward and adjusted her blanket. Then he settled himself down, closed his eyes, and drifted off to sleep too.

# CHAPTER 8 – ETRUSKAN PEBBLES

"Is this normal?" asked Volakles, pacing around the barracks chamber. "Does a Satrap usually request a private audience with the Cleansers on assignment?"

Firuzeh slid her hands into the water basin and washed her face. Once she had dried herself, she looked up at her younger partner. "A typical Satrap delegates meetings with Cleansers to their Vazirs, who in turn delegate to their deputies. But Satrap Bessus is anything but typical."

The arduous ride from Chadrakarta to the city of Zariaspa had taken several days. Volakles was becoming accustomed to the pain of horseriding. He had been awed by the city's defenses: a fortified citadel, moat-encircled wall, and perimeter of sentry towers. Firuzeh and Volakles had entered Zariaspa between the regiments of soldiers stationed outside the walls, awaiting the Satrap's orders. The Skythians were already retreating back north, but the Satrap of Baxtris was planning a punitive strike. Before his departure though, he wished to speak with the two Cleansers.

"Have you met Satrap Bessus before?"

Firuzeh shook her head. "I know little about the man, except that King Artashata trusts him to protect the inner provinces. Bessus is also a distant kinsman to the royal family, and as such you must pay him even more respect than his office calls for. Are you ready?"

Volakles adjusted his clean tunic and positioned his sheath. "I am."

They walked through the palace together. Though it lacked the perfumed luxury seen in Chadrakarta, the palace bustled with robed courtiers. Volakles watched them walk through the halls clutching scrolls, stone tablets, or trays of food. Volakles's stomach gurgled with hunger.

A eunuch ushered the two Cleansers into an antechamber filled with curtains and pillows. Satrap Bessus sat at the low table, his legs crossed on the soft, intricate rug, and a cup of tea in one hand.

"Thank you for indulging me," he said, gesturing to the pillows for them to sit on. "This matter is most urgent."

Bessus wore an odd combination of iron armor and elegant silks, as if unsure whether to summon a concubine or leave for battle. He watched the two Cleansers closely with eyes lined with kohl. He dismissed his eunuch, who closed the door.

"We are honored by this summons," said Firuzeh. "We are on our way to Kapisa, to eliminate a Soulbreaker in your Satrapy."

"Leave the girl for now," said Bessus. "There is more at stake at the moment."

Volakles glanced at Firuzeh, whose frown had deepened. "Our orders come directly from the king, Lord Bessus. We cannot violate the will of Artashata, the great and mighty."

"Surely he would prefer you to serve his interests and violate his orders, if his orders are outdated. Wouldn't you agree?"

Volakles fidgeted. Something about Bessus made him uncomfortable. Even without Aimgazing, Volakles could see the

Satrap's mind was an inscrutable, writhing mass. He reminded Volakles of a hunting dog—but Bessus only had one master and the king was far away.

Firuzeh held the Satrap's gaze. "It sounds to me—and I am certain I am mistaken—that you are advocating we commit an act of treason against our monarch."

Bessus clucked his tongue. "You Cleansers have no grasp of nuance. New intelligence has reached me since you left the capital and it is imperative that we act now."

"Send word to the capital," said Firuzeh. "If you are so certain the king would direct us away from our quarry, we can wait. Our tardiness will be understood and excused."

"I understand the desire for self-preservation only too well," said Bessus. "But I cannot contact the king. I do not trust the monks in my palace. I do not trust anyone. There is a traitor in my court who seeks to kill me, a Soulbreaker who, unlike your hapless prey, is already dangerous and intent on overthrowing the dynasty."

"In your court?" Volakles almost leapt to his feet, but Firuzeh placed a hand on his knee. She stared at Bessus.

"You know the identity of the Soulbreaker?"

Bessus's lip curled. "Obviously not. I would not take the time to speak with you if I had identified the source of my discomfort. The assassin lingers among my closest advisors and guests, unknown to me."

"And how do you know this individual exists?"

"My eunuch approached me last night, after I returned to the city. He informed me that a bodyguard tried to recruit him to kill me. My eunuchs are loyal, or perhaps the price was too low. The bodyguard told him his refusal would have repercussions— that a Soulbreaker in the palace would reward the killer, but punish the cowards."

"This sounds like an elaborate—"

"This morning my gardener found their bodies in the bushes of my garden. It seems my eunuch died for not joining the conspiracy, and the bodyguard died as punishment for letting the secret out. There is an effort, here in my palace, to end my life."

The Satrap poured himself more tea, waiting for the senior Cleanser to reply. She took a deep breath. "So your proof of a Soulbreaker among your people is rumor and two suspicious deaths. Conduct an investigation, and find the perpetrators."

"I cannot be sure how deep this conspiracy goes," said Bessus, impatiently. "If they reached my bodyguards, and almost reached one of my eunuchs, this Soulbreaker must have spun a fine snare indeed. If I rest my faith on any person I will likely die. But you are two people I can safely assume are not Soulbreakers, for you are sent by the king to rid the world of that dreadful sort."

"Perhaps we are imposters," said Firuzeh.

"Perhaps," said Bessus. He paused to sip his tea. "But I have no other options. If the two of you were part of this conspiracy, then I am already doomed. No. Only you two can conduct this investigation and root out this treacherous fiend."

Firuzeh contemplated this, then turned to her partner. "What do you think, Volakles?"

Volakles was taken aback. Firuzeh had never asked him for his opinion before. He cleared his throat. "It sounds like there is undoubtedly a plot here, but it seems unclear whether a Soulbreaker is truly involved, or simply being used as a threat to coerce others."

Firuzeh said nothing, so he continued.

"But, if there is a Soulbreaker at your court, it's odd that none of the Insightcasting monks in your service detected the distinct flavor of Depravity. So either this Soulbreaker does not exist or they are hiding their Depravity with some means other than Casting."

Firuzeh's lips formed a rare smile. "As Cleansers, we can identify telltale signs of concealment—a process made easier by a vigilant Insightcaster like Volakles. We will examine your court, your staff, your harem for these traces. If we do not find them, then it is a conspiracy beyond our scope. We cannot serve as permanent bodyguards, but we can assist you for the time being."

Bessus placed his fingertips together. "How do you recommend we proceed?"

Firuzeh thought carefully. "You must find a chamber in your palace where you will be undetectable and safe, in case our investigation prompts an immediate reaction."

"I have a secret room prepared, accessible only from a hidden trapdoor in my bedchamber. I will be safe there while you investigate," said the Satrap.

"Good," said Firuzeh. "But first you must order the palace closed entirely. Anyone who leaves will be punished with death. Put it in writing with your seal, and we will enforce it. Your soldiers can guarantee the measure will be obeyed."

Volakles spoke hesitantly. "Perhaps we can call for a banquet."

Both Bessus and Firuzeh looked at him, and Volakles blushed. "To sort out the servants from the nobles, and figure out where the trouble is coming from."

"You suspect a noble?" asked Bessus.

"A servant might be more agile in the palace," said Volakles, "but a noble would have the money and influence. It is worth investigating, surely."

Firuzeh nodded. "I agree. Lord Bessus, if we do not find a trace of the Soulbreaker or a distinct trail to the conspiracy, we must move on."

"Then let us hope fortune is on our side," said Bessus.

***

Equipped with two sealed letters, Volakles reached the captain of the guard and gave him orders to seal all the gates, then sent word to three divisions of soldiers stationed outside the city to surround the palace. His task complete, Volakles returned to Firuzeh. She had changed into a guard's cape and helmet.

"We will move more efficiently thus attired."

"Neither of us looks very Baxtrian, do we?" asked Volakles, taking the uniform she offered. "A Lydian and a Mudrayan."

"We are Farsian, and if we speak the tongue, an explanation can always be found."

"Have you alerted the kitchens for a feast?"

"They were preparing it already," said Firuzeh. "The court has been expecting a celebratory occasion to welcome Bessus back, after his so-called victory against the Skythians."

"Good," said Volakles. "And when will it begin?"

"In two hours," said Firuzeh.

Volakles looked at himself in the reflection of a glass window. The helmet was a little loose and it bounced gently on the curls of his black hair.

"What are the traces?" he asked, finally. "How can Soulbreakers hide their identities?"

Firuzeh strode ahead through the empty corridor, looking for the stairs down to the kitchen. "There are several ways. There is a frog from the client kingdom of Taxiles—small and bright blue—which can stifle one's own Cost, and exude Thirst. It must be in contact with the deceiver, and it is imperfect. It will satisfy an unsuspecting Insightcaster, but a closer glance will find the Thirst unattached to the Casting.

"Then there are Etruskan Pebbles. The Etruskans live even further west than the Hellenics. I do not know their language and customs, but the rocks from their rivers have the power to absorb any traces of a person's Cost. The energy they absorb heats up the rock. Using an Etruskan Pebble for too long will cause it first to steam, then to melt. It smells horrific and the contact with the Pebble is incredibly painful."

Firuzeh lowered her voice as they proceeded along the servants' corridor. Eunuchs, servants and slaves shot wary glances at these unfamiliar soldiers. Volakles wondered how many of them were in on the plot.

"There's also a herb, isn't there?"

"The Flower of Daoi does not replace one Cost with another: it only creates a cloud of deflection. If you focus your Insight directly on the suspect, we will not have a problem."

Volakles considered what he had learned, smelling moisture in the subterranean air. He cleared his throat. "Any clues from examining the bodies?"

"Unfortunately not," said Firuzeh. "In fact, I could not determine the cause of death."

Volakles stopped. "What?"

Firuzeh touched the pommels of her swords. "There were no wounds, no signs of strangulation. If they were poisoned, the healers have not detected a toxin. They might have died of shadow infection and a Lightcaster can kill without leaving a mark. Perhaps—"

"It was a Shadowcaster," said Volakles, firmly. "I have no doubt."

Firuzeh closed her eyes. "You suspect the same woman who kidnapped the princess?"

"These traitors are looking to destabilize the kingdom. It must have been her."

"I thought you suspected a noble, or a guest of the Satrap."

"I do," said Volakles. "But it's still possible that she hides among the servants."

Firuzeh started walking again. "She is being hunted by the best Cleansers in the kingdom. She does not have time for this distraction."

Volakles scowled, and said no more. They found the detachment of soldiers Firuzeh had requested, and immediately divided them into three parties of ten.

"Bring all servants into the holding cells, then conduct a thorough investigation of the palace. Use Lightcasting to find anyone hiding their presence with Shadowcasting. If you find such a person, be prepared for a battle. Understood?"

The soldiers saluted and headed off. Firuzeh turned to Volakles. "We will attend to the kitchens ourselves."

The smell of onions and sizzling fat wafted through the long room. Cooks stirred cauldrons with stews while slaves stoked the fires and added wood. A row of ovens blazed, bakers pulling out steaming sweetcakes and fresh loaves of bread. The heat escaped through the network of chimneys and the narrow windows that opened to a garden.

"How many?" asked Firuzeh, before the servants had become fully aware of their presence.

Volakles closed his eyes, breathing in and feeling his consciousness bump over every presence in the room. "Fifteen in the room, another three in the pantry."

Firuzeh nodded and raised her voice. "Attention. We are looking for a Soulbreaker among you. If you have nothing to hide, step forward and let my partner examine your mind. We have no interest in any petty crimes or associations."

A few cooks quickly removed pots from the heat and everyone gathered around. Volakles had sensed a hint of power in Firuzeh's words, her subtle Obediencecasting almost undetectable. The first slave held out her hand to Volakles, and he placed two fingers on her open wrist.

"She's no Soulbreaker," said Volakles, certain he would know the woman when he saw her.

"Say what she is," said Firuzeh. "In case a Flower of Daoi dulls your inquisitiveness."

"Fatigue," said Volakles. "Next."

Those with Costs of Fatigue or Hunger received additional scrutiny from Firuzeh, the senior Cleanser exerting her dominance over any potential Hydration Frogs hidden on their person. Then Firuzeh thanked them, and told them to return to their work. She was about to leave the kitchens, when she stopped.

"A tray of those sweetcakes," she said. "My partner needs his sustenance."

"You didn't have to ask that," said Volakles, carrying the tray out.

"You will need your strength," said Firuzeh. "The kitchens employ a fraction of the servants. We have much work to do in the holding cells."

It was a brutal two hours. The dungeon was warm with body heat and anxiety. He glanced into every face, determined to see the woman from that terrible night hiding in the linen tunic of a servant, but to no avail. Some were ordered by Firuzeh to strip off their clothes to expose any hidden items, but many were simply dismissed back to their duties. It was especially uncomfortable to examine the bodyguards, all of whom were outraged at the suspicion.

"Are there any in the palace who will not be invited to the feast, and who are not servants?" asked Volakles, after they released the final, nervous gardening boy.

"No sir," replied one of the guards. "We made a full sweep of the palace, and only those at the feast have not been examined. Even the personal servants of guests have been interrogated."

"Is there a chance the individual could have escaped before we locked down the palace?" Volakles continued, picking up a sweetcake and devouring it to appease his Hunger.

"It is not impossible," said Firuzeh, as they climbed the stairs out of the dungeons. "But I doubt they would have known in time. We moved quickly."

"Could Bessus have been mistaken?" asked Volakles, rubbing his neck. His head ached from the concentration it took to perform precise Insight. "Perhaps there is no Soulbreaker."

"Four servants returned to me after I dismissed them," said Firuzeh. "They said they had also been approached in some fashion and recruited, and they had been too afraid to refuse. But they begged for clemency and protection. Bessus is not entirely wrong."

Volakles had been far too focused to notice any conversations Firuzeh had conducted on the side of the chamber. He felt his heartbeat pick up. "What did you learn from them?"

"Very little," said Firuzeh. "Their duties were to observe their fellow servants and guards—to see who was susceptible to being influenced or coerced. Whoever recruited them did not reveal their identity and paid well for sources near the Satrap."

"Then it must be one of the nobles," said Volakles. "Or a guest."

"It seems to be the most likely solution," said Firuzeh as they ascended to the Satrap's ceremonial dining room.

Volakles had rarely seen such culinary splendor before. Silver platters, glittering goblets, broad fruit bowls and silk napkins covered the banquet table. Steaming dumplings burst at their seams with caramelized onions, beef, and pork. Dishes of rice and beans breathed sharp herbs and lime into the air. Fried pastries with candied pistachios stuck to the platters as noble fingers greedily tried to pull them free.

Volakles swung his gaze across the twenty figures seated on tasseled pillows, noticing the silk and fine thread of their robes, the splendor of their turbans and their scarves. Gold bracelets jangled as they reached for Hellenic wines and Harauvatian spirits. There were Vazirs, tribal chieftains and superior merchants. The Shadowcaster was not among them.

"What's our strategy?" asked Volakles.

"We tell them the truth," said Firuzeh, simply. "Or at least some of it. Seal the doors."

Volakles closed the portal behind himself as his partner strode forward to the front of the table and stood behind Bessus's empty spot. Her stride caught the attention of the diners, one by one, and by the time she stood still, all were quiet.

"Good evening," she said. "This dinner was not intended as a culinary indulgence—it was a snare to catch the individual trying to murder the Satrap. In your midst sits a Soulbreaker, and it is our duty, as Cleansers, to expose and eradicate the threat. Surrender yourself now, for there is no means of escape. Accept your fate quietly."

An immediate uproar filled the room. A corpulent man with a shining bald head and a thick beard slammed his fist on the table. "These accusations should shame you! We are no Soulbreakers. We are the friends of the Satrap and loyal servants of the king!"

Others joined in the chorus, and they only quieted down when Firuzeh drew her sword. "You must excuse my lack of etiquette, but I must have your cooperation if we are to reveal the serpent among the sparrows. You will hold out your wrist and allow my partner to examine the surface of your soul."

The guests complied, and Volakles stepped forward, heart slamming. If they were correct, and the Soulbreaker resided within these walls, he was about to touch the killer. Volakles would be the first one killed if the Soulbreaker decided to strike. But this was his duty, and he had to fulfill it.

He walked up to the woman sitting to the right of Firuzeh, an elderly lady with minimal jewelry. Volakles resisted the urge to apologize, and put his fingers on her skin.

"Hunger," he called out, and she let out a relieved breath.

"Am I free to go?" she asked.

"No," said Firuzeh. "No one leaves the room until the Soulbreaker is dead. Stay where you are."

The nobles exchanged panicked looks, but stayed in their seats. Volakles wished Firuzeh had at least promised false clemency. A cornered Soulbreaker might still overwhelm and destroy them. Every nerve in Volakles' body was primed as he touched the wrist of the second noble.

"Aging," he announced.

Firuzeh nodded, her gaze swinging back and forth across the room. Volakles kept going, heart pounding as he called out Costs, over and over again. When he had finished with the penultimate dinner guest, everyone tensed and looked at the last man.

"It's not me!" he cried angrily, holding out his wrist. His mustache fluttered in annoyance.

Volakles touched his wrist, closed his eyes, then opened them again. "Hunger."

Firuzeh's eyes narrowed as an uproar began again, the guests shouting at Firuzeh for her violent interruption of their peaceful meal.

"Again," said Firuzeh. "And this time, tell us what their Casting art is."

Volakles felt his stomach contract and a gurgle escaped. Embarrassed, he looked away from the piles of food, which were driving him crazy.

"Here," said the man, holding up a tray of roasted chicken. "Replenish yourself."

"Thank you," said Volakles, but he elected instead to pick up a peach. Fruit, for some reason, refueled his Casting more effectively than other foods. He wiped some of the juice from his cheek, then started with the mustached man.

"Temperaturecaster with Hunger," he declared, after a little more investigation.

"I did not know you were a Temperaturecaster, Vazir Ekmut," said the woman Volakles had first examined, the Vazir Parastu.

Ekmut bowed his head. "It is no secret. As a man of status, I have no reason to use my Casting on a daily basis."

"You could lower the temperature in this room," said one of the merchants, to a few laughs.

"Lightcaster with Thirst," said Volakles, touching the Vazir of Suguda's wrist.

It was a natural progression for such an investigation, Volakles knew. If there was no mistake, they would next demand a performance of casting. What if nothing came up? Had they just violated all these provincial nobles for nothing?

But to Volakles's shock, Firuzeh did not demand a show of casting. Instead, when Volakles made his final declaration for Vazir Parastu, the Cleanser's face fell in despair.

"I am sorry," she said, not looking at any of them. "It seems we have made a grave mistake."

Parastu glared at the Mudrayan Cleanser. "You think because you have the mandate of the king, that you do not have to respect us. I am glad no one has been hurt, but I am gravely upset."

"Of course," stammered Firuzeh, and Volakles was beginning to question everything. This was not Firuzeh. She did not make mistakes. She did not become anxious. What had happened?

"I have had my fill for tonight," said the merchant with the richest silks. "I wish to retire to my chambers."

Several others got to their feet and called for their release, and in the small chaos Firuzeh took two steps forward, as if by accident. For just a second Volakles wondered why Firuzeh hadn't put away her sword yet, if she was ready to dismiss these nobles. Then a second passed, and Firuzeh's blade was buried in Vazir Ekmut's chest. The nobleman stared in shock at the weapon cutting through his body, blood spilling forth. In the next moment he was struggling for breath, and after that he was dead.

Several screams filled the chamber but Firuzeh shouted for silence. "Sit back down, all of you. I have saved all your lives from this man, and I will prove it."

The nobles sat back down, all staring in horror at the open eyes of Vazir Ekmut as his blood spilled over the pillows and seeped into the carpet. Firuzeh drew her other sword and opened

Ekmut's robes with them. Triumphantly she reached in and picked up a smooth, perfectly black stone.

"The Etruskan Pebble is a Soulbreaker's only friend, for it hides the keeper's own evil nature beneath a spiritual mirror. If an Insightcaster gazes into them, the Insightcaster will see their own Cost, and think it belongs to the target. I knew it was a pebble at play by a process of elimination. There are only three methods of concealment: I could sense no Hydration Frogs, and Volakles's focus ruled out a Flower of Daoi. I knew the Soulbreaker would be someone with the apparent Cost of Hunger."

The nobles were listening now, as were the soldiers. Firuzeh paced back and forth slowly.

"But how would a Soulbreaker keep their Etruskan pebble from heating up? I made the process intentionally long and arduous, so that the pebble would expose itself. But would there be any other way to keep the stench of the melting stone from revealing the Soulbreaker in the room?

"It had to be a Temperaturecaster, who could force the pebble to conform to his body temperature without much effort, and thereby maintain a permanent mask, unless we ordered everyone to remove their clothes. Once I knew that Vazir Ekmut, the only Temperaturecaster to present the Cost of Hunger, was the traitor, I had to lull him into lowering his guard with my bluster. Now it is over. You are dismissed, and may return to your chambers."

Volakles watched, stunned as anyone, while the dinner guests departed, trembling or leaning on each other. Some threw awed glances back at Firuzeh—others only looks of fear. Once they were gone, soldiers hurried forward to secure the body of Ekmut. Volakles approached too.

"That was incredible, Master Firuzeh."

"It would not have been possible without your assistance," she said simply, pulling her sword from the Soulbreaker's chest. "I thank you, Volakles. Now, let us find Lord Bessus, and then find our beds. It is time to retire."

Volakles glanced back at the body of the Soulbreaker, then followed his mentor from the chamber.

# CHAPTER 9 – DROWNERS

Even growing up around goats did not prepare Zemfira for the stench of this odorous barn, but the pouring rain limited their options. At least it was warm and mostly dry. When they awoke the next morning, the downpour had stopped. They returned to the muddy road, heading southwest.

"So," said Paniz, who still had straw in her hair. "How far away does Zemfira's uncle live?"

"Another ten days of walking," said Kuzro, massaging the stiffness in his neck. "But thankfully we—"

"Ten more days!" exclaimed Paniz. "The Cleansers will surely pick up our trail by then!"

"We will not be walking the entire way," said Kuzro. "We're nearing the Helmand River. At the town of Barkana, we will take a ferry downstream, and save ourselves a great deal of time. We will be in Rasparad in just a few days."

"Aha! You said it!" said Paniz, triumphantly. "Now we know where we're going!"

Kuzro smiled. "We have to tell the ferryman our destination anyway, so you might as well know now. We should think of a good story to tell, in case anyone asks us where we came from."

"In case the Cleansers ask them," said Zemfira.

"Exactly."

The clouds were coming apart in pieces above them, tendrils of gray spilling into the blue of the sky. Zemfira felt greasy and tired; they hadn't found a good bathing stream the day before. The novelty of the journey had receded and her preoccupations had returned. She still was eager to see more of the world, to see Rasparad, to travel the kingdom like Baj, perhaps. She wondered if the fear would ever fade.

A distant rumbling made them stop. It sounded like thunder, but it was rare for thunder to make the earth vibrate. Something had disturbed the natural equilibrium. Within seconds the sound faded, the earth settled. They exchanged glances.

"It couldn't be a Shadow Beast, could it?" asked Paniz, trying to sound casual.

Kuzro was silent, but his hand was on his seed pouch. Naturally, they were familiar with the atmospheric distortions caused by Shadow Beasts prowling a moonless night. Everyone would barricade their doors and hope the terror would pass on by... but Shadow Beasts did not roam while the sun shone.

"We should move," Kuzro said.

Zemfira followed her father and Paniz, glancing side to side at the surrounding trees. Her sword was still latched to her pack, unused but in easy reach. That reassured her a little.

Barkana was a cozy river town with cottages built from rock and timber. A bridge spanned the water and several boats docked in a man-made harbor. A mill groaned as the wheel turned through the flowing flume. The villagers were friendly, especially when Kuzro paid in coin for new rations and an additional wineskin. Then they looked for the ferryman.

He sat on the dock jutting into the harbor, cleaning a fish he had caught earlier that day. Little guts spilled across the wooden planks and the ferryman swept the fish through the water a few times.  He was not fat but heavy, his arms well-muscled from working on the river.  He scratched his stubble with long fingernails, looking at the three of them.

"You'll have to wait until tomorrow," he said, pooling a load of phlegm in his mouth and spitting it onto the planks. "I'm not taking my ferry out today, not when there are strange rumors floating around."

"What rumors?" asked Kuzro.

The ferryman tossed his fish into a woven basket. "The rice merchant said he saw a Scorpion Man scuttling through the canyons at twilight—one of our herd boys claims a Shifting Hound killed some goats.  When fiendish things are on the move, it's best to let them pass."

"But you are a ferryman," said Paniz. "Those things can't reach your boat in the water."

"Impertinent whelp," muttered the ferryman. "You know nothing of the river.  There are beasts in the depths that are worse than anything you can imagine."

Fire flashed in Paniz's eyes, but she said sweetly, "I only meant, sir, no creature of the river is a match for you and your piloting—you can steer your way out of any hazard, I am sure!"

The ferryman grimaced. "These creatures are not hungry often, but when they want to devour a human soul, it is hard to stop them.  Better to wait and let them settle back down.  There's enough danger in our lives already."

"I can pay extra," said Kuzro, pulling a handful of coins from his pocket. "If we leave today—we need to get to Rasparad quickly."

The ferryman narrowed his eyes. "Why?"

Kuzro fumbled at words until Zemfira said, "My mother is dying."

The ferryman missed Paniz's and Kuzro's looks of shock, which was lucky. "Dying? What from?"

"An illness," said Zemfira, quietly. "We only heard about it a few days ago—my aunt had to sell her necklace to send us a message via an Insightcasting monk."

The ferryman rubbed his nose and stood up from the dock. He surveyed the shifting clouds, then the rush of the river. "Perhaps only this area is feeling the tremors—to the southeast all may be calmer. I will take three coins for each of the girls, and five for you, good sir."

Kuzro counted the coins up, and reluctantly handed them over.

"When do we leave?" asked Kuzro.

"In an hour," said the ferryman, picking up his basket of fish and walking toward a nearby cottage. "I must first convince my sons to join me in this madness."

Kuzro waited for the ferryman to head for his cottage before turning to his daughter. "That was—that was some quick thinking with that story."

"I couldn't think of anything else," said Zemfira. She couldn't look directly into her father's eyes, afraid she would see some pain brought up by the invocation of Roshni. "I wanted to be convincing."

"I understand," said Kuzro. "Go relax by the water. Both of you. I'm going to keep an eye on the ferryman—just in case."

The girls meandered from the pier along the river's edge. Paniz ran her fingers along the stalks of the reeds. Zemfira glanced up at the sun, as it endeavored to emerge from the clouds. They took a seat on the muddy bank.

"Missing home?" asked Paniz, removing a boot and flexing her toes.

Zemfira didn't look at her. "I've never seen a river like this one: it's so wide. Almost difficult to see the other bank. Do you think an ocean is this big?"

"Your father says oceans go on for days and days, even with a sail and the fastest winds."

"He must be exaggerating."

"Only one way to find out," said Paniz with a wink. "Oh —look at what I managed to do!"

Paniz held out her hand, squeezed her eyes closed, and a ball of fire ignited in her palm, swirling and hissing. Zemfira stared.

"Wow," she said. "How are you doing that?"

"I can't explain it, exactly," said Paniz, the fire illuminating her grin. "But casting is starting to make sense to me. You have to visualize what you want to cast—then channel that desire through the movement of your body. It's like pulling on a string inside your soul so that you can push something heavy with your other hand."

"That's just more confusing," said Zemfira, and Paniz laughed.

For a while they sat in silence.

"Are you sad that you can't cast?" asked Paniz, her question tentative.

"I was," said Zemfira. "But I don't have to rely on my Casting—I will become better with a sword—I will become stronger and then maybe I'll travel to lands far away. I don't know."

"Like your uncle's wife! From the land where they don't kill—"

Zemfira nudged Paniz hard, not wanting to be overheard. She looked around the riverbank, but there was no one around. Only the whispering of insects was audible.

***

The ferryman prepared to cast off as the sun reached its zenith. The day was growing hot. The air was thick as sweat, and they were eager to get underway. Zemfira, Paniz and Kuzro climbed aboard, joining the ferryman's two sons, both of whom were burly and tall.

The boat was not elegant, but the wooden frame looked solid. It stretched about ten meters in length. Oars were pressed to the sides and a mast jutted up through the center of the vessel. The ferryman clambered aboard, settling himself at the tiller near the back.

"This ship can handle the currents and the rapids?" asked Kuzro, glancing uneasily over the side.

The ferryman snorted. "Have you ever been on a boat before?"

"Not for many years," said Kuzro. "I was just picturing a sturdier vessel."

"Don't worry," said the ferryman. "Both my sons are Stonecasters—they will demolish any rapids that pose a threat. If a storm comes up, I can mitigate it easily."

Zemfira and Paniz settled into the niche at the stern as the older son pushed off from the dock. The boat slid into the current and an anguished, feral howl rose in the distance, echoing between the mountains. The ferryman stood still, his bravado receding into concern. But he shook his head and steered the ship out into the middle of the river.

For a while, Zemfira lost herself in unfamiliar landscape. They passed irrigation channels cut into the countryside between the rice fields. She marveled at the dense forests stretching all the way to hazy mountains. These trees were new to Zemfira's eyes—these did not grow around Nebit or the valley.

They encountered mills and fishermen, but the brothers commented that the banks were usually not so empty. There had been no new howls, but tension hung in the air, dimming the sunlight and making the hairs on Zemfira's arms prickle. Paniz, unconcerned, dozed against Zemfira's shoulder.

They spent the night on an island in the middle of the river, pulling the ferry a few meters up onto the sand. They sat around the campfire, speaking infrequently, mostly listening to the noises of the night. Paniz volunteered to keep watch during the dark hours, since she had slept all afternoon. She sharpened her knife against her shoes, as if daring the ferryman and his boys to try anything uncouth. They had no such intentions, and everyone except Paniz slept fitfully.

The morning fog was already lifting as they clambered aboard the ship and continued downstream. Even though the day was bright and full of birdsong, everyone was still on edge, listening and glancing to either side of the river.

"We will reach Rasparad by evening," said the ferryman, to which Kuzro gave a curt nod.

The river narrowed, and submerged boulders became a frequent obstacle. The brothers pulled the oars back into the ship and positioned themselves on either side of the girls. Paniz examined their biceps with interest, and raised an eyebrow at Zemfira, who rolled her eyes.

Their technique was unrefined, but effective. When boulders formed too narrow a passage, one of them would bring his fists together and shatter it, creating rubble which the boat floated over with ease.

"Something's wrong," said Zemfira. She stood up, trying to figure out what was making her stomach churn, what was making her skull ache. "Does anyone else feel that?"

The ferryman's hands were tight on the till. "Something is following us. I can feel it in the water. You—" he pointed to Kuzro. "Look at our wake, tell me what you see."

Kuzro walked to the edge and Zemfira joined him, squeezing his hand to reassure herself. Something shimmered between the white foam and the rushing of water over the rock. Zemfira squinted, and then a creature jumped out of the water and slid back under the surface. Kuzro's neck muscles tightened.

"What was that?" asked Zemfira.

"It looked like a thick, silver snake," he said.

In the brief instance of its leap, Zemfira had seen the empty yellow eyes. It was not a normal thing to see in a river. Even she knew that.

"Saam," called the ferryman, looking only ahead, "focus on the rocks by yourself. Davud—come back here. Perhaps we can fight the Drowner off."

The older brother hurried to stand next to his father, facing back. Zemfira reached for her pack and unlatched her sword. She could sense the ferryman's controlled fear.

Saam studied the Drowner's movements, watching it squirm between rocks, its serrated fins breaking the surface of the water. Then, when it darted to the left to squeeze between two boulders, Saam moved his arms together, and the boulders came together, trapping the creature. The casting was well-timed, but the boulders had been large. Saam stumbled back, coughing.

"Water," he croaked, and Zemfira handed him some, which he drank greedily. He returned the wineskin to her, then faced their wake again. The trapped Drowner was already beyond their line of sight.

"Why are they called Drowners?" asked Paniz.

"I think you can guess," said Davud, shuddering.

Kuzro stood there too, looking out over the water. "I think it got free," he said.

"What?" said Saam. "It couldn't have—not already."

"Look," said Kuzro, pointing. "It's after us."

The ferryman's brow furrowed. "Are you sure it is the same one?"

Zemfira's stomach sank. "I don't think it is. This one's longer."

"Yes," agreed Saam. "And look, there's another one."

"Three of them, in one day?" cried Davud.

A rippling of fins rose above the foam, and Zemfira knew it was far more than three. Saam called from the front again, saying that there were more Drowners up ahead, on either side of them.

"We need to go faster," said Kuzro, opening a pouch and rummaging through it.

"We can't go faster unless I conjure up some wind," said the ferryman. "And doing that on rough waters is suicide. I have never seen Drowners move like this: like a unit."

"What can they do against us?" asked Paniz, just as something hit the underside of the boat, tilting them.

"It depends how long it has been since their last meal," said the ferryman, gritting his teeth and steering the ferry to the right. "We have to hope—"

Another shove, and then an impact, as if a Drowner had rammed itself against the boat at full speed. The vessel shifted to the left again, but the ferryman returned them to the course.

"Look up there!" shouted Paniz.

Zemfira could barely take her eyes off the creatures teeming under the surface, but when she looked up, she saw what was causing Paniz's additional panic. On a stone ledge above the water stood a silhouette, dark against the cloudy sky. It had the muscular torso of a man and the lower half of a giant scorpion. The black pincers and long tail flexed as the creature stared down at the approaching boat. The Scorpion Man bellowed with triumph and menace.

"What is happening?" screamed Davud. "How are all these creatures out beneath the sunlight?"

The Drowners surged forward—not to knock the ship to pieces, but to guide it into a narrow passage between the rocks, towards the Scorpion Man. It was coordinated. But since when did Drowners and Scorpion Men work together? Each hungered for human souls, but neither would share. How were they cooperating?

"I can't stop them," shouted the ferryman. "Saam, Davud, you have to get rid of them—hit our ship with underwater rocks if you have to!"

But it was too late. The Drowners pushed the ferry and with a crunch, jammed it between the rocks. The impact knocked the passengers down. Before the Stonecaster sons could get back on their feet, let alone break the stones that trapped their boat, the Scorpion Man jumped down onto the vessel. Wood splintered as the creature's mass smashed through the planks. There was a second of horror as the bald head turned this way and that—the pure yellow eyes focusing on each of them. Then it lunged at the ferryman and knocked him in the water.

"No!" screamed Saam. He ran forward, an oar raised like a spear, but the creature's tail whipped him across the deck. Paniz barely dodged one of its legs as it turned to focus on Zemfira, claws clicking.

Kuzro stepped in front of his daughter and raised a fist. Zemfira's heart pounded. She couldn't bear to see her father knocked down into the writhing mess of Drowners below. But before the Scorpion Man could strike, Kuzro tossed his fistful of seeds down onto the deck, which exploded into twisting brambles and thorny vines. The Scorpion Man recoiled as the vines curled around his legs and caught his torso, drawing purple blood.

The Scorpion Man growled and whipped his tail around again, trying to hit Kuzro with his stinger. Kuzro flung himself backwards and Davud ran forward now, picking up his brother's oar and slamming it against the creature's neck. It barely noticed, too busy tearing itself free from the vines.

Again the Scorpion Man approached Zemfira but Paniz jumped onto its back and dug a knife into its shoulder. Zemfira screamed for Paniz to let go, but she pushed the knife in deeper. Then the tail whipped up and a barb buried itself in Paniz's back. Paniz gave a cry and fell off the creature, landing hard on the deck.

The horror unfroze Zemfira's body. Unsheathing her sword, she rushed forward. She couldn't remember any of Old Navid's lessons, but she struck anyway, desperate to protect the others. Before the blade could make contact, the Scorpion Man caught her in his pincer, lifting her up as she flailed.

"No!" shouted Kuzro, and he tossed more seeds, but these were a random assortment and they created only a brief explosion of leaves and thorns. Saam smashed the creature in the ribs with a chunk of floating rock, and the Scorpion Man stabbed him in the stomach with his other pincer, tail jabbing Davud in the shoulder. They were all about to die.

Zemfira raised her sword in her free arm and buried it in the elbow of the creature, which released her with a bellow of pain and anger. He pulled out the sword and tossed it over the side of the ship, flecks of purple blood spattering the deck. And just as the Scorpion Man raised a leg to crush Kuzro, the sunlight intensified.

Zemfira, bruised and on her knees, looked up to see a shining figure flash down out of the sky, brilliant wings spread. She stared as the humanoid figure with a falcon's head drew a sword made of light, even brighter than itself. The being skidded across air, then dashed straight for the Scorpion Man. Zemfira squinted and saw the avian beak open, the eyes shining like silver, and a blinding slash cut the Scorpion Man in half diagonally.

Zemfira watched the corpse disintegrate into a thousand purple fireflies, but the shining figure was not done. With feathery wings extended, it pointed its sword at the water and shot a beam of light into the rapids. The water boiled and screams rose into the air. Countless Drowners fled, up and downstream, as their unlucky comrades turned to brilliant dust.

The being circled once and alighted on the bow of the ship. Its glow had dimmed enough to reveal the sleek contours of its body. Two feathers fluttered off one wing, lost to the wind, and the bright creature sank into a bow. Then it rose and turned to light, vanishing again among the rays of the sun.

Zemfira could not move. She was shaking. She wanted to vomit, to cry. But she had to help Paniz, who was gasping in agony, help Saam who was bleeding, and Davud who was muttering frantically to himself.

A Celestial One had saved their lives. A Celestial One had just bowed in front of Zemfira.

# CHAPTER 10 – FIRUZEH

When the clouds began to curdle and cracks of lightning shot across the sky, Firuzeh and Volakles sought shelter in a shrine beside the road. The smell of ozone filled the atmosphere, and heavy raindrops collided with the stone pillars and the tiled canopy. Water dripped along the edge of the roof. They sat on either side of a crude stone statue, watching their horses grazing beneath the tree cover.

"The delay is no disaster," said Firuzeh, assuming the cross-legged position and folding her hands in her lap, as if she were cradling an egg. "We will rest at the Hunger Temple ahead, and check in with the monks at Kapisa. Enjoy the respite."

"Thank you, Master Firuzeh," said Volakles, removing his armor and stretching his biceps. He tried to meditate, but he was exhausted from travel. They had spent the last two days riding hard, and Firuzeh had not wanted to talk about the killing of Ekmut. Volakles watched the rain.

After a protracted silence, he asked, "how did you become a Cleanser, Master Firuzeh?"

Firuzeh did not open her eyes, but took in a deep breath. "My father encouraged me to join the army, after my mother's death. I proved myself to the Satrap of Mudraya, and Captain Sahin needed an Obediencecaster. Thus I became a Cleanser."

"Wow," said Volakles. "You chose this life to please your father?"

"No," said Firuzeh. Her words were calm but a muscle in her wrist twitched. "I joined the army to learn how to kill, so that I could kill him."

Volakles wasn't sure he had heard her correctly. "I'm sorry?"

Firuzeh breathed in and breathed out. "It is irrelevant to our task at hand."

Volakles looked at the shrine's statue, dedicated to a long-deceased pilgrim. "I would like to learn more about you, Master Firuzeh. If we are partners now, perhaps we should know something about each other."

"Very well," said Firuzeh, opening her eyes. "I told you that I am from Thebai, in Mudraya. My father served in the army of King Arsames, forty years ago. Mudraya had been recently pacified, after an attempt at secession. To strengthen his legitimacy, the new Satrap launched a campaign to the south, raiding in the lands known as Kusiya. The campaign was ruthless. After razing villages and massacring those who resisted, the Farsian soldiers gathered the able-bodied survivors and hauled them into the kingdom as slaves."

Firuzeh looked at her calloused hands. "My father, a common soldier, took a village woman prisoner, making her his slave and then his wife. Her name was Dahketo, and she suffered at my father's hand. My birth was a miracle. I should not have survived the many beatings he gave her. Despite my mother's strong spirit, she could not stand up to him. But she told me everything, so that I would know what sort of a man had brought me into this world."

Volakles felt something lodged in his throat.

"Her village was burnt to the ground—I tried to find it many years later, but there was no trace. Only slaves survived, and they are all dead now. My father felt no remorse. He said he was saving my mother from death in a burning village, that he had given her a chance at life. With him, she was the wife of a soldier. A fine sentiment, but he was a man of great cruelty. In time, I learned where the bruises came from. Many slaves are not beaten as savagely as she was—it's wasteful to subject property to such treatment."

Firuzeh picked up one of her swords and put it on her lap. "She died when I was thirteen, giving birth to my sister, who also did not survive. I resolved to achieve posthumous justice for her and so I joined the Cleansers. I told Sahin I wanted to become stronger: I wanted to learn to kill without flinching, to serve justice. He gave me the best training I could ask for, and I returned home after my third assignment, ready to complete my just revenge and—"

She tightened her grip on the handle of the sword. "I could not do it on the first night. I stood over him as he slept, knife raised, ready to kill a man as wicked as the Soulbreakers I had killed for the king. But he was so old, so pitiful. I returned to my room and meditated, waiting for him to wake so I could confront him and could make him atone for his crimes before I killed him—but he never came. He died that night, peacefully in his sleep."

She drew her sword now and held it up, staring at the sliver of her reflection. "I felt robbed again, a last affront to my mother's memory that left me entirely alone. But alone is safer, safer for your body and in other ways too. I live for my kingdom now."

She slid the sword back in its sheath and fell silent. Volakles tried to find adequate words, but failed. Instead he asked, "You serve the same army that enslaved your mother?"

"Yes. But I serve to make the kingdom better. I seek a world with less evil—and I am willing to pay my own innocence to protect the innocent. I don't do this for wealth, or status, or slaves. I am not here because I failed in my original duties."

Volakles swallowed and lowered his eyes. Firuzeh's harshness softened.

"I am sorry," she said. "That was unkind."

"It's true, though," said Volakles. "I did fail—I lost the princess and I lived. Sahin offered me death or service, and I fear death."

Firuzeh looked at him. "I don't imagine you neglected your duties. They knew the defenses too well. You cannot blame yourself."

"I wish I had a different Casting art," said Volakles, quietly. "I wish I had something where I could defeat my opponents, instead of just seeing how they intend to kill me."

Firuzeh barked a laugh. "That is your youth speaking, Volakles."

"I've been casting for ten years!"

"Not long enough to understand the true value of your gift. Insightcasters are crucial to Farsia. Without your Casting, our Unclaspings would be haphazard—Soulbreakers would escape and stumble into depravity. Without Insightcasters, communication would be restricted to messengers. As for its value in combat, Sahin told me you survived against the Soulbreakers because of your Insight."

Volakles lowered his head. "I am not ungrateful, only frustrated I cannot be stronger in battle."

"I used to believe the same about Obediencecasting. But I've learned techniques that can be just as destructive as Infernocasters. Mastering your Casting takes time. You must not give in to haste. Deliberate action will be your salvation."

"I was so accomplished in my little village," said Volakles. "After my Unclasping, I could already sense the presence of others around me. I could even Aimgaze with almost no training. My mother disapproved of how much I was casting, since food was scarce and she had many mouths to feed. So they sent me off to the army, and I went happily, eager to pursue my greatness, only to discover that I am not great. The Insightcasters I've met are so subtle, discerning and quick. I'm constantly reminded of my own limitations."

Firuzeh waited for a rumble of thunder to pass. "You will grow and keep getting stronger, but unless you can appreciate your limitations, you are doomed. Nothing is boundless, except the Casting of the Celestial Ones, and the depravity of the Shadow Beasts."

Volakles ran his fingers along the bricks of the shrine. He thought about when he visited the temple in the neighboring village as a child, sitting before the monks and listening to their lessons. They had taught him that every being in the universe falls on the side of good or evil—creation or chaos. With the help of the Celestial Ones, humans fought a war that did not end in death. It only ended when the depravity that spawned Shadow Beasts was vanquished. "Are we fighting the Eternal Crusade, Firuzeh?"

"Of course we are."

He reached for the right words. "Sometimes—sometimes it doesn't feel quite so clean and easy."

"True, we are not in open combat with chaos itself," said Firuzeh. "But we fight the advance guard—the Soulbreakers—and yes, some Shadow Beasts too."

"But we're also fighting the Skythians, the Hellenics, the Nandans and so many more. They should be our allies in this cosmic war."

"Other nations do not believe in our creeds," said Firuzeh. "Until they do, they are not our allies."

He opened his mouth to say more but she held up a hand. "I understand your sentiment, but it should be your concern. Do your duty, and you will have played your part in the conflict."

*  *  *

The rain finally slackened and they resumed their journey. The horses trotted along the soft earth. The mountains on their side of the valley grew taller, the distant peaks pinched with snow. They did not speak, but focused on the uneven road. Only when the temple was in sight did Firuzeh turn to face Volakles.

"I would like you to kill the Soulbreaker in Kapisa," she said. "I think you are ready to accept the burden."

Volakles swallowed. "I am scared I would hesitate, or even falter."

"You are a better soldier than you believe. I will assist, but you will take charge."

He stared straight ahead. "We should contact the monks at Kapisa this evening. It is essential we stay informed."

They stopped for the night at a small temple, with only ten monks and a handful of disciples. Volakles and Firuzeh paid their respects to the Targu, then took their sleeping mats to the corner assigned to them. Volakles was putting down his pack when one of the monks approached, an elderly woman with smooth skin and the tattoos for Stormcasting on her forehead and palms.

"I do not wish to disturb your rest," she said, her voice like two flowers brushing up against each other. "But our Insightcaster monk is feeling unwell and is unable to perform the communication you requested. My sincerest apologies."

"That is no problem," said Volakles, setting his boots aside. "I can communicate myself, if your Targu has no objection. Where is your Temple Stone?"

She led him through the temple to a chamber too small for three people. A mineral sat on a stone table, the crystal glowing faintly from within. Volakles thanked the monk, took a seat in front of the stone, and placed his fingers on the uneven surface.

The connection hummed through his body, his awareness amplified, spiraling out all around him and brushing up against other Temple Stones, many kilometers away. He focused, not wanting to expend himself by spreading his consciousness across the entire kingdom, instead directing his thoughts eastward, towards the specific Temple Stone at Kapisa. He reached mentally for it, and waited for someone to reciprocate the connection.

Volakles felt the crackle of the link and sensed the other monk before he spoke.

"I am Gahnandar, monk of the Kapisa Temple."

"And I am Volakles, Cleanser of the king. We will reach your temple within two days. What is the condition of the target?"

There was a brief pause. His heightened awareness allowed Volakles to glance at the monk's emotions, to notice his unease.

"She and her father have not arrived yet," said Gahnandar.

Volakles tightened his grip on the Temple Stone. "What? She isn't there yet?"

"No," replied the monk. "She left the Temple at Velvu Hill three days ago, but we have not sighted them yet."

Volakles scanned out again, touching the Velvu Hill temple with a mental finger. "But it is a two-day walk at most—have they been detained?"

"We do not know."

Volakles felt his jaw clenching. "Have you sent out a welcoming party? A scout? Someone to see what has happened?"

This time the hesitation was longer. "Our Targu believes such action would alert the Soulbreaker to our knowledge of her Depravity. And that would endanger—"

Volakles tried to keep his annoyance in check, but no doubt Gahnandar could sense it. "I must speak with my partner, but I will contact you if there are any changes. We shall arrive in two days."

"We look forward to your visit, Cleanser," said Gahnandar, and the connection ended. Volakles removed his hand from the stone and took a deep breath.

"She already knows," said Firuzeh, when he relayed the information from Kapisa. "And she is on the run."

"How could she know?" asked Volakles.

"The Targu in Nebit mentioned they were not entirely convinced the girl believed them," said Firuzeh. "Her examiner had never seen a Soulbreaker before, and reacted with fear. Her journey to Kapisa was a ruse to get herself away from Nebit. At some point after Velvu Hill, she must have changed course. Get out your map: we will see where she might be going."

Volakles retrieved it from his pack and carefully unfolded the papyrus. "You don't think she's hiding in one of the villages between Velvu Hill and Kapisa? Thanks to the Helmand River, the land is fertile. And the surrounding area is mountainous, plenty of places to hide."

Firuzeh frowned. "Contact the Temple at Velvu. We are changing our route and heading there."

"What?"

"Then contact the Nebit temple, and order them to send a runner with an article of the girl's clothing to meet us there, by the will of the king."

"Master Firuzeh, are you sure—"

"We must alter our thinking, Volakles," said Firuzeh. "This has become a hunt, and we shall begin at Velvu Hill. Is that understood?"

Volakles, heart pounding, nodded. "Yes, Master Firuzeh."

# CHAPTER 11 – ALONE IN THE DARK

Zemfira looked upon their haphazard camp at the edge of the forest and fought her sense of helplessness. Saam lay unconscious, his stomach bandaged, but both Davud and Paniz were delirious, curled on the grass and muttering to themselves. Kuzro was digging through his pouches again, taking out seeds and turning them hastily into medicinal herbs.

"I'm no healer," he muttered, pushing a few leaves into Paniz's mouth and touching Davud's forehead. "They need proper help quickly. You have to find someone."

Zemfira swallowed. Her father was right. She was no use here, watching Paniz slide towards madness. She had to do something.

"How far away is Rasparad?"

"Hard to say. It might be only a few hours away, but you will have to run."

Zemfira adjusted her tunic and tightened her boots. Her sides still hurt from the Scorpion Man's claw, but the pain was bearable. Kuzro handed her all the coins in his pockets, and she took off running, following the river southwest.

The forest soon gave way to an open, dusty plain, and Zemfira increased her pace, each breath coming fast and painful, each step draining her.

Why had the Celestial One saved their lives, but left them wounded and poisoned? What was stopping the Celestial One from using its unlimited casting to heal them and give them a chance? Zemfira thought about the Drowners leaping in and out of the water, and she shuddered. She hoped the ferryman's death had come quickly, that he had not suffered. If it had not been for the Celestial One, they would have all ended like that: devoured and lost to the world.

Or would they have? Zemfira stumbled over a loose stone but regained her foothold. The Scorpion Man had focused on her twice but hadn't attacked her in the same way he attacked the others—not stung, stabbed or swatted, but *grasped*. It was almost as if she had been targeted to be...captured.

The sky was darkening by the time she saw the river outpost. River pirates were uncommon, but merchants were comforted by outposts of soldiers stationed at narrow points on the river. Zemfira, feet aching, increased her speed and arrived at the stout tower, gasping for air.

Soldiers were harvesting cactus pears from the garden next to the defensive structure. They looked up as she approached, shouted out a greeting, and even exchanged a laugh. Zemfira's face filled with heat at their lack of concern.

"I need help," she called, once she had regained enough air to speak. "My companions were attacked by Shadow Beasts—they're injured!"

"What's the matter?" called an officer, striding out of the tower. "Who are you?"

"My name is—is—Roshni," said Zemfira. "Please, it is urgent."

The officer was clean-shaven and stern, but he listened patiently as Zemfira explained the ambush.

"What a mad story," he said. "How did you possibly survive the Scorpion Man's attack?"

Zemfira swallowed, unwilling to mention the Celestial One. It would sound preposterous to claim divine intervention had saved them from doom. "I don't know. I—um—passed out and only woke when it was dead and the Drowners were gone."

"Did your father see what happened?" asked the officer. "Or one of the pilots?"

"I'm not sure," said Zemfira. "My father might have. He told me to find help."

"We cannot do anything tonight," said the officer. "The river is too dangerous, especially if Drowners are active, as you say."

"No!" cried Zemfira. "No, we must go now! They're suffering! They're going to die!"

The soldiers exchanged looks, then glanced up at the fading sunlight. The officer remained firm. "It is no service to your companions if we die too."

Zemfira sank to her knees, tears climbing to her eyes. She looked up at the man, at his uniform. "Please," she said. "Please help us."

The officer considered Zemfira. Then he took a deep breath, turning to his fellow soldiers. "If they have information on mass movements of Shadow Beasts, the Vazir will want to know. Mehrzad, take the boat downstream to Rasparad. Then, alert the local healers and order a ship sent upriver at daybreak."

"But that will be too late and—"

"Rambod, you will ride with the girl back to her fallen comrades. Take the antidote against Scorpion Man venom and ensure they survive the night. You can use my horse."

The two soldiers bowed and hurried off to complete their missions. The officer turned to the girl and heaved a sigh.

"Roshni, I hope for your sake that your tale is true—but for the sake of the kingdom, I hope you are lying. There is too much wickedness happening at once."

"What do you mean?" asked Zemfira.

"Have you not heard?" asked the officer. "The Hellenics are attacking Farsian territory—they have landed in Lydia and are capturing cities. The Satrap of Lydia is gathering forces to repel them from our shores."

"They're raiding?" said Zemfira. "I thought they were fighting amongst themselves. Since when are they unified enough to attack us?"

"They have a king now," said the officer. "King Eskandar. He crushed all resistance and is ready for a larger foe."

"But Hellenics only have petty kings."

"This one came down from the north—they say he's more Skythian than Hellenic."

"They don't call them kings," amended another soldier. "They have their own word for it. Hegemon."

"Enough chatter," said the officer. "We have larger issues at hand, so let us attend to them."

***

Kuzro sat in the gathering shadows and thought about the day his wife had died. Her anguish had been terrible, none of the herbs seemed to quell her pain. When his sister said she would not survive, he had told her with savage certainty that Roshni would live. He had been wrong, of course. As Roshni took her last breaths, Kuzro had vowed no harm would befall their children: he would not allow them to suffer. Jabo was safe enough, welcomed by Gozeh into her home. But now Zemfira

114

was out of his sight, out of his meager protection, and it filled him with panic.

The moon was still far from rising, and he heard Davud moaning softly, but there was nothing Kuzro could do. He was almost out of seeds, and his stomach begged for sustenance. Casting had weakened him considerably. His Hunger made his eyesight foggy. Foolish, he thought. If anything came to attack, even a wolf or bear, he would be unable to protect the others or himself.

With an effort, he raised himself onto his elbows and struggled to his pack, fumbling through it for a piece of meat. He found one, stuffed it in his mouth, and collapsed onto his back. His jaws were too weak to chew, so he let it slowly dissolve on his tongue, savory spittle dripping like broth down his throat.

"Please," whispered Paniz, only a few meters to his right. "Please come back."

With great effort, Kuzro bit down on the dried meat, and it came apart in two pieces, both lodging in a separate cheek.

"Don't leave me here," she cried. "Please don't do it—I can't—"

"She's coming back," mumbled Kuzro, chewing with difficulty. "She'll be back soon, Paniz."

"Zemfira, I'm sorry—I don't know what I did, but please —no,      Kavoos—I      can't      keep      up!"

He thought for a moment she was saying his name incorrectly, but then Kuzro remembered—Kavoos was Paniz's older brother. She spoke from some twisted dream, unaware of where she was. Were the herbs wearing off? He had tried to salve her wound—siphon out the pus—but even traces of Scorpion Man venom were potent.

The girl cried out, but there was a hint of ferocity behind the anguish.

"You can't leave me here! Come back! Please!"

From his wanderings as a young man, Kuzro knew the venom of Scorpion Men unleashed more than horrific physical agony: it manifested a victim's greatest fears in hallucinations. Kuzro swallowed another small piece of the dried meat, and felt a little energy return to his body.

"I won't be left alone in the dark," she mumbled. "Even if you're gone I will find you! Agh!"

She convulsed and Kuzro wiggled another piece of dried meat from the bag. He needed more nutrients, otherwise he would be no help at all. His fingers touched a dried apricot, and he snatched at it. Paniz gritted her teeth and growled, tossing back and forth. What was happening to her? And if they had been struck by the same poison, why was Davud unaffected?

The moon rose now, spilling light over the dismal scene. Chewing urgently, Kuzro fought his way onto his knees. He had to be careful with his casting. What seeds would best calm this feverish hallucination? He rummaged through his pack, hoping there were enough left.

"I want to belong," said Paniz. "I won't be forgotten—and I'll show all of you."

Kuzro stared. The girl's skin was glowing, as if with the passion of her words. Kuzro marveled at the gentle light Paniz now exuded. Her breath rose as steam.

"Paniz," he said, sharply. "Paniz, snap out of it."

"I am not alone," she said, hands convulsing into fists, and her skin glowed brighter still. "No matter what you say—I know I am not alone."

Kuzro backed away. She was not only glowing brighter, but becoming warmer—waves of heat radiated away from her body. Was she burning up? Was the venom using her Casting against her? But no—Kuzro realized it was *Paniz* using her casting against the venom. With a roar, a tongue of flame whipped from her mouth and slashed the air, turning to nothing—and the glow dimmed.

Slowly, Kuzro lowered his hands from his eyes. The hairs on his arms were singed. He felt sunburned. What powerful Casting had just occurred? Had Paniz been Infernocasting in the grips of a venom fever?

The provisions had restored him enough to move, and he crawled over to Paniz. She lay still. He touched her wrist, which was hot, but cooling quickly to a normal temperature. She was taking slow breaths, and releasing them. Then she gave the smallest of snores, and smacked her lips. Kuzro couldn't believe it. She was asleep. She had gone from the madness of the Scorpion Man venom to utter tranquility: she had burnt away the poison. How had she known to do that?

Unsure what to make of the situation, he ate another apricot and examined the other victims. Saam's wound was bleeding again, and Kuzro applied more bandages, but he was afraid. He did not know how to deal with such wounds. Saam needed a healer. Davud's sting was not inflamed, but it was still taking its toll on the young man. Beads of sweat dotted his furrowed forehead, and he was shivering.

Where was Zemfira? Would she return tonight? He swallowed. What if someone discovered her Cost and attacked her? He was still grappling with the knowledge that a Celestial One had saved them. But why? Kuzro was so tired. His eyes itched, his back hurt, his fingers felt raw.

His plan to save his daughter had been so simple, but fear of the Cleansers had driven him to start the ferry journey too soon. His haste had caused the death of the ferryman—it had almost killed them all. But he could not give up. He had to keep fighting until Zemfira was safe.

In the distance he heard hooves and sat up. Wiping at his burning eyes, he watched a soldier and Zemfira enter the clearing. He was relieved that she had brought a healer. She dismounted, and he stood up to embrace her, his relief flooding through him like a restorative draft.

# CHAPTER 12 –
# THE FERRYMAN'S WIDOW

There was a downside to using Temple Stones. Volakles stepped out of the temple, his skull throbbing and ears ringing. The dry grasses around Velvu Hill rustled, and the mountain ranges all around them quivered in the summer haze.

"What's the news?" asked Firuzeh.

She was scratching behind the ears of two enormous dogs. Their fur was gray and indigo, their bodies sleek and muscular, their collars studded with metal.

"Still no sign of the girl at Kapisa," said Volakles. "Um— where did these dogs come from?"

Firuzeh shrugged. "While you were busy with communications, I purchased these beasts from the local estate. Fine creatures, don't you think?"

One of them growled at Volakles, then stopped when Firuzeh gave it a harsh look. "And why did you purchase them?"

Firuzeh held out the girl's patched scarf to the hounds, who sniffed it with interest. A few days ago, Firuzeh had instructed the monks of Nebit to deliver the garment safely to Velvu Hill. It would be key to tracking the target.

119

"She cannot escape, Volakles. We have your Insight and my hounds. Any other news?"

Volakles grimaced. "The Hellenic raid on Lydia is worse than we imagined. The Hellenic Hegemon keeps winning battles and has started turning the allegiance of some Lydian cities."

"Any word from Bessus?"

"The Satrap sends his thanks and heads north to crush the Skythian threat."

Firuzeh gazed up at the afternoon sky, eyes watching a distant bird of prey. "And what do the local temples say? Any rumors about a girl and her father?"

Volakles shook his head, his headache forcing him to close his eyes.

"Then contact more temples tomorrow in an increasing radius. Have them ask every traveler and pilgrim to report any sightings. We will not let her escape."

Volakles blinked a few times and rubbed his head, remembering. "There have been some disturbances in the Helmand River valley—a migration of Shadow Beasts, moving east."

Firuzeh nodded slowly. "The monks were discussing it. They're consulting old texts, trying to understand the phenomenon."

"And do they have any answers yet?"

"No, not yet," said Firuzeh. "Though if you wish to learn more, you can ask them yourself. I must meditate."

He was tired from the Insight communication and craved sleep, but a shaming voice inside him whispered that he was becoming complacent, not improving himself even though he had been paired with an expert Cleanser. He cleared his throat.

"I was wondering if—if we will be training together, at some point." Volakles spoke hastily, almost tripping over the words.

"Train how?" asked Firuzeh, raising an eyebrow.

"Well, I need to stay fresh with my swordplay, and—"

"You would find me a disappointing opponent. My military experience is quite different from yours, I am sure."

"You have been a soldier for much longer! I'm sure you can teach me many things."

Firuzeh gave a low chuckle. "Perhaps another day. Get some rest. The trail only gets more difficult from here."

***

They left early the next morning, their horses trotting behind the massive canines, whose dark fur glistened in the light of dawn.

"Surely the trail is cold," said Volakles, adjusting himself in his saddle. "They passed here many days ago!"

Firuzeh smiled. "A trace always remains. In hounds like these, I can amplify the necessary senses with my Casting. We can pursue the girl to the edges of the world."

They rode past canyons marbled by centuries of erosion: a beautiful but pitiless landscape. They had packed additional water and quenched the thirst of the dogs at regular intervals. By afternoon their path climbed through the foothills, towards a mountain pass which was too steep and narrow for horses.

Firuzeh studied the path her dogs were straining to investigate further. They were not bound by leashes, but by the Obediencecaster's will. She dismounted and consulted her map, which was showing signs of wear.

"This girl and her father are more clever than I gave them credit for. They took a difficult path here to dismount us, and slow us down. Devious. Let's see if we can predict their likely trajectory..."

"What are we going to do?" asked Volakles.

"We split up," said Firuzeh, attaching her swords to her pack and lifting it onto her back. "I'll proceed with the hounds, and you take the horses along the road to Barkana. If our quarry did stop in Barkana, you will either find them or find a clue regarding their true destination. I'll meet you there, once I've double-checked this trail."

Volakles chewed his lip. "And how long will it take you?"

"I won't arrive before tomorrow."

Volakles didn't like the idea of going off by himself, nor did he like the idea of leaving Firuzeh on her own, to face a potential ambush. She seemed to know his mind.

"I have two powerful hounds with me," she said. "She may try to cast against me, but she is not reckoning on this much destructive force. I am not concerned."

"Then I'll hurry ahead to Barkana and see you when you arrive."

"Good," said Firuzeh. "Take my horse's reins. I have commanded her to follow you, but my Casting will diminish as our distance grows. Best of luck, Volakles."

\*\*\*

Volakles missed the sea. The coast of Kappadokia was so far away from these Baxtrian mountains. As he galloped along the dirt road, he craved the salty edge on the wind, the call of the gulls as they flew low over the calm waters. It was a strange flare of nostalgia, since home had never satisfied him—though after Firuzeh's story, he would never complain about his young restlessness again.

He wasn't sure he wanted to find the Soulbreaker and her father in Barkana, but he wanted this ordeal to be over. Then he could plead with Sahin for the assignment of tracking Princess Stateira. He missed feeling pride about his service. He hated how this work made his stomach writhe.

Slowly, the canyons and stubbled foothills faded into a grassland, fed by the Helmand River. By afternoon his exposed skin felt raw from the sun, and the rest of his body itched from the mix of leather and sweat, but he had reached Barkana. Exhausted, Volakles dismounted.

He led the horses forward and immediately knew something was wrong. Closing his eyes and spiraling out his awareness, he detected a tight cluster of people by the river. He heard crying as he approached.

A woman dressed in wool and linen sat on her knees by the water, hands raised and anguish pouring from her lips. Villagers surrounded her, heads bowed with empathy. She was calling two names out, over and over again, then bursting into sobs.

Volakles took several steps forward, then stopped. It was not his place to ask questions of this grieving woman, but his curiosity prevented him from leaving. He simply watched until a hand gripped his shoulder, startling him.

"Welcome to Barkana, traveler," said an older man. He spoke Farsian with a rough accent. "You have found us at a time of sorrow."

"I am sorry to disturb you," said Volakles, "What tragedy has occurred?"

The villager sighed. "Hamide just lost her husband and son to Shadow Beasts."

"My deepest sympathies," said Volakles, bowing his head. He paused in deferential silence before speaking again. "Please pardon my haste, but I am a soldier of the king, and it is my duty to enquire on such matters. How did the Shadow Beast attack? Where?"

The man frowned. "Let us go speak to Hamide and pay our respects. She will tell you if she wishes—it is not my business to gossip."

They approached. Volakles felt his insides clench, seeing the widow with her hair strewn like gray brambles, dabbing her crimson eyes. He greeted her with the proper formalities, and the woman regained her composure.

"Are you one of the king's Champions?" she asked, her accent even heavier than the man's.

He hesitated. "I hunt Soulbreakers, not Shadow Beasts," he said. "But as an Insightcaster I can relay what happened to the Champions and you will have your revenge."

"Revenge has been served already," said Hamide. "But it will not bring my child or my husband back."

"Already been se—is there a Champion in the area then? A division of soldiers?"

Hamide gave a mirthless laugh. "My husband is—was—a ferryman. He and our sons were taking some travelers down to Rasparad, when they were ambushed by Drowners and a Scorpion Man. My husband died in the attack, my older son died from an infected wound and my youngest is recovering from Scorpion Man venom. The healers have sent a messenger to—to inform me—"

Her eyes filled with tears, but she choked them back. "The messenger informed me of the deaths, and that my youngest son will make a full recovery."

"My deepest condolences."

"Thank you."

"Did they say how your son survived?"

Hamide shook her head. "They're saying in Rasparad that a Celestial One saved them, that my son and the travelers were spared by celestial grace."

"But that's impossible," said Volakles, exchanging a look with the man who had brought him forward. "A Celestial One has not been seen since—since—"

"Since the great war with the Hellenics, yes," agreed the man. "It is a most baffling account, but the survivors seem to agree."

Volakles listened as others added detail, but there was some confusion as to whether one of the travelers was a boy or a girl. The child had short hair.

"Is anything known about the travelers on the ferry?" asked Volakles.

"Not much," admitted the first man. "All unclasped, but the man was older. The two younger ones could have been his children."

"And they came from Velvu Hill?"

"On that road, yes," said another. "We didn't ask where they came from. They were eager to be on their way."

"Why would a group of Shadow Beasts attack them?" asked Hamide, staring at the water. "Was this a result of the migration, or does it have something to do with those travelers?"

Volakles decided it would be safer for the villagers to know the truth, in case Zemfira and her accomplices doubled back. "One of the travelers is a Soulbreaker. It's possible that her wicked presence stirred the surrounding Shadow Beasts. Perhaps she caused this herself."

"Is the girl an Obediencecaster?" asked the widow. "Did she commandeer Shadow Beasts with her Depravity?"

"She's a Lightcaster," said Volakles. "It's possible that in her casting, she was mistaken for a Celestial One. And if she's already breaking her soul to fuel her Lightcasting—then she's already descending towards rampancy."

The villagers provided him accommodations. There was an empty bed where the widow's son would sleep no more. He lay awake that night, anticipating Firuzeh's arrival the next day. Together they would travel to Rasparad, locate the fugitives...and then Volakles would have to do his duty for the king.

# CHAPTER 13 – OMID AND JIA-FAN

Rasparad lay a few kilometers north of the Gedrosian Desert. Perhaps to spite the murderous desert, the city's inhabitants had built luxurious parks behind their sandstone walls. Their elegant fountains proclaimed the glorious wealth of the Helmand River. The Vazir collected stiff taxes from caravans and merchants, who made their city rich with silks and spices from the east, and silver, gold, and iron from the west.

"I had no idea Harauvatis was so much grander than Baxtris," said Paniz, looking at the city architecture, with its great arches and columns. "A little pretentious though. Where do we find this uncle, then?"

They had been released from the healers' care with many whispers. Davud had raved as the poison flowed out of his system—and everyone knew what had happened on the river. The news would spread quickly to temples, where it would be relayed to the nearest Cleanser.

"I—um—don't know exactly where he is," said Kuzro, stepping aside as several silk-clothed citizens walked past them.

"What?" asked Zemfira. After all the chaos, the pain and the fear, she had hoped they had finally reached a sanctuary. Rasparad was large enough to hide in its multitudes, and the prospect of finding her uncle reassured her.

"I am not sure where Omid lives," said Kuzro "But he's a merchant, and he's probably on the market square. We merely need to ask for directions."

Paniz pushed her lower lip forward. "We don't even know if he still lives here! He might have left! He might be in a caravan somewhere, doing whatever merchants do!"

"I have faith that the Celestial Ones guide our journey," said Kuzro. "We will find him."

They reached the marketplace via the brick road. All around, the smell of animals, dried herbs and honey spilled into the air. Colorful fabrics created a vivid tapestry of commerce. A few chicken feathers blew on the wind and caught on Zemfira's cheek. In the middle of this glorious market stood Omid, next to his wares, just like Kuzro had predicted.

"You will not find better silk than here," said the merchant, adjusting his turban as he adjusted the tone of his voice. "My wares come from a Zhou temple where the silkworms are fed a diet of gold leaves, making the silk they produce glitter like the treasure of a hundred kings."

Omid was taller than Kuzro, with a broader waistline and a mustache that curled magnificently. He comported himself with a fluid grace: he didn't walk as much as he flowed around his stall. Out of his left eye he watched the two girls and the man, and ignored them at first. When they came nearer, he reappraised them, eyes fixating on Kuzro.

"I do not believe it," he said, voice losing all jovial inflection. "You have come here, after all these years, after Roshni's—"

"Omid, we need to talk."

"You need to leave. You are no kin of mine: I owe you nothing."

Kuzro lowered his eyes. "Yes, you owe me nothing—you have many reasons to disdain me. But Zemfira is your kin, and she needs your help. Will you refuse your sister's daughter, because you bear a grudge against me?"

Omid clenched his jaw and looked at Zemfira. Zemfira met his eye until he turned back to Kuzro.

"You are a manipulative charlatan, Kuzro," muttered Omid. "Wait here while I pack up my stall. You are probably costing me great business today."

Zemfira watched Omid's workers deconstruct the cloth canopy that protected the delicate silks, and load the commodities onto a mule cart. Omid followed his wares as the cart trundled down the road. Kuzro, Zemfira and Paniz followed him.

"I've heard the rumors," he said, without looking over his shoulder. "You chose a disruptive entrance to Rasparad, didn't you?"

"Disruptive?" cried Zemfira. "We were attacked!"

Omid waved a hand. "On the river when the Shadow Beasts are defying their own laws—what were you thinking, Kuzro? You're not traveling by yourself anymore. Other lives are at stake."

Kuzro said nothing. Zemfira was growing disenchanted with her uncle, and although Paniz tugged on her sleeve in warning, she could not contain herself.

"Why are you disparaging my father?" she asked. "You're speaking to him like he's some miscreant!"

Omid laughed. "You must not know your father as I do, girl."

"Are you accusing my father of something?"

The merchant glanced at Kuzro, who was looking at the cobblestones. "The streets are not the best place for these particular conversations."

Omid's house was several stories high, replete with its own little courtyard. Zemfira blinked as servants welcomed them and offered refreshments. Omid dismissed the servants with an irritable hand. He led them through several carpeted hallways to a little library, full of scrolls.

Omid directed them to sit on the thick rug, where he himself took a seat, looking grim. "What brings you out of those accursed mountains?"

Kuzro rubbed his forehead. "Zemfira has the Cost of Depravity."

Understanding flashed into Omid's pistachio green-brown eyes. He placed a broad hand on Zemfira's wrist. "I am sorry to hear that, my girl. Fortune has dealt you serpents."

"My father says you can help me," Zemfira said. "That you can protect me."

"Your father... is not entirely mistaken," admitted Omid. "I know how you can survive with your curse. I know a place where you will be safe. In a few days' time, I can take you there."

"I don't know if we have a few days," said Kuzro. "The Cleansers must know by now that we gave them a false trail, and with the incident on the Helmand..."

Omid leaned back, tugging at his mustache. "Perhaps it would be best if you first tell me everything."

Kuzro explained the events that had led them from Nebit to Rasparad, with Zemfira filling in details that he omitted. Omid listened with his brow furrowed and his thumb pressed against his chin.

"Remarkable," he said, eyebrows condensing. "I must inform Roya as soon as possible. And you are sure it was a Celestial One?"

"I do not know what else it could have been," said Zemfira.

Kuzro nodded his agreement.

Omid pushed himself onto his feet and started pacing. "I have a few guards in my pay—they will let us know when Cleansers pass through our gates. They probably won't arrive for another three or four days, which gives us time to prepare for our journey."

"Are we safe here?" asked Zemfira.

"There is only one place you will be safe," said Omid. "And that's where I'm taking you. Until you arrive there, true safety will remain outside your grasp."

"Where will be we going?" asked Paniz.

Omid raised an eyebrow. "Do you also have the Cost of Depravity?"

"No," said Paniz. "My Cost is Fatigue."

"Then you won't be coming," said Omid. "I will just take Zemfira."

Both Paniz and Kuzro immediately spoke up, their complaints crashing over each other. Omid scowled at their noise.

"This sanctuary is for innocent Soulgivers. Since you are not Soulgivers, you do not belong there."

"Soulgiver? Since when are Soulbreakers—"

"Those who reckon with the Cost of Depravity do not consider themselves Soulbreakers," said Omid. "They consider themselves Soulgivers, because they aren't breaking their souls for their Casting—not the way you're imagining it. They don't want to be demonized in their own sanctuary."

"You're not a Soulbreak—a Soulgiver either," said Kuzro. "If you're going, I'm going. I want to make sure you don't sell my daughter to the Cleansers."

"Have you lost your mind?" spat Omid. "You think I would treat my kin as merchandise?"

Kuzro hesitated, trying to maintain their fragile peace accord. "Is that not how you came by your wife?"

Omid's face turned purple. "I bought her freedom from the Zhou trader. Jia-Fan did not have to become my wife." Kuzro said nothing, and Omid's face contorted further. "Don't moralize with me, after what you have done! Sixteen years was not long enough, Kuzro."

Zemfira looked at her father, who didn't say a word. For a moment Zemfira suspected Omid would toss them onto the street. Then the merchant let out a long breath.

"I have guest rooms available for you, but realize the risk I take in letting you stay. I ask nothing in return except that you do not increase the risk—keep a low profile until we can depart."

"All of us," said Paniz. "We are not leaving Zemfira."

"You will be safer and happier if you return to your village—I will pay for your passage, if necessary. But if you insist on coming, I will not stop you."

Kuzro rose to his feet as well. "Thank you, Omid. We appreciate your generosity."

Omid clenched his jaw. "My servants will show you to your rooms. I must begin preparations as soon as possible. We shall speak at dinner."

***

Zemfira gazed around the private room assigned to her, marveling at the luxury. The windows had glass panes, a painting representing the nine Castings decorated the wall, and a Chatrang board stood on a spindly wooden table. Zemfira knelt down and examined the little wooden figurines of the King, the Charioteer,

132

the Vazir and the Archer, each piece a work of art. The mattress was filled with feathers, not straw. Zemfira collapsed onto the bed and smiled at the extravagance of it all.

She could hear Paniz unpacking in the room next door, could hear her singing the songs from their village. Zemfira was deeply relieved her friend could still express joy, after nearly dying of Scorpion Man venom. She was also grateful Paniz was not abandoning her on the next leg of the journey. She closed her eyes, and silently thanked her father for all he had done.

And yet, Omid's smug disgust made her uneasy. Her father rarely talked about Roshni. He said it was too painful to discuss. But what did that mean? Zemfira had never pressed him to explain, not because she feared punishment, but because she did not want to distress him further. Perhaps there was something else her taciturn father wasn't telling her.

A knock sounded at the door. Zemfira called, "Come in!" assuming it was Paniz. But of course, Paniz would never have knocked. A woman with shiny black hair and narrow eyes entered. A Zhou woman. She smiled at Zemfira, straightening her silk robes and cotton tunic, her bare feet lightly touching the carpet.

"You must be Zemfira," said Jia-Fan, taking a seat on one of the pillows. "Then I am your aunt. It is a pleasure to finally meet you."

"Um, thank you!" said Zemfira. "It is a greater pleasure for me. Thank you for welcoming me into your home. We are all so grateful."

Jia-Fan's left cheek was beautiful and smooth, but her right cheek bore a burn mark. The burn twisted when she smiled. "We cannot turn away from your plight—the days since your unclasping must have been a nightmare."

"Yes," agreed Zemfira. "But I'm lucky I've made it this far."

"It will never be entirely over," said Jia-Fan. She spoke Farsian crisply, every word pronounced correctly despite her unusual accent. "If you are a Soulgiver, you have to bear that burden until your death... as long as you remain in Farsia."

"Farsia is my home," said Zemfira. "But if staying in this kingdom costs me my life, of course I would rather leave and learn a new tongue."

Jia-Fan nodded. "Many Farsians Soulgivers choose that path—but you need not be among them. There is one sanctuary for Soulgivers in Farsia: a place where you can be safe, where you can belong."

"Is that where Omid intends to take me?"

Jia-Fan nodded. "He has long been an ally to our kind. He knows we are not the wicked creatures the Cleansers believe we are."

"How can there be a place in Farsia that the Cleansers do not know about? How can so many Soulbreakers— sorry— Soulgivers hide?"

Jia-Fan smiled. "Because it is a sanctuary in the Lut Desert."

Zemfira frowned. "I am not familiar with it."

The Zhou woman inclined her head. "The people in Harauvatis also call it the Empty Desert, because it bears no fruit and barely a stalk of grass. No one bothers scouring the most desperate corner of the kingdom, not even when hunting for a Soulgiver. Omid will explain."

Zemfira did her best not to stare at the burn mark. Jia-Fan wore earrings and no scarf, but perhaps this was more the custom of Rasparad than of her Zhou heritage.

"You are curious," said Jia-Fan, slyly. "I can see it in your eyes."

"No, no," said Zemfira, her cheeks heating up. "I'm sorry for staring."

"If you wish to ask something, I will not take offense," said Jia-Fan, draping her long hair over her right shoulder. "We are family and I want you to feel comfortable under this roof, even if the world beyond is a terrible place. You have aunts in your village, yes?"

"One aunt. My father's sister."

"And now you have one more. I am here for your questions."

Zemfira lowered her gaze in embarrassment. "I have been wondering how—how you came here, from so far away. My father did not know exactly, and—"

Jia-Fan laughed, and Zemfira could see the subtle creases from many years of smiling. "Perhaps your father feigned ignorance to protect your delicate ears. You see, I was part of a merchant's caravan, from Jicheng to Babilim, a large party that brought silk and tea to the Farsian people. I was not involved in the trading, of course. I was a concubine."

Zemfira said nothing.

"The caravan leader was a cousin of my father, who took me off my father's hands when his gambling debts needed to be forgiven. I spent several years with the merchants, some good, some horrible. I started younger than you are now, and only escaped when your uncle purchased me. That was twenty years ago."

"What happened then?"

Jia-Fan smiled sadly. "At first he tried to treat me as a concubine—and I obliged him. It was a better life than the dirty tents, the drunk men, the bruises and..." her fingers brushed her burnt cheek unconsciously. "But Omid could not manage it. He had many conversations with his Targu, but could not shake the guilt of owning another human being. So he manumitted me, saying I could go wherever I wanted. He even put silver coins into my hand. Then he asked if I wanted to be his wife. I accepted."

Zemfira could see what her father had been implying now. Omid's offer at freedom, even if genuine, had been empty. What could a Zhou woman, who barely spoke Farsian, do in Harauvatis with a few silver coins?

"And he knew you were a Soulgiver when he proposed?"

"I told him before the wedding, so that he could reconsider. Naturally the revelation upset him, and he spent the night meditating on his doubts, but in the morning he said it made no difference to him. He spent the next three years searching everywhere for a way to protect me. Eventually, he found it."

Paniz entered the room, hair all wet and spiky, as if she had dunked her head in the courtyard fountain. Her eyes grew wide when she saw Jia-Fan.

"Sorry," she said. "I didn't mean to interrupt!"

"Not at all," said Jia-Fan. "Please join us. Paniz, is that correct?"

Paniz nodded, and plopped herself down on a pillow. "That's me. You must be Jia-Fan, the Soulgiver who has avoided capture in the heart of Farsia."

Jia-Fan laughed at this. "It's far more mundane, I'm afraid. I was never pursued because no Insightcaster unclasped me, as Zemfira was. I don't use my Casting, so there is little evidence of my true nature. I eat a few herbs every day to minimize my trace, and I am practically invisible to the king's soldiers. I'm afraid Zemfira does not have that luxury—she must turn to Roya for proper protection."

136

"Who is Roya?' asked Paniz.

"The most dangerous traitor in the kingdom, and a friend to all Soulgivers."

"She wants to remove King Artashata from the throne?"

Jia-Fan shook her head. "She wants to do far more than that. She intends to end the Haxamanis dynasty, to disband the Cleansers and to exact revenge for innocent lives lost."

Zemfira chewed her lower lip. If Roya was using her Casting to achieve revenge against the crown, she might not be a safe ally for long. This Roya would soon descend into rampancy. Jia-Fan seemed to intuit her thought process.

"Roya will do far more than hide you from the Cleansers, Zemfira," she said. "She will teach you how to use your Casting."

"What?" gasped Zemfira.

"That's madness," said Paniz. "It's not safe to cast if you have the Cost of Depravity!"

Jia-Fan smiled. "The truth is not quite so simple. You'll see." She turned to her niece. "Whether you wish to explore your Casting, or whether you choose to abstain from it, as I do, I promise you this—soon you won't have to run from danger anymore."

\*\*\*

Dinner was opulent but Zemfira had little appetite. She ate a few dates, drank the Fars wine, and consumed two quail eggs. Next to her, Paniz was devouring stewed oranges, roasted goat, and marinated aubergine. Across the table, Kuzro put food into his mouth at a polite but constant pace. Jia-Fan ate mostly bread soaked with gravy from the goat, but Omid made full use of the menu.

137

"It's good to have guests again," said Omid, putting down a chicken bone and taking a sip of wine. "Even if the company is mixed."

Kuzro put an olive in his mouth, saying nothing. Zemfira was suddenly struck with an idea.

"Uncle Omid," said Zemfira. "What was Roshni like? What can you tell me about my mother?"

As predicted, Kuzro choked on his olive, and he spat out the pit with olive flesh still clinging to it. Paniz looked up from her vegetable stew nervously. But Omid only rubbed his mustache.

"Surely you remember something about her," said Omid.

"She died when I was five," said Zemfira. "My few memories are hazy. I want to know more about her when she was younger."

"Ah, my sister was an amazing woman," said Omid, gazing up at the painted stars on the ceiling. "Very gifted, you know. She tricked the visiting Vazir into teaching her how to read. She was two years younger than me, but you never would have known that. She was tall, and graceful and proud."

"You both grew up here in Harauvatis?"

Omid nodded. "Our father was a captain among the Eternal Cavalry, and his raids made him a rich man in our town. Our mother grew disenchanted with our new comfortable life and turned her attention to spirituality. She joined the local temple and—"

"And became the Targu," said Zemfira.

"Yes," said Omid, a little surprised, looking over at Kuzro. "She had to abandon the pleasures of life, including ready access to her family. She could only visit us on festival days. She used those visits to teach Roshni how to be efficient with her Fatigue. Our town was close enough to the desert that Fatigue

138

and Thirst were dangerous Costs but Roshni excelled. She kept our house cool during heatwaves and made glass sculptures out of sand."

"Wow," said Zemfira.

Omid sighed. "But she was waiting for her chance to leave. We should have seen it coming—she had read all the scrolls in the temple and was bored. One day she joined a group of pilgrims heading for Parsa, and apprenticed with a scribe at the royal court. Our father was furious. The goldsmith's son had planned on marrying her and now our father had to deal with the goldsmith's disappointment. But I was glad she was pursuing her destiny."

"Liar," said Kuzro.

"I was," insisted Omid, shooting Kuzro an angry glance. "Perhaps I did not realize it at the time. My father ordered me to bring her back, so I took a camel to Parsa and tried to talk to her. I communicated our father's threat of disinheritance. He just wanted her back. Our father was lonely ever since our mother's choice of the temple over the hearth, and my apprenticeship with the local merchant. But Roshni would not come back."

"I had no idea she was almost married to a goldsmith," said Zemfira.

Omid looked at Kuzro, then at Zemfira, then at Kuzro again. He burst out laughing—the sound like a thousand joyous frogs. "You have not told—"

Kuzro stood up abruptly. There was no laughter in his face. His eyes looked like raisins. "I think it is time we retire for the evening."

"If the girl has more questions, she should ask them," said Omid, hiding his grin behind another sip of wine. "It is not so late that we cannot continue our conversation."

139

"Zemfira," said Kuzro. "We could use a good night's rest. Let's get to bed."

Zemfira was not tired. She wanted to know what Omid knew, what her father had kept from her. But she could see the sorrow in Kuzro's eyes, and the fear. She could not do that to him. She would ask him about it later and perhaps he would tell her, with his own words.

"I would like to retire myself," said Zemfira. "I still owe Paniz a game of Chatrang."

Paniz nodded, sliding an orange into her pocket.

Omid sighed. "Rest, and tomorrow we shall discuss details for the upcoming journey. Sleep well."

They exited the dining room, Zemfira followed by Kuzro and Paniz. Kuzro put a hand on his daughter's shoulder. Zemfira saw the sorrow in Kuzro's eyes and squeezed his hand.

She could be patient.

# CHAPTER 14 – THE SHADOWCASTER

The barracks at Rasparad were modest at best. Volakles could not help noticing the faded banners, the broken training dummies, the age of the sentries' uniforms.

"I cannot offer much support," the captain of the guard informed Volakles and Firuzeh, leading them across the courtyard to the armory. She wore a short blue cape over her leather battle gear. "Our soldiers are occupied with patrols and sentry duty. Those we can spare have never dealt with a Soulbreaker."

"We are not talking about a fully-fledged bandit," said Firuzeh. "We are talking about an untrained girl. She may be volatile, but she is not fully rampant yet."

"I understand," said the captain. "But our guards lack combat experience—they cannot cast in coordinated maneuvers."

Volakles clenched his jaw. For three days, he had been on edge. Waiting for Firuzeh had been stressful enough, but journeying down the river had been worse. They had to force a ferry to take them down the river at swordpoint. No one wanted to brave those waters. Now that they were in Rasparad, the gravity of their mission was inescapable. They would eliminate the girl before she could disappear.

"I am not expecting trained Cleansers, Captain Atafeh," said Firuzeh. "The task of cleansing falls on our shoulders, but taking precautions is advisable."

The captain led them through the sheltered walkway and into the armory. "I received a scroll from the healers, a report on the target and her accomplices. This way, to my private offices."

"Your private office is the back of the armory?" asked Firuzeh, eyebrow rising.

"Unfortunately so," said Atafeh, offering her guests a stool each. "The Vazir has provided limited funds, and we must make the best of them. Please, take a seat."

Volakles was astounded by the dearth of resources, considering the wealth of the city beyond the barracks. How could a city so beautiful invest so little in its protection? Did they not worry about Shadow Beasts coming out of the desert to the south?

Atafeh pushed aside two arrow quivers to access her shelf of scrolls. She extracted one and unrolled it.

"You say the target's name is Zemfira?" asked the captain. "She used a pseudonym and claimed ignorance regarding what killed the Shadow Beasts around the boat. In the accounts of the father, Kuzro, and the friend, Paniz, they say it was a being, descended from above. Then there is the confused account of Davud: he claims the girl Zemfira killed the Scorpion Man, but his account seems as unreliable as the others."

"Before we discuss the strange incident on the boat," said Firuzeh, "let us review what we know about our targets. The father, Kuzro, is a Sproutcaster with the Cost of Hunger. Not an altogether dangerous casting art, but we found dried vines on the wrecked boat, so we can assume he has used Sproutcasting in battle before."

Atafeh inclined her head. "It stands to reason."

142

She had gray in her short hair, but with her smooth skin and fit body, she looked younger than Firuzeh. Her eyes were softer, and she lacked the coldness of some officers Volakles knew.

"Next, the girl Paniz—" said Firuzeh.

Atafeh nodded and glanced at the scroll. "Infernocaster with Fatigue."

Volakles chewed his tongue. "With training, such an opponent would pose a threat."

"Thankfully, this is not the case," agreed Firuzeh. "But we will be careful nevertheless."

Volakles frowned. "I hope we can dispatch the Soulbreaker without harming the other girl. It's bad enough we have to kill one of them."

"They are in defiance of the king," said Firuzeh. "The protection of Soulbreakers is punishable by death, and they know this. You cannot hesitate—they are all fugitives."

Volakles nodded glumly.

"Let us return to the question of the Celestial One," said Firuzeh. "Was it an illusion, a hallucination, or a misinterpretation of the girl's powers? The only reliable witnesses are a part of the conspiracy—the boy Davud was addled by Scorpion Man venom. So, do we believe a Celestial One would protect the life of a Soulbreaker, or do we think the event was a burst of destructive light, cast by a Lightcaster who does not know her own powers yet?"

Volakles scratched his ear. "If it was a Celestial One...could it have been protecting someone else? Maybe it is not about the Soulbreaker at all. Maybe it was protecting the other girl."

"We lack information," said Firuzeh. "If we can take either the father or the other girl alive, we can ask them for a more honest account—but our priorities remain unchanged. We must kill the Soulbreaker before she uses more of her power and descends into her inevitable depravity."

"You have already tracked their general location?" asked Atafeh, passing the scroll to Firuzeh.

"The warehouse of a prominent merchant by the name of Omid," said Firuzeh. "Are you familiar with this man? Could he be hiding them?"

"Doubtful," said Atafeh. "He is interested in profit, and there's no profit in Soulbreakers. We suspect they are hiding without Omid's knowledge, since his warehouse is large. But shall we track the merchant's movements?"

"Yes," said Firuzeh. "Until sunset at least. We are always better equipped with more information. You have all the gates out of the city covered?"

Atafeh nodded. "We will close them at sundown and they will be trapped within our walls."

"Good," said Firuzeh. "Then we can plan our assault."

\*\*\*

It was a simple stratagem. Volakles would monitor the warehouse until all were asleep while Firuzeh summoned the stray hounds of Rasparad to her position. Once the three were unconscious, Firuzeh and her legion of stray hounds would break down the wooden door and overwhelm them. If convenient, the accomplices would be spared for interrogation, but the girl would die immediately.

"Stay nourished," said Firuzeh, positioning herself with her dogs in an alley near the warehouse. Evening swept darkness across the sky. Volakles took a seat against the wall of the warehouse, disguised in a beggar's garments. He bit into his peach, which gave a satisfying crunch but was too young to exude any flavor. He closed his eyes and focused his mind.

Cities made directing his meditative perception difficult: the teeming mass of humanity clouded his observations. But with a concerted effort, he became aware of Firuzeh in the alley, of street urchins playing with rocks in the road, of the mercantile laborers in the warehouse next to Omid's.

He pushed the ebb and flow of his focus towards the three presences within the walls behind him. They were huddled together in the far back of the building, far enough to muddle the connection. He could gauge their breathing, their body heat, their casting art, but he really had to focus to determine their Costs. He first pinpointed Kuzro, confirmed his Cost of Hunger, then Zemfira the Soulbreaker, and finally the girl with Fatigue.

He wanted to move closer to better monitor their movements. Even without Aimgazing, he could tell that they were not hectic, but calm. The girl, Paniz, seemed to be eating something.

Volakles stood up and walked over to Firuzeh, surrounded by the sleeping forms of her various strays.

"Well?"

"They're still there," said Volakles. "But not asleep yet. They seem relaxed."

Firuzeh nodded. "Keep your mental gaze on them. We will wait until they have dozed off. In the dark, both you and my dogs will perform much better than they can."

"They have an Infernocaster and a Lightcaster though."

"We won't give them time to use their Castings," said Firuzeh. "Captain Atafeh says there is a side door into the warehouse, through which we can enter rapidly."

"Shall I move nearer?" asked Volakles. "I'm afraid my awareness is a little fuzzier at a distance, and I don't want to miss any subtle changes."

"I want to keep you in my line of sight," said Firuzeh. "And moving all these dogs will arouse suspicion. Resume your original position."

So Volakles returned, taking a seat and another bite of his peach. He wiped away the dribble of nectar and focused his mind again. His awareness scrolled out, gyrating around the nucleus of his being, and for a moment, he panicked. Kuzro's larger presence was not where it had been before. But then Volakles found him, walking around the warehouse.

Volakles could feel Kuzro zigzagging between large crates, like city blocks. He occasionally paused, his presence flaring from time to time. Volakles frowned. Why was the Sproutcaster using his abilities? Surely he wasn't spending his energy on botany at a time like this... perhaps he was bored.

Hours passed with brutal lethargy. Volakles stayed focused, waiting for their muted activities to end. Paniz was asleep—those with the Cost of Fatigue slept early and often. If the others would just join her in slumber, they could be dispatched.

But then something strange happened. Kuzro vanished from Volakles's awareness. Volakles opened his eyes wide, then slammed them shut and tried to locate the man. He was not in the warehouse. But a moment ago, he had been next to the girls. How could he possibly get so far away so quickly from Volakles's awareness? Unless—

He hurried over to Firuzeh and informed her of Kuzro's disappearance.

"Under what circumstances can one vanish from an Insightcaster's awareness?" asked Firuzeh.

"There are certain methods of Shadowcasting," said Volakles. "Immensely complex and difficult to use—and then there is death."

"Is it possible that the Soulbreaker killed her father?"

"I don't know. I didn't feel her presence spike."

"Return and signal to me if any other strange developments occur. Whatever happens, do not lose track of the target."

Volakles returned to the other side of the dark street. The moonlight made everything look unnatural. The shadows felt all too dark, the stars too faded. He sent out his awareness again, but this time, only found Zemfira. Both Paniz and Kuzro were gone. Agitation sparked in the corners of Zemfira's presence, but that did not explain the disappearances. What had happened? Should Volakles and Firuzeh wait until she vanished too, or should they act now?

His decision was made for him. Zemfira's presence vanished. He had been focused on her, had no one else to distract himself with, and yet the special consistency of her presence had disappeared, leaving only the faintest trace. He signaled for Firuzeh and she strode to his position.

"The other girl is gone too," he said. "I can't detect her."

"I see."

"Could this be a trap?" asked Volakles.

"Not impossible," said Firuzeh. "But we have no choice. Let's go."

They hurried for the side door, along the weeds and scattered rocks of the alley. Volakles took three quick bites from his peach, then tossed the fruit aside. He discarded the disguise, drew his sword and adjusted his buckler.

Firuzeh, ahead of Volakles, used her twin swords to slash the lock and pull open the door. The hounds rushed in, but within seconds Volakles could hear squeals. In the minimal moonlight, Volakles saw thorny vines in which the dogs had tangled themselves, drawing blood.

"They knew we were coming," said Firuzeh, entering. "I must alert Atafeh."

One of the dogs peeled away from the rest, and rushed back up the alley and toward the barracks.

"What do we do?" asked Volakles.

"We confront them," said Firuzeh. "We never flinch away from Soulbreakers. Follow and guard my flank."

She slashed her way through the network of vines. They extended from the dirt of the warehouse floor into the rafters: a barbed jungle made more dangerous by the lack of light.

"Wait," said Volakles. "We have reinforcements coming."

A few soldiers, having seen the commotion, were hurrying down the alley now. Three were all Atafeh had been willing to spare, but two were Infernocasters. Their Castings would make short work of the thorny impediment.

The two assumed casting stances, flames glowing in their hands. Embers fluttered forth, attaching themselves like insects to the vines and burning them to charred crisps. Volakles focused on the surroundings, but there was no one in the warehouse about to ambush them. Firuzeh and her hounds advanced over the dead plants, scanning between the crates and rolls of silk.

"This Sproutcaster," she growled, "has caused us too many problems. Let us end this."

He followed behind her, fingers tight around his sword's hilt, coughing on the smoke. "Firuzeh, I still don't detect anyone here. Is it possible that—"

He stopped talking and felt his muscles go rigid. Standing amidst the burning vines and half-concealed in the haze stood a woman. Her long black hair was pulled back to reveal purple

148

eyes. It was her. It was the Shadowcaster—the Shadowcaster from Princess Stateira's chambers.

"She's there!" shouted Volakles.

"Who?" demanded Firuzeh. "Do you see the target?"

"Not Zemfira, it's *her*! It's the Shadowcaster from—"

She was walking towards them, amused. Firuzeh still wasn't looking at her, as if she couldn't see the enemy. Her hounds sniffed the air, snarling. On instinct, Volakles stepped in front of Firuzeh, sword extended before him.

"Volakles, get back now."

"I can fight her," said Volakles. "This time I'm ready."

He rushed forward before Firuzeh could renew her command. The Shadowcaster was only twenty steps away. Her weapons were not drawn yet. He would strike her down and end this now.

"Pitiful," she said, raising a hand, and Volakles collapsed to his knees. His vision went dark and his brain filled with needle-sharp agony. Her Shadowcasting was strong, powered both by the night and her Cost of Depravity, but Volakles did not need to see to fight her. He struggled against the pain and the despair she was pouring into him and with a great effort, he got back on his feet.

"Volakles, no!" shouted Firuzeh. "Come back and—"

He didn't hear the rest of her words. Something in him was primed—he could finally sense the Shadowcaster. Her presence was muted by many layers of concealment, but it was not enough to hide from him—not at such close range.

He sensed her surprise at his resistance. Without hesitation, she drew her weapons—a sword and a knife—and attacked. He blocked the sword with his buckler and slammed his sword against her knife, the power imbalance knocking the Shadowcaster back. His eyes could see nothing so he closed them and fixed his Aimgazing upon his opponent. He advanced again, shield raised. He did not care about the young Soulbreaker —he had to kill this one before she killed them all. She dodged backwards, drawing him back.

The scent of rain and ozone filled the space, and before Volakles could comprehend what it meant, a bolt of lightning knocked him off his feet and flung him over the dirt. Coughing, limbs shuddering, he sat up, barely raising his buckler in time as another lightning bolt slammed into it. He was still blinded by the darkness, but didn't need vision to know when a Stormcaster was attacking him.

"Roya, be more careful," called a man's voice. "I cannot fight these dogs and your battles at the same time."

"I know this one," said Roya. "He must have survived execution at the palace. He's an Insightcaster who resists shadows."

"Switch, then. Fight the Obediencecaster, I'll take him."

Volakles's heart pounded. He had to fight the Shadowcaster himself—Firuzeh would be unable to defend against her powers. He sprang to his feet and ran from the Stormcaster. Volakles staggered into a crate and almost fell. He could sense the Stormcaster, could sense Roya moving towards Firuzeh, but he couldn't see any of it.

A bolt struck the crate next to him, forcing Volakles to roll away. But something was wrong—the Stormcaster's attacks didn't have the same emptiness that defined the Cost of Depravity. Volakles could detect the subtle aroma of Thirst. Could the man attacking him be the owner of the warehouse, Omid the merchant? Was that even possible?

One of the soldiers shouted and shot a volley of stones at the Stormcaster, forcing him back. Volakles seized the moment and got back to his feet, running straight towards Roya's presence. He had to get to her first, had to stop her. Then his foot caught a coiling vine, tripping him, and he hit the ground hard.

"You will not achieve your mission," said another voice, and Volakles could sense the aura of Zemfira's father. "You will not harm my daughter."

"Surrender her," shouted Volakles, refocusing his Aimgazing on the Sproutcaster and picking up his sword. "Don't let her become a monster."

"The only monster is you," growled Kuzro, and Volakles tensed as he felt the father preparing to cast.

Kuzro slammed a fist into the ground, causing a root to erupt from the dirt and knock Volakles across the floor. His chest ached from the impact, but his body armor had cushioned most of the blow. His stomach growled a warning at him, but if he stopped Aimgazing, he would die.

He rolled backwards into a crouch, dodging more roots as they burst from the ground, and Volakles braced for the next attack. But Kuzro didn't strike again—the goatherd hurried along an aisle of silks. Why wasn't Kuzro attacking?

Volakles ran forward as a stack of fabrics burst into flame. In the periphery of his Insight he detected the Infernocaster soldiers, hurling flames at Kuzro and the Stormcaster. Blinded by the darkness, their aim was not very good, but it still forced the enemies to find cover.

The heat intensified, billowing through the warehouse. Dogs barked, metal clashed, people were shouting. Smoke stung Volakles's nostrils. Breathing was becoming difficult. He scanned for Roya's presence but only detected Kuzro, still ahead of him. He would have to be killed first.

More textiles ignited as Volakles closed the distance to Kuzro. The man stumbled back, weaponless, and Volakles's buckler slammed him to the ground. The Cleanser's sword cut along Kuzro's arm, tearing the sleeve and drawing blood. Before Volakles could strike to kill, another bolt hit Volakles in the back, locking up all his joints. Kuzro took the opportunity to twist a vine around his ankle and yank him up into the air. Volakles felt his sword slip from his grasp, landing in the dirt.

"They've raised the alarm," shouted Roya. "Get out of here before reinforcements overwhelm us!"

Serrated thorns dug into Volakles's ankle as he swung, upside down, disarmed. Blood rushed to his skull. Roya would have reached Firuzeh by now. Could Firuzeh have held her own against a Shadowcaster with Depravity? Perhaps the hounds were not so easily bent by shadows. Skilled Obediencecasters could use the senses of an obedient animal as their own.

He reached into his belt, pulled out his knife, and hacked at the fibrous vine. Kuzro and Omid had fallen back, fighting off the Infernocasters. He cut the vine again and it broke, sending him crashing to the ground. He fumbled for his sword, but even as he did, he sensed the Shadowcaster coming. Her murderous intent was so overwhelming, it was made nauseous. Her sword swished through the air and pure darkness curdled in her free palm.

"I admit, I didn't foresee your abilities," she said. "I intended to kill two Cleansers without detection—but you can see through my Shadowcasting. How inconvenient."

A dog lunged at her and she caught it by the throat with her shadowy hand. It whimpered and went limp. She tossed it aside, advancing on him. Volakles could see blood dripping from her arm and a cut across her cheek. He struggled to get up, but his body hurt too much.

*It is just like last time,* he thought. *But now, she is going to kill me.*

He lifted his buckler as she released more shadows from her hand. The impact of the casting hit his shield with such force that the enchanted metal vibrated and made his body shudder. The force of the vibration increased. Then, with a metallic shriek, the shield split in half. It had been forged with silver to repel all casting, but even silver had failed in the face of such power.

Volakles lay on the ground with no sword, no shield, no hope to survive. She approached him now, stood over him and let the darkness swirl in her palm. The entire warehouse was trembling, beams groaning and wood splintering, but Roya was focused on him.

"I want you to suffer before you die," she whispered. Then she kicked him onto his back and punched down into his stomach.

The punch winded him, but it was only a mechanism to force the shadow energy into him. He screamed as the pain wriggled into his body. If only he could pass out, if only he could die. Anything was better than such unutterable agony. His sanity was evaporating in a sweltering crisis of anguish.

Then it was over. Firuzeh was bending over him. "Volakles?"

"Where—where is she?"

"Escaped," said Firuzeh. Volakles could make out burn marks on Firuzeh's arms. "Atafeh has brought her full garrison here—but they're too late."

The fires had been extinguished, but everything smelled of ash and blood. The bodies of a few dozen hounds lay on the ground, as did two soldiers.

"She is the one from the palace—the kidnapper—"

"I know."

"Where did they—"

"Here, have this."

The plum tasted like nothing. He coughed half of it back up, and struggled into a sitting position. He took several difficult breaths.

"Let me scan the area," he said. "Maybe I'll find a trace —"

"Don't bother," said Firuzeh. "The Insightcasters among the soldiers have already attempted it, with no results—they are beyond our scope."

But Volakles clenched his teeth. After two encounters, he knew the subversive flavor in Roya's cloaking. He would find her, all he had to do was scan the—

The pain was instantaneous. As he reached for his casting, his whole body seized up. Every color drained from his mind. Gasping, he stopped attempting to access his powers, and the pain decreased to a dull throbbing—but it did not go away.

"What did she do to me?" whispered Volakles, hot tears burning his cheeks.

There was alarm in Firuzeh's eyes, and she stared down at him. "Let me get you to the healers, now. We'll have someone else use the Temple Stone."

"Temple Stone?" mumbled Volakles. "Why?"

"We need to tell Captain Sahin what has happened," said Firuzeh. "Rest now. We have lost this battle."

# CHAPTER 15 – THE LUT DESERT

Zemfira shuffled forward through the dark, narrow tunnel, wishing it would end. Behind her, she could hear Paniz muttering to herself. Zemfira kept one hand on the silver-plated rock wall, and the other out in front of her, in case Jia-Fan came to an abrupt stop.

"Calm your breathing," said the Zhou woman, her voice echoing. "This tunnel is safe, you do not have to panic."

When Omid had realized they could not leave town before the Cleansers arrived, they had planned to ambush the Cleansers and stop their pursuit. He explained that his warehouse had a concealed tunnel that led out of the city. Because it was lined with silver, no Insightcaster would be able to sense them once they were inside.

But Zemfira had not realized the Cleansers had been outside the warehouse, nor had she heard them enter as she descended the ladder beneath the trapdoor. The Cleansers were so close to catching them that Kuzro refused to go forward—he joined Omid and Roya in buying them more time. The barking of dogs and the cries of battle faded as Paniz pulled Zemfira into the tunnel, into the absolute darkness.

"How much further is it?" she asked, voice cracking.

"Relax Zemfira," said Jia-Fan. "We're almost there."

155

Omid had told them to depart as soon as they reached fresh air, and to meet at the rendezvous point, in case the trapdoor was discovered. What if Kuzro, Omid and Roya didn't follow? What if they were captured—or killed?

She heard Jia-Fan stop and climb another ladder, her palms slapping the metal rungs with dull reverberations. Still blind, Zemfira followed. Before long they emerged from underneath a dusty carpet into a small junkyard, which opened out to the broad plains around them. Zemfira immediately felt a chill from the wind, and wrapped her cloak more tightly around herself.

"This way," said Jia-Fan, after Paniz emerged. They moved between broken carts and cracked ploughs to a group of camels and the boy who was guarding them. The boy grinned, adjusting the hood of his traveling cloak. He was unclasped, but it must have been recently.

"Who's the pretty one?" he asked Jia-Fan, pointing at Zemfira, and Paniz kicked him in the shins. With an exclamation of pain, the boy stumbled backward.

"This is Zemfira and her friend Paniz," said Jia-Fan. "Girls, this is Ardeshir, another recent addition to our sanctuary."

"A—a pleasure," he gasped, eyes watering.

"We need to go," said Jia-Fan. "Zemfira, you ride with me. Paniz, you will ride with Ardeshir."

"I will not," said Paniz.

"No time for arguments," said Jia-Fan. "Come, let us go."

The camels were far hairier than Zemfira had imagined, and they smelled worse than her father's goats. Jia-Fan gave her a hand up and they followed Ardeshir's camel out of the junkyard. Paniz looked grumpy.

The starlit road was empty, snaking northwest across the grassland. The air sunk its icy teeth into Zemfira's ears and toes as she turned to glance back, hoping to see her father emerge from the junkyard.

"They will be fine," said Jia-Fan. "Roya is very powerful, and Omid, though his appearance would not suggest it, is a capable Stormcaster."

They reached the acacia trees and dismounted. Paniz walked a few steps back to the road, looking back.

"I can see them!"

Three camels trotted along the road toward them, barely visible against the night around them. Zemfira's heart leaped, and she tightened her scarf around her ears, hiding a smile. Her relief didn't fade until the three riders dismounted and she saw their wounds.

"Father! You're bleeding!"

Kuzro grimaced. "Not a deep cut, don't worry. The Cleansers somehow managed to pierce the Shadowcasting. We were not expecting such determined fighting."

"I've never seen an Obediencecaster command such an army of animals," muttered Omid.

He was bleeding worse than Kuzro was. Omid had suffered several bites on his arms, which Jia-Fan examined and tended with a few bandages, before kissing her husband on the cheek. Roya seemed unmoved by her injuries, though they looked painful too.

Zemfira had not gotten a good look at the Shadowcaster when the two of them had passed each other in the warehouse tunnel. Her hair was long, her sharp nose had a scar across it, and her lips were pressed so tightly together that no air could escape. When she sheathed her weapons Zemfira saw her arms were toned with muscle. She looked to be around thirty years old.

"You have been expensive to extricate," she said, grimly. "We have lost a key resource in Rasparad thanks to you—Omid and Jia-Fan will never return to their home."

Zemfira swallowed, turning to them. "I'm sorry—"

"Your apologies will bring nothing back," said Omid. "Give me some time, and my rage will subside."

Jia-Fan smiled. "Don't fret, Zemfira. Your life is more valuable than a silk warehouse and a city home. And Omid agrees."

"Of course her life is more valuable," Omid snapped. "But I can still be furious, can I not? I can still blame Kuzro."

Kuzro nodded, looking down.

"Calmly," said Roya. "Omid will be richly rewarded once the revolution comes. Had we more time, we might have slipped away without revealing Omid's true allegiance, but no matter now. Every Soulgiver's life is worthy of sacrifice. If what I've heard is true, you may be more valuable still."

Zemfira did not like Roya's intense eye contact. It felt as if she could gaze into her thoughts without any Insightcasting. "Because of what happened on the river?"

Roya's pupils widened with private amusement. They reminded Zemfira of plums—dark and juicy.

"This is not the place to discuss the matter. We will talk once we reach Jalehravan. Ardeshir, you did a good job with the camels."

Ardeshir grinned. "Anytime, Master Roya!"

"Do you feel capable of raising the temperature for our ride?"

"Easy!" he said, climbing back onto his camel. Paniz, annoyed, climbed up behind him.

Ardeshir raised his hands and made fists, and almost instantly the frosty edge of the night lifted. The air turned mild.

158

Satisfied, Roya led her camel along the road, the others following behind.

With her father riding next to her, Zemfira began to feel sleepy. She wrapped her arms around Jia-Fan and leaned her cheek against her back. She slept through the sunrise and only woke when Ardeshir had switched his energies from warming the night to cooling the day.

The journey was long and no one was inclined to speak. Omid looked especially grim and Zemfira wondered how much he resented her for costing him his business and status in Rasparad. His dedication to his sister's memory or to Roya's cause must be profound.

The day turned to evening and the grasses gave way to canyons and rocks. Even with Ardeshir's Temperaturecasting it had been hot, but not unbearable. They rested in a clump of boulders, tired and sore, and soon drifted off to sleep. Roya slept in a sitting position, her cloak pulled around herself, while Omid lay on his back, starlight falling on his cheeks. Zemfira slept again, her mind weary from the sun.

"We are lucky," said Roya, as they set off before dawn the next morning. "We have not been pursued yet. It seems the trapdoor was concealed by sufficient rubble. They must believe we're still hiding in the city."

They passed imperceptibly out of western Harauvatis into eastern Mada, and soon entered the Lut Desert. Zemfira stared in awe. The canyons broke into sandstone rubble as sweeping dunes spread glittering sand across the dawn. The desert also made her anxious. There was no end in sight and they had only refilled their wineskins the day before. It was a lifeless expanse, with no signs of mercy in the terrain. She could already sense the temperature rise as the sun peeled over the horizon.

"Ardeshir!" called Roya from the front. "How are you doing so far?"

"The weird girl is making fun of my breathing," called Ardeshir. "But I'm confident I can handle the Lut heat."

"Not his breathing," corrected Paniz loudly. "When he casts, he grunts like a goat. And he gets so sweaty."

"You have to control a larger radius now," Roya reminded the boy, ignoring Paniz. "We have five camels and seven people. If you feel yourself succumbing under the weight of your casting, let me know."

"That won't happen," said Ardeshir.

Their camels trotted steadily as the road became sandy and more difficult to see. The rising sun made the air shimmer and soon Zemfira felt sweatier and hotter than she had ever felt before. The morning was still young and already Zemfira's skin was glowing from heat.

"I've set the temperature," called Ardeshir. "Within the sphere of my Casting, it won't get any hotter than this."

And so they continued. While the air stayed at a constant heat, the sand started to sizzle and radiate heat against them. It was like walking over smoldering coals. The space outside their little bubble rippled menacingly and the dunes swam in refracted light.

Zemfira watched the boy as he took deeper breaths. He looked over and gave an encouraging smile. "It's going to get very hot today—I can sense it already. But don't worry."

Zemfira couldn't help worrying. Despite Jia-Fan's insistence that Soulgivers could cast safely, Ardeshir was breaking his Soul to keep them cool. What if he lost control? What if he went rampant and attacked them?

They continued along the outline of the road, camel hooves treading over grains of sand. Once they reached a broken

160

boulder, however, Roya took a sharp left turn and rode into the dunes. For a moment Zemfira thought the camel had disobeyed the Shadowcaster, but Omid and Kuzro followed.

"Jalehravan is not easy to find," said Jia-Fan. "Only those who know its existence would be foolish enough to investigate the deserts of Lut. Those who do stumble across it can be killed and no one would be surprised. This desert is ravenous."

Zemfira could only imagine the brutality of that sun without Ardeshir to weaken it. He was struggling, but unwilling to admit it. Roya gave him a concerned look, then glanced at Paniz.

"Girl—pay Ardeshir a sincere compliment."

"What?"

"Do it."

Roya's tone did not invite defiance, and so Paniz, face contorting into a grimace, muttered, "You're good at riding a camel. Thank you for letting—letting me ride with you."

"Another one. More superficial."

Zemfira was just as confused as Paniz, but had the privilege of being a witness to the exchange. "I—um—you have nice hair. If you had a nicer personality, I'd find you attractive."

Roya scowled. "Paniz!"

Paniz let out a long breath. "Sorry. You're probably a loyal friend and a good helper."

Ardeshir turned around, wiping some sweat from his forehead and said, "Thanks, Paniz!"

"Now hug him," said Roya.

The interaction made no sense to Zemfira. Was the heat playing tricks on her mind? But Paniz knew better than to protest, so she put her arms around Ardeshir and embraced him for five seconds. Then she let him go.

"Thank you, Paniz," said Roya, and she spurred her camel forward to ride in the front again.

Paniz glanced at Zemfira, mouth open in utter confusion.

"What was that about?" she whispered, but Zemfira only shook her head.

The sun touched its zenith and began to descend, and the desert just continued. The air tasted so dry that it was difficult to draw breath. Perhaps it was the rivulets of sweat dripping into Zemfira's eyes, but it almost looked as if something was scuttling across the sand towards them—a black and red thing with pincers and a tail.

"Scorpion Man!" shouted Omid, jumping down from his camel, his shoes sizzling on the sand.

Paniz covered her mouth to stop a scream. Zemfira wanted to vomit. She saw Kuzro fumble with some seeds, and drop them into the sand. Jia-Fan was rigid, watching Roya step down from her camel with grace and tranquility.

"Everyone relax," said the Shadowcaster, assuming a stance and moving her hands in slow circles. "Ardeshir, maintain the temperature, no matter how close the Scorpion Man gets."

"Y—yes ma'am," said Ardeshir, his trembling causing slight fluctuations in the heat.

It was happening again. In the middle of the day she was being attacked. Zemfira knew it was somehow her fault. Whose deaths would be at her feet this time? This Shadow Beast was larger than the one on the ferry—it had a vicious underbite and spines growing out of its back.

But Roya simply walked forward and raised a hand, making the Scorpion Man's shadow boil and splash. The Scorpion Man did not realize anything was amiss. He rushed towards her first, the easiest target, but then a black spike burst out of his shadow, lifting the Scorpion Man into the air as it impaled him.   Paniz covered her mouth as the Shadow Beast hung by its neck, swinging gently with vacant eyes.  Purple blood fell onto the sand and evaporated in pungent hisses.

Roya held her position for ten seconds, then she released the corpse to fall and dissolve into feathery bits.  She remounted, stretched her arms, and started her camel forward again.  No one said a word, and the journey continued.

Hours later, as the sun sank towards the dunes, Zemfira saw a cluster of enormous boulders.   Jia-Fan relaxed her shoulders and let out a sigh.  This had to be their destination.

The massive boulders were larger than temples, their shadows stretching far across the sand.  Roya maneuvered her camel through the gaps in the rocks, which radiated heat that Zemfira could feel on her cheeks.  She trickled water down her parched throat.  It was warm as tea, but she didn't care.

"We didn't come all this way to live in some rocks, did we?" asked Paniz.

No one answered.  The sandy ground began sloping down, becoming pebbly, then rocky.  They rode this way and that between the boulders.  Zemfira's head ached and she marveled at anyone being able to cross this desert without a Temperaturecaster.  Then the boulders ended and they stood at the edge of a marvel.

In the middle of the circular valley grew a gigantic acacia tree.  Massive branches grew from the central trunk and spread a canopy of leaves against the sky.  Beneath the dappled shade of the natural colossus was rich, clean dirt, not sand.   The soil boasted agricultural riches: grapevines, wheat, fig trees heavy with fruit.  Pigs and goats lay in the shade, sloshing their snouts in the creek that flowed from an underground spring.  As they approached, Zemfira could see an old stone temple built against the base of the enormous tree.

"Welcome to Jalehravan," said Roya, smiling.

Zemfira was speechless. They followed Roya through an archway into the blissful shade of the temple's stable. An audience wearing cotton robes and tunics greeted them as they dismounted. Some even cheered.

One robed figure hurried forward to take the camels from them. The travelers descended a spiral staircase on wobbly knees, and Kuzro forced a wineskin into Zemfira's hands, imploring her to drink more.

The first floor below was a dining area, filled with low tables and cushions. The next floor was lined with practice swords and casting targets—a training space. Zemfira noted how the acacia tree and its roots integrated into the very structure of this subterranean temple, and she wondered how deep it went. The third floor was a dormitory, partitioned with several stone walls. Roya led them to the furthest niche of eight beds and indicated they should put down their loads.

"This is your new home," she said. "The Cleansers cannot reach you here. The king cannot find you. You are safe."

"What is this place?" asked Paniz.

"A temple," said Roya, simply. "The only Soul Temple in the kingdom. Rest now, and we will answer your questions soon enough."

She walked away, back up the stairs. Paniz and Zemfira collapsed on their sleeping mats, while Kuzro leaned against the wall, twisting his beard. All three were too exhausted to say a word.

# CHAPTER 16 – THE GLOOM

"Odd," said Lieutenant Bishen, examining Volakles in his hospital bed.

"What is odd, sir?" asked Firuzeh, who sat by the window.

"The entire situation is odd, Firuzeh," said Bishen, his polished boots clacking on the stone floor as he paced. "The warehouse ambush, the disappearing presences, the Shadowcasting Soulbreaker, and of course: the fact that Volakles has encountered her twice now, and survived both encounters."

Captain Sahin had sent Bishen to assess the situation in Rasparad, which demonstrated how seriously he took the turn of events. Bishen was Sahin's most trusted deputy and had killed more Soulbreakers than any other Cleanser. His eyebrows were bushy, but he kept his face clean-shaven. He was from the small eastern kingdoms incorporated into the Satrapy of Harauvatis, but he spoke Farsian without an accent.

"Are you accusing Volakles of something, Lieutenant Bishen?" said Firuzeh.

"Treachery was on my mind before I spoke to the healers," admitted Bishen with nonchalance. "Surviving twice seemed too coincidental."

"I am not a traitor," said Volakles, trying to sit up, but the pain in his chest forced him back down. Two days had passed since the warehouse battle, two days in which he had been unable to reach for his Casting without intense agony. Now mere movement hurt. Volakles knew something was very wrong.

"I cannot exculpate you either," said Bishen, as if Volakles had not spoken. "I cannot prove definitively that you are innocent. This conundrum makes me pine for the beautiful clarity of mathematics—systems of numerical precision devoid of human scheming. Alas, I cannot have my wish. I am uncomfortable with the coincidence of your two encounters, but I am more uncomfortable with the idea that you would risk the Gloom to further any sort of scheme. It's perplexing in either direction."

Firuzeh took in a sharp breath and Volakles's eyes widened. "What is the Gloom?"

"A poisonous curse only a powerful Shadowcaster can create," said Bishen. "It attaches itself to your soul and the moment you access your Casting, the Gloom begins to seep into your soul, like blood filling the lungs of a dying man."

"But—but—"

"Calm yourself," said the Lieutenant. "Panic will not save you."

"Calm myself?" gasped Volakles. "This Gloom is destroying me from within! It will kill me!"

"Most likely yes," agreed Bishen. "The healers are mixing rare herbs that can slow the advance of the Gloom. That can extend your life."

"What about a cure?"

Bishen frowned. "The Gloom is not cured. It is either revoked by the hand that cast it, or it kills. That is a hard truth you must accept."

Firuzeh stood up and put a hand on Volakles's shoulder as he started breathing rapidly, the pain intensifying in his chest. He was afraid to cry, even if all dignity was long gone. Bishen watched him suck in air and press a fist against his stomach, as if he could stifle the pain.

"How long do I have to live, Lieutenant?" asked Volakles.

"The medics give you another twenty days," said Bishen. "As long as you do not use your casting."

Deep despair washed over him. Volakles stared at his wrists, at his mortal body.

"But there is a way," said Firuzeh. "You said so, just now. We must find this Roya and force her to reverse her actions. That will end the Gloom."

"Yes," agreed Bishen. "But as you realize all too well, pinning our hopes on such an event is laughable. This woman has broken into the palace and escaped with the princess: she has bested you both in the warehouse. If we confront her, we must kill her. She is too dangerous. And I do not know whether killing her would lift the curse or not."

"But surely her defeat is a top priority," said Volakles. "She has Princess Stateira! Roya is central to whatever conspiracy has Soulbreaker assassins in the courts of Satraps and in the palace."

"She does present a significant threat," agreed Bishen. "But the situation in Lydia has become dire. The Hellenic Hegemon has met the Farsian army in battle and triumphed over our soldiers."

A new pain, duller but heavier, struck Volakles in the stomach. "The—the king lost?"

"King Artashata did not take the field himself," said Bishen. "The Satrap of Lydia led our armies, with assistance of the Hellenic mercenary Memnon. Naturally their defeat is a grave concern. The Satrap underestimated the enemy, and now our soldiers have retreated by sea. Some are saying the Hellenic Hegemon is a Polycaster."

"But there's no such thing. Mortals only have one art of casting," said Volakles.

"It is unconfirmed, of course," said Bishen. "But Polycasters do arise every century or so. Most fail to master their nine Castings, and die quickly. If the Hegemon has conquered Polycasting, then it might explain why the Hellenics have been united under his banner."

"Then the Celestial Ones have turned against Farsia," said Firuzeh.

"The omens are grim, but we are far from defeated," said Bishen. "And the Hegemon is the king's headache, not ours. As Cleansers, we must ensure these Soulbreakers don't strike while we are most vulnerable. It is critical that we end this sedition." He turned to Volakles. "But I will not lie to you and pretend that Roya will be vanquished in just twenty days."

Volakles just stared at the straw poking out of his mattress.

"Sir," said Firuzeh. "Would you allow me to pursue this woman? May I join the strike force?"

Bishen looked at her, his large nose twitching slightly. "Loyalty to your partner is commendable, but no justification for re-assignment, I am afraid. I believe there is an unclasped Soulbreaker in Tatagus you were instructed to kill."

"I understand," said Firuzeh. "But I would be useful in pursuing the Shadowcaster. I can track her. I fought her using three of my dogs and I even scratched her skin—I know her scent and I know the traces of her energy better than I know that of the Soulbreaker girl we were pursuing originally. I will be more effective than any other Cleanser you deploy on this assignment."

Volakles saw the steel in her eyes. She had slept for a day and a half after the battle, having spent an unhealthy amount of energy, but her ferocity had not diminished.

"You're probably right," said Bishen, thoughtfully. "Apart from your partner, you have the most experience with this fiend, and he cannot hunt. You shall lead the primary team."

Firuzeh's eyes widened and she inclined her head. "I will not disappoint you."

"Even your expertise will most likely yield no results," cautioned Bishen. "The full power of this Soulbreaker remains unknown. Do not engage her recklessly: gather information. We must comprehend a foe to beat a foe. Do you understand?"

Firuzeh set her jaw. "I do. But if an opportunity presented itself, you would not punish me for a successful capture of our nemesis?"

"I would not be here now if I was not pragmatic," said Bishen. "Such a result would be rewarded: but if I am to lose more capable fighters, I do not want them lost in vain."

Firuzeh sank to one knee. "I will serve with distinction."

"I expect nothing less," said Bishen. "Go speak with Kallisto and assemble your team. Prove yourself with results, not passions."

Firuzeh rose and looked Volakles straight in the eye. "Don't give up. Don't die. We will find her."

She strode out of the room, already repositioning her swords and putting on her helmet. Bishen watched her go, then looked down at Volakles.

"From what Firuzeh has told me, you resisted the Shadowcaster's power enough to engage her in combat," said the Lieutenant. "That was proof of the talent Captain Sahin saw in you. It was also very brave."

169

Volakles said nothing.  Bishen took a deep breath and smoothed his eyebrows with a broad finger.

"You are not the first victim of the Gloom I have spoken to, not the first subordinate of mine to receive this death sentence. Do not despair.  Call upon whatever resources you desire. Attempt to survive or make the most of your remaining mortality. You have earned that much, at least."

With the Gloom bubbling within him, Volakles wondered if he could enjoy himself with fine foods, or sensual pleasures, or even poetry.  Sahin had not saved him from death in that dungeon, he had merely postponed it by a month.

"I would like to be transferred to the nearby Hunger Temple," said Volakles. "Even if I cannot access my Casting, I would like to speak with those who understand my soul better than I do."

Bishen nodded solemnly. "It shall be arranged.  I have no doubt you will show courage as you face inevitable death.  You have my premature condolences."

\*\*\*

The Hunger Temple at Rasparad had a small room set aside for the dying. Volakles shared the space with an old woman who could barely open her eyes.  Watching the monks care for her from his mattress punctured his self-pity, but seeing her last breath rise from her lips amplified his fears.

The room smelled of stone and sprigs of rosemary. Volakles sipped the broth provided by the monks every few hours, read scrolls that described the origins of the universe, and tried to sleep.  Perhaps it was his anxiety, perhaps it was the Gloom dripping into his soul, but nightmares tumbled through his mind as soon as sleep found him.  He woke in sweat, surrounded

170

by darkness, unable to move because the pain in his torso was pushing him down.

He did not fear the dark. The dark was where he hid when his father was drunk. But since his unclasping at fifteen, he could always rely on his Casting to help him sense his fellow creatures when night robbed him of his vision. Of course, he could not access that power now.

Firuzeh would not find Roya in time. Bishen and Sahin did not realize what a threat she posed. They did not realize she could have killed the entire royal family that night, but she had chosen to only take the princess. Roya had something else in mind, something far crueler. This meant impending tragedy for the kingdom and death for Volakles.

And so he read the passages describing the Eternal Crusade, the battlegrounds beyond death in the abstract realm where the virtuous continued to fight the forces of chaos. He prepared for death to strip his soul of its memories, rendering him a pawn to aid the Celestial Ones. It was a noble fate.

The monks visited him, sat with him, even attempted to comfort him, but his mind could not be so easily calmed. His mind perceived the pain radiating from his core and knew it would soon rip his life from his body.

"How was the broth this morning?" asked a monk Volakles hadn't seen before. He stood at the entrance of the chamber, unusually sharp sunlight pouring in behind him. "Did you notice anything about the flavor?

Taken aback, Volakles considered his empty bowl. "It tasted like pepper, but my afflictions were disturbing my taste buds. It seemed more likely than a monk serving spices in their temple."

The monk chuckled. "I am no typical monk—I hoped some spice might life your spirits. Did it work?"

"I'm still dying," said Volakles.

"Mm, yes," said the monk. "And dying men are notoriously melancholy. No matter. My name is Danyal, and I am a Shadowcaster."

"A pleasure," said Volakles. "I presume you know who I am already."

Danyal smiled. "You are the Kappadokian Cleanser by the name of Volakles. You are the one afflicted with the Gloom."

Danyal was a short man with receding hair and uneven teeth. His round face was blotchy, and despite the order for all monks to stay clean-shaven, Danyal had missed a few patches that morning. There was sympathy in his eyes as he watched the young Cleanser.

"I have not seen you before, Master Danyal."

Danyal inclined his head. "I have been traveling. The local villages have been suffering from an increase in Shadow Beast aggression, and I was preparing a few defenses for the nighttime."

Volakles frowned. "I did not know monks engaged in military matters."

Danyal laughed. "Not often, but a good monk uses their wisdom for the benefit of others. And since the army has called upon every garrison from Tatagus to Byzantion to link up in the west, local protection is being neglected."

"What a crisis," mumbled Volakles. "A powerful Hellenic invasion, a rebellious cadre of Soulbreakers—and the Shadow Beasts are on the rampage."

"Dark times indeed," agreed Danyal. "But not your concern at the moment."

Volakles set his jaw. "True. I will not live to see any of these disasters come to pass."

"Not if you fail to shed this curse," agreed Danyal.

"But I cannot shed it," retorted Volakles. "My partner is hunting the woman who did this to me, but she won't find her—and I only have days left to live."

Danyal put a hairy hand on Volakles's trembling fingers. "There is another way."

Volakles stiffened. "What?"

Danyal shrugged. "You can save yourself of the Gloom without the assistance of the one who cursed you. You can accomplish it all by yourself."

"Why did no one tell me this?" demanded Volakles, heart thudding and the pain in his chest sharpening.

"Because I was not here," said Danyal. "And it is by no means a guaranteed solution. You may simply lose your life faster."

"I am willing to try it," said Volakles, sitting forward. "Please, Master Danyal—tell me how I can save my life."

"And you would prefer to pursue this unlikely path to salvation, rather than find inner peace and prepare for death?"

Volakles clenched his jaw. "Yes," he said. "If death takes me, so be it—but there are things I want to set right first, if I can."

Danyal smiled. "Excellent."

He positioned himself on the stone floor just next to Volakles's bed mat, assuming a meditative posture with his hands in his lap. "You have spent many years learning to meditate, have you not?"

"Of course."

"But how deep can you go, Volakles? How effectively can you leave your physical form?"

"I      can't      leave      my      body,      I—"

"It is not a matter of leaving your body, per se," said Danyal. "It is a question of entering the labyrinth of your soul."

Volakles felt his mouth go dry. "Only a few Targus every century achieve such clarity."

"True," said Danyal. "But thanks to the Gloom you have a conduit into your soul."

"What do you mean?"

Danyal smiled. "The pain, my boy. The pain links your physical body to your soul—the connection exists and you may achieve your clarity by dint of your curse. You said you are willing to try—is that still the case?"

Volakles stared grimly at the monk with his sly smile.

"I'll do it," he said, defiantly.

"Wonderful," said Danyal. "Then we will begin training at once."

# CHAPTER 17 –
# QUESTIONS AND ANSWERS

The food, while plentiful and fresh, was simple. Zemfira ate the bread with olive oil, figs and goat's cheese, then sipped at the crisp, clean water. It tasted rockier than the water from the creek at Nebit, and Zemfira quenched her thirst with slow, deliberate sips.

They were not eating on the dining floor, but deeper in the temple, among the shrines and statues where monks sat in meditation and prayer. Roya had instructed some disciples to bring food for the three newcomers and they ate together, heads down, waiting for Roya to arrive. Stones in the floor and the ceiling glowed in the place of lamps. The smell of incense and pressed flowers hung on the air. Kuzro drank wine, but not much, and Paniz eyed Zemfira's extra figs.

"Enjoying your meal?" asked Roya, descending the stairs briskly.

She had changed from combat clothing to a silk dress and sandals. Her hair was loose and her ferocity had receded into tranquility.

"We cannot express our gratitude, Master Roya," said Kuzro. "You have saved us."

She bowed her head in acknowledgement, then took a seat. "It is time you received a few answers. I apologize for my reticence on the journey—there is always the chance of a royal ambush, where one of you could have been tortured into giving up valuable details, had you learned them earlier. Now that we are here, we can speak freely. Once your burning curiosities have been satisfied, I would like to speak to Zemfira by herself."

"Does Omid still hate us?" asked Paniz.

"He certainly does not hate you or Zemfira," said Roya. "He only hates Kuzro, but that predates recent events, I believe."

"He seems angry."

"Every merchant curses and moans when he loses material goods, but he will move on, never fear."

"I would like to know more about this place," said Kuzro. "How can Jalehravan exist in these arid lands? Since when can an acacia tree grow in the Empty Desert?"

Roya smiled. "A good question. Are you familiar with King Darayava?"

"I don't recall the name."

"He was the third king of Farsia: a Sproutcaster of legendary power. Amid his conquests and reforms, he wandered through the desert and declared a temple should stand here. His men dug deep into the ground, through layers of sandstone and rock until they reached the subterranean ocean within."

"An ocean?" exclaimed Paniz. "Under the desert?"

"A great body of water, untouched by human lips," said Roya. "King Darayava placed a seed in the water, then compelled it to grow. In the mineral-rich soil the tree grew, thrusting its way up through the opening, up into the desert sky. No matter how hot it becomes, the tree is always hydrated, and always remains healthy."

"What about at night?" asked Kuzro. "Would the cold not affect it?"

"The surrounding boulders absorb massive quantities of heat during the day," said Roya. "When the sun sets, these rocks radiate their heat and keep the area temperate until dawn, when they begin absorbing heat again. Even without our Temperaturecasters, this environment is perfectly contained."

"And doesn't King Artashata know about it, since the temple was built by his ancestors?"

"The temple was kept secret," said Roya. "A place to test the safe limits of Depravity—but the project failed. The subjects, under immense strain and tribulation, killed their overseers and escaped into the desert, unleashing their anguish out onto the people of the young kingdom. King Darayava hid the failed project from posterity to protect his legitimacy. He branded those of us with the Cost of Depravity as Soulbreakers—and Soulbreakers we have been ever since."

"Wow," said Paniz. "Then how did you find this place?"

"My grandfather saw it," said Roya. "A Celestial One visited him in his dreams and showed him the place where he did not have to run anymore."

"He also bore the Cost of Depravity?" asked Zemfira.

"He did," said. "He was young and afraid, seeking sanctuary, so he made the journey here, and started a new life. It was difficult at first, but with time, a community grew up along the creek, using the healthy soil to feed the inhabitants. Not everyone here is a Soulgiver, but everyone here is a friend to the Soulgivers—as you are both, Paniz and Kuzro."

"Is it safe to have so many Soulgivers together?" asked Paniz. "Is there a risk that—"

She stopped talking when she saw the momentary displeasure in Roya's features. "There is a lot to learn about Cost

177

of Depravity, Paniz. Let me assure you, we are no monsters. You have been taught many falsehoods about who Soulgivers are. These untruths pervade the seven Satrapies, and unite them better than language, religion or royal decree."

"I'm sorry," said Paniz, quickly. "I didn't mean to offend. I'm ignorant on such matters."

"I took no offense," said Roya. "I invited questions in order to clear up ignorance, not to shame you for it."

"What exactly do the people of Jalehravan do?" asked Zemfira.

Everyone looked at her, and she cleared her throat to rephrase the question.

"You rescue Soulgiver children like me and provide sanctuary—but Jia-Fan said you were the most dangerous traitor in the kingdom. What did she mean?"

"We do save some young Soulgivers," said Roya. "Such as you, and Ardeshir—he lived in Rasparad, which made rescuing him convenient. Most we cannot save—the Cleansers are too fast, too organized. Many die every time an Unclasping Day arrives."

She took a deep breath. "Jia-Fan is essentially correct: we are more than a shelter, more than a temple devoted to understanding and mastering Depravity. We absolutely reject the House of Haxamanis. We want to end the systematic killing of Soulgivers by any means necessary."

Kuzro put down his wine cup. "Since your very existence is a defiance to the king's authority, you must fight to ensure your survival."

"That's right," said Roya. "We must fight or hide until Artashata's lineage dies. Once that accursed dynasty is dead, we can revise the king's policy of oppression, and the healing can begin. Integration will be possible. Until then, we do not flinch from enacting violence—not for cheap vengeance, but for the survival of our people.

Paniz watched Roya curiously, turning a fig in her fingers. Kuzro chewed his lip. "And... do we have to participate in your revolution?"

"Of course not," said Roya. "You are free to leave at any time—though if you leave Jalehravan, you must leave Farsia. Your life would be in perpetual danger for aiding a Soulgiver, and you might be tempted to save your life by giving away our sanctuary's location. We would bring you to a harbor, east to Hindusia, or west to the Hellenic islands. But we strongly encourage you to stay—to fight for justice, not to run away."

"And how can we help?"

Roya smiled. "Omid tells me you are a goatherd. We are always grateful for help with our husbandry. As for Paniz, you can benefit from some direct instruction from our Infernocasters, who can teach you to control your power. Go upstairs and seek out Tryphon, the Targu of Jalehravan. He will find you an appropriate teacher. Kuzro, if you would be so kind as to accompany her, I need to speak with Zemfira alone."

"May we ask just one more question before we go?" asked Paniz. "Who are you, if not the Targu?"

"I am the leader of the rebellion," Roya replied. "While there is overlap between temple life and the revolutionary life here, they are distinct. Tryphon handles matters of enlightenment and I deal with matters of politics. When war breaks out in earnest, I will lead the charge."

"Then why did you come personally to rescue Zemfira?" asked Paniz.

Roya laughed. "I cannot sit here and grow plump—I am too restless to ignore the crises of our people. I lead from the front line."

Paniz and Kuzro thanked the Shadowcaster, exchanged nervous smiles with Zemfira, then headed for the stairs. Zemfira did not speak until their footsteps no longer echoed, and they were surrounded by silence.

"You didn't have to send them away," said Zemfira. "I will tell them anything you tell me. I trust them more than anyone."

"That is likely true," said Roya. "But I prefer giving you the choice of sharing the information. Once you understand the Cost of Depravity—you may do with that knowledge as you please."

Zemfira processed this, shifting on her pillow. Roya looked up at the glowing stones above their heads for a moment, selecting her words carefully.

"What do you know about the Spenta and the Angra?"

Zemfira blinked. She hadn't been expecting a question about cosmology. "The Spenta is the creative force of the universe, a vast deity of life. The Angra is its perfect foe, a being of absolute destruction. Their war is the Eternal Crusade, which echoes across the realms, and which every living being participates in—either on the side of order, or on the side of chaos."

Roya gave the slightest nod. "And how do the Celestial Ones and the Shadow Beasts factor in?"

"The Celestial Ones serve the Spenta, defending the living and the dead from corruption—the Shadow Beasts spawn from the chaotic hunger of the Angra, and torment our dimension. The worst Shadow Beasts are known as Devas, and bring the greatest misfortune."

"Good," said Roya. "You have received the standard, oversimplified, spiritual education. I can work with that."

Zemfira said nothing, mouth dry in anticipation.

180

"You have also been taught that the Cost of Depravity depletes your soul of generosity, sympathy and regret. You have learned that your soul is a finite resource—like your age. The more you use your soul, the more inclined you are to destroy, to consume, to murder. To use the Cost of Depravity is to defy the Spenta and declare oneself for the Angra. Not all these statements are true."

Roya held out her hand and the shadows condensed into a swirling disc above her fingers. Zemfira stared in awe.

"The truth is simple—your soul is not a finite resource. When you siphon your soul into your Casting, your soul can be restored."

"But that's impossible!" cried Zemfira.

"No, Zemfira," said Roya. "I have used my Shadowcasting countless times, and I am no monster. I do not crave violence and suffering. I remain myself, not a mindless servant of the Angra."

"How do you restore your soul?"

Roya spun the disc of shadow above her palm a few more times, then let it disperse back into the corners of the chamber.

"Through community. The way to restore your soul is through love."

Zemfira had never heard something so foolish in her life. "Love? How does *love* help you regain your soul?"

"Soulgivers are not the only ones capable of damaging their own soul. People do it unconsciously every day. When people steal, cheat, harm or kill others without remorse, they are shaking the foundations of their soul. Most do not become monsters—the healing power of caring is often enough to mitigate the evil acts. There are those, of course, who have no love to fall back upon. Those who are alone in life become alienated, become angry, become unsympathetic, and spiral into depravity. There are hundreds of looters, rapists and murderers in this kingdom—the vast majority are not Soulgivers."

Zemfira was reeling. "Then why are we targeted? Why did King Darayava give the order to hunt us down—to kill us as children?"

"Because Soulgivers are as human as everyone else—they will lie and cheat, and unconsciously undermine their souls. People do so, no matter their Cost. But if a Soulgiver begins to use their Casting on top of ordinary foibles, an oblivious community cannot repair that damage. Soulgivers are powerful and rare, which makes us inherently different. If the love we receive is distorted by jealousy and fear, it won't be enough."

"That was why you told Paniz to say nice things to Ardeshir?"

"Her negative attitude was affecting him—his soul was under strain, and he needed a boost."

"How did you discern that?"

"With enough meditation you can learn to intuit the souls around you, to test their integrity, and examine them for weakness. Paniz's words helped Ardeshir's soul stabilize, and allowed us to safely reach Jalehravan."

Zemfira stared at her hands, trying to understand this new information. If it was true, she was not condemned to a life without casting. She could develop her powers. She did not have to run away all her life.

"That's why Jalehravan is so important," said Zemfira. "It's a place where Soulgivers never feel like outsiders. Where we can reassure ourselves that we belong."

"You are bright indeed," said Roya.

"I'm curious," said Zemfira. "How exactly does one deliver love? I understand quenching thirst with water and hunger with a bowl of rice, but quenching Depravity with love seems—complicated."

Roya let out a breath through her nose. "It is complicated. Not only must the act of love be expressed with sincerity, but the receiver must also be open to the love, must appreciate it. Since Depravity is not a Cost, using Depravity isn't a simple input-output relationship."

Zemfira blinked. "Depravity is *not* a Cost?"

"Your soul is not a part of your body," said Roya. "It is tethered to your body, of course, but it is not strictly in the same category as Hunger and Fatigue. Depravity is unnatural."

"What do you mean?" asked Zemfira, heart beating faster. "I thought you just said that we belong to the community, that we can safely use our powers if—"

"You misunderstand me," said Roya. "No *human* is unnatural, regardless of birth, sex, language or casting. But Depravity does not come from within us. It is inflicted upon us."

Zemfira mouth was dry despite the water she had been sipping throughout the meal. "Inflicted upon us? By whom?"

Roya sighed. "By the Spenta. Or more precisely: by the Celestial Ones."

"*What?*"

"Inscriptions on royal monuments insist the power of the Celestial Ones is limitless, which is what separates them from humans. Some statue plinths even refer to them as Bounteous Immortals. But these immortal paragons of the Eternal Crusade do not wield power without limit. There are texts here, older than the inscriptions on monuments that explain this. Each time Celestial Ones release their power—to save a life miraculously or destroy a dark creature—they create equal, opposite darkness: a boon for the Angra. Either they spawn Shadow Beast in darkness, or they pervert the Cost of an unborn child—they make that child a Soulgiver."

"No!"

"Yes," said Roya. "Immortal beings do not suffer the price of their own powers. They cast them off onto mortals like us. Yes, our souls can heal. Yes, community and love can restore us —but it is no gift to corrupt yourself—it is dangerous to yourself and to others, especially when there are no masters to train the young and the afraid. The Cost of Depravity reflects nothing about you, Zemfira. The Cost of Depravity is a blight inflicted upon you by the Celestial Ones."

Zemfira swallowed hard. It relieved her to know her Depravity did not reflect some hidden evil within. Perhaps she really was a Soulgiver, not a Soulbreaker. Perhaps she didn't have to blame herself for everything that had happened.

"Do you understand now who you are, Zemfira?"

Slowly, Zemfira shook her head. "Not yet—but I feel closer to understanding."

"Good," said Roya. "There is a lot to absorb, I realize."

"Do you know why a Celestial One saved our boat on the river?"

Roya's eyebrows contracted. "I have a few suspicions."

"Would you share them with me? I want to understand what happened."

"Not until I have sufficient information," said Roya. "And there is plenty you need to learn while I gather that information. I shall bring some scrolls to your bed this evening."

"I don't know how to read," said Zemfira, a little sheepishly.

"Then I will assign you multiple masters—some for combat, some for spiritual matters, and one for reading. Is that agreeable?"

Zemfira was about to nod, but stopped herself. "Are you training me to become a rebel—to join you in overthrowing the king?"

"Not everyone is suited for a life of resistance," said Roya. "But you carried a sword all the way from Nebit to Barkana, did you not?"

Zemfira's cheeks glowed again. "And?"

"Swords are heavy ornaments for those who just run away. You are a fighter. I do not ask you to pledge allegiance to my cause now, but with time you will understand the necessity of our war. I want you to be equipped to make that decision."

Zemfira touched the callouses on her hands, which still lingered from Navid's training. "I would like to learn how to read, very much. As long as you can teach me how to use my Lightcasting too."

Roya regarded the girl, as if deciding what to say. "There are no Lightcasters among the Soulgivers here. Your combination of Lightcasting and Depravity is unique, more unusual than you might suspect—but we can still train you, and we will."

Roya rose to her feet and Zemfira did as well. The rebel commander extended a hand and clasped Zemfira's forearm.

"Your new life begins now, Zemfira of Nebit."

# CHAPTER 18 – VOLAKLES IN THE MAZE

The monks allowed him to meditate in a sacred chamber of the Hunger Temple. Volakles sat, legs folded, palms open in his lap, breaths coming steadily and slowly. He let his thoughts slosh back and forth until he found a gentle mental rhythm.

Volakles focused on his uncertainty about this imminent ordeal, his worries for Firuzeh's safety, his concerns for his family in the exposed province of Kappadokia. He did not let his fears burst forth and overwhelm his mind. He simply wrapped each in a thin film of acknowledgement, and pushed them aside.

He turned his attention to his physical discomfort, letting his mind sweep over the aches in his back, the cold of the stone floor, and the root system of pain spreading through his chest. Recognizing these sensations was simple, but casting them away in their own bubbles took great effort. He managed it, and this gave him time to settle himself. Death did not threaten him in this mindset.

After half an hour Volakles opened his eyes and Danyal approached him.

"Are you ready for this?"

"I don't know if I'll ever be truly ready," admitted Volakles. "But I have prepared myself in accordance with your guidance. I thank you, Master Danyal."

"I cannot tell you what lurks in your labyrinth," said Danyal. "Every internal maze is different. But if you can navigate to the center, your spirit can reclaim dominion over your soul."

"Will the Gloom affect the maze?"

"Yes. And the longer you wait, the deeper the Gloom will sink into the structure of your entity. Your presence might accelerate the process."

"Understood. I'm ready. If this is goodbye, know that I am grateful to all of you."

Danyal bowed, and Volakles closed his eyes. He let the pain surge within him, immersed himself in the agony and let go of everything else. He allowed his thoughts to fuse into the pain. He reached with his mind, almost casting but not quite. The pain became everything, and Volakles felt himself condensed, sucked, swirled and pushed deep into his very being.

*** 

He stood at the mouth of a cave. The roar of the sea filled his ears and salt stung his inflamed nostrils. Sharp rock dug into his bare feet and he shivered as droplets of water landed on the back of his neck. He could hear Kappadokian gulls circling outside, but when he turned to look there was only brightness. This was not the cave of his childhood. This was something else.

He turned from the light and walked forward into the darkness, wincing as his tender feet crossed the craggy rocks. Something glowed up ahead, casting orange light on the walls. A torch hung in a bracket on the cave wall—only the cave was no longer rocky and rough. It had become a structure of sandstone brick. The walls were as tall as the corridor was wide—Volakles could only touch the ceiling with his fingertips if he stood on his toes. He stared down the seemingly endless passage. Was this the contents of his soul?

It was strange to exist as himself within himself. Volakles walked forward, along the corridor, touching his shoulders and chest, making sure both tunic and skin felt real. But perhaps that was not even important.

"Hurry up, Volakles!"

Volakles jumped, looking all around for the source of the voice. He saw a bird limping forward, dragging one of its wings along the stone floor. Had it spoken? Tendrils of shadow were curled around its neck and legs, impeding its progress.

"What are you staring at? Hurry and get me out of this sludge!"

Volakles approached the corner where the bird was struggling, and stamped on the wisps of darkness. They retreated with angry whispers, back into the cracks between the bricks, and the quail hopped forward.

"I wondered if you'd find your way in here," said the quail. It moved its beak in a facsimile of human speech, but the words radiated from the surrounding walls and from inside Volakles's head.

"Who are you?"

The bird picked at its silver feathers. "I thought you would remember. Well, come on, lift me up."

"What?"

"Pick me up, I can't fly with my broken wing, and we need to go. If you can't feed me, you can at least carry me while you're traipsing around your soul. Let's go."

The sandstone walls were becoming neater but more and more darkness was leaking out of cracks, a few drops were falling out of the ceiling tiles.

"I don't blame you, of course," said the quail. "She was immensely powerful—but we *saw* her, we were ready, and I hoped—well, circumstances did not favor us, I suppose."

"Are you a part of my mind?" asked Volakles.

"Of course not," said the quail. "Turn right up ahead."

They had reached an intersection of four identical passageways, and Volakles followed the quail's directions. They headed along the passage until they reached a pit in the path. It descended very deep, as Volakles could see. Looking up, the hole extended up indefinitely as well. Volakles realized there were no more torches around. The stones themselves were glowing faintly and provided the illumination.

"Not yet," muttered the quail. "Jump across first."

Volakles was not sure he could make it, especially with a quail in his hands, but he took a few steps back and ran at the hole, jumping and clearing it. He didn't have long to celebrate his success, because he was facing a dead end a hundred meters up ahead.

"This is the wrong way," said Volakles.

"You have to trust me," said the quail. "Walk up to it. We don't have much time."

Volakles jogged forward, jumping over another pit and kept going. The ceiling was no longer two and a half meters above him, but suddenly ten meters above, then one hundred, then back down to the normal height. He wanted to ask the quail about the nonsensical architecture when they reached the solid sandstone wall at the end.

"Sometimes I wish your soul was less convoluted," said the quail. "Place your palm against the wall and brace yourself."

Volakles only followed half of the instructions. As soon as he had placed his palm against the wall, the entire corridor rumbled and tilted forward ninety degrees. He fell hard against the wall, which had become the floor, and he was now in an entirely different maze—but entirely the same one.

"Wow," said Volakles, standing up and gazing straight up at the long shaft down which he had walked. "It's a maze with three dimensions."

"Move!" said the quail, and Volakles darted forward in panic. He turned to see more tendrils of darkness snaking out of the stonework, ready to wrap themselves around his ankles.

"It's lurking in the mechanism," said the bird. "It retreated when you entered—but every time you turn the maze, it'll start leaking out more, and you know what that means, don't you?"

Volakles didn't want to answer. "Tell me where to go, and I'll follow your directions."

"Wise choice," said the bird. "Left, turn left!"

He leapt over two pits, then reached a hole too wide to jump over: it was about three corridor widths thick.

"Should I go back?"

"No, put your palm on the left wall. We have to go forward, or we'll be too late."

The world turned again and Volakles ran along the wall, the bricks beginning to tremble. The quail scratched its way up Volakles's tunic to roost on his shoulder, freeing up Volakles's arm for better mobility. He jumped a gap and kept running.

"To the right!"

Volakles noticed patterns in the unnatural glow of the bricks—they held the outline of shapes, characters, even hieroglyphics depicting quails, all glowing with fluid brightness. What did they signify?

"Later, later," said the quail. "We do not have time—we can't waste a second."

Darkness was creeping in around the edges of these brighter bricks, sliding down the walls and dislodging the stones. Then Volakles saw a door up ahead, a wooden door with a metal handle. Before the quail could say anything, Volakles opened it.

Inside was a village, nestled by the sea. Volakles stared at his childhood home from the grassy crag where the door stood. The sea, normally calm, raged violently. The water was dark as night, roaring up the shore and not receding, but swallowing up the little cottages and the children darting along the streets. Volakles felt sick. The flood of shadow kept rising, and he slammed the door closed.

"What was that?"

The quail looked sad. "These rooms contain the imprint of your memories. The Gloom is already breaking into them."

Volakles ran faster, putting distance between himself and the slow advance of the gloom. The deeper he went into the maze, the more frequently he was jumping over gaps. The walls on either side fell away frequently, revealing a cosmos of hieroglyphs around him. It was almost peaceful.

"Focus," said the quail, when they reached a square block surrounded by emptiness on three sides. "This part is tricky."

"What do I do?"

"Jump off the left side, and quickly tap the side so that it becomes the floor. Are you ready?"

"What? No!"

Darkness didn't frighten him half as much as falling did.

"Hurry, before the Gloom pierces into these inner sections of your soul."

Fighting all his instincts, Volakles sat down on the edge of the stone, then pushed himself off, stomach ricocheting in fear.

He spun in that second of free fall and pressed his left palm against the wall. Nothing happened. It only grated his skin and he pulled it away. He was falling now, and panic filled his brain. What happened if he died in his soul?

"Your other palm!" screeched the quail. "Quickly, you're gaining too much speed!"

Jolted, Volakles slammed his other hand against the wall and the world righted itself, and he tumbled hard along the stone corridor without walls, landing on his shoulder and back, skin scraped and in agony. His nose was bleeding, and he kept sliding with his momentum, to the very edge of the walkway, almost falling off, but grabbing hold just in time to pull himself back up.

He had no time to take a breath, because the previously tranquil stones were shaking. Roots of shadow were already pushing several bricks into the air. The Gloom wrapped around the glowing hieroglyphic tiles, breaking the maze apart.

Volakles ran left and jumped over a gap, almost losing his footing as the far brick dislodged itself and floated free. The quail told him to go right, and he did, bricks flying up into the air behind him.

"Last switch," said the quail. "Straight up ahead. You're almost there!"

Grimacing, Volakles ran straight at the stone wall, held out his right palm and rolled up the wall as it became the floor. He hurried forward along his new passage, but running had become unfeasible. He had to leap from brick to brick as a tidal wave of darkness swallowed whole swaths of the maze. There were stairs up ahead, stairs already falling apart. Volakles dashed up the steps even as they broke and he tossed himself onto the landing, which glowed with bright symbols. He gasped for breath, even as relief filled him. He had made it.

He sat in the very center of the maze. He could feel himself most concentrated here and sensed the hieroglyphics beneath him containing something crucially important, but he did not know what exactly. He stood up and walked to the stone railing, looking at the symbols glowing there. The quail dug its talons into Volakles's shoulder.

"Touch the symbol with the three ovals."

Volakles did so, and the destruction all around his little island of sanctuary slowed. The darkness still broke the network of stone apart, but at a greatly reduced rate.

"How do I stop it?" asked Volakles.

"Oh, it's too late to stop it," said a voice behind them.

A fat black toad sat on some of the glowing hieroglyphics, licking the air with a poison green tongue. The frog had too many eyes and too many legs. It looked almost as large as a dog.

"What are you?" asked Volakles.

"Isn't it obvious?" said the creature. "I am here to tear your soul apart. I am the uninvited guest, fortifying your fear, depression, and self-hatred. The more you resist me, the more your world shall crumble. Death awaits you, Volakles."

"You have to fight it," whispered the quail. "It's breaking the world down around us—your soul is only hanging together by a thread! You have to kill it, that's why you're here."

"The little pest is right," said the frog, taking a step forward with a slimy webbed foot. "You are here to fight me, to banish me. But your winged friend is useless, with or without peaches, and I am so much more than this little body. I am everywhere in you right now."

A broad avenue of the maze crumbled above them, splitting into slow-spinning bricks. The hieroglyphs, glowing all around the dark sphere like constellations, were being extinguished.

"You're the Gloom," said Volakles, to the toad. He then glanced at the quail on his shoulder. "And you are my Insightcasting."

"It took you long enough," said the bird. "But I can't help you, without hurting your soul irreparably. That's why the frog is so confident."

Volakles stood still for a moment, feeling the reverberations of his soul as it broke into pieces, the humming of darkness swallowing chunks, and he knew even if he crushed the darkness, the damage would not be reversed. He could not fight the toad.

"I can't tell what you're thinking anymore," said the quail. "He's blocking our connection—he's too strong. You have to kill him now."

"No," said Volakles. "He is too strong, you're right. But I don't want to fight him."

The frog laughed, a noise that echoed in croaks off the pieces of rock. Volakles turned calmly to the glowing symbols behind him, examining them.

"Which one opens the floor, and which one closes it?"

"No, Volakles!"

"My essence is in there—it's where you come from, isn't it?"

"It's your most vulnerable point! You can't give the Gloom access to it!"

Volakles smiled. "Not all of the Gloom—just the locus of its power. Trust me."

"It's too late to stop me," taunted the frog. "You're finished."

Volakles ignored this, focused on the hieroglyphs. He found the symbol, pressed his fingers against it, and the glowing floor dissolved. Volakles hung on by the edge, but the shadowy frog plummeted into the pit of swirling color—an orb of light kept in place by forty bolts of lightning. The toad hit the mass of light and Volakles could feel it immediately. Volakles's entire body writhed against his desires, but he fought the spasms and slammed his fist back down on the symbol, sealing the frog into his essence.

"What have you done?" whimpered the quail, hopping down from his shoulder. "Why did you do that?"

"If it's too late to fight the encroachment of the Gloom," said Volakles between gritted teeth, "then I have to make it a part of me."

"It's breaking you apart," warbled his Insightcasting.

His body shuddered, and he fell to the ground, gasping. But he clenched his jaw, unwilling to surrender. He was not afraid of shadows. If his soul had to become a realm of darkness, that was fine with him as long as the darkness obeyed his will: as long as it held all of his soul safely in its grasp.

He felt violence surge in him, an assault on his being, but he fought back and absorbed that aggression, consumed it, allowed it to swirl within him. He would make it settle. He would make the Gloom subservient to his will.

It was the only way to survive.

*** 

He woke with all the weight of his physical form, feeling the stiffness of his joints. His eyes had to adjust to the lamplight. Danyal and the other monks watched him stand up. The pain in his joints lingered. He was hungry beyond belief, his throat was parched, and he was exhausted.

"Are you all right?" asked Danyal, face tight with worry.

Volakles focused on him, taking a few deep breaths. By the time he looked up a monk had brought him a bowl of fat grapes. He ate a few of them, chewing slowly.

"Well? Did you vanquish the Gloom?"

He closed his eyes, the sweet juice and the grape skins sliding down into his stomach. He let out a sigh, but his exhaustion felt heavy.

He focused his mind and let his awareness spiral out around him. His focus was not sharp yet, but it did not matter. He had successfully used his Insightcasting without the agony of the Gloom. Danyal was smiling, opening his mouth to congratulate Volakles on his miracle recovery. But then Volakles lifted his palm and wisps of darkness rose from it, starting to spin slowly into a disk of darkness. With a wave of his hand, he let the darkness disperse.

"Impossible," whispered Danyal. "How did you learn to Shadowcast?"

Volakles didn't answer. He merely collapsed onto his bed mat and tumbled into a deep sleep.

# CHAPTER 19 – JALEHRAVAN

"If you want to channel your casting successfully, you cannot force it," said Master Kalpana. "Forced casting will be both weak and costly. Envision your casting as a tamed animal—a creature you must sustain and care for, so that it will behave according to your desires."

Dawn lessons took place outside the temple, near the grazing goats, before the sun rose to its murderous heights. Zemfira and Paniz were both still groggy while they listened to the master's instruction. Kalpana told them she could guide them both, since she was an Infernocaster and a Soulgiver.

Zemfira stood barefoot in the dirt, holding out her left hand as Kalpana had instructed, and keeping her right arm curled by her side. But when she tried to pull her soul and push light from her extended hand, it did not work. She just stood there, feeling foolish.

"You need to visualize your objective," said Kalpana, assuming the same position as Zemfira, but turning her left palm up to the air. "And take advantage of your stance. Particular stances will favor specific expressions of casting. This pose, for example, allows you to create a ball of fire easily—or in your case, a ball of light. Give it a try."

Zemfira rotated her hand so her palm faced the morning sky. Her heart pounding, she tried to pull from the center of her being and push up through her hand. Nothing. She could not believe how poorly she was performing.

Paniz, next to her, was gritting her teeth but sustaining a crackling ball of fire above her fingers, flames licking up and vanishing into the air. It was the size of the grapefruits they had seen at the Rasparad market. Paniz looked at her and winked. Zemfira scowled.

"That is incredible, Paniz," said Kalpana. "And you've had less than a month of training?"

"Yes," said Paniz, maintaining the fire and grinning. "I've had no training whatsoever."

"Self-taught," whispered Kalpana, watching Paniz's fire burn brighter still. "Incredible. You have a gift, Paniz. You can release it now—you should not exhaust yourself so early in the day."

Paniz extinguished the flame and wiped the soot from her palm. Kalpana turned to Zemfira with motherly kindness and said, "Come, let's give it another try."

By the end of the lesson, Zemfira had been unable to cast anything. Paniz's undisguised gloating made Zemfira feel worse, and she took her frustrations out on her friend during combat training where showed no mercy. Paniz left the combat training with bleeding knuckles, so furious she didn't even shout at Zemfira. Zemfira regretted her aggression, but the praise from Master Yashar, the combat instructor, felt good.

Reading lessons were almost as hopeless as casting practice. At least she and Paniz were equally incompetent with letters and symbols. They received these lessons from Targu Tryphon who had fled from Lydia sixty years ago and had not left Jalehravan since.

"I have all I need here," said Tryphon with his rasping voice. "The wonders of the world are nothing compared to the wonders of my library. My reading allows me to touch every corner of the known world without leaving the temple. If you too wish to access this knowledge, you must first learn the basics."

"Our people don't have an alphabet," said Paniz, squinting at the diagrams on the scrolls. "We tell our stories orally."

"You are not merely Baxtrians," said Tryphon. "You are also Farsians and so have a rich tradition of written record. Written narrative is our way of achieving immortality—it is communication with the dead and distant. Do not dismiss it so soon, Paniz."

Connecting the letters to sounds slowly started to make sense. Zemfira managed to recognize the pointed letter of "Gamal" which Tryphon wanted her to find. She had yet to string a word together, but she was curious to learn more.

"I was hoping we would not be so busy," muttered Paniz as they shuffled along the dining hall to the pots of stewed vegetables, lentils and rice. "Since we're not leaving this place any time soon we could space out a few of our lessons, and spend some time exploring."

"There isn't much to explore here," said Zemfira, filling her bowl and sitting down. "We're in a little valley, surrounded by the Lut Desert, and have already seen most of the temple."

The dining hall was packed with people of all ages. Some were the children of Soulgivers—others wore the tunics of various provinces. Some drank beer and wine, others gorged themselves on food. Laughter and conversation were everywhere.

"The temple has many levels, though," said Paniz, slyly. "I bet there's more to see down below. You'll come exploring, right?"

Zemfira grimaced. "Only if it's safe—and if it won't annoy Roya."

Paniz shook her head. "You wanted to see the world, didn't you? Well, this is our world now, so we should know all of it, no matter the risks!"

Zemfira touched her tongue to the stew and pulled it back, burnt. "Things have changed, Paniz. I'm a Soulgiver, and we're under the protection of rebels. If we displease them, we could get kicked out into the desert. We can't be so foolhardy anymore."

Paniz shook her head. Normally she would have tried again to convince Zemfira, but her knuckles still had dried blood on them, so she turned to her soup instead.

Ardeshir sat down next to them. "Hello, girls. How's your first day going? Enjoying life as a disciple so far?"

"We're not disciples," said Paniz, irritably. "At least I'm not. My Cost is Fatigue, remember?"

"Right," said Ardeshir. "Well, if either of you are struggling, I would be more than happy to teach you what I know."

Paniz snorted. "We'll pass, thank you."

A young man came by with a basket of bread, offering loaves with a sleepy smile. Zemfira shook her head and Paniz took two. As he walked past them, Ardeshir swung out his leg and tripped the boy up. He fell hard, several loaves spilling from the basket. Ardeshir buried his face in his stew while several of the other boys and girls laughed. The narrow boy blushed, wavy hair falling into his face, and he hastily collected the fallen bread. He hurried toward the kitchens, almost tripping again over his own feet, which caused renewed bursts of laughter.

"What did you do that for?" demanded Paniz.

"Haven't you met Hami yet?" grinned Ardeshir. "Everyone teases him a little. It's harmless fun."

Paniz stood up and walked a few steps toward the door, hesitating.

"Don't go," said Aredshir. "It'll just embarrass him. He's very shy."

And quite handsome, Zemfira thought, but didn't express it while Paniz's anger was unfurling over Ardeshir's smugness.

"You're disgusting," said Paniz, but she sat back down, staring at her stew. "I remember boys just like you in Nebit—cowards and bullies all."

"Who's a coward?" demanded Ardeshir. "Hami is two years older than I am, and much taller! If he has a problem with it, he can confront me. He knows where I sleep."

"You are pretty short," acknowledged Paniz.

"He never uses his casting," said Ardeshir confidentially. "He's a Stonecaster but he refuses to use it. He doesn't want to join Roya in raids or assassinations—he wants to spend his days cooking and serving the bread!"

"So what?" Paniz shot back. "That's no reason to torment him."

"I thought we were all supposed to support each other," said Zemfira, quietly.

"We're supposed to give each other our honesty and love in whatever form it takes," said Ardeshir. "And as I said, he's not casting anyway. He's fine."

"You seem mighty at home for someone so recently unclasped," said Paniz, staring at the boy with narrowed eyes. "You don't miss your family at all?"

Something in Ardeshir's expression collapsed, and he grew grim. He made a halfhearted joke, then took his stew off to sit with some of his friends. Paniz shook her head in exasperation. Zemfira, meanwhile, kept glancing over at Hami, while he ate in a corner by himself.

***

A mandatory hour of meditation followed the midday meal. Some took the time to sleep through the heat, but many assumed a position on their bed mat and let their thoughts float free. Targu Tryphon, however, took them down to the sacred floors to explain the purpose of meditation.

"You have lived near a temple all your life, yes?" said Tryphon. "So perhaps you noticed monks sitting with their eyes closed—some kneeling, some cross-legged."

"Yeah, we've witnessed the spectacle," said Paniz and Zemfira elbowed her.

"Meditation is a ritual for transcendence," the Targu went on. "It is our way to let the soul disconnect from the anguishes of the mortal body—it is a crucial step for those rare among us who leave our human form and become celestial."

"That's not about to happen," muttered Paniz.

Tryphon smiled. "There are practical reasons as well. To cast with precision, you must have a clear mind. You must meditate. Inner clarity allows a Soulgiver to gauge what effect the Cost of Depravity has exacted on one's soul. It is especially important for Soulgivers and the friends of Soulgivers because being better attuned to your own soul helps one gauge the condition of souls nearby. You will know who is stable and who needs support."

Tryphon had assumed his meditative stance, legs crossed and palms together, and waited for the girls to imitate him. Zemfira did, straightening her back and leveling her shoulders. She let her eyelids sink.

"Do not attempt to divorce yourself from all your thoughts and sensations," said Tryphon. "You will find that most challenging. Focus instead on the letter Shin."

"What?" asked Paniz from Zemfira's left.

"Silently, Paniz," said Tryphon. "Focus on the letter you learned today. Let the image hover in your mind. No, Paniz, relax your face. Do not exert yourself in meditation."

"The letter won't stay in my mind!"

Zemfira could hear the Targu's sigh. "Loosen your focus on the letter, my girl."

"But you just said—"

"Your mind is a slippery creature. The harder you try to pin it to an image, the quicker it will slip away. Let your mind wander, but guide it back to the letter Shin. Circle your consciousness around to land back on the original target."

Zemfira let the contours of the symbol fill her mind in the form she had seen on the scroll. Paniz was muttering under her breath. Zemfira continued the exercise, but her mind drifted to her failure at casting, to the boy Hami and his very fine cheekbones, to her father and uncle, who had been arguing outside. She centered herself again on the image, circles of her consciousness returning to a central point. It was hard work, and yet it filled Zemfira with a sense of peace.

They had no lessons that afternoon, so after meditating Paniz and Zemfira returned to their bed mats. Zemfira had intended to review the symbols they had learned but then Paniz pulled the Chatrang board from her pack, which had stood in Omid's guest room.

"Did you steal that?" whispered Zemfira, although no one was nearby.

"I did not steal it," said Paniz, taking out a charioteer piece and placing it on one of the ivory spaces. "I simply brought it along. Omid and Jia-Fan won't mind. They would have lost it anyway, now that they're known to be supporters of the Soulgivers."

"Paniz—"

"You know what your problem is?" said Paniz, placing the line of archers in front of her Vazirs. "You say you want adventure, but you're too scared to disobey, to defy, to deceive. Well, you can't have an adventure unless you break the rules. The law exists to prevent people like us from having adventures. If it's not the king, it'll be Roya or it'll be Omid, but in the end, it's up to you. Now, will you play or not?"

Zemfira looked at Paniz, at the glow in her eyes, at the bruises on Paniz's hands. "I'm only playing for a wager," she said.

"Oh, and what do you want to play for?"

"The winner gets to eat the loser's fruit rations for the next day."

Paniz rolled her eyes but Zemfira wasn't finished.

"*And* the winner chooses where we explore first."

Grinning, Paniz shoved her archer forward on the board. "Deal. Your move, Lightcaster."

*** 

Zemfira was unable to sleep that night. Even in the stillness of the sleeping niche, surrounded by the gentle noises of slumber, she could not rest her mind. No matter how much everyone told her she was safe, no matter how much she told herself she didn't have to worry, she couldn't relax. This was not home.

After what felt like hours she scaled the stairs, supposing a cup of goat's milk or just some moonlight might soothe her. She glided past the many temple dwellers, some snoring, others still awake and reading by the glow of little lightstones. She climbed the staircase, her feet slapping gently against the cool stone bricks.

Approaching the kitchen, Zemfira heard shuffling and gentle scraping. She stepped toward the doorway and saw Hami scrubbing a large bronze cauldron with a goat's hair brush. Zemfira didn't say anything, just pressed her toes against the crack between the stone bricks. She was fascinated by Hami's feet. They were a little wider than she had expected, with little black hairs growing on a few of the toes.

Hami turned and immediately dropped his brush. He opened his mouth, made some small noise in his throat, then dropped to his knees and picked up the brush, not looking at her.

"Sorry," said Zemfira, her whisper carrying through the silence. "I didn't mean to disturb you."

Hami said nothing, and Zemfira felt her heart pounding unexpectedly. She took some steps into the room and leaned against the beer barrel. The lightstones here were dimmer since the two hearths provided an additional glow. She felt the urge to leave—every instinct told her to. Yet she stayed.

"Can I help you?" asked Hami, the words falling from his lips to the stone floor.

"I was hoping for some warm milk," said Zemfira. "Is there any left?"

Hami shook his head and busied himself with the cauldron. Zemfira could see he was uncomfortable in his own body. Something about his unease spoke to Zemfira. On some instinctual level, she was sure she could trust him.

"Do they make you clean when everyone goes to bed?"

He shook his head again, standing up and rinsing out his rag in a bucket by the ovens. She was making him anxious. He was making her anxious too, but less than the other residents of

Jalehravan did. Was it simply that she found him attractive? Paniz, while willing to stand up to Ardeshir about Hami, would laugh at Zemfira if she revealed her interest in the boy.

"Can I ask you a question? About casting."

He wrung out his rag and stared at it for a moment. "Master Kalpana will be more helpful."

His words were as delicate as feathers, caught on a breeze.

"She says a Soulgiver intuitively knows how to call on their soul to access their power—but I don't have that intuition. Can you tell me how you do it?"

Hami picked up a rag and rubbed it against the cauldron, removing a patch of grease. "I don't cast."

"But you know how."

Hami scratched his nose. "I'm not the person to ask."

"Why not?"

He sat down then, staring at his bare feet. "Casting is a choice," he said. "Not everyone is willing to pay the price."

"Not even to defend yourself?" asked Zemfira.

Hami just shook his head, hands twitching nervously. On a whim, Zemfira slid off the barrel, filled a cup of water from the trough and brought it to him. He lowered his eyes in thanks and drank it. It provided her a degree of happiness to comfort him.

"Why did Ardeshir trip you in the dining hall?" she asked, quietly.

Hami rubbed his nose. "He's...just having fun. It's not serious."

"If you ever need help," said Zemfira. "Just ask me. Well, ask Paniz. She enjoys putting bullies in their place. But I'll help too, as much as I can."

Hami opened his mouth, then closed it. "That's a very nice thing to say."

"Not really."

She was blushing, and so was he. They couldn't quite make eye contact, but they were sitting only a meter apart.

"Don't worry about casting," he said. "It will come. It sometimes takes time."

"Thanks, Hami."

They sat in contented silence. The stones glowed, brighter then dimmer. Zemfira almost thought she could feel the temple breathing. Eventually Hami rose to his feet, put away the brush, mumbled a blushing goodbye to Zemfira's feet, and left. Zemfira waited for her excited heartbeat to slow, then she too descended the stairs, found her sleeping niche, and tried again to sleep.

# CHAPTER 20 –
# THE GARDENER AND THE SCRIBE

Zemfira had known life at Jalehravan would be a challenge, but she had hoped her abilities would progress. A few days into her training, Zemfira still could not release any light, and Tryphon's reading lessons were making her head spin. Combat training now incorporated hand-to-hand combat, at which Paniz excelled but Zemfira struggled.

It would have been easier if Kuzro wasn't keeping his distance. He claimed to be busy with goatherding. Whenever Zemfira asked, he told her he had to earn their stay, but she knew when he was adjusting the truth. He was giving her time to acclimate herself to her new life, to make new friends rather than to rely on her family. Zemfira suspected Roya had leaned on Kuzro to make sure Zemfira focused.

"Training needs to be your top priority," said Kuzro, leading a stubborn goat into the shade. "I will be here, but I cannot teach you what you need to know. I've done all I can."

"You're still my father," said Zemfira. "Just because you can't teach me how to cast doesn't mean I don't want your guidance—not that anyone so far has been able to teach me how to cast."

"The longer it takes to start the fire, the brighter it will glow," said Kuzro. "Don't worry."

Zemfira wiped the sweat from her eyebrows, exhausted by the late-morning heat. "Jia-Fan mentioned you were planning on returning to Baxtris," she said quietly.

Kuzro looked at the goats eating from a patch of dried grass. A little goat was being pushed aside by the others, so Kuzro held out his hand and new verdant blades sprung from the soil.

"Omid wants me to go," said Kuzro, quietly. "He does not want me to stay here."

"But why?"

"He does not trust me. He thinks I've been a bad influence on his sister's daughter."

"But why?"

Kuzro took a bite of stale bread. Zemfira saw him wince at its toughness. "I was considering whether to bring Jabo here, to safety. While he's out of my grasp he's at risk. But me going back would be dangerous for him and for myself. I am hoping his lack of involvement will keep him safe. Gozeh will protect him, I know."

Zemfira's stomach tightened. She missed her brother but could not see him living happily at Jalehravan. It was too isolated. There were no mountains to climb, no forests to hide in, no creeks to dam up with rocks.

"You think going back will make things worse for Jabo?"

"If I go back, he would have to leave with me, and I cannot guarantee his safety anywhere, especially on the road. Maybe once everything has calmed down, once Jabo is unclasped, we will find ourselves another village in Baxtris far from any temple. We can start a new life there."

Zemfira was enticed by the idea of remote anonymity beyond Jalehravan, even if she was skeptical that the idea could be realized. Before Zemfira could express this in words, she heard Paniz call her name. It was time for combat training.

\*\*\*

"The key to hand-to-hand combat is endurance," said Yashar, tightening the cloth belt around his tunic. "A real fight is about tenacity. You will sustain blows and you must learn to absorb them, deflect them, and fight through them. Everyone knows they must avoid pain and injury—novices always underestimate the effects of exhaustion."

Yashar was a formidable creature. He stood a head taller than everyone else, with a thick chest and a sharp goatee. There were gray streaks in his hair and old scars on his shoulders. He had escaped Farsia when he discovered his Cost was Depravity. He first went east to the land of the Zhou and learned their fighting style, then rode with the Skythians across the plains and crossed into the northern Hellenic territory, learning their style of wrestling and spear-wielding. Somehow Tryphon had heard of him, contacted him and finally recruited him to Jalehravan. Now he prepared young Soulgivers for a life of conflict. He had trained Roya, many years ago.

"First, Zemfira," said Yashar. "I want you to throw the punches against Paniz. Paniz will defend without counterattacking until I call a switch, and then your roles reverse. I want to see both of you exert yourself. Ready?"

Zemfira saw the challenge in Paniz's eyes. Her hair had grown messy and looked wild from a lack of bathing. On Yashar's cue, Zemfira darted forward and jabbed straight at Paniz's shoulder, but Paniz blocked it easily with her forearm,

210

moving the blow outward and decreasing its impact. Zemfira swung again, faster, and again Paniz blocked. The sparring continued, Paniz soaking up Zemfira's abuse without a problem, even smiling as she did so.

Zemfira finally landed a hefty punch on Paniz's upper arm, but in that moment Yashar called a switch, and now Zemfira was on the defensive. Paniz's blows were not individually brutal, but she kept hitting the same point on Zemfira's forearm. The hits stung, forcing Zemfira's guard to drop and allowing Paniz to land a quick jab to her stomach.

Yashar called a halt and complimented Paniz's offensive technique, but told her to employ both arms more. Her left arm was slow to respond in defending when it should have been her primary defending arm, leaving her right open to counterpunch. Yashar turned to Zemfira and counseled her with more basic advice. Her barrage had been too slow, her defense had lacked deflection. Then he told them to try again.

"This is important," said Yashar, at the end of the lesson. "Women do not have the same body strength as men, though your sex is gifted with the stronger casting abilities. Nevertheless, you must be physically strong. You must be ready for any combat situation, and sometimes casting is an unwise option."

Yashar ended the lesson by recommending Paniz join the early morning lesson with Ardeshir and Milad, which hadn't cheered Zemfira's spirits. Her sour mood persisted as she and Paniz sat down with the young Soulgivers for the midday meal. There were few others their age at Jalehravan. Apart from Ardeshir and Milad there was only Nava, who scorned the company of her peers. She spent her free time with her mother or with the monks, reading. Nava was very arrogant just because she knew how to read.

211

"Are you okay?" asked Ardeshir, when Zemfira had taken her seat. "You look a little bruised there."

"That was my doing," said Paniz, proudly.

Zemfira was about to retort when Hami passed the table with extra rolls of bread. Her heart beat faster and her negative feelings receded. They had not spoken more than a casual hello since their nighttime encounter. She cleared her throat before he moved on.

"Would you—would you like to sit next to me?" she asked, trying to sound casual about it. "I mean—only if you're not eating somewhere else already."

Hami's eyes lit up even though it took him a moment to find the words. "That would be very nice," he said. "I'll—uh—I'll just finish serving the bread and come back."

He proceeded to the next table and Zemfira hid her smile behind her bowl. Ardeshir stared at her, incredulously.

"You're blushing like an idiot because of *Hami*?" he asked. "Unbelievable."

Paniz was ready to argue but Milad preempted the matter by tousling Ardeshir's hair. "At least she managed to resist your charms, didn't she?" he grinned. "She must have some sense in her."

Ardeshir scowled and Zemfira tried not to laugh at his annoyance. Next to him, Nava sighed into her bowl of lentils. "I can't believe I'm surrounded with such vulgarity," she muttered. "I used to be served by people like you."

"Fate is a funny thing," said Milad, good-naturedly. "Even the daughter of a Vazir is hunted like an animal when it turns out she's a Soulgiver. Better to eat with dirty commoners like us than get cut down by Cleansers, eh?"

"I haven't decided about that yet," said Nava, coldly.

"What happened to your father?" asked Zemfira. "Does the king suspect he was involved in your escape?"

Nava's eyes flashed. "My father had nothing to do with it—my mother alone saved me, but he was still forced to flee for his life."

"Could be worse," said Ardeshir, not touching his soup. "Better to have one parent who cares about you than zero."

At that moment Zemfira saw her father enter the dining hall, fill a cup with cold vegetable soup, and return outside. Why would he choose eating outside to the coolness of the temple? There had to be a reason. Zemfira stood up, even though Hami would be joining their table, to sit with her. But this was more important.

"Where are you going?" asked Paniz.

"Outside," she said. "Tell Hami I'm sorry."

Kuzro sat in the shade of the acacia, bare feet in the creek. It was dangerous to spend time outside during this time of day, but Kuzro was keeping himself cool. Zemfira sat down next to him.

"I want you to tell me," she said.

"What are you talking about?"

"You know, father. Why does Omid not trust you?"

Kuzro pulled his cloth tighter around his head. "I'm afraid to tell you. You won't ever hold me in esteem, nor look to me for moral guidance."

"Nothing can change my love, father! You know that. Please, tell me."

Kuzro sighed, staring at the creek for a moment. "When I was your age—I hated Nebit."

Zemfira didn't reply and Kuzro continued. "I'm not proud of it. I yearned for my Unclasping so that I could leave Nebit and explore the kingdom. You might not believe that of your placid, goatherding father. Much changed in me after Roshni—well, I should tell everything in order."

Sweat dripped into Zemfira's eyes, and she had to blink it away.

"My father drank the little money we had away, and my mother had to resort to some—some unsavory methods to get by. My brothers were abusive—only Gozeh was kind, but her kindness was not enough. I was sick of it all. When I was unclasped I did not return home from the temple, but kept walking, down to Himdook and then west from there, to Zariaspa."

The soup tasted salty on Zemfira's tongue, but she could not take her eyes off her father. He was rubbing his beard with his knuckles.

"It's hard to live by yourself at fourteen. The Satraps and Vazirs abhor vagrants on their roads or beggars in their cities. I encountered a wandering monk all the way from Taxila who had been tuned out of his temple when he went blind. He was a Sproutcaster and he taught me much about my Casting. He taught me to regulate my Cost efficiently—how some plants wanted a slow burn of energy, while others needed a brief blast for maximum effect. And on that slow journey from Zariaspa to Margos, the monk gave me the tools to become a thief."

"No," said Zemfira. It was preposterous, but Kuzro's eyes showed no humor.

"I left the monk when he beat me for burning his food. I am not proud of that either, but I was ready to move on. The monk walked too slowly, and I was too young for patience or regret. I found some ruffians my age in Saddarvazeh who took me in based on my casting tricks, rather than any muscle or quick wit. Many of them had run away from broken homes—some had escaped hangings and beheadings for their petty crimes. They were determined to make a life for themselves outside of the law."

"This is another one of your stories," said Zemfira.

"Not exactly," said Kuzro. "But it was the inspiration for many of the stories I told you. I was the thief who lured the camels away from the caravans with a trail of delicious sprouts. I was the outlaw covered the road with vines and forced the merchants to steer into an ambush. That was how I spent my days and nights."

Zemfira just stared at Kuzro. "You're not a thief."

"Not anymore. But for a long time, I could justify it to myself. Living by the law means accepting the lawlessness of the state. The king, or so I believed, took whatever he wanted from the people in exchange for protection, but that protection was already wearing thin—Skythian raids have been increasing ever since I was born. We are worth very little to the nobles and the royalty, so we decided not to acknowledge their laws anymore. If we had to steal to fill our bellies, we would do so."

"Did you ever kill anyone?" asked Zemfira.

Kuzro shook his head. "I never had the nerve for it. But that does not exonerate me from guilt. My actions contributed to many deaths. There were deaths in almost every ambush. We were relentless on the border between Mada and Baxtris—if soldiers came to instill order, we blended in with the local populations. We were the only gang in the area, so we never went to bed hungry."

"So what happened?" asked Zemfira. Kuzro had told her many stories about one bandit leader being assassinated by a jealous underling, and she wondered how this group fell apart.

"I left," said Kuzro. "I had been feeling uncomfortable for a while, grappling with the implications of our lifestyle. Then our leader took two sisters hostage and held the unclasped girls for ransom. I was done then, and took a ferry west, to begin travels by myself."

Kuzro looked at his daughter, but could not hold her gaze. "I visited every Satrapy except Lydia and Mudraya. I traveled and offered my services as a Sproutcaster in exchange for a hearty meal and a patch of straw for the night. The more I traveled, the more I regretted my years in the border territories. Most merchants I encountered were not rich—they were just scraping by. Many borrowed heavily to finance their journey and struggled to feed their families. They cursed bandits like me, but they cursed the government too, who failed to protect them. The merchants had to hire expensive Hellenic mercenaries, cutting heavily into their profits."

"And you never stole again?"

Kuzro clenched his jaw. "Well—not quite. Once a soldier arrested me for vagrancy and found the three silver coins I hid in the leather of my boot. When I saw him pocket the coins for himself I grew angry. I expressed that anger not on the soldier, but by robbing a local market vendor when his back was turned. There were other times when a purse lay forgotten or unattended and I took it. I'm not proud of my larceny. However, by the time I reached Parsa, I had left these actions many months behind me."

"You've been to the capital?"

"I've seen most everything east of Issos. I reached the capital when I was in my twenties, feeling capable and independent. I had earned a small reputation with the rare flowers I grew, and upon hearing of my arrival, the Vazir invited me to teach the palace gardeners my technique. Despite my travels and my contempt for the tyranny of the royals, I was impressed by the palace grandeur. Over the course of several days I showed the gardeners how to apply their attention to each flower, and received a pouch of silver for my trouble."

"You've never grown flowers," said Zemfira. "Even when I implored you to grow some. You refused."

"I know," said Kuzro. "But there's a reason, and I—"

"That's where you met her, isn't it?" Kuzro had never specified where in Fars he had met Roshni.

"You know the important details already, how she watched me tending a flowerbed while she translated a document."

"I remember you telling me, but I'm not sure if it's true anymore."

Kuzro swallowed. "With one exception, I never lied to you about Roshni. She taught me how to read, she would bring me to the local tea house and treat me to the finest selections—but she was married at the time."

"You courted a married woman? A royal scribe?"

A sad smile blossomed briefly on Kuzro's face. "I liked the danger of it. Roshni did too. She was dissatisfied with her marriage and wanted something exciting. Her husband was away for long stretches of time, and Roshni's position required she stay in the capital. They had grown distant. I don't think there was any abuse, but there was no love anymore. A divorce would be prolonged, scandalous and subject to court gossip. Roshni wanted to avoid a protracted humiliation. She asked Omid what to do."

"What did Uncle Omid suggest?"

"He didn't suggest anything, exactly. He tried to kill me."

"What?"

"He recognized me, you see. I had spared his life several years before when we robbed his caravan, and he had seen my face for a good ten seconds. He had not forgotten me."

Zemfira put a hand in front of her mouth.

"I was the bandit who was ruining his sister's lawful marriage, but Roshni's pleading stopped him from calling the guards. I apologized profusely and paid him all the silver I had earned from gardening... and he let us go. We fled to Baxtris before Omid could change his mind, and we returned to Nebit. There, my family took us in. Two of my brothers had died, as had my father, and my mother felt it was a blessing that I had returned with a pregnant wife."

Kuzro cleared his throat. "I sought this new, calmer life, but I had to change. Never again would I steal, and I strictly limited my Sproutcasting. My reputation for creating beautiful plants had to remain dormant, otherwise trouble from Parsa might find us."

"She was still married to the man from the capital."

"We had a little wedding ceremony, but yes, it could not be official. She died the wife of another man—but he never came looking in Nebit. We decided our love could trump the legal niceties."

"It was Baj. He was Roshni's husband."

Kuzro's mouth opened in surprise, ready to deny it, but then he reconsidered. "Yes. That's right. He was the Royal Cartographer and she was his scribe. They worked together, then were married."

Zemfira struggled to process this. "So, all this time, you've been telling me and Jabo stories you heard from Roshni?"

"It's absurd, I know. But I could never hate him properly. He was no monster—and though he never loved Roshni with the passion I did, I bear him no ill will, wherever he is."

Zemfira dabbed the sweat from her forehead. "I don't know what to say."

"Well, now you have the truth," said Kuzro. "Perhaps knowing will make it easier to focus on your training. You won't feel beholden to your father, now that you know what sort of a man he really is."

Zemfira stood up and walked over to Kuzro, who flinched. She did not say anything, but she sat down next to him and put her arms around his waist. Bodily contact was hot and sticky but she embraced him tightly.

"I couldn't ask for a better father," said Zemfira. "And you're a fool if you think this changes anything."

Kuzro had words lodged in his throat. He drank more soup and watched the water run over his bare feet. The silence washed over them, between the waves of heat.

Finally, Zemfira stood up to go in and he placed a hand on her arm. He drew her attention to a flower growing rapidly out of the creek, the petals crimson and purple. Kuzro slowed his casting as the petals spread wide, then plucked the flower and handed it to her, wiping a tear from his eye. She kissed him on the cheek, and headed inside.

# CHAPTER 21 – STATEIRA

"Why does Hami have to come?" demanded Paniz in a whisper.

"He knows the temple better than we do," replied Zemfira, glancing around their sleeping niche to make sure they were not being overheard. "He might be useful."

"We can figure it out ourselves," said Paniz. "I thought this would just be the two of us."

"He won't disturb us, I promise."

Paniz grimaced, but said no more. They had now been at Jalehravan for half a month, both tougher, both slightly better readers, and one of them gaining a good handle on her Casting. Zemfira still showed no potential.

With Yashar on a mission for Roya and combat lessons cancelled, the time was ripe for exploring the forbidden sections of the temple. Heart pounding, Zemfira had asked Hami to join them. Then she had informed Paniz of her unilateral decision in the dark.

"Why do you like him so much?"

"I don't know what you're talking about."

"You're hopelessly infatuated," said Paniz, clucking her tongue.

"I'm not *infatuated*—I just enjoy having him around. And maybe I want to kiss him. So what? You and Milad seemed to have some fun yesterday."

Paniz moved in the darkness and punched Zemfira in the shoulder. Zemfira assumed her friend hadn't meant to punch her right on a bruise, but she couldn't rule it out either.

"I was *racing* him, that's all. We wanted to see who could get to the edge of Jalehravan's boulders and back first."

"But you let him win—and now he gets to eat a supper with you, just the two of you?"

"I didn't let him win! He's fast in the sand."

"Uh huh."

They lay in the darkness together, Kuzro snoring in his deep sleep. It was impossible to wake him with words. Zemfira remembered mornings where nothing less than river water could stir him. Paniz was quiet—quieter than she was when Tryphon guided them through meditation.

"You told him to meet you here?"

"An hour after the lightstones dim, I said. He might not even come."

"Whatever. As long as it isn't Ardeshir," muttered Paniz.

They waited and Zemfira tried to meditate. Tryphon had started teaching them the regional methods of meditation. In Lydia, with its Hellenic cities, monks dismantled stray thoughts through repetitive reasoning and philosophical proofs. The monks to the east, living in the Hindusian client-kingdoms, chanted in order to make their souls resonate. She liked the Mudrayan style of lowering or raising one's heartbeat to find mental tranquility in both stress and relaxation. She could almost sense Paniz's soul pulsing nearby, thrumming like some incomprehensible instrument.

221

Zemfira's trance broke when Hami banged into the stone wall. She and Paniz both rose and stepped around the corner to see Hami holding his forehead in the dim glow of the lightstones. Paniz walked past Hami, too annoyed to acknowledge the boy. Zemfira gave his hand a reassuring squeeze.

Thankfully, the little disturbance had failed to draw attention, and they glided through the sleeping chamber unnoticed, reaching the spiral staircase and following it further down. The air grew cooler—a strange subterranean breeze drifting over them.

"Thank you for inviting me," mumbled Hami.

"Yeah, yeah, our pleasure," said Paniz. "Now, be quiet."

Each footstep was soft, a gentle slap against the stone. They reached the floor with the statues of the bird-faced Celestial Ones, lit by inlaid lightstones. The next staircase, the forbidden one, lay on the other side of the room.

"Do the monks ever sleep down here?" breathed Zemfira as they passed an alcove of scrolls.

Hami shook his head. A small trickle of blood clung to his dark curls from his impact with the wall.

Roya and Tryphon had never forbidden them directly to descend into the temple, but masters like Kalpana and Yashar had expressed the restriction several times, not to mention Omid who had insisted the girls behave themselves. Jia-Fan told them the lower floor only contained a boring rebel armory and a tedious meeting chamber, but she failed to quell their curiosity. Zemfira stepped over the little canal of water that ran between two statues and reached the next staircase.

It was darker here. The lightstones were older and only flared up weakly when someone approached. The floor was no longer flat, but slanted deeper into the earth. Water chuckled down slanted canals along either side of the long chamber. The air smelled of earth and iron. Squinting, Zemfira could barely see etchings on the wall, an art style long since passed out of fashion. Perhaps they had been etched in the time of King Darayava—relics and images of a history long lost.

"It's the nine casting arts," whispered Paniz, slowing down behind Zemfira. "Look."

Zemfira peered more closely at the nearest wall. Paniz was right. The crude image of a genderless figure held fire in one hand and a sword in another. The next figure had three rocks floating about its head. The line of figures continued through all nine arts, leading up to a tenth figure, much larger than the others.

"Polycaster," whispered Hami, pointing a trembling finger at the figure's eight arms and the staring eye in the center of its forehead. Each hand held a different power. The crudeness of the etching unnerved Zemfira.

"Can you read these, Hami?" asked Paniz, pointing at the symbols beneath the images.

Hami squinted and shook his head. "That's not Aramaic— that's an older alphabet—from the time of the early kings."

The symbols were sharp, almost aggressive. The pulsing lightstones gave the reliefs an eerie quality, and the hairs on Zemfira's arms prickled. She kept moving, Paniz and Hami following close behind.

"How far are we going?" asked Hami, voice hoarse.

"You can go back if you want to," said Paniz.

"No! I—I was just curious."

Zemfira touched his shoulder sympathetically. "We just want to see if there's really a subterranean ocean that feeds the acacia tree. If we don't find anything, we'll turn back. I promise."

They reached a long, broad staircase and descended it. Zemfira marveled at the depth of the temple. How had they built such an elaborate temple so long ago? There must have been an army of master Stonecasters to bring this edifice into being. And where had all the lightstones come from? They were as rare as rubies and had to be handled by Lightcasters or they would lose their luminescence.

The floor leveled out and three archways in the rock appeared. Each arch was inscribed in words Zemfira could not recognize—more relics from that old alphabet.

"Where do we go now?" asked Paniz. There were no lightstones in any of the passages, so she conjured a small flame into the palm of her hand. "Do we explore each one?"

"I don't think so," said Zemfira, slowly. "I'm guessing two of them are traps."

"Hami, tell us which way to go," said Paniz.

"W—what?"

"You're a Stonecaster, aren't you? You can sense rock the way an Insightcaster can sense human presences. Which way leads to the underground ocean?"

But Hami was shaking his head, unable to control his hands. "I don't interact with rocks. I can't. I won't."

"Oh, you're kidding," said Paniz. "Even *this* is too much for you?"

"Leave him alone, Paniz."

"He's useless, Zemfira. He's worse than you! At least you're trying to cast."

Zemfira closed her eyes so that her irritation wouldn't push a scathing retort onto her tongue. But closing her eyes made her notice something. She sensed an incorporeal tugging within her body. Almost involuntarily she stepped to the archway on the left. The tugging was gentle, almost imperceptible.

"I think this is the way we need to go," she said, looking into the darkness.

224

"Why?" asked Paniz. "You're not a Stonecaster."

"I know. I just feel confident about this path."

Paniz stared at her. "Based on a feeling? Zemfira, wait!"

But Zemfira had already started walking down the gray brick path, hands out ahead of her to feel her way along the rock, clumped dirt and tangled roots. It was as if they were plunging into the heart of the earth. Paniz lit the way with her fire, and Hami, trembling, followed last.

The smell of dirt and smoke filled their nostrils as they slipped between broken boulders. When Hami stumbled Zemfira caught him and held his hand, and he squeezed hers to assure her he was fine. Finally they saw light ahead, pale as fog. Paniz extinguished her flame and they slowed down. They exchanged nervous looks and Zemfira stepped out first.

It was a sight Zemfira could not have imagined. Crystals larger than their cottage in Nebit jutted from the vast ceiling. Their glow fell like moonbeams upon a vast lake, gently disturbed by ripples on its turquoise surface. A vast network of roots descended from the ceiling and sank into the body of water, each as thick as a tree trunk. Zemfira sucked in the cool air, releasing it in a soft whistle.

"This is incredible," said Paniz.

"Is this what an ocean looks like?" asked Zemfira.

"An ocean is bigger," said Hami.

"Bigger than this?" demanded Paniz. "I can barely see the other side!"

The tug had not abated. Zemfira stepped onto a sandy bank, her bare toes curling on the granular surface. The sand glowed when her feet touched it as if the subterranean beach contained fragments of lightstone. She placed one foot in the water, its icy coolness running through her body and revitalizing her.

"What's that?" asked Paniz, pointing to the center of the lake. "Next to that large root—is that an island?"

"I think so," said Zemfira, taking another step into the shallow water. The island was not far away. She came to a decision and squashed her habitual doubts. "I'm going to swim to the island and investigate."

Hami gave a squeak and Paniz stared for a moment, disbelieving. Then she shrugged and undid the sash around her middle. "While we're here, we might as well."

"But—but—" said Hami.

"Stay here if you're nervous," said Zemfira, slipping out of her tunic. "We'll be back soon."

"He's not nervous, he's embarrassed," said Paniz. "Do you think he'll get into trouble if he's caught with two naked girls? I bet they're a lot stricter here about that stuff than in Baxtris."

"I'll keep watch," said Hami, turning away and looking back towards the tunnel. "You two go ahead."

Zemfira smiled, watching him turn and settle in the sand. His embarrassment was endearing. She pushed thoughts of kissing him from her mind and focused on the island ahead. Her curiosity was irrational and overwhelming. She had to obey.

Both Paniz and Zemfira had only swum in the creek by the village and the pond in the valley, but the intensity of combat training had strengthened them. Zemfira put her head underwater and pushed herself forward, hair fanning out around her as she kicked. It was a beautiful sensation, being surrounded by so much cold, tranquil water.

"Hopefully there are no creatures in the depths," said Paniz, panting a bit as she swam like a pale frog along the surface.

Zemfira didn't reply as she tried not to think of the Drowners.

They reached the sandy island shore and saw an enclosed shrine of rock, worn down by age and covered in lichen. Dark flowers grew around a fallen column, and a statue glowed within the small structure studded with countless lightstones. Zemfira was focused on the statue until she saw the crouched figure tied to its base. It was a little girl, wearing rags and an Iron Necklace.

Zemfira suddenly felt very exposed in her nudity. The girl looked up at her with empty eyes, her cheeks sunken, her hair oily. She seemed unsurprised and didn't move.

"Who are you?" asked Zemfira, the words catching in her throat.

The child just stared at them. Her rags looked like they had been pulled from a ditch and sewn together, but her dirty slippers were soft and silky.

"Are you not with them?" she asked. Her voice reminded Zemfira of small pieces of glass falling onto stone and shattering.

"With whom?" asked Paniz. There was a small pile of patched blankets lying next to the girl. Paniz picked one up and wrapped it around her waist.

The girl opened her mouth but froze. They could hear someone rising to their feet on the far side of the shrine. Someone had been sitting cross-legged and now approached with quick strides, around the statue. The girl covered her face in her hands and began to cry.

"Who are you?" demanded a voice. "How did you get—"

Zemfira felt something heavy settle in her stomach. It was Yashar, wearing robes and a scabbarded saber. He stared at them with just as much shock as they stared at him, but he quickly averted his eyes, realizing who they were.

"What are you doing?" demanded Paniz, voice rising. "You're—*torturing* a child here, at the bottom of the world?"

"How did you find your way here without triggering—" Yashar broke off and hurried past them to the small sandy beach. An empty boat was gliding along the edge of the lake. No pilot steered it, no one rowed any oars, and yet it moved towards the point where Hami stood with another figure. Zemfira knew in an instant that it was Roya.

"Who is the girl, Master Yashar?" demanded Paniz, while Zemfira wrapped a blanket around her shoulders. "What's happening down here?"

"I cannot tell you," said Yashar, staring at Roya who was climbing into the boat. The cowering figure of Hami remained on the shore. "You should never have come here."

"I am Princess Stateira, daughter of King Artashata, and crown princess of Farsia," said the girl, tears on her cheeks but her voice firm and determined.

Paniz and Zemfira looked from the girl to Yashar, whose knuckles had tightened around the hem of his tunic.

"Is it true, Yashar?" asked Paniz, quietly. "You kidnapped a *princess*? A little girl?"

Yashar swallowed, unable to find words that might make Zemfira doubt the girl's statement.

"Get on the beach," said Yashar. "Do not speak with the prisoner. Now!"

But Zemfira did not want to leave the shrine. She wanted to take a step forward—not towards Stateira but towards the statue. She blinked, trying to reckon with her own desire. Why did she want to do that? In her confusion she allowed Yashar to push her and Paniz out of the shrine, away from the little girl.

Roya's boat reached the shore and slid into the sand. The Shadowcaster stepped out, boots crunching, and looked at Zemfira, then Paniz. Her expression was unreadable for a long time. She turned slowly to face Yashar.

"How did this happen?" she asked, very quietly.

"I was asleep," said Yashar, sinking hastily to one knee. "I am sorry, I did not hear their approach until they discovered the prisoner."

"I know you were asleep, Yashar," said Roya. "I cannot fault you for sleeping during a five day shift—but why is the cavern entrance not sealed? Why was it open for anyone to wander in?"

Yashar's jaw worked, but he said nothing.

"Was it too much trouble, Yashar, to swim back to the shore and activate the mechanism? You did not want to bother because you assumed no one would make it so far down?"

"I am sincerely ashamed, Commander Roya. I will take responsibility for my failure however you see fit."

Roya looked to the girls now. Zemfira wondered what she would do. Surely she wouldn't kill them, would she? Zemfira felt Roya would not be so wicked—but she also never thought Roya would imprison a child in such conditions.

"Your punishment depends on the extent of the damage," said Roya, not even looking at Yashar. "And we shall determine the damage soon enough. Girls, why did you bring Hami down into the most sacred levels of Jalehravan? I know this was not his idea."

"We just wanted to explore," said Paniz.

"Despite the prohibition against descending beneath the level of worship?"

Paniz lowered her eyes. Roya glanced at Zemfira, then strode to the shrine and inspected the little girl with the chain attached to her necklace. Paniz stood where she was, but Zemfira took a step toward the commander.

"Master Roya, we have erred and will accept our punishment—but what is happening here? Why is she chained like this?"

"I made no secret of my occupation," said Roya. "I am a rebel, and I lust to topple the king's head from his shoulders. There are unsavory elements to this business, which you have now witnessed."

"How is this girl aiding your revolutionary efforts? Is she something to be *bargained* with?"

"We do not have the privilege of clemency, Zemfira. The oppressed cannot choose kindness. We want to end the systematic murder of our people. No method is beneath us."

"What are you going to do to her?" asked Zemfira.

"That is not your business."

"I want to know, Master Roya, even if it is not my place to ask."

Roya considered her. "King Artashata came to power after most of his family was killed—his children are the end of the direct Haxamanis dynasty. Once we have Stateira's sister, we will kill them both and use their corpses to shatter the king's morale. Then we will strike, and forge a new kingdom from the rubble."

Zemfira took a step back. "That's horrible."

"They cannot live, even hidden from public eyes. Their blood will always give them legitimacy, and undermine our future stability. Revolutions may be told with glory after they succeed—but to succeed we cannot stoop to sentimentality."

"She's a child! It's not her fault!"

"Rarely do the guilty pay the price in war, Zemfira of Nebit. You must cut the tender part out of your heart if you wish to change the world. It is the only way to ensure justice for the weak."

Zemfira's fists trembled. She was scared of Roya, but she could not let her fear stop her. She marched past the Shadowcaster, into the shrine, and sat down next to Stateira.

"Everything will be okay. I promise."

Roya entered, her face illuminated by the glowing statue. She watched Zemfira putting her hand around Stateira's.

"It's a shame," said Roya. "I risked so much for your safety, because of this very shrine. We don't know the names of many Celestial Ones, but this statue is dedicated to Tishtyra. I wanted to bring you down here, once you developed your Lightcasting, and matured enough to understand our cause. But it seems you neither have the power I hoped for nor the obedience I require."

"You're going to kill me, and Paniz?" asked Zemfira, calmly. "And Hami, I suppose too."

"You think I am not capable of it because I invested so much in your rescue?" said Roya, taking a step forward.

Zemfira scooted backwards, trying to position herself in front of the little girl. She wished she had a sword with her, though it would be useless against Roya's Shadowcasting. Her back bumped up against the statue and she felt a humming in her ears.

"You told me casting with Depravity drains you of empathy, makes you more willing to kill."

Roya bared her teeth for a moment. "You think I am spiraling into rampancy? It takes a damaged soul to defy a king. I have watched many people die, my companions, my friends, and my family. My soul has experienced things no amount of love can rebuild. And yet, my soul remains whole, it does not impair my judgment. My pain allows me to forge the path so that no one else must suffer what I have suffered!"

Every word came from Roya's mouth with increased

ferocity and Zemfira backed up further, pressing herself hard against the statue. Her fingers slid back, the buzzing increased and she touched the feet of the statue.

A burst of light and energy exploded from the statue, knocking everyone back and to the ground. Zemfira's ears were ringing, her head spun and her whole body felt warm. Somehow, her wet hair had become dry. She opened her eyes to a shrine devoid of shadows.

The statue was gone. The princess lay dazed between two pillars of pure lightstone. Roya slumped against the shrine wall, clutching her face and groaning. Paniz and Yashar sprawled on the little beach, seemingly unharmed. Every color seemed amplified.

"Her presence was the trigger," mumbled Roya, struggling to stand up. "I thought Lightcasting itself—but it only required touch."

On an impulse Zemfira stepped into the stance Kalpana had been teaching her and lifted her palm. This time when she reached for her soul there was a counterweight, a palpable, inexplicable pull and a ball of light blossomed in her hand. She stared at it, discerning all the rainbow's colors in its pure whiteness.

"I'm Lightcasting," said Zemfira, incredulous. "I've accessed my powers."

She felt elated, relieved, and savagely satisfied. Roya had been about to kill her, Zemfira, the only Lightcaster with the Cost of Depravity in Jalehravan? A sense of vengeance unraveled in Zemfira's stomach, but she became aware of it and quickly released the casting. The negative emotions receded. She had to be careful with Depravity.

"Come," said Roya, walking out onto the beach. "Let us sit in the sand."

Zemfira did not move and Roya heaved a sigh.

"You have nothing to fear from me. You have earned yourself a great deal of bargaining power. And to think my temper may have cost us—well, let us speak."

Zemfira, caught between unease at her unbidden emotions and confidence flowing from her unlocked ability, stepped out onto the beach. Both Yashar and Paniz were staring. Roya sank to her knees in the Zhou meditation style.

"Lightcasters are rare but Lightcasters with Depravity are almost never found. And yet, we have been waiting for a Lightcaster since my grandfather's days. A Lightcaster with the Cost of Depravity has the art and the power to open this Flash Gate."

"What's a Flash Gate?"

"A portal," said Roya with a smile. "An old artifact from the early kings that can take you to any temple in the kingdom. And once we can open the Flash Gate, we have the chance to end our struggle for good, and herald a new age for Soulgivers."

Zemfira swallowed, afraid to ask for details. "That's why you came personally to Rasparad: to make sure I survived."

"I save many young Soulgivers, even those not so valuable to the cause. But you were our top priority. You had to live."

"And now that I've opened the gate—"

"You have not opened it," said Roya. "You have merely revealed it. Opening it requires a ritual long fallen out of practice. Not since King Darayava have monks studied the art. You must now study and learn it. This gives you a great deal of leverage over me."

Zemfira took a seat next to Paniz, who was shivering. She was still wet but was looking at Zemfira with awe and fear.

"What do you mean, leverage?" asked Zemfira.

"You are now the most important resident of the temple complex," said Roya. "Indeed, more important than me. I cannot compel you into months of arduous study merely with threats. It will be more effective if you are invested in our success."

"Pragmatism," said Zemfira.

"Yes," said Roya. "What can I promise you to convince you to study the art of Lightcasting here at Jalehravan until you can open the Flash Gate?'

Zemfira's heart pounded. "No punishment or harm to Paniz. None to Hami—and please don't harm my father or Omid and Jia-Fan."

"Of course," said Roya.

She glanced back at the shrine, now glowing from the two thin pillars rather than the statue. "The princess. Don't leave her down here, please. Let her live up in the temple with the rest of us. We'll keep an eye on her. She can't run away."

Roya shook her head. "It is too risky. One of the non-Soulgivers might take her and escape to royal custody, to reap the reward for returning her, while giving Artashata our location."

"You can protect against that," said Zemfira. "You could make it my responsibility and put the lives of my family in the balance."

"You would not risk your family for the sake of our enemy's daughter."

"Just because she's the daughter of our enemy doesn't mean she must be our enemy too. If we work together, we can keep her safe from anyone trying to steal her back. Anyway, it's difficult to escape into the Lut Desert without being rapidly pursued."

The rebel commander furrowed her brow. "I will agree to these terms. In exchange you will make the study of Lightcasting your top priority. I invite you, officially, to our resistance. Your actions will lead Soulgivers into a better future."

Zemfira hesitated. "I will do what I can, but I'm not ready to become a soldier—not yet."

"You must not rush the decision," said Roya. "A volunteer always fights more fiercely than a conscript. If you are strong enough to open a Flash Gate, you have the power to end this struggle in our favor."

Roya extended her hands to Zemfira. The commander's expression was grim, but there was no malice or false kindness in it. While Zemfira did not trust Roya, she sensed the truth of the Shadowcaster's passion for justice. They needed each other. Zemfira reached out and clasped Roya's hands tightly.

"Good," said Roya. "Then let us return to your quarters. You will need to rest before tomorrow. There is much to learn."

# CHAPTER 22 – THE DUALCASTER

Volakles sat in the elevated gardens, looking out over the rippling Western Sea. The water was streaked purple and orange by the setting sun, casting itself across the rocks and crags of the coastline. The queen and the younger princess Drypetis sat on the beach, surrounded by servants and a small division of soldiers. It was difficult for Volakles to believe he was here in Issos, even after the long days of travel from Rasparad.

Being summoned to the king's presence felt portentous, though perhaps it boded well that he had not been killed immediately. The shock of the monks after his recovery from the Gloom had been nothing compared to that of Bishen, who had requested further orders from Sahin. The Captain of the Cleansers had ordered Volakles to perform combat tests in the Rasparad barracks using his simultaneous casting arts. He was still getting a grip on his Shadowcasting, but there was no denying his new power.

"You are indeed a Dualcaster," Bishen had said, after the tests were complete. "We are still uncertain whether you gained it all from the Gloom, if you had an inclination towards Shadowcasting, or if you were always a Shadowcaster, but only able to unlock your powers when the Gloom melded with your essence."

"I don't know myself," Volakles had admitted. "I'm sorry I cannot be more helpful."

"You understand why this interests us. The implications are staggering. If we can give our soldiers twice the ways to fight, or perhaps even more, this Hellenic Hegemon would pose no threat to our western coasts. We could not only stave off the Skythians, but crush them."

"It would be an honor to assist in that mission in any way possible."

Bishen had given his head a slow shake. "The king requests you at his current residence in Issos. You are to ride west immediately and prostrate yourself before him. He shall determine your future, not me."

Volakles was not anticipating commendations for his service. He could never wipe away the shame of losing the king's daughter, nor would Artashata have forgotten it. So when the king's eunuch summoned him from the garden into the elegant court, he entered with a heavy heart.

King Artashata was neither tall nor handsome, and he wore his middle age like a burden. Even the powder and eyeliner could not hide his weariness. He reclined on a wooden throne, studded with gemstones and painted gold. Scribes and advisors milled around him like bees around a hive, and he listened to their mix of omen and praise.

"Step closer, Cleanser," called Artashata. His voice, at least, had a royal power behind it. "Kneel before your divine sovereign."

Volakles did, and pressed his forehead to the carpet. He spoke the words of honor and kept his eyes down. He sensed something akin to boredom from his king, the commander of more than one hundred thousand soldiers, supreme ruler over millions of lives.

"Sahin told me about you," he said. "First when you let my daughter fall into the hands of cutthroats and anarchists, then again when you overcame the Gloom. He still thinks I should not kill you, though I am sorely tempted."

"I shall gladly accept whatever fate you give me, my king of kings," said Volakles. "My failure at the palace deserves no forgiveness."

"I am not speaking of that," said Artashata, taking a bowl of almonds from a servant and giving a nut to his taster. "I am more concerned you are colluding with those who wish to destroy my dynasty entirely."

Volakles remembered Bishen's suspicions. Since he had survived and even gained more power through his ordeal, it was conceivable that the rebel had never intended to kill him, but merely to clear him of guilt. He could say nothing to disprove such a theory, so he simply stared at the emeralds stitched into the king's slippers.

"I convened the greatest Shadowcasters in the kingdom and asked them to give their opinion, if the Gloom could be used to transfer a casting ability. They had all read the ancient texts in Thebai, in Babilim, in Tatagus, and they could find no record of such an occurrence. No Caster can give their power to another without losing it themselves. So something within you was able to evolve and adapt, and you came very close to dying. You are either a peerless traitor, deceptive in ways we cannot even fathom, or you are indeed loyal to the dynasty and to the kingdom—gifted with two casting abilities."

Volakles wondered why the king was devoting so much time to speaking to him, but then he realized Artashata would not allow him to get so close if he truly believed Volakles a traitor. He was simply trying to impress upon Volakles that he was no fool.

"My foe in the west poses a greater threat than my Satraps realize," said Artashata. "I've read the stars, I know what dangers the future may hold. When nine stars of power align during the birth of a prince, he shall wreak havoc upon the earth, cursed as a villain and applauded as a hero—with all the abilities of a Caster at his disposal. The Hellenic Hegemon Eskandar is this man. Unlike you, he displayed his many abilities since birth. If this man is underestimated, he will do more than ravage the Lydian peninsula. He could penetrate as far as the capital."

"But it's too late in the campaigning season," said Volakles, before he could stop himself. Several servants stopped their serving and paperwork to stare at him, and he pressed his forehead back to the ground. Why had he spoken out like that, without being asked to? Why had he expressed himself as an equal? But Artashata seemed unmoved.

"We near the equinox, it is true, but Eskandar seems content to stay on our soil. He has set up winter quarters in Gordion and will continue his actions in the spring."

It was unprecedented, Volakles knew. Not since the mythical siege of Illios, six hundred years ago, had Hellenic armies made such an incursion.

"I won't rush in," said Artashata. "Eskandar's leniency in Lydia has given him a base of power. If I am hasty, I will condemn myself to a tragic astrological fate. I await his move first. If he pushes east into Babirus I will scorch the land, fortify the cities, and starve him into a shameful surrender. But he will not go east. He will march south, all the way to Mudraya. According to my spies, he thinks the Mudrayan priests can tell him who his real father is."

Artashata chewed on a handful of almonds. Volakles, though fascinated, wondered why the king was telling him all of this.

"And so I remain here at Issos, readying my army myself. They must know their king stands with them—must know that this Hellenic upstart, while powerful, is no immortal. We will trap him in the pass by Issos and crush him. My concerns now lie in the troubled Satrapy of Harauvatis—which has revolted against my authority. My loyal Satrap was murdered, and a cabal of Vazirs have taken control."

Volakles had not heard of this and knew it was a bad sign. Artashata was losing the depth of his kingdom, just when he needed it the most.

"How—how may I serve you, oh king of kings?" asked Volakles.

"You will serve in my court," said Artashata. "Not as a guard, but as a Cleanser—you will ensure that there is no evil present. If there is a patient assassin, you will find them and execute them. I believe you may even be a match for a Soulbreaker now."

"I will serve with ceaseless devotion," said Volakles. "But I am still becoming accustomed to my powers and—"

Artashata waved a casual hand. "You will train with my best soldiers and the royal Targus. If you serve well, you may ascend to the rank of Zealot again—but not simply a sentinel. You could become the Captain of the Zealots if you earn my appreciation."

Volakles's pulse quickened. Had a commoner ever risen to such a rank? Not under any king Volakles could remember. But in desperate times a king would happily anger his aristocracy to preserve his throne. Was Volakles really so valuable? Was that why the monarch was speaking so candidly with him?

"You honor me beyond my merit, oh greatest of kings," said Volakles.

"It is also better, I think, to keep you in the eyes of my other trusted protectors," said Artashata, massaging his perfect goatee. "Your intent shall have no place to hide. So if your behavior is deemed suspicious, or should you fail me again, I will have you killed. Keep that in mind. You are dismissed."

Heart thudding in his chest, Volakles stood up, bowed and departed the room.

# CHAPTER 23 – SKIRMISH AT DUSK

Zemfira put down the scroll and rubbed her eyes. It had taken her months just to grasp Aramaic script, and even now she struggled with longer passages. But ever since Tryphon had started teaching her the alphabet of Elamite, her mind felt like a chunk of rotting wood. How could she learn the steps of the Flash Gate ritual if they were written in a language so old that Tryphon could barely decipher it? The old Targu attempted to translate the relevant passages, but told her a translation would never capture the intricacies of the Elamite language and alphabet.

Roya did not share Zemfira's frustrations on the occasions she visited Jalehravan.

"The ritual requires an extraordinary amount of Lightcasting," Roya had said on a cold winter evening, "A skilled Lightcaster with the Cost of Aging would shave ten years off their life for performing it perfectly—to do this right, your Casting will have to develop."

Zemfira had been improving as a Lightcaster. The lessons after that night in the subterranean lake had already yielded results. She was getting good at releasing flashes to blind her opponent. Her focus now was to master the art of light projectiles—unleashing a beam or a burst that could physically strike a target. Her healing was mediocre, and she still struggled with the Cost of Depravity itself. Sometimes it took hours, rather than minutes, for her negative emotions to recede. At least she could sense the impact her Casting was inflicting upon her soul. That was essential for any Caster with Depravity.

Paniz entered the reading niche wearing her combat gear. Her hair was shaved shorter than Ardeshir's now and she looked tougher than Zemfira could remember. While Zemfira was showing promise with her Lightcasting, Paniz had continued to make improvements too. She could not sustain long bouts of Casting like Ardeshir, Milad and Nava could, since she couldn't rely on the Cost of Depravity, but her technique was praised all around Jalehravan. She routinely beat Milad and while Ardeshir put up a good fight, Paniz had learned how to circumvent his thermal technique.

"Feeling smarter?" Paniz asked.

Zemfira laughed bitterly. "Maybe it would have been better to die on that underground island—this reading is worse than death. It's dry and boring and I can barely understand a word!"

"It's difficult being the salvation of the Soulgivers, isn't it?" sighed Paniz.

"Oh, shut up," said Zemfira. "Even if I manage to open the gate, that doesn't make me a savior."

Paniz picked up one of the scrolls, squinted at the Elamite characters and put it down. "Do you understand how Flash Gates work yet?"

Zemfira stood up and stretched. "Not really. The literature is so confusing. I've re-read it fifty times and still get confused. A Flash Gate allows you to move instantaneously through the abstract realm known as the Menog and emerge at any temple stone in an instant."

"Traveling through the Menog," said Paniz, shaking her head. "Wow."

"It sounds impossible, but if it could be done—"

"It would mean Roya can enter the palace temple in a heartbeat," said Paniz.

"No wonder the kings censored the knowledge about opening Flash Gates," agreed Zemfira. "Too dangerous to allow anyone entry in the royal temple. If someone is powerful enough to create the portal, they will be strong enough to overwhelm the guards."

Paniz let out a low whistle. "Thanks to you, Roya can kill Artashata without struggling through his heightened defenses."

Zemfira looked around, in case Stateira was somewhere nearby. While the princess was affectionate with Hami and smiled shyly at Paniz's jokes, she spent a great deal of time with Zemfira, reading peacefully. It was only recently that Zemfira's reading had outpaced the eleven-year-old girl's abilities. But Stateira must have been upstairs, or outside looking at the goats.

"I'm worried," said Zemfira. "If Roya kills the king, the Hegemon will sweep in and destroy Farsia."

"He wouldn't destroy it, even if he could," said Paniz, reasonably. "Farsia is more valuable conquered than razed. And anyway, Roya will wait until Artashata drives Eskandar back before striking. She's not stupid."

"Mmmm."

Paniz cocked her head. "You look really tired. Come on, let's go dip our feet in the creek and watch Milad try to fight Nava. I can't wait to see how it goes."

"Is he trying to make you jealous?" asked Zemfira, reluctantly putting aside the pile of scrolls and following Paniz to the spiral staircase. She had chosen not to comment on the little

244

flower tucked behind Paniz's ear, which undoubtedly came from a specific male suitor.

"Nah," said Paniz. "He's hoping to impress me. I said I won't kiss him unless he could beat me in a fight."

"So he's fighting Nava instead?"

"He's claiming he holds back against me, but he's just making excuses."

Jia-Fan was preparing bread and rice as they passed the kitchens and she waved at them. She had volunteered to be one of several wardens for the princess while Omid was bringing supplies to Harauvatis. Jia-Fan, although busy with her duties around the temple, always agreed to a game of Chatrang if Zemfira asked. She had still not beaten Jia-Fan once.

The early spring was sweltering, even near evening. The fading sunlight caught in the branches of the tree, where little leaves were budding in defiance of the dry environment. Nava and Milad stood barefoot on the dirt a hundred meters apart with Ardeshir positioned in the middle, equidistant from both of them.

"Remember the rules," said Ardeshir, in his most officious tone. "This is a skirmish, not a battle to the death. If either of you even scratches the tree or temple, I was never here and Roya will hang you by your eyelids. Otherwise, the first one to be knocked onto their back or stomach loses. Ready Nava? Ready Milad? Go!"

Both darted forward at the same time. Milad, tall and broad-chested, closed the distance with his long strides. Nava was slower, her long black braid fluttering behind her as she pulled a seed from her pocket. Leaves burst from it, curling around her right forearm and creating a verdant battle glove. Milad, with pockets of cloud floating behind him, dodged aside and tripped Nava with a sliding kick. Before she could hit the ground, Nava's left arm flexed and a root blasted out of the sand, pushing her up and flipping her back onto her feet.

"Foul!" shouted Milad. "She's using the tree!"

"That's not against the rules," snapped Nava, using the root to jab Milad in the shin. Zemfira winced, watching, as Milad beat a hasty retreat, the clouds around his shoulders thickening and turning gray. It was only with the creek nearby that the young Stormcaster could gather such moisture.

Nava lashed out again with a vine but Milad dodged. He spun a kick at her that pushed a torrent of water into her stomach, knocking her back. Grinning, Milad looked over at Paniz for approval, but Nava didn't hit the ground. Using a burst of roots, she pushed herself up and flipped herself over into a crouch. She rushed forward, tossing a seed at him which exploded into flowery tendrils and knocked him off balance. Nava punched him in the chest with her vine-encased hand, smacking Milad onto the sand, winded.

Paniz and Zemfira applauded, although neither was particularly fond of Nava's haughty attitude and self-satisfied tilt of the head. Paniz and Ardeshir went up to Milad and helped him to his feet. His nose was bleeding, but he otherwise looked okay.

"I almost had her," said Milad, blinking a few times. "It's only because she used the tree roots, and that's not fair."

"It wasn't against the rules," said Ardeshir with a sigh, supporting him back toward the temple.

Stateira and Hami approached them. They had been sitting in the reeds by the creek, playing with the mud. The princess's face was streaked with it. She had never been allowed to play with dirt at the palace.

"Hi Zemfira!"

Zemfira smiled at the girl. "Hello Stateira."

They had resolved not to address Stateira by her title. The social dynamic of Jalehravan was founded upon a rejection of the Farsian dynasty, and so the princess would be treated like any other girl at the temple. She had to wash the stone tiles with the other children and clean up after meals.

"Hami and I built a little house of mud!" she proclaimed.

"It's not a real house," said Hami quickly. "Just a very small one."

Zemfira was trying to figure out for whose benefit he was explaining this, when a howl filled the darkening sky. Everyone froze.

"Is that—is that a Shifting Hound?" asked Milad.

"Everyone get inside, quickly!" shouted Ardeshir.

But they had barely taken a step when something darted out between the boulders, jumped over the creek and ran straight at Nava. She threw herself out of the way as it lunged, reptilian jaws snapping and canine paws scratching the dirt. Stateira screamed and the Shadow Beast raised its wriggling jaws to the darkening sky and howled again.

It was as large as a hunting dog, with six legs and six eyes derived from three different animals. Talons, paws and hooves left grooves in the soil while insect, falcon and panther eyes bored into the young Soulgivers.

Reacting on instinct, Zemfira stepped forward, pulled her left arm in and released a burst of light from her extended right palm. The beam hit the beast in the side, slamming it over the dirt with squeals of pain, but the attack lacked lethal strength. It did not tear the creature in half as the Celestial One had done on the river, so many months ago.

The Shifting Hound rose again, growling and screeching. It shook itself like a dog emerging from a creek, but instead of shedding a spray of water, it shed physical features. Bits of the

Shifting Hound flew from its body and disintegrated into darkness, leaving a sleek lizard body, bat wings and the head of a wolf. All six eyes fixed upon Zemfira with hatred.

Paniz crossed her wrists in front of her torso and two bolts of fire hit the Shadow Beast from opposite directions, crushing it into a flaming mass of writhing limbs and burnt flesh. The smell and sound were awful as the creature expired. Zemfira and Hami exchanged a relieved look, but there were more howls and a bellowing. More Shifting Hounds were coming, and there was a Scorpion Man among them.

"We need to get back," said Paniz. "But don't—don't panic."

"Don't panic?" shouted Milad. "They're Shadow Beasts! They want to devour us! How are they getting past the sacred etchings on the stones?"

Two Shifting Hounds darted out from the rocks, one snarling and the other hissing. It was hard to discern what amalgamations they possessed in the semi-darkness. The young Casters backed up towards the temple, keeping the princess behind them and maintaining defensive stances. Ardeshir drew his sword, which he carried since Roya had accepted him as a rebel.

"Don't let them bite you!" he shouted. "Their teeth are more than just teeth!"

"What are you talking about?" demanded Paniz, swirling her arms above her head to create a floating ring of fire. But Zemfira understood. She had read about how Shifting Hounds could grab hold of a human soul with their jaws and wrench it from the body of their victim, if they held on long enough.

They were only thirty meters from the temple when the two Shifting Hounds rushed at Ardeshir. He held his sword in his left hand and the metal glowed red hot. Sweat dripped down the

248

boy's face from the heat he was creating. He sidestepped and slashed, the hot iron splitting one Shifting Hound in half. The second one lunged, but Ardeshir blasted ice from his right hand into its body. He fought like a typical Temperaturecaster, relying on extreme heat and cold to keep his Casting balanced.

The frost was not enough to kill the beast, but it allowed Nava to wrap roots around its many limbs and its body. As it tried to shake itself into a different form, Ardeshir stepped forward and cut off its head. The whole oasis smelled of burning flesh.

"We're under attack!" called Paniz to the temple as more Shifting Hounds emerged from the shadows. "Quickly, help us!"

The sounds of battle must have already alerted those inside. Even so, they were too far away to intercept the half dozen Shifting Hounds rushing the children now. The beasts didn't care about their individual lives. Shifting Hounds functioned as a pack: they would disorient their prey before overwhelming them with numbers. Hami was the only one who did not assume a defensive stance. He was still rushing the princess inside.

Zemfira took a step back as one of the Shifting Hounds snapped at her, long alligator jaw barely missing her neck, but its hawk talon cut a scratch along her arm as it passed. Zemfira winced at the pain but hardened her hands into fists, light glowing from within her clenched palms.

Before the beast could strike again, Zemfira slammed her fist into its neck. Without her Casting it would have been the height of folly, but the light glowing within her hand and radiating out of her skin made the punch noxious to the dark creature. The burst of light split the snapping head from the body, and the entire creature dissolved into little fireflies.

Melancholy tinged her sense of triumph, and she could sense the erosion her soul sustained as the price of Casting.

Another beast lunged, then snarled, stopped and rolled to the side, diving past her. Zemfira was stunned to see it avoiding her and going after Nava, who was already dealing with two of them. Why were they not attacking her? She shot another beam of light after the Shifting Hound, this one much thinner and more precise. It gored the Shadow Beast and lifted it into the air, where it disintegrated into particles. Malicious triumph coursed through her, and she fought to control it.

"They're still coming!" shouted Milad, keeping three of them at bay with a volley of hail, but unable to kill any of them. Paniz incinerated the creatures with controlled blasts of fire, but she was swaying. She yawned uncontrollably, even as she sent a spear of fire flying into a lunging foe. Zemfira knew her friend would soon collapse. She had killed more of the creatures than the rest of them combined.

"Paniz, are you okay?" asked Milad, as the girl sank to one knee, holding her head. The boy forgot, as the adolescents of Jalehravan often forgot, that Paniz was not one of them, and lacked the Casting endurance.

His distraction cost him. A Shifting Hound screeched down from the sky, long wings spread and jaws open. Milad was knocked to the ground but he rolled and kicked the creature aside. Just then another Shifting Hound pounced and pinned him. Milad screamed as its claws cut his skin and its panther jaws sank into his chest. Ardeshir lopped off its head in a quick stroke before it could do any serious damage, but a third Shadow Beast was at Milad's leg. The powerful jaw of the bear head bit through the bone, severing the boy's foot.

Milad's screams were shattering. Zemfira's concentration failed her and she missed a crucial strike against the Shifting

Hound. Another two knocked Nava to the ground with brutal talons. Chaos and panic were bubbling up through her thoughts. Her friends were dying. She was going to see them all die, as Depravity tore her soul to pieces. She heard Hami give a cry and saw him trying to shield Stateira from two approaching Shifting Hounds. They hadn't made it to the temple in time either. None of them would survive.

Then fire, which didn't come from Paniz, burst like infernal flowers around the Shifting Hounds, consuming the beasts in the brightest orange. Rocks thudded out of the earth, rising from the dirt to spin through the air and smash the creatures. Several Shifting Hounds slowed their attack and began gnawing at each other's throats. Five Soulgivers and Kuzro had emerged from the temple to drive the Shadow Beasts back.

"Zemfira, get your friends inside!" shouted Kuzro, throwing several seeds into the earth that twisted together into a thick tendril of vine. "We don't know how many more are coming!"

Zemfira nodded and rushed forward, blinding the nearest Shifting Hounds with quick flashes. She wanted to attend to the fatigued Paniz first, but knew Milad was a bigger priority. He was alive and still possessed his soul, but the bleeding was bad and the gore made Zemfira sick. This was worse than the awful battle on the ferry.

"I'm going to die," moaned Milad.

"You're going to be fine," said Zemfira, unsure who she was trying to convince. "Just keep breathing—try to meditate. I'm going to get you inside."

Nava was getting back to her feet, shaken but not wounded. She helped Zemfira carry Milad while Ardeshir hoisted Paniz and carried her inside, passing the adult Soulgivers who advanced on the Shadow Beasts. They were going to live.

Now at the door to the temple, they would be safe. It would be all right.

"Stateira, come back!" shouted Hami.

Zemfira turned to see the princess running barefoot from the temple, towards the rocks and the desert beyond. Was she trying to escape? Hami was running after her. After a moment of indecision, Zemfira gave Milad over to Nava and took off running too. They would not lose the princess: there was enough blood and pain in their peaceful oasis.

Stateira was sprinting across the sand, glancing back at the carnage and chaos, not seeing the glowing eyes ahead of her. Hami was screaming at her to stop, to come back, as the towering Scorpion Man emerged between the rocks, pointed legs digging into the sand.

Panicking, Zemfira released a beam of light. Her aim was poor and the light glanced off a rock, only distracting the creature for a moment. Her soul shuddered, already overexerted. There was nothing else Zemfira could do, she was too far away.

"Hami! You've got to do something!"

"I—I can't—"

"Hami!"

Stateira saw the Scorpion Man now and stopped. She stared at it as it approached, pincers clicking in the twilight. Stateira stood frozen. The creature snarled at the night and reached for the little girl with its claw.

Hami darted forward and pulled the princess to the ground just in time. The Shadow Beast bellowed, a sound like all the evil in the world laughing. It took a step closer to kill them both, but Hami raised a fist. For just a second Zemfira thought he would have the strength to shift one of the boulders and crush the Shadow Beast. But instead the sand began to tremble, then floated up into the air. Zemfira stared at the spectacle. Hami was Stonecasting.

Hami moved his arms with a grace that would have pleased Master Kalpana, bringing countless little grains of sand into a swirling arc. The controlled sandstorm surprised the Scorpion Man, but he was a creature of the desert. He had nothing to fear from a little sand. He lunged, and Hami punched his fist forward.

The grains condensed into a pillar, hard as rock, in front of the Scorpion Man's torso, blocking his lunge and he recoiled from the obstacle. But Hami's fingers were clenched into claws and there was an anger in his eyes that Zemfira had never witnessed before.

The pillar of packed sand pulled back and slammed into the Scorpion Man's sternum. The force pinned the Shadow Beast against the rock, limbs splayed. It was far from dead, however, and Hami dispersed the pillar back into its component grains of sand, swirling them above himself like a curse of locusts.

Just as the wounded Scorpion Man peeled itself off the stone, Hami pointed his fingers straight at the creature and the sand shot towards him, a million invisible rock fragments moving at incredible speed.

The tiny projectiles cut straight through the Scorpion Man, shredding the purple skin and spattering the stones with dark blood. Screaming, the Scorpion Man fell to the ground, physical form disintegrating into a swarm of insects. Hami collapsed into the sand, hands wrapped around his knees. Stateira sat next to him, staring at the young man as tears fell from his eyes and soaked into the sand.

"You're a talented Caster," said Zemfira, kneeling next to him, gripping his shoulder. "But you kept it to yourself."

"I—I only practice when everyone is asleep," said Hami, shuddering with sobs. "And I only use sand. I can't—I won't use rocks."

Zemfira picked him up and hugged him close to her. He had never told her why he refused to use his powers. Now she was worried, not sure Hami's soul had been stable enough to use such an extraordinary amount of Casting on one occasion.

"I killed it. I didn't mean to kill it. I didn't want to kill it."

"You had to, Hami."

"No, no, no," he whispered, in utter anguish. "What have I done?"

Zemfira had to focus. "It's over. You can relax. Come, let's get inside. Stateira, you too. There's only more danger that way. Let's find you your bed and settle you in."

The Shifting Hounds had fled. Without the commanding influence of the Scorpion Man, they had been easily dispatched and scattered by the more talented Soulgivers. Zemfira, Hami and Stateira made their way back to the temple where Kuzro was trying to ease Milad's pain with strong herbs. The smell drifted on the night, masking the odor of blood.

Yashar put a hand on Zemfira's shoulder as she passed. "Are you okay, Zemfira?"

"I'm not the one in need of care," said Zemfira. She could see Kalpana nursing a bleeding gash across her stomach, which Zemfira prayed was shallow. There were other injuries among the monks and revolutionaries. Zemfira helped Hami into the temple while Yashar kept guard at the temple door.

"What does this mean?" demanded Ardeshir, pacing the lower floor. "Why are Shadow Beasts launching coordinated attacks? Why are they overwhelming the sacred lines and boundaries? This is a temple! Shadow Beasts avoid skilled Casters and prey on the weak!"

"We do not know yet," said Tryphon, looking wearier than Zemfira had ever seen. "It appears to be part of a larger trend."

"This is her fault!" shouted Ardeshir, pointing at Zemfira. "The Shadow Beasts are after her. First on the river, now *here*!"

"Calm yourself, boy," said Tryphon, tightening his headband. "You do not know what you are saying."

"It's because of her Lightcasting," said Ardeshir. "That's why the beasts are chasing her. That's why Milad—"

There were tears of anger running down Ardeshir's face. Milad was in too much pain to care. Two monks were bandaging his leg, and the bleeding had abated, but Zemfira's heart was heavy.

"I need to check on Paniz."

Ardeshir didn't say anything else, just folded his arms and watched her go. Nava and a monk were carrying a sleeping Paniz downstairs. Zemfira couldn't help so she just lingered, hovering behind them as they descended the stairs.

"Don't listen to him," said Nava. "He doesn't mean it, and he doesn't know what he's saying."

"Maybe he's right," said Zemfira. "I think one of the Shifting Hounds stopped attacking when it realized it was me, just like the Scorpion Man on the boat—"

"It doesn't matter," said Nava. "You can't blame yourself for Milad's injuries. You couldn't have prevented it."

Zemfira wondered why Nava was being so friendly. Perhaps the sudden onslaught of monsters had rattled her. She might have been the daughter of a Vazir, but fighting against imminent death could humble even the proudest.

Nava and the monk set Paniz down on her bed mat and Zemfira thanked them. They left her alone with her best friend. Zemfira swallowed, hands on her knees. She could still hear the snapping of so many changing jaws, and the screams. She rubbed her forehead, pressing her eyes closed.

Perhaps there were advantages to having the Cost of Fatigue. Zemfira knew there was no way she could fall asleep that night, no matter how hard she tried.

# CHAPTER 24 – THE BAIT

The Baxtrian road needed repairs, prompting Firuzeh to slow her horse's canter. She stared straight ahead, trying to ignore the aches and pains that had settled into her body over the last months. It was rare for her to dwell on physical discomfort, but after thirty years of service as a Cleanser, she felt her age now in a way she had never felt it before.

Children were playing in the melting snow, laughing and shrieking at each other. Firuzeh observed them, wondering if her target was among them. Not that it mattered. She would have to contact the Targu and the child's guardian before departing Nebit anyway.

The cottages were quaint, each billowing a trail of smoke into the cloudy sky. Sticks and wood pieces were piled in dwindling stacks before the closed doors. Firuzeh sniffed and pulled her cloak tighter around herself. She had not expected winter to keep its grip upon these foothills, but then again after scouring the Lut Desert for months, the mere sight of snow seemed like a miracle.

When Bishen had promoted her to lead the investigation, Firuzeh and her hounds had tracked the Soulbreaker delegation into the sands, but winds and heat had ended the trail. It had been crushingly disappointing to find no trace of them. Without a

Temperaturecaster, Firuzeh and her canines had retreated from the awful heat. At the nearest temple she sent a message back to Bishen and one to the city of Saddarvazeh, the largest city on the far side of the desert, in case the Soulbreakers fled there. With that done, Firuzeh began to think.

There were safer, faster ways to lose a trail than taking a detour through the Lut Desert. Certainly, a trail could go cold in those blistering sands, but only one road led through it, and it was easily blocked. And if these Soulbreakers knew the desert well enough to ride across the dunes, perhaps they knew how to hide within its dangerous interior.

When scouts and spies reported nothing from the far side of the desert, Firuzeh asked Bishen for resources to examine Lut more closely. She set up a base of operations southeast of the desert, where the temperatures were harsh but less lethal, and sent scouting parties of three Temperaturecasters at a time, equipped with maps and water. Methodically they combed the area around the road for any sign of human activity, but the sand revealed no secrets.

The lack of progress displeased Bishen. He informed Firuzeh that the traitor Roya had been sighted in the Satrapy of Mada and should be pursued immediately. Firuzeh obeyed. On her way, Firuzeh stationed a few of her men in a northwestern outpost along the desert road. If Firuzeh's hunch was correct, they would catch Roya on her return.

There had been no trace of the rebel commander anywhere in Mada. A witness claimed a Shadowcaster had come to abscond with an unclasped Soulbreaker, but arrived too late. A pair of Cleansers had already dispatched the young threat. The claim interested Firuzeh. Perhaps this Zemfira was the rule, not the exception. Was there really a relationship between the anarchists and the occasionally disappearing Soulbreaker children? She had just assumed they had died or fled the kingdom entirely, able to escape due to the incompetence of her fellow Cleansers—but how much was the king underestimating the Soulbreakers?

Returning east, Firuzeh had stopped at the outpost to hear the reports from her sentries. She found nothing. There were no bodies, no signs of human habitation. They were untraceably gone.

"These disappearances do not prove that Roya frequents the Lut Desert," Bishen had said, not looking up from a scroll he was reading. "Consider the alternatives. A Shadow Beast, or a contingent of Shadow Beasts, may have attacked your soldiers. The deserts are home to many such dangers. They might have encountered bandits, and tried to stop them, without success. Or they could have deserted."

"My soldiers would not leave their duty," Firuzeh had snapped back. "Not when their duty was so crucial and not when their assignment kept them out of Lut. Something happened."

"There are rumors of Soulbreaker activity throughout Harauvatis," said Bishen. "Your attention is better suited there than in the Empty Desert."

"If that is an order, I will obey," said Firuzeh. "But if you merely make a forceful recommendation, I respectfully disagree. I know this desert has secrets, and I will expose them."

They had found a compromise, and Firuzeh had sent her best soldiers and Cleansers east to gather information while she remained. Months of observation continued. Based at the Fatigue Temple of Izad, on the desert's edge, Firuzeh spent her days channeling her being through the bodies of desert animals, scrutinizing the vast emptiness of the sweltering sands. With time, Firuzeh wondered if her obsession with the desert meant she was losing her mind. She wondered if the lizards and snakes were rubbing off on her thoughts. She often had to sleep for days after using her Obediencecasting to examine the desert vicariously, and feared she was missing many important occurrences during that time.

But then a migration of the Shadow Beasts had crossed into the desert. Firuzeh had prioritized this phenomenon, knowing Bishen's concerns about erratic Shadow Beast behavior. She dominated a sand lizard and pushed it deep into the desert, after the Shifting Hounds.

She watched them gather before a collection of boulders, far from any road. There were dozens of Shadow Beasts, and yet, incredibly, the direct sun did not appear to bother them. They were at no risk of dehydration, but Shadow Beasts hated sunlight, which diminished their powers. Hours passed. A sandstorm swept through, but the Shifting Hounds never moved.

With her concentration waning she had needed a respite and so she slept until dusk. It was a risk, but Firuzeh knew the Shadow Beasts would wait until sunset to make their next move. And when she reasserted control of the lizard, she saw the Shadow Beasts still gathered by the rocks. Details were distorted by the lizard's eyes, but Firuzeh had registered a Scorpion Man prowling behind the Shifting Hounds, like a sergeant inspecting a regiment of soldiers.

When the sun set, the beasts moved into the cluster of boulders. But why? Such rock formations were common in the desert, but the radiating heat meant no human would linger near them for long. Firuzeh tried to follow, but as she did she felt her control of the lizard unraveling, her channeled vision become blurry. Something about those rocks was distorting her Casting, so she pulled the lizard back, just in time to witness the Shifting Hounds fleeing into the darkening desert.

The Soulbreaker girl had been attacked by Shadow Beasts before, on their way to Rasparad. For some reason, Shadow Beasts had pursued the girl with unnatural coordination. Had that happened again, here in the desert? Perhaps the girl was somewhere in those rocks, which could lead them straight to the commander, Roya.

Firuzeh resisted the urge to ride straight for the rocks to investigate. She did not want to die like the soldiers she had posted on the road—she would not be ambushed. This time she would make sure she had the advantage. And so, a plan was born.

***

Firuzeh dismounted her steed in front of the temple and asked for the Targu's audience.

"I know you are a servant of justice, Cleanser," said the Targu, quietly. "But this course of action makes me uneasy."

"Had you and your monks managed to keep Zemfira here, we would not be having this conversation. We would be done with the matter."

The Targu shivered in his robes as a chilly breeze flecked his face with droplets of rain. "I cannot prevent you, of course, but it is most irregular."

"We live in dangerous times," said Firuzeh. "Please relay my arrival to the Hunger Temple at Rasparad. Then, once I depart, inform everyone in Nebit of my actions. Express that unease as passionately as you desire, I don't care."

"To the village? You wish me to—"

"It is essential that the news travels at a speed to match my horse."

"But—"

Firuzeh was already walking away, leading her steed down the muddy lane. She raised the cowl of her cloak, hoping the rain would abate. The task was unpleasant enough.

Bishen had informed her of Volakles's miracle recovery, but of course had not let her return to congratulate her partner on his success. Her mission could not stop. Killing Roya was still a matter of utmost importance.

She had dreaded the prospect of Volakles dying—especially since the young Insightcaster reminded her so much of her former partner. Firuzeh still dreamed about Sephr and his demise, about his final scream as the tower fell and the stone bricks crushed him. Firuzeh had delivered the news to Sephr's widow and children. Their anguish had cemented Firuzeh's determination—she would never again make the mistake of showing mercy to a Soulbreaker.

Firuzeh dismissed her personal thoughts and focused on her task. The Targu had described the house and she located it without haste or a slackening of her pace. It stood beside a crooked pine tree: a spacious cottage with a refurbished barn connected to the main living quarters. Firuzeh knocked on the door.

A young girl opened the door, greeted the Cleanser politely, and hurried back into the house to fetch her mother. Firuzeh adjusted her cloak to hide her twin swords, not because she wanted to reduce her powers of intimidation, but so that she could reveal the blades as an unspoken threat, if necessary.

"Can I help you, ma'am?"

The woman had a sturdy frame and hands grown tough from domestic life. She adjusted the scarf around her neck and ran her fingers through her hair once.

"You are Gozeh?" asked the Cleanser, calmly.

"I am."

"You are the sister to Kuzro, aunt to Zemfira."

The color in Gozeh's cheeks drained. "That—that's correct."

"And you are the current guardian of your nephew Jabo."

"Well, my husband is the guardian to Jabo and—"

"Tell the boy to pack up whatever belongings he has immediately."

"But there must be some mistake. Jabo is only eleven years—"

Firuzeh fixed a stern look upon the woman. "His age is of no concern. I am an envoy of the king, it is my duty to enact his will. I am to bring Jabo to Ragai without delay."

"To Ragai? Where is Ragai?"

"It is a city in Mada."

"In Mada? That must be halfway across the kingdom! I promise you, Jabo has done nothing wrong."

"That is irrelevant. Bring out the boy immediately. Anyone who defies the divine orders of the king is a traitor and will be punished."

Firuzeh watched with interest as the woman's jaw tightened and her fingers turned to trembling fists. Gozeh could do nothing, knowing she would risk the safety of her family if she disobeyed. She walked back into the house. A fly buzzed around the door frame and Firuzeh contemplated taking possession of it, to make sure Gozeh was not plotting something, but Firuzeh hated pushing her obedience upon insects. They had no sense of self, and their awareness was so multifaceted that it gave her a headache.

Gozeh returned with her nephew, who clutched a small sack in his arms. The boy was bony with dried mud on his knees and patches on his tunic. He looked sullen, and unimpressed by the Cleanser towering over him.

263

"Where are you taking me?"

"Ragai, in Mada," said Firuzeh.  It was important that Gozeh remembered where she was headed.  Gozeh probably did not have a direct connection to the traitors in the Lut Desert, but the information would reach the enemy eventually.  If rumors were slow, one of Sahin's agents could spark them again in Harauvatis or in Rasparad.

Jabo followed Firuzeh to her horse without complaint.  She had to help him up and decided to walk beside the beast until the road evened out.  Gozeh watched them go, calling to Jabo words of affection, but the boy did not bother waving goodbye.  His face was contorted with controlled anger.

"You were not happy living there," said Firuzeh, once they had left Nebit behind.

"Why do you say that?"

"You don't look sad."

"I'm not sad," said the boy. "I just hate everyone."

Firuzeh stopped her horse by raising a hand, then climbed on behind Jabo.  The boy did not seem to mind.  Firuzeh did not need reins to ride a horse, but it was more efficient to guide the animal without resorting to her Casting.  She had to conserve her strength if she was going to be this boy's keeper.

"Your father and sister left you here when they ran away."

Jabo's body was tense. "So you're going to kill me because you can't find them?"

"I imagine your father was protecting you," said Firuzeh. "If you were caught with them, you would be hanged, regardless of your age.  You are innocent of their treachery and therefore cannot be touched as an accomplice."

"Of course my father was trying to protect me," said Jabo. "He thinks I'm just a child.  He thinks I'm no use to him and Zemfira.  He always liked her more than me."

Firuzeh didn't know much about a father loving his child from personal experience, but she doubted whether a child of eleven could accurately gauge the complexities of an adult's mind.

"You won't be killed," she said. "Wanton vengeance is unprofessional. You will merely be the bait."

"They won't come for me," said Jabo.

Firuzeh hoped the boy was wrong. Her entire plan relied on luring Kuzro from whatever lay beyond the rocks. If Kuzro or anyone appeared on the Lut Desert road, she would have her evidence for Bishen to call in every Cleanser to assist in the assault. Then the Soulbreakers could be extinguished permanently.

The drizzle beat down on them, and upon the mountainous land.

# CHAPTER 25 –
# A PRIMER ON SHADOW BEASTS

Zemfira found Hami hiding deep within the temple, seated in front of the three archways on the forbidden floor. He sat in darkness, a little halo of sand swirling around him. He didn't react to Zemfira's glowing light, nor did he look up when she sat down next to him.

"I know you don't like to talk," said Zemfira. "And you don't have to. But you shouldn't stay down here. You shouldn't think that you're alone."

"I like being alone," said Hami.

"But it's dangerous, Hami," said Zemfira, exasperatedly. "It's dangerous for you and me. We're more at risk than regular people."

"This is why I don't Stonecast," whispered Hami.

"You're Stonecasting right now," Zemfira pointed out. She had spent far too long looking for Hami to put up with this indulgent self-pity.

Hami pressed his eyes closed and the sand fell to the ground in a shower. "It was an emergency. Last night. If I didn't —"

"I know," said Zemfira. "I was there."

Hami turned away and began tapping his fingers against his forehead. "I just want to be alone, please. You can't help me."

Zemfira took a deep breath. Soul regeneration was a complicated matter. It was not enough to love someone: a Soulgiver had to be open to love in order to restore their inner world. Hami had refused to let anyone get close to him, even Zemfira. Perhaps her personal frustrations stemmed from her disappointment. After all these months, after the midnight excursions to the creek and meals shared beneath the acacia tree, she would have assumed he could trust her.

"I'm not a warrior like you," said Hami. "I don't enjoy fighting."

"You don't try!" Zemfira burst out. She grimaced, knowing she had to be gentler. "You're gifted, Hami, and even if you're afraid—"

"I am afraid, Zemfira," said Hami, his voice firmer and louder than before. "You know what happens when people fight? People get hurt. People die."

"No," said Zemfira, angrily. "That's what happens when people *don't* fight. If you don't resist, people will die—the people you love and care about will die if you don't become strong."

"Who have *you* protected?" asked Hami.

Zemfira punched his shoulder with a force that caught Hami off guard. He gasped in pain and turned away.

"I'm sorry," said Zemfira, regretting the action immediately. "I'm really sorry, Hami."

He trembled and Zemfira bit her lip. She rarely had such trouble resolving matters with Paniz—Paniz did not have the patience for a grudge and always was ready to talk.

Zemfira changed tactics. She assumed the position Tryphon had taught her and closed her eyes. Hami wasn't interested in conversation, so she sank into meditation, pushing away her anxieties and frustrations. She took deep breaths, and let Hami's presence press against hers. The sensation was blurred, vague and muffled, but she could feel the spherical pressure of his soul, throbbing. His soul was unstable. There was a residue of damage. Swallowing, she opened her eyes.

"You're right," said Zemfira. "I haven't saved anyone. In fact, I'm the reason two people died on the Helmand River. I'm probably the reason Milad lost his foot. But it's because I can't fight. I can't defend myself so I can't defend anyone else—and I hate it. I can't even learn as much as the rest of you because I'm busy deciphering ancient scrolls with Master Tryphon. But I'm not giving up. I have to get stronger with my Casting and with my sword."

Hami sat back up and held out his hand. The gesture caught Zemfira by surprise: Hami rarely initiated anything as intimate as physical contact. His fingers felt warm to her touch, and she squeezed his hand.

"I grew up in a village near Ektabana, in Mada. When I was unclasped, the monk did not bother lying to me. He simply had me locked up in the stone tower that served as the village prison and told me if I tried to escape, my family would be killed. And so I waited in that cold, unfriendly room, day after day, for the Cleansers to arrive."

Hami's voice shook and his words spilled forth in a nervous flood. He ran his fingers through his hair.

"I was so scared, Zemfira. I didn't want to die. My parents were not allowed to see me but they begged for leniency—I was always a tender child. But when I saw the two Cleansers ride up to the village from my tower window, my panic rose. I didn't realize my father was arguing with them, trying to block their way, trying to protect me. I heard voices and footsteps and I panicked.

"I feverishly tried to cast, even though I didn't know what I was doing. I was terrified for my own survival. I attempted forcing the door open by breaking the stone doorway, I didn't understand how much power I had. I didn't know my own strength."

Zemfira tightened her fingers around Hami's and she was determined not to let go. She had to hear everything.

"I shattered the tower. Bricks began breaking apart, and I couldn't stop them. I was thrown against the wall as the building began to collapse. The bars of my window had fallen away and I dove out, tumbling into the acacia trees, breaking my arm and spraining my knee. I was alive and heard the screams and laments for the dead—town guards had perished, so had one of the Cleansers—and my father, too."

He pulled his hand free and wrapped his arms around his knees. Zemfira tried to find something meaningful to say, but she had nothing—no comfort, no gentle advice.

"Every time I see Kuzro, I'm hit with guilt, Zemfira," he said, hiding a stammer. "Your father saved your life—and I killed my father."

"Hami, don't say that!"

Hami pulled on a few strands of his wavy hair. "You blame yourself for the deaths of the ferryman and his son, you blame yourself when you were attacked—but you won't let me feel anguish for being the direct cause?"

"It was an accident! There was no malice in it!"

He grabbed her shoulders and stared at her, incredulous. "You and Paniz and Ardeshir—none of you understand! Even without malice, I'm the reason those people died! I can't be excused because I was afraid, because I didn't know what I was doing! Even good intentions lead to death. The Cost of Depravity is no reward, Zemfira. It brings death to everyone

269

whom it touches. That's why I don't want to fight—it's too—it's too dangerous for me."

"You fought for Stateira."

"I almost didn't," said Hami, his voice sinking to a whisper. "But I knew it would be better—better for me to cause her death—than if the Scorpion Man took her soul and—"

He tried to bring his breathing back under control. Zemfira wrapped her arms around Hami and embraced him so tightly that his bones dug into her. He had to know that he wasn't alone. With her eyes closed she could almost feel his soul: the scrapes on its surface, the deep grooves cut by time and depression. But the damage to his soul had not ruined his empathy or generosity—the pain was digging most deeply into his self-worth.

"You need to forgive yourself," said Zemfira. "It doesn't bring your father back, but you've mourned and grieved for two years—and that's too much. It's ruining you, Hami."

"I know it's ruining me," said the boy. "But I don't deserve a healthy soul. I don't need one to help around the temple. I resolved that I can still be of assistance, but I never want to take up arms—not even against the Shadow Beasts."

They lay together on the stone floor for several minutes. Zemfira stared up at the glowing white orb suspended above her. Its glow bounced off the lightstones and illuminated the Elamite engravings. She had learned Hami's most painful secret and she had no intention of letting him hold it by himself. His soul needed emotional comfort in order to regenerate itself.

"Listen, Hami," she said, moving even closer to him. "I've resolved to be utterly obnoxious to you from now on."

Hami blinked. "What do you mean?"

"Every day, I'm going to work on making you laugh. I will tell you jokes, I will draw funny pictures of you, and if that doesn't work, I'm just going to tickle you."

"You do that already—except for the tickling."

"But now I'm not going to accept a reluctant smile. I want to hear you laugh."

"Zemfira—"

"No, there's more. I'm going to learn how to sing well."

"Sing?"

"Master Tryphon has a lovely voice, when he clears his throat and chants in Harauvatian-style prayer. I'll ask him to help me. I want to wake you every morning with glorious songs—I will create a ballad for you."

"But you wouldn't do that in front of everyone else—"

"I'll have to. This way you'll sleep more at night—if you're tired all day, you'll go to sleep earlier."

"Zemfira, it doesn't work that way!" Hami was getting frustrated, which Zemfira thought, perhaps unhelpfully, was very cute.

"I'm also going to ask Master Hooshang to teach you how to Stonecast properly—not for combat, I promise. I want you to be confident in your powers—I want you to be able to control them so that you don't fear them. You never have to be a warrior, but you have to be a Soulgiver. That's who you are. Do you understand?"

Hami closed his eyes. "Zemfira—I'm not worth the effort. It's not going to work."

"I thought you might say that, and I have the perfect answer to it. Tickle penalty!"

Zemfira ran her fingers under Hami's armpit and he gave a little screech of surprise and squirmed vigorously.

"No, Zemfira, stop! Don't! I'm not a child."

Reluctantly, Zemfira leaned back. "You are—a little bit. You are letting tragedy define you—you're abdicating the responsibility for your life. It's easier to lead a life that doesn't matter than one that does—but your life does matter, and as long as you pretend otherwise, I won't give up."

She waited for him to react with another sigh, to evade conceding to her point. Instead, he looked at her with sorrowful eyes.

"Why, Zemfira? Why spend all this effort on me?"

"I like you. Isn't that obvious?"

"Why not invest your energies in Ardeshir? He's confident and funny—and I'm sure he's a wonderful kisser."

Zemfira smiled. "I doubt that. His feeble mustache is probably very scratchy."

Hami blushed. "I—uh—I like you too, Zemfira."

And Zemfira, seizing the initiative with a galloping heart, leaned in, pressing her lips against his. Hami was surprised, but he kissed back clumsily, as Zemfira ran her fingers through his hair, pulling him closer.

When the kiss ended they simply lay together in the faint luminescence of the lightstones, tangled around each other. Zemfira stroked Hami's face.

"If I can learn how to open a Flash Gate," she whispered, "you can learn to accept yourself. Once Roya goes through the Flash Gate, we can go wherever you want! We could go to Harauvatis, then keep traveling east, into the empire of the Nanda, into deepest Hindusia. We can find our own happiness, far from the Farsian regime and Roya's uprising."

Hami mustered a small smile. "I might like that."

Zemfira pulled him closer to her. It was a good start, and she would claim it as a victory.

***

While Zemfira enjoyed the challenge of cajoling Hami towards self-acceptance, most of her energies had to be devoted to the Flash Gate ritual. Master Tryphon assisted in small ways, re-reading the long inscriptions while Zemfira went through the steps and the motions.

"This ritual is practically a dance," said Tryphon. "And you are channeling so much power from your soul that it will take a serious toll, even when executed perfectly."

"I've feared as much," said Zemfira, standing in the middle of the large tile, holding her arms out in front of her and moving in accordance with the specified patterns.

It was Paniz who was nimble on her feet and precise in dance. Zemfira had to repeat steps over and over again until she could remember them. It was worse than baking bread. Zemfira grimaced, stepping forward, turning her shoulder, spinning her body in a graceful arc.

Slowly, she was beginning to understand the ritual. The movements were not random—they had to match the rhythm of her Lightcasting. To open a Flash Gate, Zemfira needed her body to resonate perfectly with her soul. Throughout the process she had to remind herself that she was loved, that she was worthy of love. Each rendition was physically and emotionally exhausting.

"You're making progress."

The comment didn't come from the Targu, but from Roya. Zemfira slowed her motions, wound them out into nothingness and bowed to the commander of the rebels.

"Welcome back to Jalehravan, Master Roya."

The commander looked exhausted. A few streaks of gray were visible in her hair and a bandage was wrapped around her

273

left forearm. Zemfira had never seen Roya properly injured. But her passion was not diminished.

"The Harauvatian uprising is faltering," she said. "A pity, after all the energy I put into destabilizing the Satrapy. Now, the damn royal army is quelling the voice of the people. When a king cannot hold onto his legitimacy he must impose it, and we did not have the numbers to stop them. Our local allies have retreated to the mountains or surrendered their weapons."

Zemfira's sympathy naturally lay with the Harauvatians. Discovering what it meant to be a Soulgiver had really eroded whatever loyalty she had towards the king. On the other hand, she harbored doubts about sparking rebellion now, when Shadow Beasts and the Hegemon menaced the people of Farsia. Then again, there would never be a good time to stand up to the systematic destruction of Soulgivers.

"I heard of your troubles here," said Roya. "Hence why I'm back so soon. I am glad all of you survived—such an assault on our sacred oasis by Shadow Beasts is unprecedented."

"Do you know why they attacked us?"

Roya shook her head. "It disturbs me how little we understand. Nevertheless, there are ways to prepare, should it occur again. I have gathered the young Soulgivers upstairs so that I can provide instruction on Shadow Beast combat. You are not obligated to come if—"

"I could use a change of scenery," said Zemfira. "If you give me permission to go, Master Tryphon."

Tryphon smiled. "I will wait here until you are done. Take your time."

Zemfira followed the rebel commander up the stairs, feeling uneasy. Roya's presence always put her on edge. They climbed the stairs in silence, nodding at the many monks and soldiers they passed. They reached the combat floor to see everyone assembled, even Milad, who sat on the ground with his leg bandaged.

"I must say this bluntly," Roya said, as soon as Zemfira took a seat between Hami and Paniz. "I cannot protect you when I am away. Since there is much for me to do, you need to protect yourselves. You already demonstrated incredible ability, but it was not enough."

Milad grimaced. He had wanted to assist Roya in storming the palace at Parsa. Now he was destined to a life as a monk. Zemfira knew he was suffering, but he always smiled and said he was simply glad the wound hadn't gotten infected—that he had kept his life and his soul.

"I will give you a primer regarding Shadow Beasts, so that you know how to combat them in the future. There are nine different species—Shifting Hounds, Meadow Gaunts, Blaze Beetles, Drowners, Starmouths, Scorpion Men, Golems, Delta Vipers and Voidicants. According to many, these monsters each correspond to different casting arts."

"What about Devas?" asked Darya, a tall Insightcaster who was a few months older than Hami.

Roya inclined her head. "There are also Devas, wicked creatures that rival the Celestial Ones in power. But you do not need to fear these, since they do not venture out of the abstract realm—they will not menace you."

"Have you encountered all nine Shadow Beasts?" asked Paniz.

"I have," said Roya. "When I was younger and long before I became commander, I thought I could serve my kingdom and people best by hunting down the unthinking brutes that prey on human souls. With time, I realized how futile it is to hunt them down: they always come back. The Celestial Ones constantly create more through their divine administration of justice. So I turned my attention to the threat to Soulgivers posed by fellow humans: by King Artashata and his dynasty."

"Which Shadow Beast is the most deadly?" asked Ardeshir.

The usually exuberant boy looked grim and sleep deprived. He had been training on his own, occasionally asking for guidance from Master Giv but scorning all peers except Milad.

"Patience," said Roya. "Let's start at the beginning. You fought Shifting Hounds, so you know what they are: multiple carnivorous animals meshed into one body, recklessly unstable and constantly shifting to exploit the environment. They rarely travel alone. If you are by yourself, do not attempt a pitched battle. If you must fight, use your casting for ranged attacks. Beams and projectiles are your best chance. They are simple creatures, and often bow to the command of a Scorpion Man or Voidicant."

Zemfira glanced at Paniz who was listening intently.

"Meadow Gaunts do not chase you. They hide in grassy, flowery places, buried in the soil with greenery growing out of their mud-like skin, a single, yellow eye extending like a meadow flower. They only move beneath the surface of the earth, but if you approach one it will wrap its tendrils around your leg and pull you into its hole—to slowly devour you with long rows of sharp teeth. Be cautious if the scenery looks too pretty, or if the earth grumbles beneath you. If you are a Stormcaster you can drown them in their warren and Infernocasters can burn up their underground network with a controlled blast."

Milad swallowed hard. He looked like he regretted coming to the meeting. Hami, next to the injured boy, also looked nervous.

"Blaze Beetles are immune to fire. In fact, flames will only make them stronger. If lightning strikes, they will emerge from the trees, logs and shallow caves where they hibernate. They will dig into your skin and suck out your blood with their tiny incisors. Kill them quickly. I find conventional weapons and fire-resistant boots are the best methods for eliminating these creatures."

"Could Blaze Beetles or Meadow Gaunts attack us here?" asked Nava.

"It is unlikely," said Roya. "But the only species I would not worry about at Jalehravan are Drowners. If you do encounter a Drowner, pray your weapons are sharp—otherwise Lightcasting, Shadowcasting, or lightning Stormcasting will be most effective.

"Starmouths are rare. For a time, the royal Champions believed they were the companion creature to Shadowcasting, but this is not the case. They absorb the light in their vicinity and hide it between their jaws. They make almost no sound, and approach their prey on padded paws. If your surroundings seem unnaturally dark, there may be a Starmouth stalking you. They take almost no damage from casting or weapon—until they open their mouth. Be careful of the blinding light and the sharp teeth. If you can react quickly enough to strike into the gullet, it will die."

"What do they look like?" asked Darya.

"I can't say for certain," said Roya. "By the time you kill one and restore the light, the Starmouth is half dissolved—but they share similarities with the panthers of Hindusia—only with much longer jaws and too many legs."

Zemfira knew about some of these creatures already, from the stories children told after dark to scare each other—but she had written off many details as preposterous. Now, Roya was verifying these nightmares.

"Scorpion Men are straightforward—powerful, fast, poisonous and clever. If they fix you with their gaze, they can dominate your mind—if there is a hierarchy within the Shadow Beast world, the Scorpion Men are near the top. Fight them with allies. Target the tail or the legs. Try to wound it before going for the throat or eyes."

Zemfira's memory filled with the three Scorpion Men they had encountered so far—and how they had each been destroyed by overwhelming force. Even with some training, Zemfira doubted she could face one on her own, Lightcaster or not.

"Golems are found on the coast of the Western Sea, mostly around the city of Gaza. They are beings constructed of rock, and held together by enchanted mud. A talented Stonecaster can break away chunks of a Golem, but unless you dislodge the jewel at the center, these behemoths will not relent. Temperaturecasters can exact damage, as can a Sproutcaster. Just be careful: they have a tendency to sneak up on their prey, for they too make no noise.

"Delta Vipers commonly live along the Hapi River in Mudraya and always predict what you are going to do. They are six meters long, shaped like a cobra. Fight them with a comrade, since they only register one mind at a time, or learn to shield your own mind from inquiry. That requires refinement and many years of training."

Roya paused and looked around at the young Soulgivers, and at Paniz. All watched now with rapt attention. All wanted to know about the final Shadow Beast: the most terrifying of all.

"Voidicants, of course, are associated with Shadowcasting. They sometimes resemble the hollow outline of a woman. Sometimes they take the form of your greatest fear.

They are the purest Shadow Beast, because they make no illusions of their emptiness. They use their own lack of essence to consume yours, either through seduction or gravity. I tried to fight one once and I had to flee. It is hard to kill something that wants anything, and it's harder still to take away from something that is nothing. Voidicants are paradoxes with appetites."

"Then how do you defeat them? How have they—they not—"

"They are not invincible," said Roya. "They can be trapped by their own reflection, if they have assumed a physical form. You can build mirrored cages for them, from which they cannot escape—but to kill one—I do not know. They are uncommon, but since the Shadow Beasts are on the move, we must prepare. Are you ready for practical training?"

The drills were simple, limited by the lack of real Shadow Beasts. Roya paired Ardeshir with Zemfira, and they monitored each other.

"We're delaying the inevitable," said Ardeshir, creating a triangle with his outstretched hands which pulled all the heat into its center. He aimed at the target on the wall and released the blast of hot air. It left a small crack about a meter to the left of the bullseye.

"You think there'll be more Shadow Beasts?" asked Zemfira, as Ardeshir shook the heat from his fingers with a grimace.

The boy focused his fingers again, this time releasing a blast of cold, which slammed ice crystals into the target, even closer to the center.

"I think the Angra is rising," said Ardeshir. "It senses the divisions within Farsia. It knows we are not united against chaos: we're fostering it. The Angra will overwhelm the Spenta, and we'll become slaves to chaos and death."

279

Zemfira frowned, switching places with the boy and positioning her own hands. "From what I've learned about the Eternal Crusade, we feed the Spenta with good acts, regardless of our devotion. We shouldn't give up hope."

"There are few good deeds in a time of war," said Ardeshir, sagely. "And the Shadow Beasts know the end is coming. They parade through the sunlight, they strike at temples, the very bastions of compassion and goodness. They'll overrun Farsia while Roya and Artashata struggle over the throne."

"I thought you've declared yourself a loyal rebel to Master Roya."

"I have," said Ardeshir. "Her cause is righteous—but the Angra knows how to exploit our righteousness to undermine our world."

Zemfira's beam struck a few centimeters above the target, a bright flash that stung her eyes and left the smallest scorch mark on the sensitive stone.

"Does this truly feel like the end of the world to you?" she asked. "It's a calamity, yes, Farsia is in trouble, but do you believe we are nearing the climax of the Crusade?"

Ardeshir's jaw set. "I've seen it in dreams. The Shadow Beasts keep coming—they shake the earth and boil the seas—the world splits in half and collapses on itself. Unless the Spenta can overpower the Angra, we are approaching the end."

\*\*\*

When supper was served, Nava, Darya, Paniz and Ardeshir hurried upstairs, eager for food. Roya followed them, most likely to talk with Yashar and Kalpana. Hami and Zemfira stayed behind with Milad.

"I'm useless," he muttered. "I can't Stormcast like this—I can't balance, I'm physically weak and—what's the point? I'm as good as dead."

"What are you talking about?" said Zemfira. "Some of the greatest casters were maimed. Think of Bozorgmehr who fought on the Hellenic mainland! He was a Stonecaster who moved a mountain, and he only had one hand!"

"I'm no hero!" said Milad, angrily. "I wanted to become a hero but—but every time I try to cast, I just think about that night."

Hami helped Milad up, supporting him as the boy put his weight on his good foot. Milad's grimace and the flaring of his nostrils made Zemfira's stomach squeeze.

"Is there something I can do to help?" she asked. "Anything at all. I'd even challenge fate and cook something for you."

Milad glanced at the ground. "There is something I've been meaning to ask you, but I've been too ashamed to do so until now."

Hami looked very uncomfortable, but kept silent and lowered his eyes, as if that would give Milad and Zemfira some privacy.

"Don't be ashamed," said Zemfira. "What can I do?"

Milad looked like he regretted bringing up the matter, but said, "I was wondering if you could talk to Paniz for me. She— uh—she hasn't wanted to spend time with me since—"

Milad broke off and rubbed his crooked nose. Zemfira blinked.

"Paniz hasn't spent any time with you? Did you two fight?"

He shook his head. "We haven't spoken. I think she's avoiding me, but I don't know why."

Zemfira frowned. "I'll talk to her, don't worry, Milad. Can I bring you some soup?"

"No thanks. I think I'll get to bed. Ardeshir found a scroll for me with a story in it—and I want to read it before I go to sleep. Hami said he'll help me down."

Zemfira kissed Hami on the cheek and watched them descend the stairs. She was about to climb up to get some food when she saw Roya descending with a loaf and a plate of salted meats.

"Oh," said Roya. "I thought you would have already gone down to rejoin Tryphon. I was bringing your supper."

Zemfira wanted to say she had to speak with her friend, but knew Roya would not think it important. So instead she lowered her head and followed the commander down the stairs, to resume her studying.

# CHAPTER 26 – KUZRO'S DECISION

Despite her promise to Milad, Zemfira didn't manage to speak with Paniz for several days. Roya and Tryphon kept her practicing the ritual, over and over, only letting her escape for a few hours a day. During those hours Paniz was out between the rocks in the staggering temperatures. Master Kalpana had described a method of fighting which gave an Infernocaster immunity against heat, making their entire body hot and deadly, and Paniz was determined to learn the technique.

"She's insane," said Ardeshir, slurping from his ration of beer in the cool dining room. "Her soul's affinity with Infernocasting is astounding. Paniz practically speaks fire with every movement, and yet she's not satisfied."

"Of course she isn't," said Zemfira, massaging her feet which still ached from practicing the ritual. "Her Cost is Fatigue. She feels inadequate with us."

"That's why she's insane," said Ardeshir. "She's easily the best Caster among us—limited only by her Cost—and yet she wants to transcend that, for what? Pride?"

Zemfira shook her head, but she didn't know.

She ended her exercises with Tryphon early that evening, taking a few scrolls back to her bed mat and waiting for Paniz. Hami sat with her for a bit, and she would scratch his back from time to time.  Eventually, however, she kissed him on the cheek and told him to look after Milad.  She suspected Paniz was arriving soon.

"I'm utterly exhausted," Paniz announced to Zemfira, stumbling into the sleeping niche, taking off her sandals and falling onto her wool blanket. "I've been learning how to acclimate my body to immense heat and it's not easy.  I can stay cool in a fire for a minute now before my Casting falters.  Even Master Kalpana can only hold it for five minutes, and she's been casting for years!  Well, good night, Zemfira."

"Wait," said Zemfira, as Paniz curled up and yawned. "We need to talk about Milad."

Paniz didn't open her eyes, but her body was too rigid for sleep. "Tomorrow, perhaps."

"No.  We have to talk now."

Paniz sat up with a groan. "Why do we have to talk?"

"Are you not speaking with Milad anymore?  What's going on?"

Paniz wouldn't look at Zemfira. "He asked you to talk with me, didn't he?"  When Zemfira didn't say anything, Paniz heaved a sigh. "I don't know what to say to him. If I try, I'll say the wrong thing, so I think it's better that I don't try at all."

"Does his injury make you uncomfortable, or do you not like him in the same way anymore?"

Paniz curled her toes. "It's—it's both."

"Both."

There were tears welling in Paniz's eyes—tears of emotion and exhaustion. "Do you hate me, Zemfira?  Do you think I'm a monster?  Because that's what I am."

Zemfira reached out and held Paniz's hand. "You're not a monster."

The young Infernocaster pressed her eyes closed and wiped at them with her free hand. "I never liked Milad as much as he liked me. He's nice, and pretty handsome, but he wasn't important to me the way Hami is to you. But I admired his tenacity, his desire to prove and improve himself. But now—"

"Paniz," said Zemfira. "I love you, but this is incredibly selfish."

"You think I don't know that?" demanded Paniz. "But what does Milad want from me? Marriage? I can't marry him—I wouldn't have, even if he hadn't been attacked."

"I'm sorry that you lost your most willing sparring partner," said Zemfira. "But he lost his foot, his mobility! You will always find someone willing to fight you. Everyone wants to see the marvelous Paniz display her Infernocasting, but what can he do? His life is altered permanently."

"I know," said Paniz. "I know, I know! What can I do though? Hold his hand every day, tell him he's still a good person, still has a bright future? Should I abandon my training? Should I become his servant?"

"You know that's not what I'm asking you to do."

"What *are* you asking me to do?"

Zemfira gritted her teeth at the petulance, but knew it was just Paniz's exhaustion.

"Tell him the truth. Be sincere, and be a friend. You do not have to devote yourself to him, but you have to support him as much as you would if Ardeshir or I lost a foot or a hand."

"But I don't—I can't—"

"Milad's not an idiot. He knows what you're saying with your absence. Don't give him any false hopes. Give him your support. He needs that, you know."

Paniz sat up, wrapped her arms around herself and stared at her blanket. "It's all my fault."

"What are you talking about?"

"That night—I just ran out of steam so quickly. I wanted to burn up the Shifting Hound attacking Milad, I wanted to stop it from biting off his—but I knew one more strike and I'd lose consciousness. I should have done it, I should have—but I didn't want to die. I was scared."

Zemfira gripped Paniz's forearm. "We were all doing the best we could. You can't blame yourself for the violence of the Shifting Hounds."

"I have to blame myself," said Paniz. "Otherwise I won't drive myself to improve. Otherwise it'll happen again, and you'll be attacked, or Hami, or Nava. I can't let that happen. I won't let my weak Cost stop me—I can't."

Zemfira let Paniz sleep then. She wondered, vaguely, what would have happened if their fates had been reversed, if Paniz had faced the lying monk at Nebit. Paniz had a drive that superseded Zemfira's. Both wanted to improve themselves, but Zemfira was fighting because she wanted to be self-reliant and thus protect others from suffering on her behalf. Paniz was training to become the best. If she had been born with the Cost of Depravity, she might have changed the trajectory of history.

*** 

Half a month passed. Summer was approaching fast. Roya had gone, leaving her lieutenant, Musa, in charge. One sunny morning a rebel caravan arrived with fresh supplies, including seeds for Kuzro. He examined the pouch in the dining hall with great excitement. Zemfira could not tell what was so important about the seeds. The three little piles looked fairly similar to her, but Kuzro rubbed his hands gleefully.

"Go get Milad. I have a surprise for him."

Milad's mood had settled over the last few days. He was still unhappy, but had accepted his situation. He limped up the stairs, leaning on his staff. Despite his missing foot he was keeping fit, working his arms and torso to keep himself mobile.

"Nava, get me some dirt, please," said Kuzro, motioning Milad to take a seat. The young Stormcaster sank down, suspiciously.

"If you're trying to cheer me up by entertaining me, save your energies. I'm not enthusiastic about flowers."

"No, no, no," said Kuzro. "Nothing so mundane, I promise."

Nava returned, scowling when Kuzro accepted the bowl of dirt with only a nod of appreciation. Despite a friendlier acquaintance with Zemfira, she still looked down on Kuzro for being a mere goatherd. Kuzro either didn't notice, or he didn't mind.

"Look here," he said, placing a seed in the dirt, watering it from his cup, and then squeezing his fist tight. Kuzro's Casting twisted a small tree from the soil, with an immensely stubby trunk and vine-like branches. Kuzro beamed at the results of his casting, and took a bite of bread to satiate himself.

"What is it?" asked Milad.

"This is your wooden leg," said Kuzro. "With a little padding—some moss will do the trick, you can step into the groove at the top. I'll help you—like so—perfect—and then—"

Kuzro raised his hands and the fibrous branches wrapped themselves around Milad's leg. Milad gave a gasp as the branches formed a flexible cast, supporting his leg up to his bent knee without constricting the blood flow. Kuzro reached down and tapped the wood, then smiled with satisfaction.

"All in order. You can step out with it—the roots are very shallow."

Milad exchanged a nervous look with Ardeshir, who gave him an encouraging nod and grasped his arm for support. With a deep breath, Milad lifted his left leg, pulling the little tree from the soil and placing his weight on it. It matched his other foot perfectly in height.

"It won't give back what the Shifting Hounds took away," said Kuzro. "But at least you can be mobile."

"Do I have to keep it on my leg all the time?" asked Milad.

"Not as long as you have a Sproutcaster nearby," said Kuzro, smiling at Nava. "The tree is still living. As long as you occasionally dip it in water it will stay alive, and the branches can be easily manipulated. You can untie them yourself, but they will be less cooperative with you."

Milad took a few steps across the dining room. The monks watched, eyes wide. A few revolutionaries at a far table glanced over at the boy with mild interest. Everyone was quiet.

"This is incredible," said Milad, making his tender way back to Kuzro and extending a hand. "I cannot begin to thank you, Master Kuzro. How did you know about this tree?"

Kuzro smiled. "Many years ago, a friend of mine suffered a similar fate as yours. I'm just glad Master Giv knew a merchant in Chadrakarta who sold the seeds. I can teach Nava and the other Sproutcasters how this plant is best raised from the seed. As long as you keep them happy, you'll be able to walk."

Amidst the celebration, Zemfira saw Tryphon talking to the rebel who had brought Kuzro the seeds. Neither looked excited by the little miracle. At first this annoyed Zemfira, who thought their behavior reflected their opinion of Kuzro, but then she began to worry. Tryphon was not a petty man. This had to be something severe.

Milad and Ardeshir wanted to enjoy the clean morning air before it became painfully hot, so they ascended outside. Darya and Paniz followed, as did Master Yashar, who seemed determined not to let the ambush of the Shifting Hounds repeat itself. But Zemfira stayed behind, more curious to talk with the Targu, who was approaching Kuzro with a deliberate stride.

"May I speak with you for a moment?" he asked, solemnly.

Kuzro's face fell. "I hope I did not violate temple protocol with Milad. I wanted it to be a surprise."

"That is no issue," said Tryphon, his wrinkles deepening. "I am glad to see a solution to Milad's problem."

"That's a relief," said Kuzro.

"But I have a private matter I wish to discuss with you. Would you mind following me downstairs?"

Kuzro shrugged. "Sure."

"May I come?" asked Zemfira.

"Not this time," said the Targu. "Go and enjoy the daylight."

Reluctantly, Zemfira emerged and saw the rebel envoy from earlier, handing a bow to Paniz and Ardeshir.

"I can't believe it," said Ardeshir. "These are so nice! And they belong to us?"

The rebel bowed his head. "Commander Roya believes our warriors should know how to fight in many different ways, and we must ready ourselves for what is to come. You must learn to wield a bow."

Paniz held hers up so that the sunlight glinted off the polished wood. "Ride a horse, fire a bow, cast with caution, tell the truth," she whispered, repeated the four abilities that defined the ideal Farsian. Even in Baxtris, where Farsian identity could be tenuous, they all knew the mantra.

The rebel handed her a quiver, and Zemfira could not watch anymore. She strode up to Paniz, touching her shoulder. "So, you're joining the fight against the king?"

Paniz looked surprised. "Of course. Aren't you going to?"

"I haven't decided," said Zemfira. "I don't feel ready to decide yet."

"It's not a decision you need to think about," said Paniz, unstringing the bow and taking the short sword the envoy handed her. "You're either a fighter or a meditator. And if you're the former, you'll fight for the rights of Soulgivers."

"But you're not a Soulgiver!" said Zemfira. "This is not your fight!"

"Of course this is my fight," said Paniz. "I don't have to be oppressed to join a just cause. I thought you were going to open the Flash Gate for us."

"I am," said Zemfira. "But Roya did not say I had to fight."

"Why are you so reluctant?" asked Paniz, slamming the sword into its sheath. "You always wanted to see the world, to fight off bandits and save villages from marauders. What's changed?"

"We're no longer children," said Zemfira. "We can no longer just dream. If we fight, we have to be ready—and I'm not ready yet."

"You won't ever be ready," said Paniz. "War is for fools and heroes. You just have to rise to the occasion."

Zemfira was about to reply when Kuzro stormed out of the temple, Tryphon several meters behind, trying to catch up with the goatherd. Kuzro reached the envoy, eyes hard like metal fragments.

"Do you have any spare swords? I don't have much money, but—"

"Has Roya or Lieutenant Musa extended an invitation to join the revolution?" asked the rebel.

"No," said Kuzro. "This is a personal matter, and I—"

Tryphon put a hand on the goatherd's shoulder. "Calm yourself, Kuzro. You cannot rush into battle."

The rebel looked aghast at Tryphon. "You told him? I thought you were going to wait until later to—"

"If my son is in peril, I cannot sit idly by, Targu," snarled Kuzro. "I need a camel and a sword. I'll figure out the rest from there."

Zemfira grabbed hold of Kuzro's wrist. "What did you say? Is Jabo—"

Kuzro's face softened and he choked away tears. "Some Cleansers are taking Jabo to Mada. They took him out of Nebit and are escorting him west."

"But why?" asked Zemfira. "Jabo hasn't done anything!"

"He's bait," said Tryphon. "It means you've evaded their capture, so they resort to this. You cannot go. You must accept your son is dead, regardless of your action."

Kuzro gritted his teeth. "Zemfira was dead, regardless of my action, and then I acted. If I can save her life, I can save Jabo's. I should have brought him along from the beginning. I have to rectify my mistake. With these new seeds, I will have the power I need."

"You're not thinking clearly," said Tryphon.

"You don't have children," said Kuzro. "If I let Jabo die, if I could have tried to prevent it—"

"I'll come with you," said Zemfira. "You won't have to do this alone."

"You're not coming along," said Kuzro. "I need to know you're                                                                          safe."

"Not to mention your task," said Tryphon. "Lieutenant

291

Musa reports sightings of Cleansers and soldiers lurking on the edges of the desert. The Harauvatian uprising has been dispersed. Once King Artashata deals with the Hegemon, he will turn all his attentions to finding Jalehravan. Then there will be no sanctuaries left for us."

Zemfira also knew how Roya would react if she abandoned her one duty, and could not let that happen. She had to complete her task. She was so close.

"Father, please wait," said Zemfira. "Let me open the Flash Gate. Then we can both go through and find Jabo. We can surprise his captors and make our escape. Please don't be rash."

"I—I won't be returning here," said Kuzro. "I know a place in Ektabana where Jabo and I can hide—I'll leave details with Jia-Fan. I promise I won't lead them back here—I'd poison myself with my own seeds before I put any of you at risk. But I am a free man—and I must protect my son."

Yashar approached, looking grim. "We won't stop you, but we cannot spare anyone to help you. We are gathering our free Soulgivers now, to be ready for Zemfira's triumph. You have to do this alone."

Kuzro wet his lips, staring out at the sizzling sky beyond the rocks. "I know."

"I'll go with him," said Ardeshir.

Everyone stared.

"What?" demanded Zemfira.

"At least to the edge of the desert," said Ardeshir. "He needs to make it out of Lut alive, doesn't he? I'll guide him out."

"Thank you, Ardeshir," said Kuzro.

Ardeshir shrugged. "I need to practice maintaining a cooler temperature anyway—plus perhaps your daughter will repay me with a kiss."

Zemfira rolled her eyes.

"I don't like this," said Yashar. "It's a huge risk. If the Shadow Beasts strike again—"

"They might strike here too," said Ardeshir. "And then I'd survive for not being here. Sometimes you have to take a chance."

Yashar grimaced. "Roya won't like this."

"She doesn't have to find out," said Ardeshir with a smile. "I'll be back before anyone knows I'm gone."

"Very well then," said Yashar. "Let's gather some provisions for the both of you and find a pair of camels. You leave tomorrow at dawn."

# Chapter 27 –
# Chatrang on the Beach

To avoid talking about her father's departure, Zemfira took her training further underground, down to the subterranean lake and island. There she practiced the ritual steps, spins and stances in front of the pillars she needed to activate. The lightstones reacted as her feet moved over the surface of the glittering dais. Whenever she grew frustrated by the Elamite scrolls, or sensed her soul needed time to replenish itself, she would undress and dive into the water, savoring its cool embrace.

Tryphon came down with her, leaning against his staff and giving occasional suggestions. More and more, however, he simply meditated, sometimes for hours. When a swim didn't calm her down, Tryphon invited her to join him in clearing her mind, and letting her body draw closer to her soul. She was getting better at sensing the Targu's soul beside her, as her Lightcasting developed. His presence helped her soul regenerate faster.

"I'm so close," muttered Zemfira, crossing her legs next to the Targu. "The pillars start glowing brighter when I reach the end of the ritual, but it's just not quite—"

"It will come," said Tryphon. "I have watched many monks and disciples develop their abilities. None have made such quick progress as you have."

"Except for Paniz," said Zemfira.

Tryphon shook his head, without opening his eyes. "There is more to casting than winning battles, Zemfira. To channel the urge to survive is only one manifestation of ability. I speak without flattery when I say your accomplishments here set you apart from your peers."

"Thank you, Master Tryphon."

"You will ascend to heights unknown. I would invite you to study further here at Jalehravan, once there is peace for the Soulgivers. I would like to see you succeed me as Targu."

"But that's ludicrous," said Zemfira. "I'm barely sixteen!"

Tryphon smiled, reminding Zemfira of an owl. "You do not have to ascend the position tomorrow, but Casting is etched into your future."

Zemfira stared up at the glowing crystals in the ceiling, then down at their imperfect reflections on the gentle water. "I don't know, Master Tryphon. I believe there will be more chaos before we have peace. After King Artashata repels the Hellenics, he won't just surrender his throne. It won't be easy to fight him."

Tryphon nodded sorrowfully. "I know Roya has a plan of action, but I fear the death toll will be staggering."

Zemfira chewed her lip. "Ardeshir returned today."

The Targu inclined his head. "Yes, my child."

The boy had seemed content, his mission complete. He had said Kuzro had left the desert to the northwest with confidence, but Zemfira was still afraid. She wished she could have stopped Kuzro's departure, and yet a part of her endorsed the mission, utterly foolish as it was, if it would save Jabo from royal violence.

295

"Do not discount your anxieties," said Tryphon. "But master your feelings. Those who let emotion or desire guide them will find trouble within. Especially Soulgivers like us."

Zemfira pursed her lips and nodded.

\*\*\*

As each day folded into the next, Zemfira found herself completing the routine from beginning to end with almost no flaws. Occasionally she would push her foot a little too far to the left, and sometimes her spin was imperfect, but she had the ritual memorized. When she lay down to sleep, her mind churned with the three hundred distinct motions. Tryphon kept telling her to slow down, to make sure her soul remained stable, but she knew she had more to give.

She experimented with different pacing: going faster, then slower, for the scrolls gave little instruction in that regard. She could see the effect of her adjustments in the pillars. Sometimes they would glow brighter, other times they became dull. There was a song behind this ritual, a song long lost to living ears. If she could grasp the pace, that song would flow through her and open the Flash Gate.

Half a month passed with no word from Kuzro when Stateira came down into the cavern, followed by Jia-Fan. The princess's tunic was dirty and she was missing her scarf, but she looked healthy and content. Zemfira wondered what brought the princess to her former prison cell.

The princess stumbled out of the little boat and onto the sandy bank, hugging Zemfira, then stepping back.

"It's nice to see you again," said Zemfira. "How are things upstairs?"

"She wants you to teach her to play Chatrang," said Jia-Fan, holding the board under one arm. "I told her you're busy, but she wanted to ask you anyway. I hope you don't mind the interruption."

"Not at all," said Zemfira. "I'd gladly take a break. Shall we play now?"

"On the far side of the beach," said Stateira. She considered for a moment, then added, "Please."

Zemfira glanced at Jia-Fan, who shrugged. "As long as I can see her, I don't mind."

"Of course," said Zemfira, holding out a hand to the girl. "Come on Stateira, let's play."

Stateria took the board from Jia-Fan and Zemfira carried the pouch of pieces. They sat down, the sand crunching delightfully as they settled. The princess glanced around while Zemfira decided how best to summarize the rules.

"The goal in Chatrang is either to capture every one of your opponent's pieces except the king—or just capture the king. To start, you place your archers on the second line, one chariot on each corner, and next to them you have the equestrian, then the war elephant—"

Zemfira broke off when Stateira placed all the pieces on the board in their correct positions. The little girl stared up at the Lightcaster, a daring defiance in those brown eyes.

"You can go first," said Stateira.

"You already know how to play?"

Stateira nodded, adjusting one of Zemfira's archers so that it matched the others. "I wanted to talk with you—alone."

Zemfira glanced over at Jia-Fan, who was covertly building a little castle in the sand, next to Tryphon. The meditating monk did not look up.

"Is something the matter?"

"You need to help me escape."

The request hung in the air. Zemfira took a deep breath, wishing the girl would break her intense eye contact. "You know I can't do that," said Zemfira, quietly.

"I know what they're planning," said Stateira. "They want to kill my father."

Zemfira knew she couldn't deceive this girl. "They're angry," said Zemfira. "Your father has killed many of them—many of us. They want to prevent future Soulgivers being killed."

"My father is not evil," said Stateira, making a fist. "You still haven't gone."

"What?"

"It's your move first, remember?"

Zemfira moved one of her archers forward. "Until my Unclasping, I thought Soulgivers were wicked, so I can't blame your father for acting on that mistaken belief. He was trying to keep the people and the kingdom safe. But he's wrong. Murdering Soulgivers is indefensible."

Stateira jumped her equestrian over her archer diagonally. "Roya kidnapped me."

"She also saved my life."

"I watched her kill Zealots who tried to save me from her. She killed one after another. Then she wrapped me in darkness so that my screams were silent and everything felt like a miserable dream. I thought she was going to feed me to a Voidicant. Instead she put me down here. And soon—soon she's going to kill me."

Zemfira tightened her fingers around her War Elephant piece. "Why do you say that?"

"I'm not stupid," said Stateira. "I have ears. I hoped they'd sell me back to my father, but I know better now. If you succeed, Roya will kill my father and my family. Then she'll have no more need for me. That's when I die."

Zemfira placed her piece and did not look up from the board. She tried not to think of Jabo, tried not to think how a king, driven mad by grief, would exact revenge on a boy connected to the Soulgivers. Jabo was as involved in the resistance as Stateira was in the oppression.

"Stateira, I don't think—"

"You know it's true. You're just scared of Roya."

Zemfira could not argue with that.

"Zemfira, save me and my family: open the Flash Gate and let us go through together."

Zemfira pushed an archer forward one space. "You know that's impossible. The moment I master the technique, Roya will want to use it for her own purposes."

"She won't know if you learn in secret," said Stateira. "If you get me home safely, my father will release your brother. I'll make sure he pardons you, and Kuzro and Hami and Paniz. My father will listen to me."

Zemfira closed her eyes. Stateira couldn't know how much Zemfira wanted to resolve this matter before Paniz entered the revolutionary battle. She wished her family was safe, but she was no fool. She would be surrendering herself to the mercy of King Artashata. Without the Flash Gate, the revolutionaries would be thwarted and with skilled torturers at the ready, Artashata could extract Jalehravan's location from Zemfira's family. There would be no mercy for those who kidnapped the king's daughter.

"Do you know where your father is right now?" asked Zemfira, tentatively.

"Of course," said Stateira. "He is at the royal palace. Where else would he be?"

299

Zemfira closed her eyes. "He isn't there.    He's—somewhere else."

"You know where he is, yes?"

Zemfira shook her head. "I can't let you go there. Your father won't spare any of our lives—and even if he did pardon me, I could not live with the guilt."

"So, you're going to let me die."

"If this war resolves itself, maybe Roya—"

Stateira began to cry.  Jia-Fan looked up and rose to her feet but Zemfira held up a hand, telling her it was okay.

"I'm so scared, Zemfira.  They're going to kill me. Please."

"I'll talk to Roya.  I'll bargain for mercy.  She might listen to me."

Stateira stared at her for a long time, then moved her Vazir forward. "If I win, you have to help me.  If I lose, I will die without complaint."

"No," said Zemfira. "I'll advocate for you, but I can't make any promises."

Stateira stood up slowly, wiping her nose with her hand. "You're no better than the rest."

"You're right," said Zemfira. "I'm not."

Stateira walked back to Jia-Fan, leaving Zemfira with the board, the shadows of each piece flickering in the light of the minerals above.

*** 

Hami found her the next day, still practicing relentlessly. The pillars had started glowing with a new intensity, pulsing in rhythm to Zemfira's movements, but by the end her concentration had slipped just enough to make the pillars dim again.

"I can't do it. It's impossible."

"You're very close," said Hami. Tryphon had returned by boat to the shore, looking for a few hours of rest, and Hami had swum over.

"Close is not enough," snapped Zemfira. "I'm not good enough to do this."

Hami looked uneasy in his shrunken tunic, moving his weight from one foot to the other. He was twisting his hands and refusing to make eye contact.

"What's going on?" asked Zemfira, suspiciously.

"We just received word," said Hami. "Your father has been captured near Ragai. He's being taken west for questioning. He's—he's probably at Issos by now."

Zemfira took a deep breath, then sat down on the edge of the shrine. She tried to keep calm and choose her words carefully. "When did we find out?"

"This morning," said Hami. "Roya did not want to tell you, not until you completed your task—but I thought you would want to know."

Zemfira felt cold, but could only say, "I thought it was morning. I've lost track of time down here."

"It's almost evening," said Hami. "Zemfira, I'm so sorry, I —"

Zemfira held out her hand, and Hami took it, sitting down with her. "I thought they would just kill him... but this is worse. They're going to torture him, they're going to use him to reveal the location of Jalehravan. They'll threaten him with hurting Jabo, and in the end—"

Hami mumbled something, but it was incoherent.

"I have to save him," said Zemfira, getting to her feet.

He opened his mouth. "What? No, you won't reach them in time, even with a horse!"

"I don't intend to travel there by horse," said Zemfira, turning to face the two pillars. "I have another means in mind."

"Zemfira—"

"Tell Roya I will have the gate ready in an hour."

"An hour? But you can't—"

"She's been gathering all her revolutionaries, hasn't she? Tell them to be ready—and then come back down here. It's comforting to have you with me, but now I need to focus."

She moved through the steps, faster and faster, her whole body vibrating with light energy. She felt it in her anger, in her fingers, in her thoughts. Her bare feet made the floor bright with their touch. She made no mistakes, and felt the power build. The pillars were glowing brighter and brighter, two beacons of collapsed rainbows. The energy became so intense that Zemfira could hear the light particles screaming.

With all her will she pushed the flat of her hand forward, finishing the stance and feeling the energy burst from her, through the two pillars, rendering them not merely bright, but connected with a shimmering film of flickering substance. She struggled to stay on her feet, soul rippling with tremors, body drenched in sweat.

"You did it already?"

Zemfira turned to see Hami, standing there, tunic soaked. Had he swum across again? She hadn't noticed anything during her performance of the ritual. How long had she been engaged in it? Hami's eyes were wide.

"Have you told Roya that—"

Hami let out a squeak and fell to his knees. Zemfira felt the substance of the air change, sensed a deep warbling. Even before she turned, Zemfira knew someone had just stepped out of the Flash Gate.

It was hard to distinguish the figure from the portal—both were so bright they hurt Zemfira's light-resistant eyes. The figure was tall, a muscular form wrapped in a shifting spectrum of colors. The graceful figure was naked, but as the brightness dimmed, Zemfira saw no sex organs: just a smooth avatar of human form. The neck transitioned from bright skin to silver feathers, forming the head of a falcon, with eyes like dripping amber. Wings spread from its back, momentarily dimming the Flash Gate, before the Celestial One folded them.

"I am Xavapar," said the creature, its voice touching her mind, her ears and her soul simultaneously. "Greetings, Zemfira of Nebit."

# CHAPTER 28 – THE CELESTIAL ONE

"How did you step through a Flash Gate?" Zemfira's words sounded far away, and so pointless. "I thought Flash Gates only worked in one direction."

Xavapar stepped forward, stretching his arms as he did so. He stood about two and a half meters tall—a specimen of divine purity.

"I am a Bounteous Immortal," said Xavapar. "I come from the abstract realm, the Menog. I sensed you had completed your task, succeeded in opening the portal and so I have come, to speak with you."

Zemfira backed up to kneel next to Hami. Beyond the Celestial One, Zemfira could hear the humming of the Flash Gate. Out of instinct, the girl and the boy both bent their foreheads to the ground.

"Lord Xavapar, how may we serve you?"

The elegant ankles and feet stepped forward, still glowing, but no longer blinding. Zemfira could see the rich hue of the Celestial One's skin as it exuded light.

"I have watched you for many years, Zemfira," said Xavapar. "Both of you may gaze upon me. You are not obliged to avert your eyes. I can perceive your respect."

Zemfira looked up and noticed something etched on Xavapar's chest—almost like a star with forty points. It was a strange flaw upon such a perfect body. Did all Celestial Ones carry such a mark?

"There is great evil afoot," said the immortal. His feet left prints in the sand but he himself cast no shadow. "You have noticed it. The movement of the Shadow Beasts, their migration across eastern Farsia: it is no accident. There is an intelligence guiding these hungry beings to its banner."

"Is it the Angra? Is it rising?" asked Zemfira.

The avian eyes stared calmly at Zemfira. "No. It is a Celestial One whom you have to blame for the attacks on you: both on the river and here in the oasis."

Zemfira was at a loss for words. "But Celestial Ones never work with Shadow Beasts."

Xavapar nodded. "When Drvaspa turned against the Spenta and wrought havoc as if she were a servant of the Angra... the betrayal was horrible. We did not know a Bounteous Immortal could break from the Spenta's cause."

"Why would she break away from the path of creation? Why pursue death and chaos? Why pursue me? And why send Shadow Beasts if she's a Celestial One?"

Xavapar took a seat in the sand, which made Hami and Zemfira draw in their breaths. They had never pictured a Celestial One assuming a meditative posture, like a mere monk.

"Centuries ago, when Drvaspa was discovered in her wicked pursuits, she was imprisoned. Her prison was not sealed in the Menog, but in this dimension, upon holy ground. She lies in a temple complex buried deep in the jungle. For centuries we have kept Drvaspa securely imprisoned, but with time, many of my brethren have ascended, shedding their immortal forms, to join with the Spenta. As we have become fewer and involved

305

ourselves less in human affairs, Drvaspa has begun to flex against our control. Her prison is cracking and as it does, her influence seeps between the stones, finding its way into Shadow Beasts."

Zemfira listened in awe. Xavapar fixed her with his golden eyes once more and continued.

"Drvaspa seeks full release. To open the prison, she requires five Lightcasters to break the five locks: one with Thirst, one with Hunger, one with Fatigue, one with Aging—and one with Depravity."

Zemfira swallowed. "So that's why she wants me alive."

"Yes," said Xavapar. "She needs you. The other four are already her prisoners and have been in her power for many years. They remain alive because Drvaspa has been waiting for you. She has been waiting for a very long time."

"*Her* prisoners?" asked Hami. "How does she have prisoners? I thought she was the prisoner."

Xavapar showed no annoyance at Hami's interjection. "She is imprisoned, but cannot be too closely guarded. We never enter the temple complex for fear she might infect us with whatever brought the darkness into her essence. And so she holds a sphere of influence around her cell. During the phases when her power is waxing, she has extended her power over the locals who live in that jungle, and over the Shadow Beasts who hunt them. She commands obedience with an ease the rest of us do not possess. These unwilling servants bring her Lightcasters and care for them, so that she may be ready when a Lightcaster with Depravity arose."

"Why don't you kill her?" asked Zemfira. "Why lock her up if she's so evil?"

"Celestial Ones do not die. We only transcend immortality when we are ready. And even if we could kill Drvaspa, we would not do so."

"But why—"

"Because we are the force of creation, Zemfira. We do not kill. It goes against our nature."

"You kill Shadow Beasts."

"We create balance within Shadow Beasts. They are empty beings, and we exist to oppose them. Unless Drvaspa decays into a Deva, we cannot end her existence. As long as she remains a being of creation, she is beyond our jurisdiction."

Zemfira heaved a breath. "So I must wait until Shadow Beasts drag me to my doom?"

"No," said Xavapar. "There is another path. If you take this Flash Gate straight across the continent, you will enter the temple and bypass the Shadow Beasts that lurk in those perilous jungles. You can safely enter those sacred grounds without resorting                    to                    battle."

"But won't I simply fall under the spell of this Celestial One?" asked Zemfira.

"Her influence fluctuates," said Xavapar. "It grows, then it ebbs back, almost to nothing. However in the last twenty years it has waxed far more than it has waned. In the past, she could only exert her influence one day every ten years—she has expanded her influence into a month every year. Her power is currently receding like water from the shore, meaning you have a chance to strike: seven days before she regains her strength."

"How?" asked Zemfira, frowning.

"The crystals that energize the prison have dimmed, as lightstone tends to over many centuries. They must be recharged, and you alone among mortals can do so. It is a time-consuming process, and will leave your soul fragile, but once you do this vital work and free the prisoners, you can escape to safety, knowing that a most dangerous being is once again locked away."

Zemfira frowned, wondering how Xavapar intended her to fight her way out of the temple, through the hordes of Shadow Beasts and into an unfamiliar jungle. Then comprehension dawned. "There's another Flash Gate in the prison, isn't there?"

The Celestial One nodded. "You will go with a few companions. After each exertion you will draw on their comfort and sustain your soul. Within four days, you will be free of this duty."

"Four days?" cried Zemfira. "But I do not have time, Lord Xavapar. My father and brother are in peril!"

Xavapar's beak tightened. "Yes," he said. "Your brother may survive and become a slave, but your father is being held by the king's torturers. Presently they will begin their interrogation, which will end in his death. You have my condolences."

"I can't let them die. I must save them!"

"You cannot sacrifice the kingdom and the continent for the sake of kin. Act selflessly now and protect millions: otherwise many shall die to the advances of the Shadow Beasts, and Drvaspa will eventually escape her shackles."

"Then can't you save my father and brother? Can't you appear before the king, tell him what threat menaces the land? Can't you counsel him to let the Soulgivers live?"

Xavapar folded his hands in his lap. "We no longer intervene in Farsia, especially not to counsel kings. Our primary duty requires we keep greater evil at bay, but we cannot teach goodness. Virtue which flows from the threat of violence is no virtue. The motivation for good must come from people themselves. I speak with you because your morality is not muddled. You see the complexities, and fear absolutes. I can neither expend myself to save two human lives any more than I can order a monarch to decree equality. It would be meaningless, in the end."

"Meaningless?     Preserving hundreds of innocent Soulgivers?  How is that meaningless?"

Xavapar shook his head. "You do not understand.  It is with the vantage of time and experience that one can see suffering and pain.  Human hands must fix matters.  I can provide the agent, you, with the knowledge you need, but I cannot be the agent myself.  There is a Deva emerging from the Menog, and I must combat it before it makes contact with Drvaspa and wakens her from that forced slumber."

"I'll do whatever you want, just save my family.  Please, Lord Xavapar."

The Celestial One rose slowly to his feet.  "I cannot fight to save your family without creating more evil in the world, wickedness that preys on other families, on other children.  You know there is no infinity: that is merely the illusion of the gods.  You can thank me for your gift of Depravity, or curse me for it.  My actions against a Voidicant in Lydia, sixteen years ago, took a feather from my wings and pierced it through your soul.  If you wish to prevent a similar fate for your successors, to prevent deaths like those you've witnessed, you will step through that portal and find the temple complex in eastern Hindusia, and seal the prison."

"You want me to abandon my family?  You think I can let them die?"

"If Drvaspa triumphs, the world will end.  She will destroy it and we cannot stop her.  Consider the stakes.  Choose wisdom over selfishness: protect many lives, rather than a select few."

"If you help me, I will do what you want."

The Celestial One glowed.  "You cannot bargain with me. I fight a crusade against dissolution: conceding on principles is a tactical defeat.  Your choice is part of that war—and you must make your decision, uncompelled. I must leave now—you do not have much time left."

"Why is there not much time?" demanded Zemfira.

"May fortune bless you," said Xavapar, and he stepped into the Flash Gate. The brightness overwhelmed Zemfira momentarily, then the Celestial One was gone. The particles in the air calmed. The light returned to a steady glow.

"I don't believe this," said Zemfira, as Hami took her hand. "I have to—I have to go to this temple, and—and stop this being                from                escaping."

"I'll go with you," said Hami. "As long as I can help, I'll come along. You won't be alone."

Zemfira hugged him. "I can't put you in danger," she said. "You should stay here, or—"

There was a rumbling above. Both froze, and listened. The earth trembled, a few loose crystals jangling. The rumbling receded, and again all was calm. They looked at each other, hearts slamming against their chests.

"What was that?"

Zemfira shook her head and stood up. "We need to think of what to do. We need to inform Roya of the situation—and we need supplies. Give me just a minute."

Hami remained seated as Zemfira paced, fists clenched. How could a Celestial One, a being of pure virtue, put her in such an awful position?

"I don't know if I can do it," said Zemfira. "How could I live with myself if I didn't try to save Jabo and Kuzro? Kuzro risked everything to save me. I can't let him die. I just—"

"Roya's coming," said Hami. "Maybe she can go to Issos while we go east."

Zemfira looked up and blinked as she saw a bridge of darkness extend over the water and Roya walk across it, hands held out on either side. She stepped onto the sand, looking grim. She noticed the open Flash Gate, but only nodded.

"Do not go through that gate until everyone has passed through it, or it will close."

"Everyone?" said Zemfira. "Why everyone? Aren't most people staying here? Master Roya, we just encountered—"

"I cannot waste time with speech," said Roya. "Hami, protect her from any falling debris. Keep her alive at all costs."

"What's going on?" asked Hami, voice trembling.

Roya was already casting a bridge back to the far shore. "We are under attack," said the rebel commander. "And we won't be able to fend them off. We will evacuate everyone, or die trying."

And she strode back across the bridge, drawing a long knife and her sword.

# CHAPTER 29 – CLEANSING

Firuzeh waited until dusk had settled on the desert before ordering the attack. She had been itching to begin the assault for days now, waiting with boiling impatience in the tents by the dunes. Now it was time to bring an end to this blight of Depravity. Now it was time to exterminate the Soulbreaker resistance.

Sandstorms had prevented Firuzeh's lookouts from seeing Kuzro leave the rock formation, but a hidden sentry sighted him on the desert road, clinching the matter for Firuzeh. There was no place for the man to come from, except through the rocks. She had called for reinforcements, and continued to steer lizards between the boulders. This proved difficult: they did not last long in her control, but she did manage to glimpse the valley, the tree, and the temple.

Capturing the father had been simple. He had some skill with Sproutcasting, but he was hopelessly outnumbered. Firuzeh had wanted to kill him immediately, but Sahin had requested him brought to Issos. The Soulbreakers' hideout was already known, but the Captain of the Cleansers was curious about the finer points of the rebellion. It would also free Firuzeh from the burden of taking prisoners. With the exception of Princess

Stateira, were she even still alive, everyone within could be killed without hesitation.

Firuzeh had fifty Cleansers and three hundred soldiers under her command, not to mention the small army of Temperaturecasters who were being kept in reserve. She sent her Insightcasters and Shadowcasters to blind and confuse any rebels who could raise an alarm. Then Firuzeh commanded the Infernocasters and Stonecasters to unleash their power upon the temple. Boulders flew like meteors and flames surged upon the enemy base. Firuzeh heard the first screams, then the remaining forces advanced on the damaged temple and began the slaughter.

Firuzeh led the main battalion. Without any viable animals nearby, she would rely on her own senses. She led the Sproutcaster division at the center of the advance. There was no time to marvel at the tree, growing in the desert of emptiness. Her mission came first.

Bodies already littered the stone bricks as they descended the tight staircase. There were screams and clashes of metal—dull explosions of Casting battles.

"Why is the assault slowing?" demanded Firuzeh, drawing both her swords.

"There's resistance at the bottom of the staircase," said a soldier. "When we break it, we can crush them and they'll have no place to go."

These words displeased Firuzeh. An ancient temple like this, having already been weakened by their initial assault, could be brought down by too much Stonecasting, killing soldiers and rebels alike. If the Soulbreakers realized their cause was hopeless, they might undermine the temple themselves as a final, suicidal, act of revenge. Firuzeh wondered what tricks Roya would employ to escape this time. Firuzeh didn't intend to give her the chance.

They pushed down the stairs, reaching a broken dining area. Tables lay smashed and flames flickered over shattered ceramic shards. Monks and children fled down a further staircase, while rebel warriors stood their ground and wrought havoc. One woman, an Infernocaster with billowing robes, wove rings of fire above her head. She hurled the flames at individual soldiers and Cleansers, consuming them in a deadly blaze.

"Stormcasters, now!" shouted Firuzeh.

Howling winds surged from their coordinated strike, blowing flames back onto the Soulbreakers, but this did not deter the Infernocaster. She transformed her embers into javelins of fire, which shot through the wind and struck unprepared soldiers with an eruption of sparks. Firuzeh had to use both swords to deflect a javelin shot at her and smashed it into the tiles. The heat of the projectile turned the stone to dripping magma.

"Quench her!"

The remaining Stormcasters released a torrent upon the defenders. The rush of water dislodged the Soulbreakers from their position and sent them retreating towards the staircase.

The Infernocaster did not flee. She struggled to her feet with water weighing down her robes, ready to fight. Before she could cast, two soldiers cut her down. The Infernocaster lay dying in a puddle, her own blood spilling out and running between the tiles. The remaining stragglers were massacred. Not wasting time, Firuzeh's forces advanced towards the stairs and the floor below.

Vines shot up between the tiles, scattering the attackers. The rebels knew they had nowhere to run and fought their inevitable doom with ferocity and desperation. Firuzeh decided to add a flank to this vertical battle. She ordered her Stonecasters back across the waterlogged chamber, to create an opening in the floor and flank the Soulbreakers.

Firuzeh's Stonecasters smashed through the tiles and formed an uneven ramp from the rubble. Rebels screamed as royal Infernocasters and Shadowcasters descended and unleashed mayhem from behind. Firuzeh stayed with the frontal assault on the stairs, which gained ground as Soulbreakers broke off to repel the new attackers.

Firuzeh slashed a Soulbreaker's throat open, pushing the body down the last stairs, and reached the floor of bed mats. The defenders were fleeing again, presumably to make a final stand deeper in the temple. Injured rebels and monks trying to hide among the corpses were efficiently dispatched.

"Regroup here," called Firuzeh. "Casters, replenish yourselves. Fortify—"

Before Firuzeh could finish the order, two girls and a boy emerged from a sleeping niche, swords drawn. The boy slammed his palm against the tiles, spreading icy particles across the floor that froze Firuzeh's boots to the ground. He pointed his sword at the nearest Cleanser, the blade glowing red from his heat, and released a blast of hot air. The force knocked the soldier across the room and into the stone wall, skin blistered.

One of the girls spun a tail of fire around herself, and her whole body began to glisten with flames. She lacked the precision of the Infernocasting Soulbreaker above, but she didn't need it. She released a wave of fire that scattered the royal battalions—those who had blocked with their bucklers were now isolated.

"Stormcasters!" shouted Firuzeh. "Wash them away!"

But this was a mistake. The last girl, ready for the torrent, tossed handfuls of seeds into the water, seeds that burst into networks of seaweed and thorny vines. The new foliage rooted itself to the submerged tiles, impeding the soldiers' advance.

Undeterred, Firuzeh waded the swamp, blocking gusts of fire with her silver-augmented swords. A wave of cold hit her, but it was delivered too quickly to pierce her enchanted armor. She slashed forward, sliced through a snaking vine and knocked the boy's sword from his hands. The Infernocaster girl tried to intercept Firuzeh, but she kicked the brat away and stabbed the Sproutcasting girl through the stomach. The Sproutcaster's eyes went wide as Firuzeh pushed her into the water.

"Nava!" screamed the boy.

Firuzeh swung her sword at him, but an iron spear blocked her killing stroke. A broad-shouldered and well-armored man had returned from the fleeing rebels to protect these whelps.

"Get back," he shouted. "Get out of here!  Now!"

He lunged his spear at Firuzeh, forcing her back. The Sproutcaster girl lay dying in the seaweed she had created, but the other two made their escape while they could. Firuzeh would kill them as soon as this Soulbreaker was dead.

"What's your name?" he demanded, swinging his sword against her swords in a scream of metal. "I like to know the names of my opponents before I kill them."

"I am Firuzeh," she replied, calm and almost amused.

"And I am Yashar," said the Soulbreaker. "Your massacre ends here."

He attacked again. Firuzeh intended to block, slide in, and slice the man's throat, but the blow was too strong—it jarred her, numbing her arm. His physical strength was staggering.

"I forgot how cowardly you Cleansers are," said Yashar. "Eager to surprise a settlement and murder unarmed monks, but unable to match us in combat."

"You are verbose," said Firuzeh, ducking under the spear and trying to slide along it to strike a quick blow from the sword, but Yashar shifted his weight and delivered a sharp kick. His armored boot hit her in the chest and knocked her into the water, one sword spinning out of her grasp.

Yashar didn't waste time gloating; he lunged for the kill. Firuzeh tried to fling herself aside, but she was too winded. His muscles tensed as he thrust his spear downwards, when a bolt of bright energy hit Yashar in the eyes, making him recoil. A royal Lightcaster had intervened, just in time. Then a vine whipped up through the water and caught Yashar's ankle. He cut himself free and stabbed blindly at Firuzeh with his spear, the heavy blade catching the edge of her wet cloak.

A stone hit Yashar in the chest, knocking him back and disarming him. He did not fumble for his dropped spear, but drew his sword and blocked the next rock aside, then stamped down on Firuzeh's ankle. She gasped, and cut at his thigh, which made him back up. An arrow stuck Yashar in the shoulder as Firuzeh staggered to her feet. He tried to attack but two more hit his arm and stomach.

The wounds slowed him, giving Firuzeh the opening to pivot and ram her sword through the Soulbreaker's neck. His death was swift and bloody. Yashar's body fell into the water, just as Nava expired next to him. But there were also many dead and wounded Cleansers, brave soldiers who had fought valiantly for the safety of the kingdom.

"Onward," said Firuzeh, feeling her ribs and wincing at her tender ankle. "Reassemble your groups. We must cleanse this hell of its demons."

The Soulbreakers continued their retreat. Despite their greater power, they lacked the cohesion of the royal army. The element of surprise had been decisive. Firuzeh monitored her warriors, making sure none were too drained. As long as they did not break formation, this rebellion would be crushed.

There were etchings on the wall, Firuzeh could see—etchings she would try to preserve for Sahin's curiosity. Blood was already drying on symbols Firuzeh could not read. But this floor was almost deserted. The royal forces advanced, cautious of any ambushes.

"Lightcasters," called Firuzeh. "Illuminate."

The Lightcasters sent out orbs that floated over the statues and scattered scrolls. The passage ended in tunnels, into which wounded Soulbreakers were filing. Firuzeh raised a hand and archers drew their bows, downing the last few stragglers as they attempted to escape further into the earth. The soldiers advanced, two hundred and fifty able-bodied fighters. The Soulbreakers had no chance against them.

As the advance troop reached the tunnel and killed the moaning Soulbreakers who had survived the arrow volley, they encountered a wall of fresh rock. Their quarry must have erected it, a frantic attempt to delay the inevitable. Firuzeh called on her Temperaturecasters to heat up the rock, making it easier for Stonecasters to blast their way through. The stone was thick, but it would not stop a disciplined legion of Stonecasters.

After a great effort, the royal forces punched a hole through the rock and scattered fragments. Immediately, a tongue of darkness lashed through the opening and wrapped around a screaming Cleanser. He was dead before a Lightcaster could sever the connection. Firuzeh smelled a familiar odor of rotten flesh, which she remembered from the warehouse in Rasparad. She knew who was Shadowcasting.

"Lightcasters, strike now!" shouted Firuzeh. "Roya is here. She's the head of the rebellious viper. Cut her down and we will quell this depravity!"

Archers shot beams of light through the gap while the Stonecasters battered the stone. But the resistance was fiercer—the Stonecaster who had erected the barrier was flinging stones back—hitting the archers with a maelstrom of gravel. Roya stood just beyond their reach, tendrils of darkness uncurling from her fingers, driving themselves into Cleanser after Cleanser. She was not hasty: she focused on each target and killed them. Firuzeh beat back the darkness with her augmented swords. Roya would not get the best of her again.

Slowly, the barrier was breaking, despite the losses Firuzeh's troops were sustaining. Roya changed tactics, drawing a veil of darkness down like a curtain, which the royal Lightcasters had to counteract. This darkness was so thick that it was difficult to breathe: Firuzeh resisted even as she felt the shadows pervade her brain with fear and despair.

"How many are through the gate?" Roya's voice was loud, a shout to a lieutenant in the chaos of the battle. Firuzeh frowned. What was the rebel commander talking about?

"Have Hami maintain a sand bridge," came her voice again. "He can go through with Zemfira, at the end. Go."

Firuzeh closed her eyes and scanned the presences around her. There was so much human energy around her, rich with the scent of killing and terror. She perceived a few rats and she focused on one, exerting her dominion on it. She had to see what was happening.

The rat had poor eyesight, and relying on smell was difficult, given all the blood, but Firuzeh forced the rodent up over a corpse to observe Soulbreakers falling back through a tunnel. Roya stood in the passage, darkness flowing from her skin in deadly ribbons. She noticed the rat.

"Squash it," she said, the words distorted by the rat's sensory organs.

A Stonecaster raised a rock and dropped it on the little creature. Firuzeh tried to dodge away, but pain overwhelmed her and ejected her from the dead being. As she shuddered back into her human body, the darkness lifted.

"Go, Master Roya," shouted the Stonecaster. "I'll hold them. You cannot be lost here."

Pitiful, thought Firuzeh. She strode forward, among the Lightcasting archers, and flung her sword at Roya. The Shadowcaster dodged it and with impossible speed, grabbed it by the handle from the air. Still using her momentum, she spun and flung it, impaling a Lightcaster against the stone. She was weaving between the gleaming arrows, knocking several aside. She was terrifyingly powerful.

"The ceiling!" called Firuzeh. "Stonecasters, Stormcasters: strike!"

Roya was not invincible. She had to retreat as lightning and water rushed from the front and stones fell from the ornate ceiling. The other Soulbreaker stayed. He spun the rocks out of the air, hurling them back. Firuzeh lunged forward, sliding beneath a blast of rock and kicking the Stonecaster off balance.

Disoriented, the Soulbreaker stumbled and an arrow hit him first in the arm, then in the eye—a ray of light that did not fade until the Soulbreaker collapsed. It had been an expensive kill, but Roya was running, and there was no one to seal up the gap.

"Our quarry is running out of hiding places," shouted Firuzeh. "Advance and destroy them."

The Lightcasters hurried forward, sending light ahead to show them the way. The remaining Stonecasters followed, to deal with any blockades or falling rock. Firuzeh led the Stormcasters, ready to end this uprising at the end of the tunnel.

They emerged onto a beach in a vast, lake-filled cavern. Roya was running along a bridge of sand, which led across the water and to a glowing island. A Lightcasting Cleanser ran forward but the bridge collapsed under his feet—it only supported the rebel's weight.

"Archers and Temperaturecasters!" shouted Firuzeh as Roya reached the island. "Form up and end this!"

But Firuzeh could see Roya jump through the gleaming light and vanish, saw a malnourished boy kiss a girl on the cheek and jump through. Then Firuzeh saw the girl who had eluded them for over a year: the girl who had escaped them in Rasparad. She stepped through and was gone.

Firuzeh stood still, the light spiraling into nothingness. The cavern was quiet. She gave a toneless order—told the Temperaturecasters to freeze a path across, to investigate. Firuzeh knew they would find nothing on the other side. Despite the devastating assault Firuzeh had unleashed upon the Soulbreakers, the accursed Shadowcaster had slipped through their fingers.

"It's a Flash Gate," reported one of the Lightcasters. "They could be anywhere."

"And none of you can open it," said Firuzeh, flatly.

They Lightcasters exchanged looks. "We have not learned the ritual, and only with the Cost of Aging could a skilled Lightcaster have enough power."

Firuzeh nodded, keeping her savage disappointment in check. "Search for any remaining Soulbreakers and kill them. We will set up camp in the upper levels. Tomorrow, we depart for Ektabana."

She retraced the path through the tunnel. She could not blame herself for a Flash Gate: it could not have been foreseen.

But she was curious where the rebels would turn up and how they would be thwarted. She had to contact Sahin immediately.

# CHAPTER 30 – ISSOS

Zemfira's consciousness was fused with her soul and amplified and expanded beyond mortal comprehension. She sensed a whole world spanning vast continents, felt the presence of each temple on these continents as throbbing heartbeats, and knew where she had to go. On the edge of her awareness, far to the east, her objective pulsed like an ethereal heart: the temple prison for Drvaspa.

But to the west, Zemfira felt a tug—a collection of points by the coast of the Western Sea. She had never seen the Western Sea, had no intimate knowledge of Issos. But the heartbeats representing temples spoke to her, telling her their names in countless languages: she knew which temples were for Hunger, which ones belonged to Aging. She could even tell which temples had buried Flash Gates: they exuded deeper pulses. She wondered if this was how Celestial Ones perceived things—if they simply knew the world in its detail without being there.

Xavapar had been clear. She had to save the kingdom and surrender the lives of her family. She had begged Roya to help, but Roya had not given her an answer, being more preoccupied with evacuation. Roya would go with her soldiers and civilians. There had been no time to assemble a rescue team, no time to save two lives when so many were already dying. And Zemfira knew she was going to disobey Xavapar.

"Are you sure about this?" Hami had asked. "You don't want to go to the temple of Drvaspa? I'll come with you. I'm not afraid."

"Go to Harauvatis with the others," said Zemfira. "I have other business to attend to."

It had been awful to see the panic in all the faces running for the Flash Gate, but worse were the faces she hadn't seen. Nava, Yashar, Kalpana—worst of all, Tryphon. According to Milad, the Targu had been meditating at the entrance of the temple and was the first victim of the Cleansers. Falling stone killed him. Perhaps he did not even feel it.

Zemfira could not linger forever in this limbo state. She guided her flowing presence to the west, to the pinprick on a little glowing palace, reserved for royal monks only. Approaching it in this ethereal manner Zemfira sensed a great swell of humanity, represented by pulses to the north—was it the Farsian army stationed at Issos? She poured herself towards the royal temple and instantly physicality encircled her, the expansive sense of geography vanished, and she felt her body again. She was in the royal temple at Issos.

She landed in a crouch, sword strapped across her back. Her eyes adjusted. The dark room glowed from the crystal behind her, not unlike the minerals hanging from the cavern she had just departed. The air tasted different: both like perfume and salt. In the distance she could hear birds chattering, despite the nighttime darkness. She edged forward along a passage bathed in moonlight. There were glass windows in this modest temple. Monks slept on linen bedrolls. None of them stirred.

Zemfira was about to exit the temple and enter the rest of the palace when she heard hurried footsteps. Not knowing what to do, she tucked herself behind a statue and hoped the shadows would hide her. She held her sword ready, heart thudding.

A palace servant rushed past and shouted. "Wake, wake! We must depart, one and all!"

"What is the purpose of this noise?" asked a monk. "We are not the maids or cooks —what justifies such rudeness?"

"I apologize," said the servant. "Forgive me, but the kingdom is doomed. King Artashata was defeated in battle."

"What?"

"A messenger has just arrived, running straight from the routed army. If we are to stay free citizens of Farsia, we must flee."

"We are royal monks," said the Targu, an old woman with a headband laced with gold. "We will not be harmed. The Hellenics respect our rights as vessels of divinity."

"Do you not understand?" cried the messenger. "King Artashata was defeated! His army was scattered, his mobile treasury abandoned, but his queen and daughter are still here. The Hellenics are coming, and there won't be any respect for your sanctity now! King Artashata cannot protect you. You must flee!"

The monks exchanged looks. Zemfira held her breath, hoping none of them was an Insightcaster. Thankfully they were too preoccupied with the staggering news to notice her.

"If the Hegemon is on his way, then the queen and princess must be the top priority," said the Targu.

"They will be escorted east by the Captain of the Cleansers and the King's Dualcaster, but they cannot move faster than the Hellenic cavalry. We servants are retreating south, to Mudraya. The Satrap can make a stand at the delta. It is our best hope."

The monks murmured with each other, then the Targu nodded. "Monks are always welcome in the land of the pharaohs. We will join you."

Zemfira waited, each minute an agony, as the monks left their quarters, bed mats rolled and few possessions bundled. She wished she had learned what was happening to the prisoners, but perhaps this environment of confusion would work to her benefit. Maybe the prisoners would be abandoned—but maybe they would be slaughtered.

After waiting another minute, making sure the monks did not return, Zemfira darted out and ran along an elevated courtyard. She passed a splashing fountain and a hanging garden, then came to an abrupt stop as she caught sight of the ocean. The moon flickered off its surface, and even at a distance, Zemfira was awestruck by this massive sweep of water. How could the king dominate this expanse with mere ships? But she had to focus. She set off running again, bare feet skimming the steps soundlessly.

The dungeons would be at the bottom of the palace. She slipped through a door to the servant staircase and dashed down it. This was not the main palace in the capital. This one was smaller, as regional palaces tended to be, yet she still found herself descending hundreds of stairs.

"Where are you going?" demanded a servant, who was hurrying upstairs with clean blankets.

Zemfira almost lost her nerve, but said, "One of the Zealots forgot their sword, so I'm bringing it to—"

"Don't wave it around like that, you idiot," snapped the servant. "This is no time to pretend to be a warrior. The Hellenics are not that close yet."

Zemfira bowed her head, hoping the servant wouldn't register her Baxtrian accent. She sheathed the sword, and continued her descent.

"Which way to the dungeons?" she asked a cook who was hastily pulling provisions from the kitchen cupboards.

"Why?" asked the cook, voice sharp. "And who are you, carrying a sword?"

"It's for one of the guards."

"They're evacuating, haven't you heard? What useless courtier recruited you?"

"What about the Sproutcaster who helped the Soulgiv— um—the Soulbreakers?"

The cook was looking suspicious now. "Captain Sahin interviewed him this afternoon, he was slated for execution tomorrow, but after all this—"

"Which way? It's urgent."

"Get out of my way. Go down the corridor and down the stairs to the right—but this is no time to think about prisoners, unless you want to become one yourself!"

Zemfira rushed down the stairs, a stitch in her side. She smelled the wet stone and tasted the dampness.

There were no guards. Torches flickered and sputtered, slapping the rusty bars with waves of orange glow. She drew her sword. The sound of sliding metal was comforting, but it echoed in the silent space. But Zemfira could hear soft crying.

"Father?"

The crying stopped. "Who's there?"

It was not Kuzro—the voice was far more high-pitched and nasal. Zemfira didn't answer, but advanced slowly. The cells were dark, even with the torches, so Zemfira pulled an orb of light into the palm of her hand and sent it up to float. The little glow illuminated the tight cells. Most were empty, but some had

327

cowering, huddled figures. Zemfira could smell the mess of urine and feces.

"Do you have the keys? Can you get us out?"

The voice was desperate and shrill. Zemfira saw the man in the next cell, mostly naked and emaciated. His eyes were very wide. Zemfira swallowed, but she had to move on.

"Kuzro?" she called. "Are you here?"

"Who are you looking for?" snarled a gruffer voice.

"My father. The Sproutcaster who the Cleansers—"

"Right at the end," said the man, coughing up phlegm. "He's—he's still alive."

"And his son?"

"Probably."

Zemfira thanked him, but wished she hadn't looked into his cell. There were cockroaches crawling over his naked limbs and beard. Zemfira hurried on, checking every cell, just in case. One woman, she was certain, was dead.

She found her father at the very end, sitting in the center of his cell with an Iron Necklace digging into his throat. He stared vacantly ahead—not seeing her. His beard had grown messy and his cheeks had hollowed.

"Father! Father!"

"Zemfira? Is that really you?"

She almost did not recognize Jabo. He had grown in the past year—taller and narrower than she remembered. His prison tunic was too small, and he looked sick. Zemfira wanted to cry, and she felt the tears heating up her eyes.

"It's me. I'm going to get you out."

"But how—aren't the guards—"

"They're all gone. The Hegemon is approaching, and they all fled. I'll get you out."

"Hurry," said Jabo. "They did something to Father—he's trapped, somehow."

Zemfira could now see the dark halo swirling around Kuzro's head, wobbling slowly over his eyes. It exuded an aura of incomprehensible whispers.

"Wait," said Zemfira, "I'll hack the lock open and then we'll deal with—"

"Zemfira, look out!" squealed Jabo.

Zemfira turned to see a cloaked figure on the far side of the corridor, a sword in one hand, a silver buckler on his arm. He wore royal armor: a strange combination of a Zealot's helmet and a Cleanser's metal-studded boots. He was young and bearded, with a strange intensity in his eyes.

"I detected a Soulbreaker nearing the royal quarters, but then you darted into the prison—why?"

He spoke with an accent like Tryphon's. Zemfira assumed a defensive position, sword held in both hands. She wished she could tie her hair back, but there was no time. What could she do with her Lightcasting that would stun him long enough to land a lethal hit?

"Who are you?" demanded the royalist. "What are you doing down here? Are you here to rescue the—" The man broke off, and almost lowered his sword. "You're—Zemfira, aren't you?"

Zemfira said nothing.

"But how did you get here? How did you get to the top of the palace without being noticed, only to descend—unless you're with—"

"I'm not with anybody," said Zemfira. "I'm here for my father—and I'll kill you if I have to."

He looked disconcerted. "I'm Volakles."

Zemfira's jaw tightened. "How do you know who I am?"

329

"He's the Cleanser who was chasing you," said Jabo. "He's the one Father fought in Rasparad! He was here when they interrogated Father!"

Zemfira looked at Volakles, wondering what words could save her. "Why don't you go protect your queen? I—we're not evil. We're just trying to survive."

"I don't think I can let you go," said Volakles, flicking his sword twice. "Not even if the king is running for his life. You are still my objective—even deferred, that does not change. I would rather not do this in front of your father and brother—but I have no choice. No Soulbreaker will get anywhere near the royal family."

"You're a monster," said Zemfira. "Just let us go, you know we mean the king no harm!"

"You've been living with the woman who stole the princess for a year."

"Wouldn't you? If you were hunted and almost killed? How loyal would you remain, if you knew your king disdained and feared you?"

"I am a soldier," said Volakles. "It is not my place to question the monarch. I only carry out orders."

"Why?"

"Because—" Volakles froze. Even forty meters away, Zemfira saw his body tense, saw him turn to face the steps. He glanced back immediately at Zemfira.

"Was this your plan? To distract me, delay me, trap me? You—"

"What are you talking about?"

"You said you were alone! I should be wiser than to take the word of a Soulbreaker, but—"

Zemfira heard the boots clacking down the steps and saw the dark form of Roya approaching. Her heartbeat sped up.

Roya had come to assist her and save Kuzro. She didn't have to worry about any single Cleanser now. She had the rebel commander with her.

"I know you," said Roya. "But you shouldn't be alive."

"I was hoping you would come eventually," said Volakles, his voice becoming grittier. "I just hoped I'd encounter you better prepared, not trapped in a corridor."

"How did you survive the Gloom?"

"I found a way."

Roya walked forward calmly. "It doesn't matter anymore. Now, if you wouldn't mind, let me pass. I have no quarrel with you—if you wish to fight me later, that is your right. But right now, I have some business I need to finish."

Dread coalesced in Zemfira's stomach as memories on a cavern beach floated back to her.

"What?" asked Volakles. He had his back to the wall, sword and buckler at the ready to engage. "What business?"

"You followed me here—to kill me?" asked Zemfira.

"Necessary and unavoidable," said Roya. "This is not revenge, merely politics."

"Politics?" asked Zemfira. "Because I didn't join up? Because I had doubts?"

Roya walked past Volakles, who tensed but did not strike. He seemed unwilling to begin fighting—was he trembling?

"Not anything so emotional," said Roya. "The fiasco at Jalehravan will be blamed on me, while you will be lauded for sending the survivors to safety. Some might even consider you an alternate leader within our cause, and I cannot risk you weakening my authority. There is too much at stake. You have served your purpose."

She drew her sword and knife. "If you had only completed the task a few days sooner, all of this could have been avoided—but I'm afraid this must be the way."

"You're going to kill her?" asked Volakles, dumbfounded.

"You should run now if you wish to live," said Roya. "I have spent enough time toying with you. Bother me anymore and we'll see if you can escape death with a severed head."

"I'm not letting you escape," said Volakles.

"If you wish to fight me," said Roya, "Wait until I have finished her—my expended energy may give you the chance to match me."

Volakles lunged forward. "Don't tell me how to fight!"

Roya turned, knife clashing on sword, sword clashing on shield. Volakles's cloak billowed and his sword hummed through the air. Metal screeched as Roya struck, again and again. Her unpredictable sword slashes and her rapid knife jabs forced Volakles back. Roya dodged forward and kicked her boot against Volakles's exposed shin, causing him to stumble.

"What are you waiting for?" asked Jabo. "Aren't you going to fight?"

Zemfira had been transfixed by the flashes of steel and wanted to help, but didn't see an opening. If she struck at the wrong moment, she would doom Volakles and herself.

"You've improved," Roya said, feinting left and flicking a shallow cut across Volakles's wrist. "But I still wield the power of Depravity. You cannot compete on my level."

Roya swung her sword, the blade arcing with a trail of darkness. The blade hit Volakles's sword with so much power that the sword fell from his grasp. Volakles blocked and retreated, using his shield and Insight to stave off Roya's attacks. Even so, Volakles was straining against the vicious assault, jabs from the knife catching his arms and thigh. He was in trouble.

Zemfira ran forward. Light formed in her mind and energy coursed through her blood. She knew how to channel her Casting for combat, she had fought under Yashar's guidance for many months. Light curled around her blade and Zemfira struck.

Roya turned and blocked Zemfira's attack, but the strength of the blow made the rebel commander stumble. She had to twist away as Zemfira slashed again, sparks flying from her sword

"How did you learn—" Roya pivoted left and spun the shadows around her dagger. She pinned Zemfira's sword with her own, then stabbed with her knife at Zemfira's neck. Acting on instinct, Zemfira flashed light from her palm into Roya's eyes, dodged the knife and twisted her sword free. She backed up as Roya's eyesight returned.

"Clever trick," she snarled. "But my version is more effective."

Roya was now delving deeper into her Depravity, causing darkness to spill from her in spiraling tongues. The shadows blinded Zemfira and muffled all sound. She backed up, suspecting Roya would kill her first, since she wore no armor. Zemfira ignited a ball of light in her palm but the darkness was oppressively thick. The shadows devoured her light hungrily. Zemfira struggled to breathe. It was almost like being under water.

Unwilling to give up, Zemfira unleashed a radiant star to cut through the shadows. The star spun and shredded the oppressive veil around her, letting her breathe. Then Zemfira realized that the darkness must be pressing on Jabo and her father too. She had to do more than escape it: she had to repel it.

Her soul shuddered, a sign that she was expending herself, but Zemfira didn't care. She pushed light through the glowing star in her palm, through the blade of her sword, through the surface of her skin. She pummeled the darkness with

333

illumination, even as her Cost pummeled her soul. There was no fight beyond this struggle: if Roya attacked now, she was doomed, but Zemfira could not stop.

The darkness fragmented. Patches of visibility opened, and Zemfira's glowing sword struck the darkness with a blow that pushed it back, revealing the fight between Volakles and Roya. He had regained his weapon, and was blocking the rebel commander from reaching Zemfira.

"You cannot be a Shadowcaster," Roya said, slashing at Volakles ferociously. "You are an *Insightcaster*!"

"You should have killed me properly," he said, parrying her strikes. "I am the product of your Depravity. I absorbed your curse and turn it back upon you."

"But you don't know how to use it," sneered Roya. "You are afraid."

"I don't need it," said Volakles. "I am not reliant—"

A black spike shot from his shadow on the wall and pierced him through the chest. He stared at it, shocked, as Roya raised her sword for the killing blow. Zemfira aimed her blade and released a burst of light. The bolt struck Roya in her raised arm and she gasped, sword falling from her grasp.

Zemfira could not sustain the bolt—her soul was too battered. It needed time and love to recover. But now Volakles was back on his feet, pale and determined.

"I told you, your Shadowcasting no longer works on me!"

There was a black burn on his armor, but he looked undeterred. He struck, faster and faster, pushing Roya back with his shield. Without her sword, Roya was using her Shadowcasting defensively while Volakles pushed his advantage. He smashed her in the chest with his shield and she fell to the ground, rolling twice. The knife, too, had fallen from her grasp.

Zemfira ran forward, but Roya turned to her with venom in her eyes, and made a fist. Darkness spiked out of the ground, out of her shadow, impaling Zemfira's calf and anchoring her to the spot. She screamed. The agony was not just in her flesh and bone, but in her terror, her despair, her anguish.

Another spike shot through her right thigh, then one pierced her shoulder. The pain was so intense it dissociated her from her body. Zemfira vaguely felt herself being lifted up by the darkness. She could sense her shadow bubbling beneath her. Roya would kill Zemfira in the moment of her own death, a final revenge. Volakles couldn't save her. But Zemfira couldn't let herself die, not when there was so much to do. She had to save her family.

Her determination crystallized her soul, and she tugged it, drawing energy into herself and expanding light from her body. She had to produce no shadow: she had to become as luminous as the sun or she would die. Her whole body glowed, growing warm, and the banded rainbow of light flooded from her skin. Hatred and bloodlust filled her thoughts, but she refused to validate the depravity, refused to give in, refused to break her concentration. The swirl of light stripped the dungeon of shadow and disintegrated the spikes impaling her. Zemfira fell to the ground, still wounded, but no longer in mortal peril.

She heard Roya's scream of frustration, and opened her eyes just in time to see the scream cut short by Volakles's sword. Zemfira closed her eyes again—she did not want to see the gore and blood—she just wanted to rest. Her soul was slowly stabilizing, despite the calamitous damage it had sustained. She had come close to losing control. She had almost given too much. She wondered if the Cleanser would kill her now too. She could not stop him without ruining her soul entirely.

She felt his hand on her shoulder. "Are you all right?"

"I don't know," she said.

She felt his fingers touch her calf and thigh where the dark spikes had penetrated. The tactile contact rekindled thoughts of drowning, of falling from high cliffs, of burning to death, and she gasped, but he was moving his fingers in little circles, drawing out the residue of shadow—leaving only flesh wounds.

"Are you going to kill me?" asked Zemfira, sitting up slowly.

Volakles wiped blood from his cheek where Roya's knife had cut him. He was bleeding from his shoulder too. He stared at her for a long time, eyes distorted by uncertainty.

"I should," said Volakles, sitting back and breathing hard. "It is my duty, but—"

"But you're a Soulgiver too, aren't you?"

"A Soulgiver? Do you mean Soulbreaker?" Volakles paused while Zemfira stayed silent. "When my partner and I were hunting you in Rasparad, Roya laid a curse upon me, which I survived only by absorbing it into my being. The curse became my Shadowcasting. For a while my new Shadowcasting had the same appetite as my Insight, but as time went on, it started— separating. I am not a regular Dualcaster—I don't feed two Castings with one Cost. Hunger gives me Insight and I trade Depravity for Shadow."

"Your fellow Cleansers attacked our Sanctuary tonight," said Zemfira. "They murdered dozens before we could escape: dozens like you, who didn't choose their fate."

"Hiding my truth has been my gravest shame these many months," said Volakles. "But once again I chose life above honor. I am, at my core, a coward."

"Me too," said Zemfira. "But you saved my life."

"As you saved mine," said Volakles. "Just as the world is ending."

"Because of the defeat of the king?"

Volakles nodded. "I do not know if Farsia can stop this Hegemon from marching all the way to Hindusia. The king was cautious: he prepared for every contingency, utilized every advantage, employed the best commanders... yet our army still failed. My home in Lydia is already firmly under Hellenic control."

"The world is changing," said Zemfira. "But it is far from over. Would you join us? We can join the surviving Soulgivers in Harauvatis, where we can build a new resistance, and—"

Volakles shook his head. "I cannot betray my oath."

"You've betrayed it already," said Zemfira. "You did not speak the full truth—you hid yourself from the king's judgment. Please, you can help us, help my father and brother, and we can help you."

"Even if I could, we cannot travel to Harauvatis—not speedily, and not while your father has been placed under the Dark Mirror."

"What is the Dark Mirror?"

Volakles shook his head. "An evil art of Shadowcasting, a way to trap a rebellious mind within their soul, to put a person in conflict with itself—less fatal, yet still worse, than the Gloom."

"How do you undo it?"

"Captain Sahin would have to, but he has already left with the queen, the dowager and the princess."

Zemfira stared at her father, and at her brother who still sat with his hands clutching the bars. "Please bring Jabo to safety. Take him south, to the next town. I will bring my father back."

"South? You said the goal was Harauvatis—to the east."

Zemfira nodded. "But there's a Flash Gate buried deep beneath Thebai, in Mudraya. I sensed it as I traveled here. If we get there, we can reach Arakhotoi much faster and link up with the other Soulgivers."

"You can open a *Flash Gate*?"

"It's how we arrived here."

"But you're barely an adult!"

Zemfira almost smiled. "Please get Jabo to safety. Knowing he's safe will restore my soul. We'll follow, I promise."

"The Hegemon—"

"I need to do this."

She held out her hand to him, and a momentary hesitation on Volakles's part, the Dualcaster took it, clasping it briefly.

"I've been having strange dreams," he said. "Not a premonition, but somehow, I knew this was the way it would be."

Zemfira bowed her head. "We have much to discuss, very soon. I am in your debt."

She hugged Jabo when Volakles let him out of the cell, feeling his brittle body. He was crying, and she was too.

"It's okay," she said, quietly. "I just need to help Father, and we will rejoin with you. I just can't concentrate if you're still in danger."

Jabo dripped snot from his nose. "I don't want to be separated again, it was too much, too horrible, to—"

"It won't be for long, and you can trust him, okay?"

"But he wanted to kill you."

"Yes," said Zemfira, looking into Volakles's ashamed eyes. "Yes he did. But he won't kill you. If he tries, he will have to deal with me. Go now."

The boy and the man hurried out of the prison, and Zemfira entered her father's cell. He still sat there, eyes vacant, a ring of darkness swiveling before his eyes. She sat down in front of him, crossed her legs, wincing at the pain from the wounds, and clasped his cold hands. She squeezed warmth into them, and closed her eyes. She would meditate, gather herself and find a way to release her father's soul.

# CHAPTER 31 – THE AFTERMATH

The air was heavy in the Satrap's dining room even with its arches open to the air. Paniz sat on the Harauvatian carpets with the others, listening to the chaotic dawn pull the city of Arakhotoi out of the night. The sounds of battle had passed, and the hacking of metal into flesh had ceased. A few fires still burned in the lower levels of the Satrap's palace, but these too were being extinguished. The atmosphere was almost calm.

"What is Lieutenant Musa doing, do you think?" asked Milad in a whisper.

There was no rule against speaking loudly, but since most Soulgivers here were tending to their wounds, sleeping or drinking tea, Paniz understood Milad's tone. Ardeshir leaned in, dabbing ointment on his burn.

"He's just securing palace defenses," said Paniz. "The Satrap isn't offering much resistance anymore."

When they had all tumbled through the Flash Gate and Roya had not appeared, her second-in-command, Musa, had taken charge and led the battered Soulgivers on a brutal capture of the palace. Caught off-guard, the Satrap's soldiers fell quickly and many were taken prisoner. Within hours, the Harauvatian capital lay in the hands of the rebels. Paniz wished she had seen less killing that night. Now she, Milad and Ardeshir were stuck with the children, the monks and the injured. Even Hami had been called away to duty, rebuilding archways that had collapsed.

"I wish Zemfira was here," said Ardeshir. "And Roya: I just don't understand how they could have missed our destination."

Jia-Fan sat with the princess in another corner. The girl had been drugged, rendered unconscious , so that Jia-Fan could bring her through the portal without her choosing a different location. Paniz wondered what would become of the girl. Would Roya still keep her alive, after the disaster at Jalehravan? She agreed with Ardeshir: she wanted Zemfira and Roya to be in Arakhotoi with them.

The doors opened and Musa entered, leading a nobly clothed woman by the collar. Several Soulgivers followed, as did Omid. Jia-Fan's eyes widened and Paniz too was shocked to see how much weight the merchant had lost, at the bandages covering his left cheek. His months of clandestine work in Harauvatis had taken their toll.

"We have news from the west," said Musa, releasing the lady and letting her collapse onto the carpet. "The king has been defeated in battle. The Hellenic Hegemon is ascendant."

Musa was stocky, with short hair and a prickly beard. He had spent little time at Jalehravan over the past year, preferring to seek out Soulgivers and protect villages from tax collectors. He was a Stormcaster of incredible strength, and a friend to the common people, unaware of what his Cost was.

"The king has been defeated? In pitched battle?" asked Darya, shocked.

"Yes, Insightcaster," said Musa. "It is good news: it will give us a chance to begin a true revolution here in Harauvatis, this time with our full attention and our total resources. We will create a state of true equality, free of oppression, and we will spread our message westward. With unity between all Casters, Farsia will rise again and the Hellenics can be driven into the ocean."

The woman on the floor was bleeding from her mouth, and spat on the ground. Musa noticed her now with a raised eyebrow. "Ah, Satrap Marmar—you put up a good resistance, despite our element of surprise and superior forces. Do you have something to say before I make you my offer?"

"Soulbreaker scum," she growled.

"I see," said Musa. "Can you overcome your prejudice for the sake of your kingdom? You see, we have the princess of Farsia here, the heir to the throne should the king die. Master Roya wants her dead, but I intend to persuade her of Stateira's utility. The girl shall be the reigning queen, under our guiding hand and protection. It is your choice, Satrap Marmar, if you wish to join the new government of Farsia, or if you cannot stomach such—"

"I'll never support you fiends," growled Marmar.

Musa sighed and drew his sword. "Goli, go execute her family."

And in a simple motion, he cut off the Satrap's head. Several Soulgivers, especially the children, screamed. Paniz's stomach twisted. Milad vomited. Musa seemed bored by the proceedings.

"It would have been nice to have a noble Satrap guiding the princess, but I have little patience today. Until Master Roya rejoins us, I will be the Satrap of Harauvatis. We begin our new revolution here. No more hiding. No more fear. The age of Soulgivers has finally arrived."

Paniz, shaking, stood up. Milad was still wiping his mouth but he tugged at her tunic to get her to sit down.

"Master Musa," said Paniz. "I believe the new capital should be in Baxtris. It is much safer there. No royal or Hellenic army will be able to penetrate safely. We would have a great advantage."

Musa smiled. "A strategic mind—what is your name?"

"Paniz—but I am no Soulgiver—merely an ally."

"It commends you to support us when your life is not on the line," said Musa. "But we cannot move against the Satrap of Baxtris yet. Satrap Bessus is loyal to the king and commands a strong army. For now, we will consolidate our position here. We will redirect the tribute from Taxiles, Abisares and Poros to us. Once we are strong enough to challenge Bessus, we will take his Satrapy from his oily fingers."

Jia-Fan stood up now too. "Where is Master Roya? And where is Zemfira, the Lightcaster who brought us here?"

People joined in, asking more questions and voicing their doubts. No one wanted to focus on the dead body lying in front of them, with blood seeping into the carpet.

Musa's lips tightened. "I cannot say. Master Roya told me to lead the mission, and she would send word soon. Until then, I am in charge. As for the Lightcaster girl—perhaps she returned home."

But Paniz knew where Zemfira would have gone. Only one location made sense. Did Zemfira really have a chance to save Kuzro and Jabo?

"This palace shall be our residence," Musa continued, "until we can exert our control over the city and the surrounding province. We must earn their loyalty as well as their submission. They will serve their young queen Stateira. Find rooms, find rest and comfort. This war is far from over, but we have escaped death and we will fight until we are victorious."

Paniz, Ardeshir and Milad looked for a room together, and found Hami sitting on the floor of a child's bedroom, holding a little doll in his hands. Paniz saw there was blood on the doll.

"They just took out the body," whispered Hami. "I—I don't think she was even four years old, but they killed her."

"War is ugly," said Ardeshir, hand trembling. "Uprisings are even uglier—but there's no other way to start over."

"Zemfira said we should build a good society on a good foundation—judicious kings and queens ruling over peaceful people."

"Zemfira isn't here," said Milad. "She's gone."

"She'll come," said Hami. "We just have to wait for her."

He touched his cheek absentmindedly, lost in memory. Paniz looked around the room, at the delicate nets constructed against vicious jungle mosquitos, at the small bed, at the little pillows. She placed her bed mat down on the carpet, next to a Chatrang board of ivory.

"I'll stay here," she said. "And tomorrow, I'm going to help Musa and Roya to win this war."

Milad's jaw set. "He's a monster, Paniz."

"Nava's dead," said Paniz. "Yashar is dead—Kalpana, Tryphon—they lost their lives because of this king. We can't let more of it happen—it's not right, and if you won't fight for yourself, I will."

Milad stared down at his leg. "Maybe I'm not meant to be a warrior, Paniz—perhaps this was a blessing, not a curse. I'm going to find Master Laleh, and see if she will accept me as a monk. She's taking over for Tryphon, as our spiritual leader."

Ardeshir helped his friend up and walked with him from the room. Hami did not look up from the little doll and the blood on it.

"What are you going to do?" asked Paniz.

"I'm going to wait," said Hami, very quietly. "As long as it takes. I know she's on her way. It's only a matter of time."

Paniz sat down next to him, and clasped his arm. "Want to stay here with me? I don't think I want to be alone when I sleep."

Hami nodded solemnly. "Thank you. I don't want to be alone either."

They sat together in the room, watching the sun spill over the Harauvatian horizon.

# CHAPTER 32 – ESKANDAR

There were dark splinters digging into her father's soul. Zemfira could sense them, deep within her meditation. She felt herself as she had in the Flash Gate—omnipresent and disconnected. Light surged through her being. She hoped it would be enough to save her father from his prison within a prison.

Months ago, Tryphon had explained how to discern the surfaces of people's souls: sunny or barbed, sanguine or shrill. Zemfira was decades away from such enlightenment, but the splinters piercing Kuzro's soul jutted into the meditative world, and Zemfira could follow them to the border of her father's being.

She found herself bolstered by his proximity. Zemfira pushed her presence along a splinter—focusing her Lightcasting on a fixed point, to pull and dislodge the shadowy thorn.

It was arduously. The effort cost her all her strength, but finally, the dark ailment came free. It fell into the infinity of the mental landscape, and Zemfira turned to the next spike.

Kuzro's small relief permeated into Zemfira's consciousness. She gritted her teeth, located the next thorn, and focused her mind on removing it.

One by one, the splinters fell away, clattering into the void. With each splinter removed, her father's soul breathed, relaxed. But each succeeding thorn took more effort. She had to exert her will, exert her love. There was no other way.

The last splinter clung on desperately, but Zemfira channeled everything into her endeavor. Her soul groaned, straining to hold itself together at her exertion. Then the splinter came free and fell into the void. All she sensed now was a band around her father's soul: the Iron Necklace that prevented him from casting. She could not sever it, even if she had the energy. She felt her concentration evaporating, and she returned to waking, and felt arms around her. Kuzro was awake.

"Where is Jabo?" he asked hoarsely. "How did—"

"We're free," said Zemfira. "The king is gone, the palace is empty. We survived, Father."

His embrace was determined, but weak. Zemfira helped him up, feeling herself unsteady from the battle with Roya, from the concentrated effort of recovering her father. They stumbled together past the staring eyes of the rebel commander, lying in her own drying blood.

They reached the stairs only to hear footsteps descending —the slap of sandals on stone. In the next instant, a man appeared.

"What's this? More Farsians?" he said, surprised. "Are you prisoners of the king?"

Zemfira didn't say anything. The man spoke Farsian like a barbarian. He was paler than Volakles, with Hellenic cheekbones and green eyes. He smiled easily, but Zemfira saw a sword at his belt and a shield on his back.

"What are your names?" he said. "I am a Ptolemaios, a friend of the Hegemon. You are fortunate to be liberated on such an auspicious day."

Zemfira mumbled her name, and her father's.

"You do not look well," said Ptolemaios. "Come, let's get you upstairs."

It was a blur. Zemfira was so deprived of sleep, so tender in her soul, that she could not process the chiton-wearing Hellenics, the shining armor of the soldiers, the banners being hung in the palace. Zemfira slept on a corner of carpet, ate a hot meal of gruel and beer with the other servants and prisoners, and let Kuzro braid her hair.

Zemfira knew they had lost their chance to escape. She had taken too long down in the dungeon and they were now at the mercy of a Hellenic man who had just conquered the largest army in Farsia. Had Volakles and Jabo made it to safety? Would they wait or flee in the face of this peril?

"Come," said Ptolemaios, red cloak billowing behind his stride. "All of you, it is time for your audience with the King of Asia."

Zemfira, Kuzro and the dozen Farsians followed Ptolemaios along a passage to the throne room. Several Hellenic spearmen followed and no one tried to flee.

The Hegemon Eskandar sat on his throne, surrounded by wives, servants and soldiers wearing red cloaks like Ptolemaios. One of these men sat on the arm of the throne, laughing with Eskandar. The Hegemon only wore the lower half of a chiton, exposing the tanned muscles of his chest. No diadem decorated his curls. No jeweled slippers obscured his feet. His sandals were dusty. He had a handsome, shaved face, and a broad grin. He was younger than Volakles, perhaps only five years older than Zemfira herself.

The Hegemon rose, still smiling about the joke, and stretched his arms above his head. His sword leaned against the throne, the blade bisected with gold.

"I am Eskandar," he said. "And I have freed you from your tyrant. He flees, a coward clothed in the finery of his office. I am not here to pillage, to take slaves back to Makedonia. I am here to succeed Artashata on the throne. You are my subjects now, not my prisoners. I have treated the people of Lydia with kindness and clemency. I will do so with you, as well. Pledge yourselves to me, and you will be dismissed. Each in your turn, step forward, press your foreheads to the ground, and call me your king."

Several servants exchanged looks, nervous about giving such an oath so easily. They knew the Farsian code of honesty and honor. Yet no one refused. Zemfira's heart was racing. They still had a chance to escape—all was not lost. One after another, servants and prisoners stepped forward, and prostrated themselves before the Hegemon. Eskandar watched with sly pleasure, an intelligence in his eyes far deeper than his easy smile.

Kuzro approached the throne, pressed himself to the ground and declared his allegiance to the Hegemon. He was allowed to depart, but he waited for Zemfira at the door of the throne room. Zemfira stepped forward, but before she could even get on her knees, the Hegemon rose to his feet and stared at her. Zemfira was so shocked she took a step back, averting her eyes and falling to her knees.

"You," he said, his voice like wild honey; spicy and sweet. "So it is."

Zemfira had no idea what the Hegemon was trying to communicate, but she was terrified.

"No need to be afraid," said Eskandar. "I mean you no harm. What's your name?"

She swallowed, then mumbled, "Zemfira, sir."

"What's that?" called the Hegemon, grinning. "Speak up, not everyone in my court can hear as clearly as I can."

Zemfira cleared her throat, and repeated herself. She wanted to get out of the throne room, wanted to find Jabo and that Dualcaster, wanted to reach her friends and safety. But the Hegemon was rubbing his hands together.

"Wonderful," said Eskandar, settling himself on the throne again, and pressing his fingertips together. "I should have known this moment would come. Perfect."

"Is she the one from your dreams?" called one of the red-caped bodyguards.

"She is indeed, Hephaistion," said Eskandar. "She looks a little younger, perhaps, but it's her. Destiny, Zemfira, destiny guides us. This encounter was inevitable."

Zemfira bowed her head, heart racing. What was Eskandar talking about? What was going on? "Ah, you don't understand," said the Hegemon. "Let me explain, then. From now on, you will be attached to my court. You will join the campaign as I conquer Farsia, Satrapy by Satrapy."

Horrified, Zemfira looked over at Kuzro, but he looked just as helpless. There was nothing to be done against a man who called himself King of Asia.

"You look like you have something to say," said Eskandar, walking forward. Zemfira could feel the air prickle as he drew closer: his mere presence was warping the world. "Go on, speak."

"I am honored by your attention, great Hegemon," said Zemfira. "But I have traveled a long way to find my father and brother. Please, if you find it within your clemency, release me to return to my family."

The Hellenic Hegemon shook his head. "No, I'm afraid not. You see, you are a Lightcaster with Depravity—a combination I have been unable to find on the Hellenic islands, the mainland, Makedonia or Lydia. It is only fitting I find you after I defeat your sham-king Artashata, a reward for my hard work. You are the key, you see—the key to my greatest desire."

"What is your greatest desire?"

"To be the strongest, of course," said the Hegemon. "To prove myself. And to do that, I need to go east. There's a certain temple, buried in the jungle. My destiny leads me there—it leads *us* there, I should say."

Zemfira dared to look into his eyes. They were no one color, but swirled with a spectrum. Zemfira understood then. Eskandar wanted to release Drvaspa. He was conquering eastward to reach that distant temple.

"You're making a mistake," she said, indifferent to whatever punishment would follow such insolence. "You will fulfill no desires there, only unleash destruction: for yourself, for your people, for all of Asia."

Eskandar laughed. "You have both intelligence and naïveté. I admire that. Perdikkas, bring her an Iron Necklace. Welcome to your new life, Zemfira."

She saw Kuzro at the door, struggling to get back in, past the guards with those long spears—but they thrust him out. He called her name, but they slammed the door. Zemfira closed her eyes as one of the red-cloaked men walked up and placed the Iron Necklace around her throat. She felt it clasp, and fought back tears. She had been so close to salvation.

Zemfira opened her eyes again and looked at Eskandar. He smiled as she stared defiantly, hands balled into fists. She didn't have to say anything. He could read her intent, and he just shook his head.

"An admirable spirit," he said. "But you will learn peace and obedience, as they all do. My era begins now—and I will write the rules in blood, stone and steel."

351

He was still laughing as two guards led Zemfira away, to her own room. Tears didn't come, even locked in the small room with the little window. She would fight. She would find a way.

She lay on her back, cushioned by the soft mattress, and stared at the painting on the ceiling. She would not despair. She still had plenty of time to escape the Hegemon. She closed her eyes and let sleep turn her anxieties and anguish into dreams.

***

Volakles had been waiting just outside the palace with the boy. Jabo had not fully recovered from his ordeal in Prison—his Iron Necklace looked dark against his sickly skin—although the sunlight was restoring him. Then Kuzro came into view, running down from the palace gates, past Hellenic soldiers, past servants and slaves. Volakles snagged his attention with a jab of Insight, and Kuzro stopped, trembling.

"Where's Zemfira?" asked Volakles. "What happened?"

Kuzro was struggling to recover his words. He was crying and shaking. With his dirty clothes, ragged beard, and dungeon stench, he looked like a lunatic. Volakles grasped his forearms to calm him.

"He—he's taken her prisoner," he said, trying to compose himself. "He's not letting her go, and I couldn't—I wasn't able to —"

"Who? Eskandar? The Hegemon?"

Kuzro buried his face in his hands. "My fault. All my fault."

Volakles glanced around, though the soldiers were not taking any notice of them. "Come, let's get into town. The cottages are abandoned, and we might be able to scavenge some —"

"Don't you understand? I have to save her! I have to—I have to make this right!"

"No," said Volakles, firmly. "You can't save her. Let's get your son to safety."

His fingers had tightened around Volakles's wrists. His bloodshot eyes widened. "You're right. I can't. I can't do it. But you can."

Volakles blinked. "What? No, I can't—"

"Please," whispered Kuzro. "Please. Promise me— promise me you'll save my daughter. Swear that she'll be freed."

Volakles stared at this broken father, glanced at his quivering son. They were in no condition to get to safety. They were barely surviving as it was.

"We need to get you both fed, and washed. You need to rest."

"If you have any goodness in your heart," whimpered Kuzro. "Promise me: get my daughter out of the Hegemon's clutches."

Volakles swallowed. He could see the soldiers milling just out of earshot, soldiers who had defeated the King of Farsia in open combat. He couldn't fight them. He couldn't outwit the Hegemon. But he knew what would happen if he refused Kuzro's request. The Baxtrian father would die in his own futile attempt. And this boy, Jabo, did not deserve to be an orphan.

"I promise," whispered Volakles. "I'll get Zemfira out of there. You have my word."

To Be Continued...

# GLOSSARY
## CASTINGS

**Infernocasting**
Power over fire.

**Insightcasting**
Power to read intention, to gauge casting and cost, sometimes to read one's thoughts. Can be distorted by the presence of silver.

**Obediencecasting**
Power over animals, sometimes humans.

**Lightcasting**
Power over light. Can be used for healing.

**Shadowcasting**
Power over darkness and shadow.

**Sproutcasting**
Power over plants.

**Stonecasting**
Power over stone, sand and sometimes the earth itself.

**Stormcasting**
Power over wind, weather and water.

**Temperaturecasting**
Power over temperature, raising and lowering.

# COSTS

## Cost of Aging

Casting makes the caster older. Overuse causes death from old age.

## Cost of Depravity

Casting makes the caster's soul deteriorate. A deteriorated soul has less compassion and amplifies any violent instincts. Overuse causes self-loathing, overwhelming bloodlust, and hatred for all living things.

## Cost of Fatigue

Use of Casting makes the caster tired. Overuse causes collapse and involuntary sleep.

## Cost of Hunger

Casting makes the caster hungry. Overuse causes starvation.

## Cost of Thirst

Casting makes the caster thirsty. Overuse causes extreme dehydration.

# NATIONS

### The Kingdom of Farsia
A multiethnic empire whose people worship the Celestial Ones and study the mysteries of Casting through temples. The King of Farsia is an absolute monarch, supported by seven Satraps who govern the seven Satrapies, and fifty Vazirs who govern the smaller provinces within the Satrapies.

### The Hellenic States
A fragile alliance of Hellenic city-states, located on the islands west of Farsia. In times of crisis, the city-states elect a Hegemon who has the mandate to lead the states against a sufficiently threatening foe. At the time of Eskandar's conquests, the Hellenic States are dominated by the kingdom of Makedonia, and are forced to elect King Eskandar of Makedonia as the Hegemon.

### The Kingdom of Makedonia
A kingdom north of the Hellenic States with many Hellenic influences. Makedonia is often considered barbaric by their southern neighbors, due to Makedonia's proximity to Skythia. Under King Philippos, father of King Eskandar, Makedonia defeated and united the Hellenic States.

### The Karganate of Skythia
The confederation of Skythian tribes and people united under the authority of the Kargan. Skythians fight with horse and bow, and are often nomadic. However, they do have villages and winter retreats.

## The Land of the Zhou

A kingdom located northeast of Farsia. Silk traders travel through Farsia to bring their wares west. No diplomatic ties exist between the Farsian King and the Zhou Emperor, so knowledge is exchanged through commerce alone.

## The Empire of the Nanda

A nation east of Farsia in the land of Hindusia. The Nanda Empire is at peace with the Kingdom of Farsia.

# SATRAPIES

**Fars**

The first Satrapy. It is located in the south of the kingdom. The capital of Fars is Parsa, which is also the capital of the kingdom.

**Mada**

The second Satrapy. This central Satrapy contains large cities, open plains and harsh deserts. The capital of Mada is Ektabana.

**Lydia**

The third Satrapy. It is the westernmost territory of the Farsian Kingdom, with many Hellenic-speaking subjects. The capital of Lydia is Gordion.

**Babirus**

The fourth Satrapy. This land has a rich history from before the Farsian state annexed it. Legends say that the art of Casting was first discovered at the Satrapy's capital: Babilim.

**Mudraya**

The fifth Satrapy. Mudraya was once its own kingdom, ruled by a pharaoh, but fell in the military conquest of Farsia. The capital of Mudraya is Memphis.

**Harauvatis**

The sixth Satrapy. This easternmost territory includes client kingdoms, which are loyal to Farsia while maintaining some independence. These small states form a buffer between Farsia and Hindusia. The capital of Harauvatis is Arakhotoi.

## Baxtris

The seventh Satrapy. Baxtris lies north of Harauvatis and east of Mada. The terrain is exceedingly mountainous. Baxtris forms a border with Skythia and often faces the brunt of raiding from the north. Zariaspa is the capital of the Satrapy.

# CITIES, TOWNS AND VILLAGES

**Arakhotoi**
The capital of Harauvatis.

**Babilim**
The capital of Babirus.  It is famous for its ancient history, considered the birthplace of Casting.

**Barkana**
A town in Baxtris.

**Byzantion**
The westernmost city in Lydia.

**Chadrakarta**
A fortified city in Mada.

**Ektabana**
The capital of Mada, home of Hami.

**Gaza**
A city in Babirus, on the coast of the Western Sea.

**Gordion**
The capital of Lydia.  The city is known for its massive trees, and the network of ropes connecting them.

**Himdook**
A village in Baxtris, near Nebit.

**Issos**

A city in Lydia, on the coast of the Western Sea.

**Izad**

A town in Harauvatis on the southern edge of the Lut Desert.

**Jicheng**

A city in the Land of the Zhou.

**Kapisa**

A town in Baxtris, near Nebit.

**Margos**

A city in western Baxtris.

**Memphis**

The capital of Mudraya. On the Hapi River.

**Nebit**

A mountain village in Baxtris, home to Zemfira.

**Parsa**

The capital of Fars, and by extension, the whole Kingdom of Farsia. It is home to the royal family.

**Ragai**

A city in Mada.

**Rasparad**

A city in Harauvatis, home to Ardeshir.

**Taxila**

A city in the client-kingdom of Taxiles

**Tatagus**

A city in eastern Harauvatis.

**Thebai**

A city along the Hapi river in Mudraya, home of Firuzeh.

**Zariaspa**

The capital of Baxtris.

# LANDMARKS AND PROVINCES

**Abisares**
A client-kingdom loyal to Farsia, on the eastern border.

**Arabaya**
A province in northeastern Mudraya, which fades into the Arabayan Desert.

**Arabayan Desert**
A desert in northeastern Mudraya.

**Armina**
A province of northwestern Mada, near the Satrapy of Lydia.

**Etruskia**
A territory far to the west, home to the Etruskan people and Etruskan Pebbles.

**The Faveh**
A poor neighborhood in Chadrakarta.

**Gedrosian Desert**
A desert in Harauvatis, south of Rasparad.

**Hapi River**
The river running through Mudraya, up into the Western Sea.

**Helmand River**
A river in southeastern Baxtris.

## Hindus River
A river that separates eastern Harauvatis from Hindusia.

## Iaxartes River
A river that separates northern Baxtris from Skythia.

## Kappadokia
A province of northern Lydia.

## Kusiya
The lands south of Mudraya.

## Lut Desert
A massive, deadly desert in eastern Fars. Contains the sanctuary at Jalehravan. Also known as the Empty Desert.

## Putaya
A province of western Mudraya.

## Poros
A client-kingdom loyal to Farsia, on the eastern border.

## Suguda
A province in Baxtris.

## Taxiles
A client-kingdom loyal to Farsia, on the eastern border.

## Velvu Hill
Near the Helmand River. The location of a temple in Baxtris.

# PEOPLE

**Amarxes**

(Farsian/Madan) The Vazir in residence at Chadrakarta.

**Aniketos**

(Farsian/Lydian) Brother to Volakles.

**Ardeshir**

(Farsian/Harauvatian) A Temperaturecaster with the Cost of Depravity.

**Arsames**

(Farsian of Fars) An earlier King of Farsia. Led a campaign to pacify Mudraya during an uprising of the people and led a raid on Kusiya. Deceased.

**Artashata**

(Farsian of Fars) King of Farsia. Father to Drypetis and Stateira.

**Atafeh**

(Farsian/Harauvatian) The captain of the guard for the city of Rasparad.

**Avalem**

(Farsian/Baxtrian) A Monk at the Temple in Nebit. Sproutcaster with the Cost of Thirst.

**Baj**

(Farsian/Mudrayan) A Royal Cartographer.

**Behrouz**

(Farsian/Madan) One of Firuzeh's and Volakles's targets. An Obediencecaster with the Cost of Depravity.

**Bessus**

(Farsian/Baxtrian) The Satrap of Baxtris.

**Bishen**

(Farsian/Harauvatian) The Deputy Captain of the Cleansers. A Stormcaster with the Cost of Fatigue.

**Bozorgmehr**

(Farsian of Fars) A Legendary Hero of Farsian Epics, fought the Hellenics during the Hellenic War. Moved a mountain by himself. A Stonecaster with the Cost of Aging.

**Dahketo**

(Kusiyan) Firuzeh's mother. Enslaved by and married to Firuzeh's father. Deceased.

**Danyal**

(Farsian/Harauvatian)
A monk who assists Volakles in the Hunger Temple of Rasparad. A Shadowcaster with the Cost of Hunger.

**Darayava**

(Farsian of Fars)
The Third King of Farsia. Long deceased. Created the oasis at Jalehravan in order to better understand the Cost of Depravity. A Sproutcaster with the Cost of Aging.

## Darya

(Farsian/Babirian) An Insightcaster with the Cost of Depravity. A young member of the Soulgiver Resistance.

## Davud

(Farsian/Baxtrian) The son of the ferryman in Barkana. A Stonecaster with the Cost of Fatigue.

## Drypetis

(Farsian of Fars) A Farsian Princess, daughter of Artashata. Not unclasped.

## Eskandar

(Hellenic/Makedonian) The King of Makedonia, Hegemon of the Hellenic States. A Polycaster with the Cost of Thirst. Gains immense power by drinking the blood of Bucephalas.

## Ekmut

(Farsian/Baxtrian) A Vazir at Satrap Bessus's court in Zariaspa. His Casting and Cost initially unknown.

## Firuzeh

(Farsian/Mudrayan) A Cleanser. An Obediencecaster with the Cost of Fatigue. Partnered with Volakles and tasked with killing Zemfira.

## Golzar

(Farsian/Madan) Zealot and friend of Volakles. Perishes defending Princess Stateira. An Infernocaster with the Cost of Aging.

**Gozeh**

(Farsian/Baxtrian) Zemfira's aunt and Kuzro's sister. A Temperaturecaster with the Cost of Thirst.

**Gahnandar**

(Farsian/Baxtrian) A monk residing in the Temple at Kapisa. An Insightcaster with the Cost of Aging.

**Garguk**

(Farsian/Madan) A combat monk assisting in the training of Cleansers. A Shadowcaster with the Cost of Fatigue.

**Giv**

(Farsian of Fars) A member of the Soulgiver Resistance. A Temperaturecaster with the Cost of Depravity.

**Hajgo**

(Farsian/Madan) A combat monk assisting in the training of Cleansers. A Shadowcaster with the Cost of Aging.

**Hami**

(Farsian/Madan) A Stonecaster with the Cost of Depravity. An avowed pacifist.

**Hamide**

(Farsian/Baxtrian) Wife of the ferryman in Barkana.

**Hooshang**

(Farsian/Harauvatian) A member of the Soulgiver Resistance. A Stonecaster with the Cost of Depravity.

**Jabo**

(Farsian/Baxtrian) Zemfira's brother and Kuzro's son. Not yet unclasped.

**Jia-Fan**

(Zhou) Sold to Omid by merchants, became his wife. A Sproutcaster with the Cost of Depravity.

**Kallisto**

(Farsian/Lydian) A Cleanser reporting directly to Bishen.

**Kalpana**

(Farsian/Harauvatian) A Resistance Fighter and Casting Instructor at Jalehravan. An Infernocaster with the Cost of Depravity.

**Kuzro**

(Farsian/Baxtrian) Zemfira and Jabo's father. Formerly married to Roshni. Makes his living as a goatherd. A Sproutcaster with the Cost of Hunger.

**Malek**

(Farsian/Baxtrian) A village boy from Nebit.

**Mehrzad**

(Farsian/Harauvatian) A soldier stationed on the Helmand River.

**Memnon**

(Hellenic) A mercenary general, loyal to King Artashata.

**Milad**

(Farsian/Mudrayan) A Stormcaster with the Cost of Depravity.

**Musa**

(Farsian of Fars) Roya's deputy. A Stormcaster with the Cost of Depravity.

**Nava**

(Farsian/Madan) A Sproutcaster with the Cost of Depravity, who was unclasped and reached the safety of Jalehravan in the same year that Zemfira did.

**Navid**

(Farsian/Baxtrian) Lives in Nebit. Veteran from the royal army. A Stormcaster with the Cost of Aging.

**Omid**

(Farsian/Harauvatian) Merchant. Zemfira's Uncle. Roshni's Brother. Married to Jia-Fan. A Stormcaster with the Cost of Thirst.

**Paniz**

(Farsian/Baxtrian) Zemfira's best friend. An Infernocaster with the Cost of Fatigue.

**Paratsu**

(Farsian/Baxtrian) A Vazir present at Satrap Bessus's court in Zariaspa. Her Casting and Cost are initially unknown.

**Roshni**

(Farsian/Harauvatian) Zemfira and Jabo's mother, died in childbirth with Jabo. A Temperaturecaster with the Cost of Fatigue.

**Roya**

(Farsian/Mudrayan) Commander of the Soulgiver Resistance. A Shadowcaster with the Cost of Depravity.

**Saam**

(Farsian/Baxtrian) Son of the ferryman in Barkana. A Stonecaster with the Cost of Thirst.

**Sahin**

(Farsian/Madan) The Captain of the Cleansers. A Shadowcaster with the Cost of Aging.

**Sargon**

(Farsian/Harauvatian) Fought against Volakles during the kidnapping of Stateira. A Stonecaster with the Cost of Depravity.

**Sepehr**

(Farsian/Mudrayan) Firuzeh's former partner and fellow Cleanser. A Lightcaster with the Cost of Aging. Deceased.

**Stateira**

(Farsian of Fars) Eldest Daughter of King Artashata. Kidnapped by Roya as part of the Soulgiver Resistance. Not yet unclasped.

**Tryphon**

(Farsian/Lydian) The Targu of Jalehravan. A Stormcaster with the Cost of Depravity.

**Volakles**

(Farsian/Lydian) A Royal Zealot turned Cleanser. An Insightcaster with the Cost of Hunger.

**Yashar**

(Farsian/Babirian) A Resistance Fighter and Combat Instructor at Jalehravan. An Obediencecaster with the Cost of Depravity.

**Zemfira**

(Farsian/Baxtrian) Born in Nebit. A Lightcaster with the Cost of Depravity.

# BEINGS

### The Angra

The destructive force of the universe. The Angra is a god who does not take humanoid form. It commands the Devas and the Shadow Beasts, as it guides destruction.

### Blaze Beetles

Shadow Beasts. Blaze Beetles are scarabs with intense body temperatures and lava flowing through their bodies. Their bite burns terribly. If controlled by a Scorpion Man, a Blaze Beetle can be compelled to explode, causing massive damage.

### Celestial Ones

Servants of the Spenta. Also known as Bounteous Immortals. Cannot die, can only transcend to the next plane of existence, becoming one with the Spenta. Some Celestial Ones are created directly by the Spenta. Other Celestial Ones are humans who reached a level of transcendent enlightenment and joined the Bounteous Immortals.

### Delta Vipers

Shadow Beasts. Delta Vipers are shaped like giant cobras, with golden eyes printed in their foreheads and on their hoods. Delta Vipers can often predict the movements of nearby creatures, making them difficult to surprise in combat.

## Devas

Servants of the Angra. While they can enter the Getig, they mostly reside in the Menog. Not as powerful as Celestial Ones, not immortal, but their power is free of counterbalance. A very powerful Shadow Beast can transcend and become a Deva. Devas have a better control over their appetite than Shadow Beasts.

## Drowners

Shadow Beasts. Drowners are aquatic, shaped like chunky eels. They have immense appetites.

## Golems

Shadow Beasts. Golems are silent creatures of clay earth and stone. They are vaguely humanoid, each drawing its strength from the jewel at the center of their being. They often steal children. In the city of Gaza, the local monks use ancient methods to pacify Golems, and even use these Shadow Beasts to bolster the city's defenses.

## Meadow Gaunts

Shadow Beasts. Meadow Gaunts are subterranean, frequently found in meadows. They wait for their prey to approach, then use a serrated tongue to drag the prey into their massive jaws.

## Scorpion Men

Shadow Beasts. Scorpion Men have the head and torso of human men but the legs, pincers and tail of giant scorpions. They are usually bald and have powers of domination over other Shadow Beasts.

## The Spenta

The creative force of the universe. The Spenta is a god who does not take humanoid form. It commands the Celestial Ones as it guides creation.

## Starmouths

Shadow Beasts. Starmouths absorb all the nearby light, creating darkness, and therefore are hard to detect. They attack by scuttling up to their prey and suddenly opening their mouths, blinding and paralyzing prey with an overwhelming blast of light.

## Tishtyra

A Celestial One, memorialized in a statue at Jalehravan.

## Voidicants

Shadow Beasts. Voidicants are rare and the most dangerous Shadow Beast variety. They often take the form of an empty woman, but they have no gender. Voidicants are difficult to kill. It is best to simply push them into the Menog, from which they cannot return easily. Voidicants are fascinated by their own reflections.

# Offices and Identities

**Champion**
A Farsian soldier dedicated to the eradication of Shadow Beasts.

**Cleanser**
A Farsian soldier dedicated to the eradication of casters with a Cost of Depravity, known as Soulbreakers. Some hunt recently-unclasped children with the Cost of Depravity. Some kill adults, who are more dangerous.

**The Eternal Cavalry**
An elite division of the Farsian army.

**Hegemon**
The leader of the Hellenic States in times of crisis. Not a permanent office, usually selected voluntarily by the member states. During the supremacy of Makedonia, the office was reserved for the King of Makedonia.

**Kargan**
The leader of the Skythian Karganate.

**Satrap**
The governor of a Satrapy in Farsia.

**Soulbreaker**
The derogative term for Casters with the Cost of Depravity.

**Soulgiver**
The affirmative term for Casters with the Cost of Depravity.

**Targu**

The head monk of a temple.

**Vazir**

The governor of a province in a Farsian Satrapy.

**Zealot**

A royal bodyguard of the Farsian royal family.

# MISCELLANEOUS

**Chatrang**
A Farsian board game involving two players. The objective is to take the opponent's king, or failing this, to take every other piece, except for the king.

**The Dark Mirror**
A Shadowcasting technique which traps the victim in their own soul.

**Elamite**
A Farsian language, forgotten but deeply associated with casting. The Flash Gate ritual is only recorded in Elamite.

**The Eternal Crusade**
The never-ending struggle between good and evil, creation and destruction, order and chaos. The forces of the Spenta combat the forces of the Angra both in the Getig and in the Menog.

**Etruskan Pebbles**
Stones that shield the bearer's Cost from observation. The stone heats up and cannot be used for long. Useful for those with the Cost of Depravity.

**Flash Gate**
A portal that can only be opened by a Lightcaster who has learned the ritual. It requires a great deal of energy, so only those with the Cost of Depravity or the Cost of Aging can open one. The Flash Gate takes a traveler to a temple of their choice, or any location with a Temple Stone.

## Flower of Daoi

A blossom which makes the bearer harder to observe with Insightcasting. Useful for those with the Cost of Depravity.

## The Getig

The physical world in which humans reside. Influenced by the Menog, but filtered into a coherent, chronological shape.

## The Gloom

A curse resulting from powerful Shadowcasting. It latches onto the victim's Casting, rendering them defenseless as it slowly kills them. No cure is known.

## Hydration Frogs

Small, blue frogs which can conceal a bearer's Cost and exude the Cost of Thirst instead. Useful for those with the Cost of Depravity.

## Iron Necklaces

Constraints made of iron and traces of silver which prevent the wearer from accessing their Casting. In the Kingdom of Farsia, Iron Necklaces are placed on every child and are removed on Unclasping Day. To remove an Iron Necklace, a Temperaturecaster and a Stonecaster must work together, the former stabilizing the gentle fluctuation of heat within the metal, the latter breaking the metal apart.

## Koptic

The language spoken by the people of Mudraya, since before the Farsian conquest.

## Lightstone

A mineral that glows in the dark. The glow fades with prolonged human contact and can only be restored through the work of a Lightcaster.

## The Menog

The abstract world beyond the Getig. Unsafe for humans, home to Devas and Celestial Ones. The Menog does not obey rules of reality: space and time are fluid.

## Temple Stone

A crystal which channels Insightcasting, allowing two Insightcasters to communicate with each other over great distances if both are in contact with the mineral. Every temple in Farsia possesses a Temple Stone.

## Unclasping Day

A Farsian ceremony held approximately every two years which frees children from their Iron Necklaces, informs them of their Casting and Cost, and designates them as adults.

# ACKNOWLEDGEMENTS

Special thanks to everyone who read during the early drafts, providing me valuable feedback ranging from improper use of em dashes to improper descriptions of bread:

Emily Ahn,
Hasan Ali,
Chloe Kaplan,
Halley McCormick,
Kenta Shimakawa,
Naomi Lee,
William Hall,
Jessie Malone,
Mieko Temple,
Colleen Hall,
Lachlan Johnson,
and Ali Holmes.

This story wouldn't be what it is without you.

# About the Author

Valentino is a recent college graduate from Whitman College, who spends his time refilling his tea mug and recommending podcasts to those in his vicinity. He's always been fascinated in time travel, so if you're from the future feel free to reach out to him on twitter at @AuthorialTino. Otherwise, see what he's doing next on his website and say hello:
www.valentinomori.weebly.com

If you enjoyed the book, please leave a review. It makes all the difference.

68935216R00234

**Life in the Ancient World**

# Technology in the Ancient World

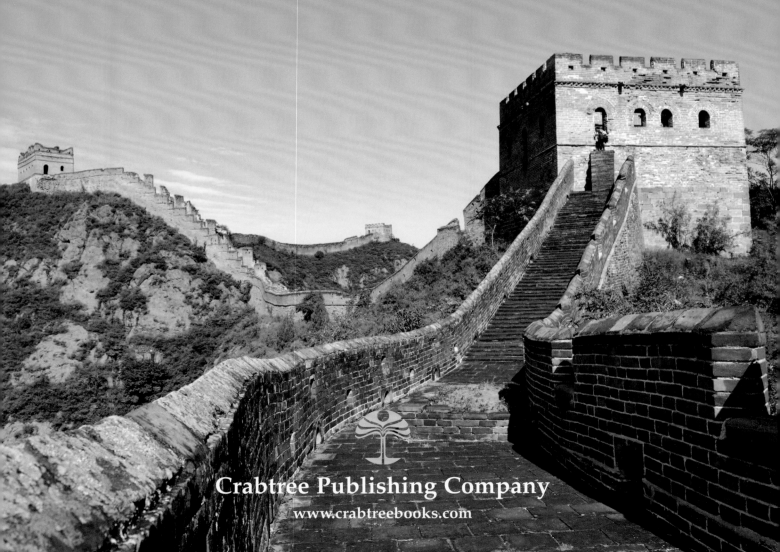

Crabtree Publishing Company
www.crabtreebooks.com

# Life in the Ancient World

**Contributing authors:** Paul Challen, Shipa Mehta-Jones,
Lynn Peppas, Hazel Richardson
**Publishing plan research and development:**
Sean Charlebois, Reagan Miller
Crabtree Publishing Company
**Editors:** Kathy Middleton, Adrianna Morganelli
**Proofreaders:** Kathy Middleton, Marissa Furry
**Editorial director:** Kathy Middleton
**Photo research:** Katherine Berti, Crystal Sikkens
**Designer and prepress technician:** Katherine Berti
**Print and production coordinator:** Katherine Berti

**Cover description:** Advancements in technology allowed ancient
peoples to build aqueducts (top), pyramid shaped tombs (front
left), fortifications, such as the Great Wall of China (middle), and
ships strong enough to travel rough oceans (front right).

**Title page description:** The Great Wall of China is located in
northern China and was built to protect the empire from invasion.
The entire wall measures 5,500 miles (8,851 km).

**Photographs and reproductions:**
Corbis: page 10; John Farmar/Cordaiy Photo Library Ltd.: 28
Wikimedia Commons: Bouba: page 4 (bottom); Parhamr: page
4 (top right); Eusebius: page 4 (top left); Cai Lun: page 6
(top);Immanuel Giel: page 6 (bottom); Yug: page 7; Marsyas:
page 15 (top right); The York Project: back cover, page 16 (top);
Yann: page 13; Ron L. Toms: page 14 (top); Oksmith: page 16
(bottom); Rémih: page 17 (top); Edwin Smith: page 17 (bottom);
John Bodsworth: page 19 (inset); Wolfgang Sauber: page 20, 29
(top middle); Lombards Museum: page 23; Kohler: page 23
(bottom); Chris: 24 (bottom left); Rama: page 27 (left); Library of
Congress: page 27 (right); Hiroyuki0904: page 27 (bottom);
Vissarion British Museum: page 29 (top)
All other images by Shutterstock.com

**Illustrations:**
Ole Skedsmo: pages 8–9
James Burmester: page 11
William Band: front cover (border), pages 12, 30–31
Roman Goforth: page 25 (top right)

---

**Library and Archives Canada Cataloguing in Publication**

CIP available at Library and Archives Canada

**Library of Congress Cataloging-in-Publication Data**

Technology in the ancient world / contributing authors, Paul Challen ... [et al.].
p. cm. -- (Life in the ancient world)
Includes index.
ISBN 978-0-7787-1736-2 (reinforced library binding : alk. paper) -- ISBN 978-0-
7787-1743-0 (pbk. : alk. paper) -- ISBN 978-1-4271-8802-1 (electronic PDF) -- ISBN
978-1-4271-9643-9 (electronic HTML)
1. Technology--History--To 1500--Juvenile literature. 2. History, Ancient--Juvenile
literature. 3. Civilization, Ancient--Juvenile literature. I. Challen, Paul C. (Paul
Clarence), 1967- II. Title. III. Series.

T16.T425 2012
609.3--dc23

2011029254

---

# Crabtree Publishing Company

www.crabtreebooks.com      1-800-387-7650

Printed in Canada/082011/MA20110714

**Published in Canada**
**Crabtree Publishing**
616 Welland Ave.
St. Catharines, Ontario
L2M 5V6

**Published in the United States**
**Crabtree Publishing**
PMB 59051
350 Fifth Avenue, 59th Floor
New York, New York 10118

**Published in the United Kingdom**
**Crabtree Publishing**
Maritime House
Basin Road North, Hove
BN41 1WR

**Published in Australia**
**Crabtree Publishing**
3 Charles Street
Coburg North
VIC, 3058

# Contents

# Technology in the Ancient World

**Most historians agree that a civilization is a group of people that shares common languages, some form of writing, advanced technology and science, and systems of government and religion. Of all the practices shared by ancient civilizations, the most innovations were achieved in technology. Many methods and processes developed in ancient cultures are still taught and applied today.**

## Technological advancements

Many elements of ancient civilizations' customs and technical advancements fall under the category of technology. Architecture, mathematics, scientific prediction for harvest and planting, innovative farming equipment such as **canals** and sewer and drainage systems, metalwork, and even medicine are some examples of ancient technological accomplishment. Trade, convenience, and quality of life caused ancient civilizations to progress and adapt the tools of their day. As people traveled and learned new methods of technology, knowledge and advancement grew, allowing a civilization to thrive and its practices to survive for thousands of years.

*A classical order is an ancient style of architecture characterized by a style of column or pillar. The ancient Greeks invented three orders, which the Romans later used and modified.*

*The first printing system was invented in China around 1040 A.D. The machine was made of clay and had moveble characters, allowing documents to be copied quickly.*

*The invention of the aqueduct supplied Roman cities and towns with water for drinking, bathing, fountains, and eventually sewer drainage.*

4

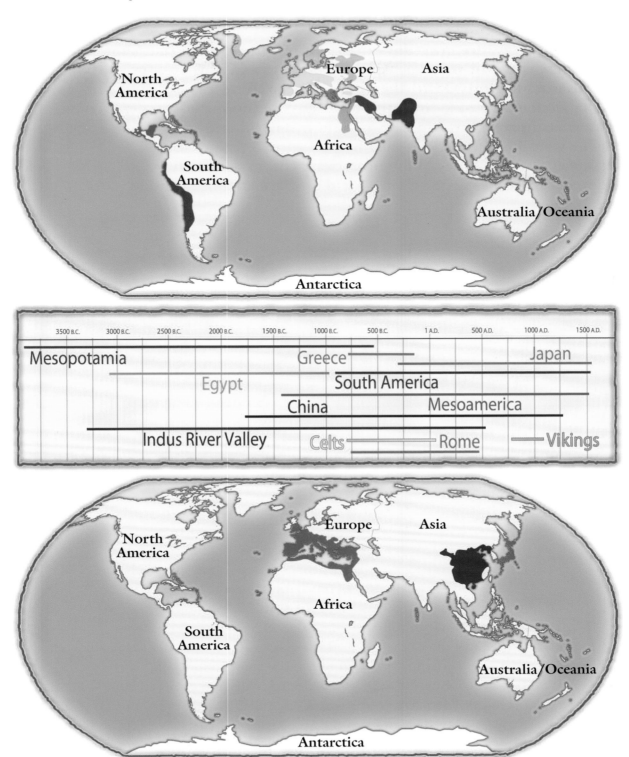

The period described as ancient history is usually defined as the time from first recorded history up to the Early Middle Ages, around 300 A.D. Some of the civilizations in this book begin well after the ancient period but are included because they were dominant early civilizations in their regions. The beginning and ending dates of early civilizations are often subject to debate. For the purposes of this book, the timelines begin with the first significant culture in a civilization and end with the change or disappearance of the civilization. The end was sometimes marked by an event such as invasion by another civilization, or simply by the gradual dispersion of people due to natural phenomena such as famine or earthquakes.

# Ancient China

1766 B.C.–1271 A.D.

The ancient Chinese were great inventors. Numerous inventions such as paper, printing, and a counting machine called the abacus, improved the daily lives of the Chinese people. The ancient Chinese invented tools that improved farming, medical procedures to improve their health, and weapons for war. The inventions also helped spread trade and religious ideas across China. Many of ancient China's advances were adopted by peoples around the world and are still used today.

## Paper

The invention of paper made it possible to record China's history. The ancient Chinese made paper by dipping a bamboo screen into a mix of crushed, or pulped, tree bark, rags, and plant pieces. As a thin layer of pulp dried on the screen, it hardened into a sheet of paper. According to legend, paper was first presented to the emperor in 105 A.D. by a government official named Cai Lun, but it is believed that paper was used in China at least 200 years earlier. Wealthier Chinese used paper for writing. The Chinese also used paper to make inventions such as raincoats, umbrellas, and kites.

*The Chinese made paper out of strips of silk and bamboo. Pulp for paper was later made from bark, hemp, and worn-out nets.*

## Making Silk

Silk was a rare and valued fabric that ancient Chinese traded with other peoples. Large-scale silk production began as early as the Zhou dynasty (1122 B.C.–221 B.C). To make silk, the Chinese fed mulberry leaves to caterpillars. When the caterpillars wove cocoons, the Chinese boiled the cocoons to loosen the fibers. Then they reeled in the fiber to produce silk. The Chinese built a network of roads and canals to allow people to trade with each other. The most famous trade route was the Silk Road, which stretched from China across Asia to the Mediterranean Sea.

*These women reel silk fibers onto a wheel, while checking carefully for flaws in the fibers.*

6

## Printing

Printing requires paper, ink, and a surface carved with letters or other symbols. Chinese **monks** developed a method of printing using marble pillars. They applied wet paper to carved sections of the pillars, which were coated in ink. The words carved on the pillars transferred to the paper. By about 1000 A.D., an inventor named Pi Sheng had created a system of moveable type that used blocks of clay to represent each of the 40,000 Chinese characters.

## Gunpowder

The Chinese invented gunpowder by mistake. Chemists were mixing two chemical compounds, sulphur and nitrate, to make a potion that would allow the emperor to live forever. Instead, it caused explosions. The Chinese used gunpowder to make fireworks. By the time of the Tang dynasty, (618 A.D.–906 A.D.), the Chinese were using gunpowder, which they called *huoyao*, in war. Fireworks were used in fire rockets, which were ignited in battle to confuse enemies.

## Chinese Medicine

Ancient Chinese medicine was closely tied to Taoism and was concerned with keeping people healthy instead of curing illness. The Chinese believed that a person became sick when *yin* and *yang*, the opposing forces in the universe, were out of balance. Chinese doctors worked to keep *yin* and *yang* in balance by using herbal cures and treatments such as acupuncture. To perform acupuncture, ancient Chinese doctors applied small needles to certain spots on the body, called meridans, where they believed life-giving energy flowed. The acupuncture needles eased pain caused by certain illnesses.

## Inventions for the World

After the Mongols invaded and united all of China, the emperor Kublai Khan opened up the country to trade with the rest of the world. In 1275, an Italian explorer named Marco Polo visited Kublai Khan. Marco Polo was amazed by the beautiful artwork and crafts made by Chinese artisans and by China's many scientific and cultural advances. He carried word of China's civilization and its many wonderful inventions back to Europe. Use of these inventions spread around the world.

Many inventions of the ancient Chinese continue to be used today. Among these are: the magnetic compass, invented to tell which direction is north; the wheelbarrow, invented to help with construction; and the stirrup, invented to make horseback riding easier.

*Zhouzhuang is a famous water village in Jiangsu, China, whereby the houses along the river were built hundreds of years ago.*

*The Grand Canal was built during the Sui dynasty to link China's Yellow and Yangzi Rivers. Boats used the canal to carry food and soldiers across the empire. Emperors forced one member from every family to work as laborers on the canal.*

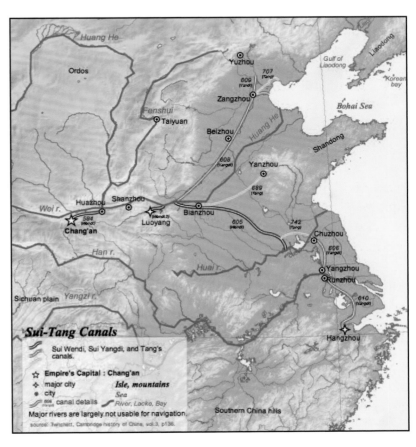

# The Great Wall

Ancient China's greatest legacy is the Great Wall. To protect ancient China from invaders from the north, China's first emperor, Qin Shi Huangdi, built a large wooden barrier called the Long Wall. The wall was later rebuilt using bricks and became the Great Wall, which still stretches 2,150 miles (3,460 km) across China.

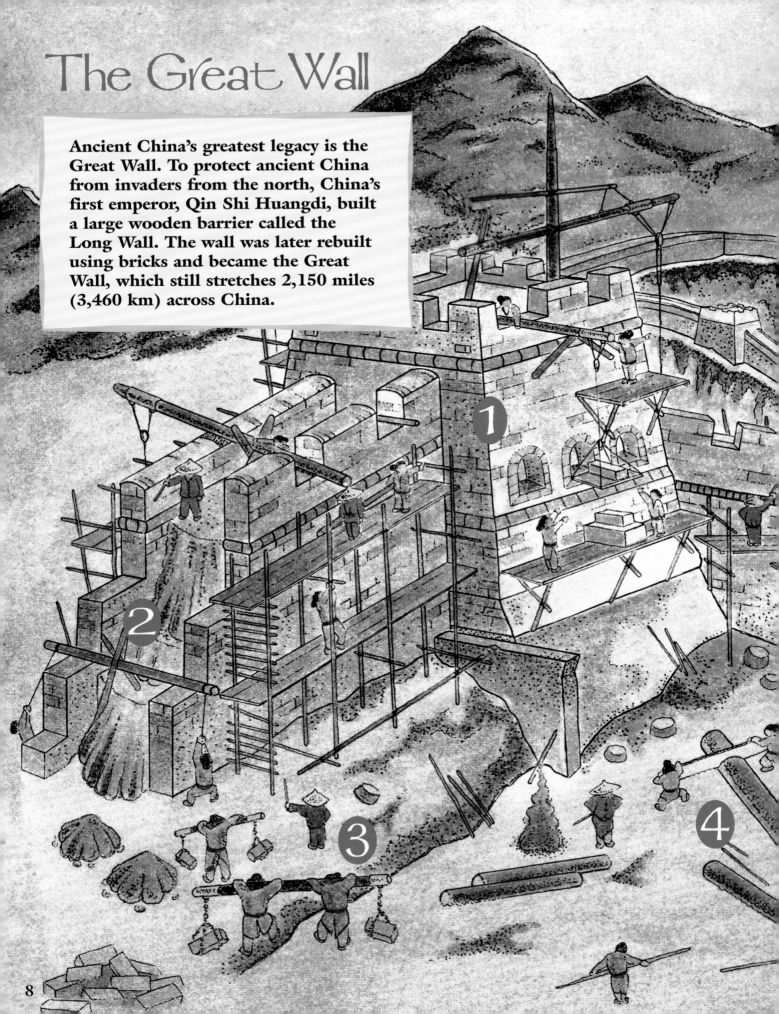

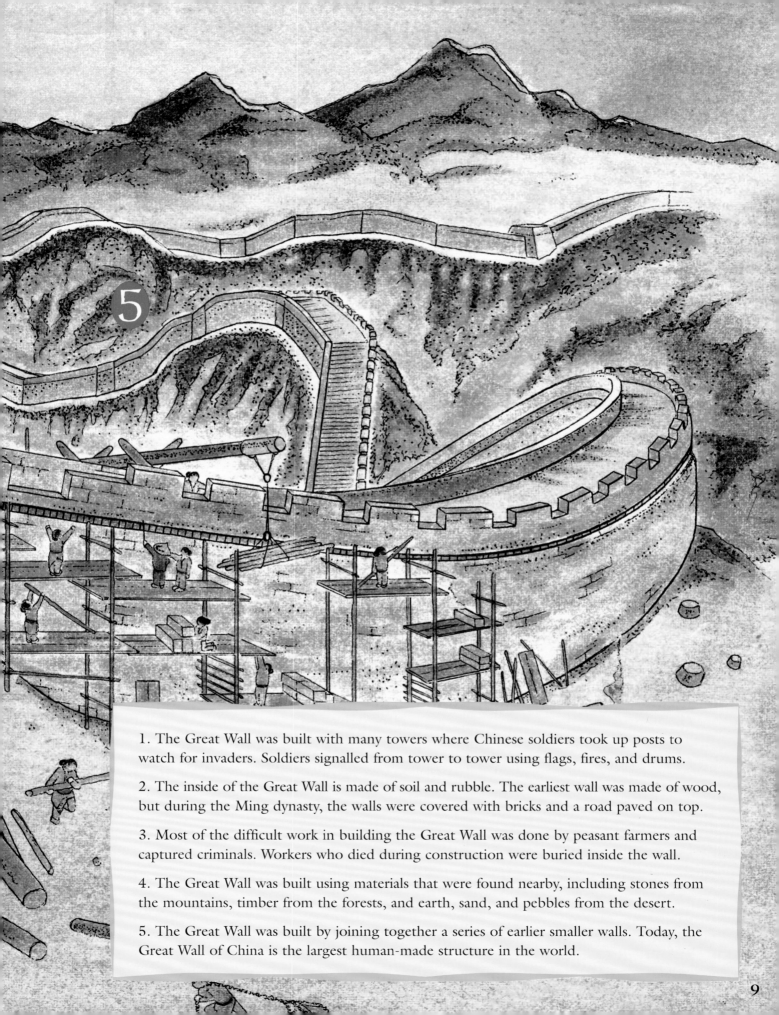

1. The Great Wall was built with many towers where Chinese soldiers took up posts to watch for invaders. Soldiers signalled from tower to tower using flags, fires, and drums.

2. The inside of the Great Wall is made of soil and rubble. The earliest wall was made of wood, but during the Ming dynasty, the walls were covered with bricks and a road paved on top.

3. Most of the difficult work in building the Great Wall was done by peasant farmers and captured criminals. Workers who died during construction were buried inside the wall.

4. The Great Wall was built using materials that were found nearby, including stones from the mountains, timber from the forests, and earth, sand, and pebbles from the desert.

5. The Great Wall was built by joining together a series of earlier smaller walls. Today, the Great Wall of China is the largest human-made structure in the world.

# Ancient Mesopotamia

3900 B.C.–539 B.C.

Ancient Mesopotamia was located between the banks of the Tigris and Euphrates rivers, in the region of modern-day Iraq. Mesopotamians developed important inventions, such as writing and the wheel, that changed the way people lived. To defend themselves against invaders, they developed styles of warfare, as well as such tools of war as the wheeled chariot, bronze and iron weapons, and protective army boots for soldiers.

## Going Places

The earliest known use of the wheel was in Mesopotamia more than 6,000 years ago. The first wheels were solid, made from planks of wood shaped into discs and held together by copper or wooden brackets. They were used on carts and chariots. The Euphrates and Tigris rivers were the main trade routes of Mesopotamia. Boats carrying goods along the rivers were often built with sails. To get the boats back home, they were hauled over land by oxen.

*(top left) Early chariots were very heavy and slow, but design improved with time and use. By the time of the Assyrians, chariots had spoked wheels instead of solid wheels, which made the chariots lighter and faster in war.*

*(bottom left) In the marshes of southern Mesopotamia, small boats were made of reeds and covered in bitumen, a thick, sticky tar. Today, people in the marshes use wooden boats.*

## Passing Time

The priests of Mesopotamia studied the position of the stars, the planets, the moon, and the sun, and they used this information to calculate dates and the start of seasons. In Sumer, the day was originally broken into 12 hours, with six hours of daylight and six hours of darkness. The new day began at sunset. The length of an hour changed to match the amount of daylight at different times of the year. The twelve-month calendar also originated in Sumer. Sumerian months were **lunar**, or based on the movements of the moon. Each month began with the full moon. The Babylonians of the city of Babylon later introduced the seven-day week.

## The Wonders of Babylon

Mesopotamia was home to some magnificent structures. Terrace walls were built around open spaces that were filled with soil and planted with magnificent gardens. King Nebuchadnezzar II ordered the construction of the Ishtar Gate, the largest of eight entrances into the walled city of Babylon. Made from bright blue glazed bricks, the giant gateway was decorated with relief sculptures of bulls and dragons. Reliefs are carvings that are raised from their backgrounds.

*The Ishtar Gate was one of eight gates that surrounded the ancient city of Babylon.*

## The need for water

Farmers developed ways to water crops before they were drowned by spring floods. They used irrigation systems to carry water away from the rivers to ditches and canals where water was dammed, and was used to water fields during the growing season. Irrigation allowed for more crops to be grown and sold, adding to the wealth of the southern region.

# Ancient Indus River Valley

**Two of the world's greatest ancient civilizations began in the Indus River Valley, in what is now Pakistan—the Harrapans and the Aryans. Five thousand years ago, the Harappans built clay-walled cities that had sewage systems for carrying water into and out of homes. They were also one of the first peoples to build sailing ships. The Harappans developed building techniques that helped them to defend their cities against floods and bring water to their fields. As skilled metalworkers, they also invented tools such as drills and needles.**

3300 B.C.–550 A.D.

## Cities Made of Clay

Ancient Harappan cities were built from baked clay bricks and had **citadels** on raised clay blocks at the center. The two greatest Harappan cities were Harappa and Mohenjo-daro. Up to 50,000 people lived in Harappa, and 30,000 in Mohenjo-daro.

Thick walls kept Indus floodwaters away from the cities. After the waters receded, the fertile soil made for excellent farmland. Every city had granaries for storing food, factories for making beads, and kilns for baking bricks.

The Harappans were concerned with bathing and cleanliness and even included bathing as part of their religious ceremonies. Every household had access to a water well, and nearly all houses had a bathroom. The Harappans had indoor plumbing and sewage systems thousands of years before most other civilizations. Clay drainpipes ran from the houses to larger, covered drainways on the streets that carried sewage and wastewater out of the city.

## Master Builders

Bricks and roads were made **standard**, and buildings were constructed using precise measurements. Their smallest unit of measure was 0.06 inches (1.5 mm). No other civilization of the time could measure anything that small.

## Fighting the Floods

The Harappans' cities were destroyed many times by floodwaters from the Indus River. There were no stones nearby to make flood walls, so the Harappans built defense walls around their cities made out of clay bricks. The bricks were baked in a large oven, called a kiln, to harden them.

*The Harappan flood defense walls were about five feet (1.5 meters) wide.*

## Magnificent Temples

The greatest artworks of ancient Indian civilization are its temples. By 400 B.C., Indians were skilled stoneworkers, having learned from the ancient Greeks, with whom they traded. From 320 A.D. to 540 A.D., beautiful stone temples with magnificent carvings were built all over northern India.

## Great Mathematicians

The most amazing ancient Indian discoveries were in mathematics. Every student in the world uses some of these discoveries. In 497 A.D., the **mathematician** Aryabhata developed the **decimal system**, which simplified calculations. He also determined that the Earth **orbits** the Sun, something European astronomers did not realize until 1,000 years later. By 600 A.D., Indians had invented the numerical symbols that evolved into the numbers 1 to 9. They also may have developed the concept of zero.

## Cotton Clothing

The Harappans were the first people to weave the fluffy heads, or bolls of a cotton plant, into thread. They passed this knowledge on as they traded with the Mesopotamians and Persians, and it spread around the world. Today, cotton textiles and clothing are still made in modern Pakistan and India and are exported around the world.

## Enduring Technologies

Many technologies used around the world today were first used by the Harappans. Bronze tools used in building, including the circular saw and drill, were Harappan inventions. **Stoneware** pottery for dishes and storage jars was designed by Harappan craftspeople. The Harappans were also the first to weave and print on cotton cloth, which they used for clothing and for wrapping goods. Farmers still use some of the technology developed thousands of years ago, including ox carts and pottery wheels.

## Exchanging Ideas

As they traded with other nations, the Harappans learned new skills. The Harappans learned how to make simple plows, called ards, from the Mesopotamians. Later, the ancient Indians began growing rice brought by Chinese traders. Rice then became a main crop of farmers.

## The Science of Life

Ancient Indian medicine emphasized cleanliness and disease prevention. India had hospitals and used herbs for medicine as early as 400 B.C. In 500 B.C., an Indian doctor named Susrata performed the first cataract operation on a patient's eyes. Doctors in ancient India were also skilled at plastic surgery. Cutting off the nose was a punishment for some crimes, and doctors found a way to rebuild the nose using skin from the cheek.

*Harappan pottery was made from clay found near the riverbanks*

*The carvings on Hindu temples such as this one depict scenes from the Vedas, the Aryans' holy books.*

13

# Ancient Greece

Ancient Greece was a group of individual island communities scattered along the rugged landscape of the Greek mainland in the Aegean Sea. The ancient Greeks developed a way of life that was inspired by their land, becoming expert sailors, traders, and warriors. They built ships called *triremes* that carried them to new lands to live, trade, and fight wars. Many people were also farmers, while others were teachers, merchants, metal workers, and marble workers.

800 B.C.–146 B.C.

## Healing Arts

Sick people in ancient Greece relied on magic charms to cure them. They flocked to shrines to make offerings to the gods, in the hope of getting relief from ailments such as headaches, blindness, and pimples. Ancient Greek doctors healed wounds caused by war and fractures and dislocations common with athletes but they knew very little about disease. Ancient Greek medicine changed with the work of Hippocrates. Born on the island of Kos around 460 B.C., Hippocrates believed that time, not temple **sacrifices**, cured disease. He also believed that disease came from natural causes, not the actions of the gods. In order to avoid disease, people had to have good hygiene and eat a healthy diet. By considering the facts and then deciding what the sufferer had, Hippocrates predicted how a disease would progress. Doctors today still take the Hippocratic Oath, which Hippocrates wrote. The oath says, "Whatever house I enter, I shall come to heal."

## Resources

The forests of northern Greece provided timber to the south where wood was scarce. Greece's rocky land provided **minerals** for tools and weapons, and marble and stone for buildings and sculptures. Mines near Athens were rich in silver, marble, iron, and lead. Slaves were forced to work these mines day and night for merchants to trade these precious items around the world.

Model of a Greek ballista catapult

## Eureka!

The ancient Greeks were clever inventors. They invented the boat anchor and the catapult, which was used in war to hurl rocks at the enemy. The most famous Greek inventor was Archimedes, and many of his inventions are still used today. One invention was a mechanical device known as Archimedes' screw. A screw is placed in a long cylinder. When the lower end of the cylinder is placed in water and the screw is turned, water is carried up through the cylinder to the top. Archimedes' screw was used to empty water from boats and to water crops. It is still used today for irrigation in the Nile River delta in Egypt.

Archimedes' screw

*Amphitheaters, such as this one in Epidaurus, were designed to hold up to 14,000 people.*

*The Greeks designed the Antikythera Mechanism, which calculates the positions of the planets, constellations, and the moon.*

## Architecture

The greatest example of Greek architecture is the temple. A temple was usually built on a hill above the city from huge blocks of limestone and marble which were brought to the construction site by ox-cart. Stoneworkers called masons carved each block into its proper size. The temple's roof and ceiling were made of wood, and its roof tiles were made of **terra cotta**.

Inside the temple, a room called the *naos* housed a large statue of a god or goddess. Only priests could enter the *naos*. This room was surrounded by rows of vertical columns. Greek architects built columns using a special technique called *entasis* to make them look straight, even though they were not.

## Dramatic Innovations

Most cities had an open-air theater, or amphitheater, where plays were performed during the day. The chorus performed in the orchestra. The orchestra was 75 feet (23 meters) wide and was generally made of sand. The auditorium, or seating area for people, was in two levels and formed a semi-circle around the orchestra. The design of Greek amphitheaters was so good that even people in the back rows could see and hear perfectly.

After 300 B.C., the actors stood on a raised stage called a *proskension*. Behind the stage was the *skene*, where the actors changed costumes. Actors entered and exited the stage through passageways at the sides called *parados*.

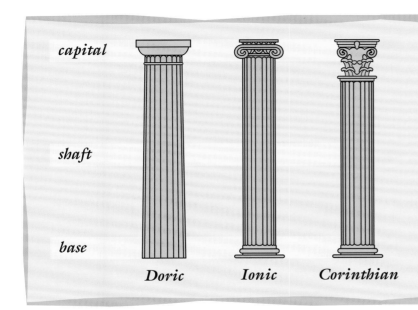

capital

shaft

base

Doric    Ionic    Corinthian

### Pillars of Society

The ancient Greeks were famous for their column-building. Three styles of columns were developed by Greek architects. Each column had three parts: the base, the shaft, and the capital. The Doric style was simple and had a plain capital. The Ionic column was narrower and had two scrolls on its capital. The Corinthian column was the most slender and had a more ornate capital. These column styles are still used today to decorate homes and offices.

# Ancient Egypt

**Egyptians were one of the earliest ancient peoples to weave the threads of civilization into a lasting nation. Egypt's enormous stone temples and pyramids took many years and thousands of workers to build, and after more than 5,000 years they still stand and amaze people today. Ancient Egyptians tracked the annual floods of the Nile River by recording them on paper. They also used simple math to create plans for irrigation projects that turned barren desert into farmland to feed a huge population.**

Ancient Egyptian architects honored their pharaohs, or kings, by building stone temples and pyramids. Thousands of workers built great cities throughout Egypt, including Karnak, Thebes, Luxor, and Memphis. Egyptians also found ways to accurately measure weights and distances, survey land, tell time, and calculate taxes to pay for the massive tributes to the pharaohs.

## Farming Innovations

Egyptians measured their fields and estimated yields of grain to provide food for their enormous labor force and taxes for their pharaoh. The Egyptians also had vineyards where workers harvested and stomped on grapes to make wine for nobles who owned the estates. Ordinary people drank a nutritious beer made from wheat and barley.

## Bringing Water to the Soil

The Nile River flooded every summer. If floodwaters were too low for several years in a row, it would be too dry to farm and there would be **famine**. Flooding forced farmers and villagers from their homes near the banks to higher ground. Workers built dikes to keep the river from flooding villages.

Big catch basins were built to trap water as the floods receded. Workers dug canals leading from these basins so the water could be used in fields located farther away. By law, every citizen had to maintain the irrigation system. The wealthy paid others to do their share.

They used the Nile's water to irrigate dry land. A network of irrigation canals supplied crops grown farthest away from the river with water.

*Oxen were used to plow the fields, and were a source of food.*

*Egyptians used a tool called a* shaduf *to lift water from the Nile to irrigate canals near fields.*

16

## Nilometer

Egyptian engineers invented a device to check water levels on the Nile River. The nilometer was a gauge to measure the rise of the river. It was a wall of stone at the riverbank with markings, like a giant ruler standing on its end, accessible by steps. The water level was checked regularly, and at various locations. Knowing the rising or falling waters of the Nile was very important because all life depended on the river.

## Sailing

Traffic was heavy on the Nile River. Merchants, fishers, traders, stone haulers, and nobles all used the river to do business. Egyptians constructed reed rafts to float through narrow canals and 200-foot (61-meter) long barges for hauling **obelisks**. They built boats to ferry people across the river. The wealthy relaxed on boats piloted by mariners to catch the cooling breezes on the Nile. Freighters carried grain up and down the river.

## Medicine

Egyptians had knowledge of the body and how to heal wounds, mend broken bones, and treat diseases. One Egyptian doctor recorded a medical textbook on papyrus that described 48 cases of injury, including wounds and broken bones. The doctor wrote how he made a diagnosis by following some of the same methods that doctors use today, including watching the patient and applying **ointments**. Treatments included healing fractures with splints and casts. Egyptians had very little knowledge about internal medicine.

## The Fall of Egypt

Egypt was invaded by several cultures over hundreds of years. The Assyrians, located in the area of the modern country of Iraq, were the fiercest warriors of the time. They captured Egypt using weapons made out of iron, a much stronger metal than the copper Egyptians used for their spears, shields, knives, and daggers. Ultimately, the country and its last ruler, Cleopatra, fell to the **Roman Empire** ending the long line of Egyptian dynasties.

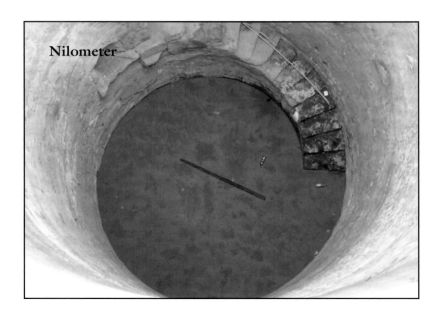

Nilometer

## Papermaking

Egyptians made an excellent lightweight paper from the stalk of the papyrus plant that grew on the banks of the Nile. Papyrus paper rolled up, and was far easier to handle than the heavy, baked clay tablets that other ancient cultures used to keep records. To make paper, workers cut ten-foot (three-meter) papyrus stems into shorter pieces and peeled them. After soaking in water, they were arranged in a double layer, covered with cloth, and pounded with a mallet until the strips matted together. The sheets were polished with a rounded stone and then trimmed and pasted end-to-end into a roll ready for scribes to write on.

*This Egyptian papyrus is the world's oldest surviving surgical document.*

# Inside a Pyramid

An Egyptian saying states that "everyone fears the passage of time, but time fears the pyramids." The Great Pyramid is the largest stone building ever built. It stands 482 feet (147 meters) high and is made from more than two million stone blocks.

## Stone and Wood

In the desert west of the Nile, the engineers and builders of ancient Egypt developed a system for cutting stone to build pyramids, temples, and statues. In a huge rock face, workers carved holes and pounded wood wedges into them. They poured water over the wedges and the swelling of the wood caused the rock to crack and split. With chisels and mallets, stonecutters shaped the blocks of stone. Teams of men transported the blocks, which could weigh up to fifteen tons (fourteen tonnes), by sledge to barges waiting along the Nile.

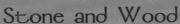

*Stone blocks of building material were unloaded from barges on the Nile to docks and construction storehouses near the pyramid building site.*

# Pyramids

The pyramid was the burial place of a pharaoh. Deep inside the gigantic monument, there was a special chamber where the pharaoh's body lay in its sarcofagus, or coffin. The pyramid contained secret passageways and rooms filled with burial goods and precious jewelry.

The great age of pyramid building lasted about 400 years. The first, built in 2630 B.C. for the powerful Pharaoh Djoser, was called the Step Pyramid because it looked like a massive staircase the king could use to climb to the sky after his death.

Less than 200 years later, the style had changed. The three pyramids at Giza looked like three-dimensional triangles with smooth sides. The largest now stands about 450 feet (137 meters) high. It required more than two million limestone blocks. The blocks weighed about two tons (1.8 tonnes) each, and were dragged by workers on oiled logs up earthen ramps. Up to 4,000 workers were used to drag the blocks up the ramps and set them in place.

The pyramids have survived the harsh climate of Egypt, war, and pollution. Today, Egyptian authorities are working hard to preserve these monuments.

*After construction of a pyramid was complete, it would be decorated with carvings and paintings honoring a pharaoh.*

# Ancient Mesoamerica

1400 B.C.–1521 A.D.

**Ancient Mesoamericans studied the stars in the night sky, believing they held the answers to their questions. In a period of 3,000 years, the Olmec, Aztec, Maya, and other peoples such as the Toltec and Zapotec, also charted the skies to tell time, built enormous pyramids in which they worshiped their gods, studied the human body, and learned how to make medicine from plants.**

## Star Gazing

Ancient Maya astronomers studied the stars and predicted solar and lunar eclipses, the cycles of the planet Venus, and the movements of the **constellations**. The Maya believed that these occurrences were caused by the gods. When constructing temples, builders made sure they lined up with the sun and stars. At Chichén Itzá, the main Maya city in the Yucatán peninsula, there is a pyramid dedicated to Quetzalcoatl, the Feathered Serpent God. At the spring and autumn **equinoxes**, the sun gradually shines on the pyramid's stairs and the serpent head at its base. This creates the image of a snake slithering down the sacred mountain to earth.

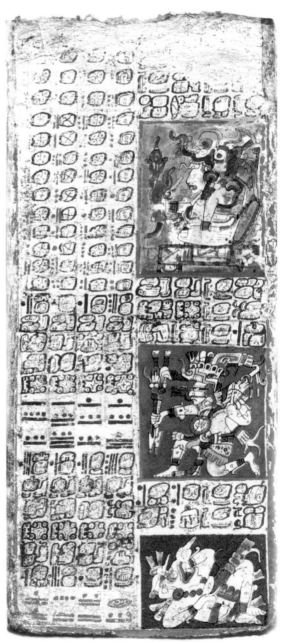

The Dresden Codex is a famous ancient Mesoamerican text that contains information on several subjects, including astronomy, medicine, religion, and natural occurrences.

*The Carocol, at the ancient Maya city of Chichén Itzá, Mexico, is believed to be an observatory. Some of its doors and windows line up with the orbit of planets.*

## Floating Gardens

On wet marshy areas, Mesoamericans built raised fields, or floating gardens, called *chinampas*. Soil was dug from the surrounding area and piled up to form the banks of a canal. Wooden stakes were hammered into the ground to reinforce the canal's banks. Trees were planted around the banks and their roots kept the sides of the canal from being washed away.

## Textile Making

Weaving fabric for clothing and other uses was the job of Maya and Aztec women. The first step was to prepare fiber either from a plant or animal. Ancient weavers spun thread themselves by hand. They used a technology of spindles and whorls. A spindle was a stick-like thread holder. As the weaver twisted fiber into thread, she wound it around the spindle. A whorl, a circular part with a hole in the middle, was attached to the base of the spindle. It provided weight to steady the spindle in its spinning motion. Whorls were made of carved wood or pottery. Weavers colored fabric with a dye made from dried, crushed bugs and plants.

For weaving, women used backstrap looms which are still used today. One end of the loom was tied to a tree or wall and the other end was tied to the weaver's waist. The weaver leaned back to keep the threads tight as she worked.

## Medicine

Maya and Aztec healers wrote about medicines that came from plants. To soothe a sore throat, a healer advised the patient to sip thickened maguey syrup. Aztec physicians used obsidian blades to cut open sores or made a cut near a swelled body part to let the patient bleed. The wound was then stitched up again using a cactus spine as a needle and hair as thread.

## Teotihuacán

In its day, Teotihuacán was the largest and grandest city in ancient Mesoamerica. It was thought to be the place where the gods were made. In 500 A.D., from 125,000 to 200,000 people lived there. Teotihuacán was the home of the largest and most famous pyramid-temples, the Pyramid of the Sun and the Pyramid of the Moon. Obsidian mines found north of the city added to the city's wealth. Around 600 A.D., the city of Teotihuacán began to decline. A severe drought that ruined crops is thought to have led to its downfall. Archaeologists believe the city may have been attacked in 725 A.D., or been the site of a rebellion. Evidence shows all the city's buildings and art were destroyed in the attack.

# Ancient South America

The peoples of ancient South America built well-planned cities out of mud bricks and blocks of stone. Farmland surrounding the ancient cities was used to grow staple crops. Expert architects and designers, the ancient Andeans built enormous pyramids and temples to honor their gods on steep mountainsides. They also built irrigation canals that allowed them to grow crops in areas with almost no rainfall.

## Pyramids

The ancient Andeans built enormous temples and flat-topped pyramids in their cities. The coastal civilizations, such as the Moche and the Nazca, used bricks made from mud to construct their buildings. In the mountains, people built pyramids from blocks of stone weighing up to two tons (1.8 tonnes) each. One of the most amazing structures of the Andes is the Akapana pyramid, built by the Tiahuanaco people. The stones were cut using stone and bronze tools. Great care was taken to cut the stones so they fit together perfectly, like an enormous jigsaw puzzle.

## Inca Stonework

A few Inca cities, such as Machu Picchu, were not damaged at all by later European invaders. Machu Picchu was built high in the Andes mountains under the Inca ruler, Pachacuti, around 1460. It consists of over 200 buildings made from granite stones that were cut to fit together. About 750 people lived there, including servants and artisans who worked for the **Sapa Inca** and the nobles who lived there. Machu Picchu was abandoned when the Spanish arrived in the mid-1500s, and was not found again until 1911.

*The stones used to build the city of Machu Picchu weighed many tons each. Archaeologists do not know how the Incas transported these giant blocks without wheeled vehicles or horses.*

*The blocks used for buildings and walls in Machu Picchu fit together perfectly without mortar.*

*The Inca temple at Pisac, near Machu Picchu, was carefully built from large granite rocks. The remains have stood for hundreds of years.*

## Terrace Farming

The steep slopes of the Andes were difficult to farm. Around 6000 B.C., the Andean people started to cut wide, flat steps into the mountains, creating terraces for planting crops. Long canals were built to channel water from mountain rivers and streams to the terraced fields. These new farming methods allowed people to grow large amounts and varieties of food, including maize, potatoes, tomatoes, peanuts, chilies, and quinoa, a cereal grain. They also grew cotton to make clothing.

## Colorful Weaving

Ancient Andeans wove cloth from cotton and wool. The weaving looms were easy to use, but weaving itself was complicated and time-consuming, because the ancient Andeans wove along the vertical threads, rather than along the horizontal threads. They chose this method because it allowed the pattern to be clearly visible on both sides of the fabric. The threads for weaving had to be very strong, so the yarn was spun many times. It took up to 200 hours to spin the wool for a poncho, and another 300 hours to weave the poncho. Most women wove only one large piece of fabric each year. Textiles were very valuable because they took so much time to make.

## The Nazca Lines

The Nazca created huge designs on the coastal plains of Peru. They cleared the red surface soil to reveal lighter soil underneath, creating line patterns and images of humans, spiders, monkeys, and birds. They also drew straight lines thousands of feet long. Some of these lines spread outward from a single spot like spokes on a wheel. These patterns are known as ray centers. Some historians believe that the Nazca lines were prayers to the gods for rain.

## Inca Medicine

Inca **shamans** used many native plants for medicine. They used quinine, a medicine from the bark of the cinchona tree to treat various ailments such as fever, and roots from the ipecacuanha tree to treat poisoning. Belladonna, a drug made from the deadly nightshade plant, was used to treat stomach problems. These herbs were prepared as teas or **poultices**. The Incas chewed coca leaves to dull pain and reduce fatigue.

## End of the Empire

In 1531, the Spanish landed in South America. Their armies killed thousands of Incas, looted treasures, and destroyed temples. The Sapa Inca fled. In 1536, he tried to retake Cuzco from the Spanish. His army, with its quilted cotton armor and spears, was no match for the Spaniards' metal armor, guns, and horses. In 1572, the Spanish killed the last Inca leader, Tupac Amaru. His death brought Inca civilization to an end.

*The Incas built roads that criss-crossed the Andes so they could travel through the mountains. The road network was called the Royal Road, and eventually ran the length of the Inca empire, covering over 14,000 miles (22,500 km).*

*The Chimu civilization, who lived on the northern coast of Peru, wove beautiful textiles.*

Cinchona

23

# Ancient Rome

753 B.C.–476 A.D.

The Romans were great builders and inventors. Near Rome there were forests of timber for building and shipmaking. Stone was also plentiful for making concrete to construct aqueducts, amphitheaters, or vast outdoor arenas. They also built temples, baths, tunnels, and an amazing 53,000 miles (85,300 km) of roads throughout the empire. Some Roman constructions were so well built that they are still used today.

## Aqueducts

The word aqueduct comes from the Latin "aqua," or water and "ducere," meaning to lead. The aqueducts carried water to Rome from mountain springs as far as 30 miles (48 km) away. Some aqueducts went through tunnels in the mountains; others were buried or were ground-level covered channels. The raised channels were held up by as many as three tiers, or levels, of arches resting on columns. Over time, eleven aqueducts, or channels, carried water to the city of Rome for drinking, washing, flushing the sewer systems, and even for filling the emperor's fish ponds.

## All Roads Lead to Rome

Wherever the Roman army went, they built roads to move soldiers quickly and make trade easier. In Britain, Roman soldiers built 10,000 miles (16,000 km) of roads. These roads have lasted so long that many modern roads in Britain are built on top of old Roman roads.

## Cloaca Maxima

The cloaca maxima was Rome's main sewer system built to drain marshlands between the Palatine and Capitoline hills. At first, the sewer was just a group of brick-lined open channels. Roman engineers enclosed the channels so they ran beneath roads and buildings. About 200 million gallons (90 million liters) of water flowed through the cloaca maxima every day.

*This three-tiered aqueduct brought water from the hills down to the city.*

*Romans built roads using stones or logs and made them as straight and flat as possible. Little attention was paid to who owned or used the land that the roads cut through.*

*The cloaca maxima, or main sewer, is still used by Romans today.*

## Arches and Architecture

The Romans were known for constructing buildings with arches. They adapted the corbelled arch from the Etruscans, from Etruria, in northern Italy, and made it strong enough to hold tons of cement and entire stories of buildings. Roman buildings were made from concrete, a mixture of bits of broken stone or brick, with sand or gravel, cement, and water. Some buildings took years to finish. The Colosseum was a 50,000-seat arena where public events such as gladiator competitions and executions were held. Construction on the Colosseum began in 70 A.D. and ended 25 years later.

## Circus Maximus

There were other circuses in Rome and the empire but the Circus Maximus was the biggest. The Circus Maximus was an enormous colosseum where chariot races were held. Romans also built spectacular buildings for worshiping their gods. The Pantheon, a round building housing statues of all the Roman gods, had walls that were 200 feet (60 meters) thick. Its dome was almost 150 feet (46 meters) around.

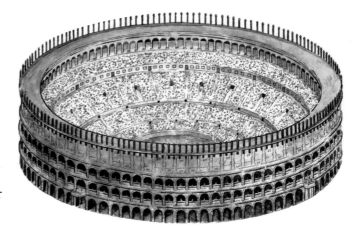

*The Colosseum hosted fights between gladiators, between men and animals, and even mock sea battles, when Emperor Titus flooded it with water. Spectators brought their own cushions for seats and often arrived before dawn to line up for events.*

*Colosseum*

# Ancient Japan

Japan is made up of a chain of volcanic islands in the Pacific Ocean, 120 miles (200 km) from the east coast of China. Surrounded by water, the ancient Japanese were cut off from other cultures developing on the mainland. As their ability to travel developed, they interacted with other cultures such as China and Korea. The Japanese took the ideas and technologies of these other cultures and adapted them into their own culture.

300 B.C.–1582 A.D.

## The Yayoi

Archaeologists believe the Yayoi peoples may have come to the island of Kyushu from the Korean peninsula around 300 B.C. The Yayoi brought many new technologies with them. They made pottery on rotating wheels that they turned with their feet. The Yayoi knew how to **forge** bronze and iron into tools and weapons. They also knew how to grow rice in wet fields, or paddies. They carved stepped rice paddies into the sides of steep mountains. These paddies were flooded in the rainy season and drained before harvesting. One acre of rice paddies could feed more people than one acre of any other crop, so rice soon became the major food crop in Japan. Over time, the Yayoi people spread out and settled on the island of Honshu.

## Herbal Medicine and Massage

*Ginger*

The ancient Japanese made poultices, ointments, and teas from plants and herbs known for their healing properties. Rhubarb was used to treat burns, while ginger was used for nausea. Headaches and back pain were treated with a special massage technique called *shiatsu*. *Shiatsu* was developed from the belief that invisible streams of energy move through the body. Some Japanese believed that illnesses were caused when the flow of energy was blocked. During a *shiatsu* massage, an expert pressed on different parts of the body to help the energy flow more easily.

*(above)* Shiatsu *massage was brought to North America, where it remains a popular therapy.*

*(left) Rice farming became so important in ancient Japan that it changed the way people lived, worked, and were governed.*

# Weapons of War

Some of the greatest achievements in weaponry were developed from the need for people to defend themselves in ancient Japan. A rich and powerful class of warrior called samurai were hired to serve as guards at the emperor's palace, as bodyguards for nobles or lords, and as police.

Samurai began training at the age of five or six. They practiced with wooden swords before they were given a steel sword. Swords were more than weapons to the ancient Japanese. They were thought to have powers and lives of their own, their strength and magic affected by the thoughts and actions of the swordsmith. A swordsmith fasted while he worked so he would be pure and the sword he made would be more powerful.

Samurai had to be very skilled to shoot bows and arrows, so they practiced all the time. They were famous for being able to shoot a bow and arrow while riding a horse. Bows, first used around 250 A.D., were made of bamboo and were about six feet (two meters) long. Eagle, hawk, or crane feathers were glued to an arrow to make it fly in a straight line. The ancient Japanese invented two types of arrowheads: a four-sided arrowhead that could pierce armor, and a three-pronged arrowhead that could cut rope. A whistle was sometimes attached to the arrow's shaft to signal the attack as it sailed through the air.

*(left) Samurai wives had to know how to defend their homes in wartime. They carried a dagger and knew how to fight with a curved sword on a long pole, called a naginata.*

*(right) Samurai wore two swords. The katana was a long sword, and the wakizashi was short. The word "samurai" means "one who serves."*

## The Kaido Roads

Well-made roads were important to the ancient Japanese because they made it easier for armies and traders to travel across the land. Around 600 A.D., the Japanese started to build a national road network connecting the capital city of Nara, on Honshu, to surrounding towns. The roads, known as *kaidos*, allowed merchants to get to seaports so that they could trade with other merchants from Japan, China, and Korea. The *kaidos* were made of pressed dirt, and many have survived to the present day.

# Ancient Celts

The dominant civilization in Europe from 600 B.C. to 50 B.C., the ancient Celts, built settlements on hilltops called hillforts, which were protected from attack by ramparts. The Celts were also the most advanced metalworkers in the ancient world. They used their skills to make tools for farming and mining, as well as weapons and armor that helped them succeed in battle.

800 B.C.–43 A.D.

## Hillforts

Many Celtic communities built stone or wooden forts surrounded by ditches and high walls on a hill to shelter in during attacks. These were called hillforts. During attacks, the local ruler and his or her family sheltered in a large, central building, while the rest of the community stayed in wooden huts built around it. Warriors defended the fort from behind the earth and stone walls.

The wall surrounding a Celtic town was about sixteen feet (five meters) high. To make a wall, planks of wood were nailed together with iron nails. Stones and earth were heaped up on both sides of the wooden wall to make a thick defensive barrier. Some towns were protected by two or more walls. Most towns had at least two entrances. These were narrow, which prevented a large group of enemy warriors from rushing the gates together. From the ramparts, defenders could easily attack anyone trying to storm the gates.

*Maiden castle, in present-day Dorset, England, was one of the Celts' largest hillforts. The Celts abandoned it more than 2,000 years ago, after an attack by Roman invaders.*

## Iron Smelting

Europe had huge amounts of iron ore in ancient times. To extract the metal from the ore, the Celts **smelted** the rock using a furnace. The furnace was a tall, cylinder-shaped chimney built from long sticks covered with clay. **Bellows** blew air into the furnace through small holes in the furnace walls, making the fire inside very hot. **Charcoal** was set on fire and poured into the furnace from the top. Then, iron ore and more charcoal were added to the furnace for over an hour or more after which raw iron had formed on the bottom of the furnace floor.

*In battle, Celtic warriors protected their heads by wearing helmets made of iron and bronze.*

## Chariots and Chain Mail

War chariots were one of the Celts' most effective pieces of battle equipment. They were used to transport Celtic warriors into battle. Pulled by two horses, the chariot cart was made of woven wicker, which made it light and quick. The cart was very low at the back and front so that warriors could climb in and out of it easily. The Celts invented iron tires for the wheels, which helped the chariot to move quickly. The Celts also made shoes for their horses from iron. Horseshoes reduced the risk of horses injuring their hooves as they galloped over rocky ground. Chain mail was another Celtic invention. Chain mail was a type of armor, usually a vest, made up of thousands of connecting metal rings.

*Chariot*

## Coracles, Canoes, and Ships

The Celts used three types of boats for traveling on rivers and across lakes: coracles, canoes, and ships. Coracles, or curraghs, were egg-shaped boats designed for one person. Consisting of a lightweight frame covered with leather, coracles were also used as sleds to haul goods in winter. Heavy canoes were hollowed out of tree trunks and used to paddle across waterways. Trading ships were even larger. Long and narrow, and equipped with leather sails, they could hold up to eighteen men, who would row when the wind was not blowing in the direction they wanted to sail.

*Coracle*

## Celtic Medicine

The Celts were skilled herbalists, using plants to treat and cure illnesses. Seaweeds were used to treat headaches, garlic was given to people with bladder problems, and the herb tansy was brewed into a tea for stomach problems. Mistletoe, a plant with white berries that grows high up on trees, was used to cure various ailments. The Celts believed that a sprig of mistletoe, especially if found growing on the sacred oak tree, had the power to heal humans of illnesses, such as swelling.

*Mistletoe*

# Ancient Vikings

The Vikings were expert ship builders, sailors, and navigators. They sailed the open sea between Scandinavia and North America in thin, fast ships called longships. The ships sailed easily into narrow ocean inlets and up rivers.

787 A.D.–1100 A.D.

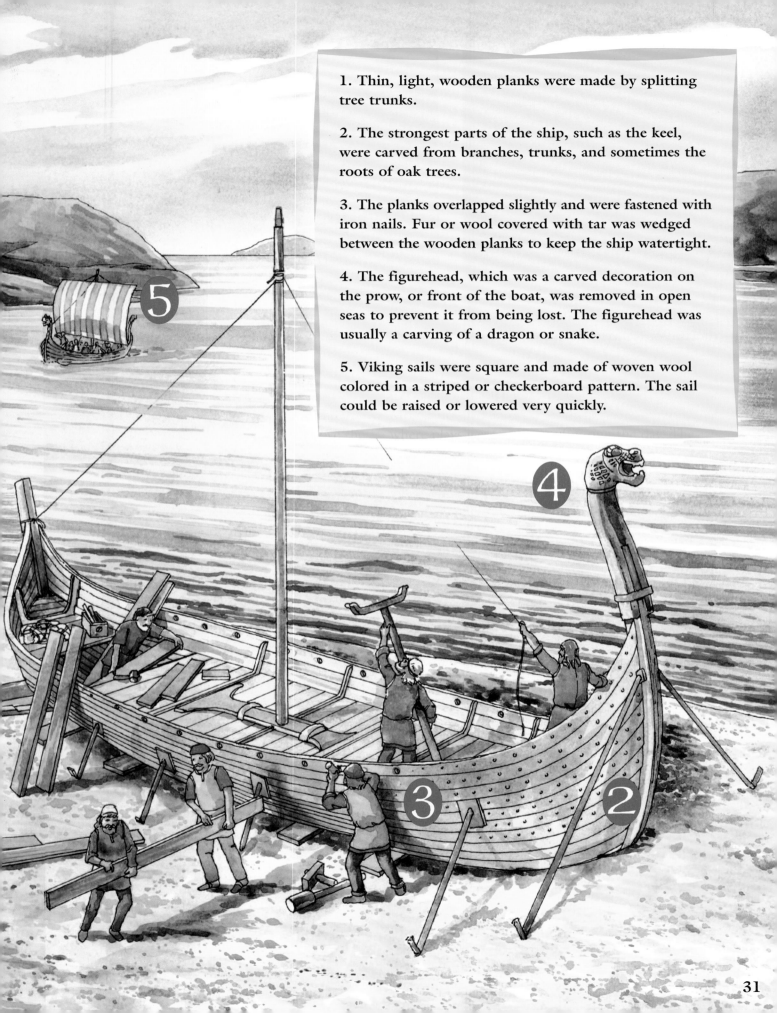

1. Thin, light, wooden planks were made by splitting tree trunks.

2. The strongest parts of the ship, such as the keel, were carved from branches, trunks, and sometimes the roots of oak trees.

3. The planks overlapped slightly and were fastened with iron nails. Fur or wool covered with tar was wedged between the wooden planks to keep the ship watertight.

4. The figurehead, which was a carved decoration on the prow, or front of the boat, was removed in open seas to prevent it from being lost. The figurehead was usually a carving of a dragon or snake.

5. Viking sails were square and made of woven wool colored in a striped or checkerboard pattern. The sail could be raised or lowered very quickly.

# Glossary

**aqueduct** A channel for carrying fresh water

**bellows** An instrument used to pump air

**canal** An artificial waterway for boats or for draining or irrigating land

**charcoal** A material made of carbon produced by heating wood or plant and animal material, and used as fuel

**citadel** A fortress that commands a city

**constellation** A group of stars that form patterns

**decimal system** A number system based on units of ten

**equinoxes** The two times each year in Spring and Fall when the sun appears overhead at the equator, and the day and night are of equal length

**famine** A great shortage of food that causes widespread hunger and starvation

**forge** The art of shaping metal into objects

**irrigation** Supplying land with water by using ditches, human-made channels, or sprinklers

**lunar** Having to do with the moon

**mathematician** A person who is skilled or learned in mathematics

**mineral** A natural, non-living substance

**monk** A person who devotes his or her life to a religion and lives in a monastery

**obelisks** Columns, or shafts with four sides that usually come to a point at the top and are sometimes engraved or carved

**observatory** A specially built structure for studying objects in the sky

**ointment** A healing substance applied to the skin

**orbit** The path taken by one body around another, such as the Earth's orbit around the sun

**ornate** Decorated beautifully with great detail

**poultice** A thick healing paste that is placed on a cut or swollen part of the body

**rampart** A wall or bank of earth raised around a structure for protection against attack

**Roman Empire** A group of territories under the control and rule of Rome

**sacrifice** An offering to a god or goddess

**Sapa Inca** A ruler in ancient South America who controlled all of the land in the empire

**scribes** People who make a living by copying or recording text

**shaman** A spiritual leader who performed ceremonies to cure the sick, make prophecies, and control natural events

**smelt** The process of removing a metal from an ore, usually by melting

**standard** A measure of comparison

**staple** A food that is part of a daily diet

**stoneware** A heavy type of pottery

**terra cotta** A hard baked clay used for pottery, statues, and building materials

# Index

# Websites

www.bbc.co.uk/history/ancient/
Amazing images highlight in-depth looks into ancient cultures.

www.historyforkids.org/
This site provides information on the history, food, clothing, technology, stories, and religion of many ancient cultures.

www.pbs.org/wgbh/nova/ancient/
Interactive videos take readers through ancient civilizations.

www.archaeolink.com/amazing_worlds_of_archaeology1.htm
This site provides links to sites with archaeological information.

# Further Reading

*Ancient Warfare* series, Gareth Stevens Publishing 2009

*Biography from Ancient Civilizations: Legends, Folklore, and Stories of Ancient Worlds* series, Mitchell Lane Publishers 2009

*The Technology of the Ancient World* series, Rosen Publishing Group 2006

*Ancient Wonders of the World* series, Creative Education 2005